FINDING DAKOTA

JENAH PIERCE

Jenah Pierce
PO Box 246
East Texas, PA 18046

First originally published by Jenah Pierce 2021.

Finding Dakota is a work of fiction. Any names and resemblances to actual events or persons, living or dead, are entirely coincidental.

The opinions of the characters expressed in this work of fiction are wholly imaginative and should not be confused with the author's.

ISBN 978-1-7369788-3-2 (Paperback)
ISBN 978-1-7369788-4-9 (Hardcover)
ISBN 978-1-7369788-5-6 (Digital)

Printed in the United States of America.

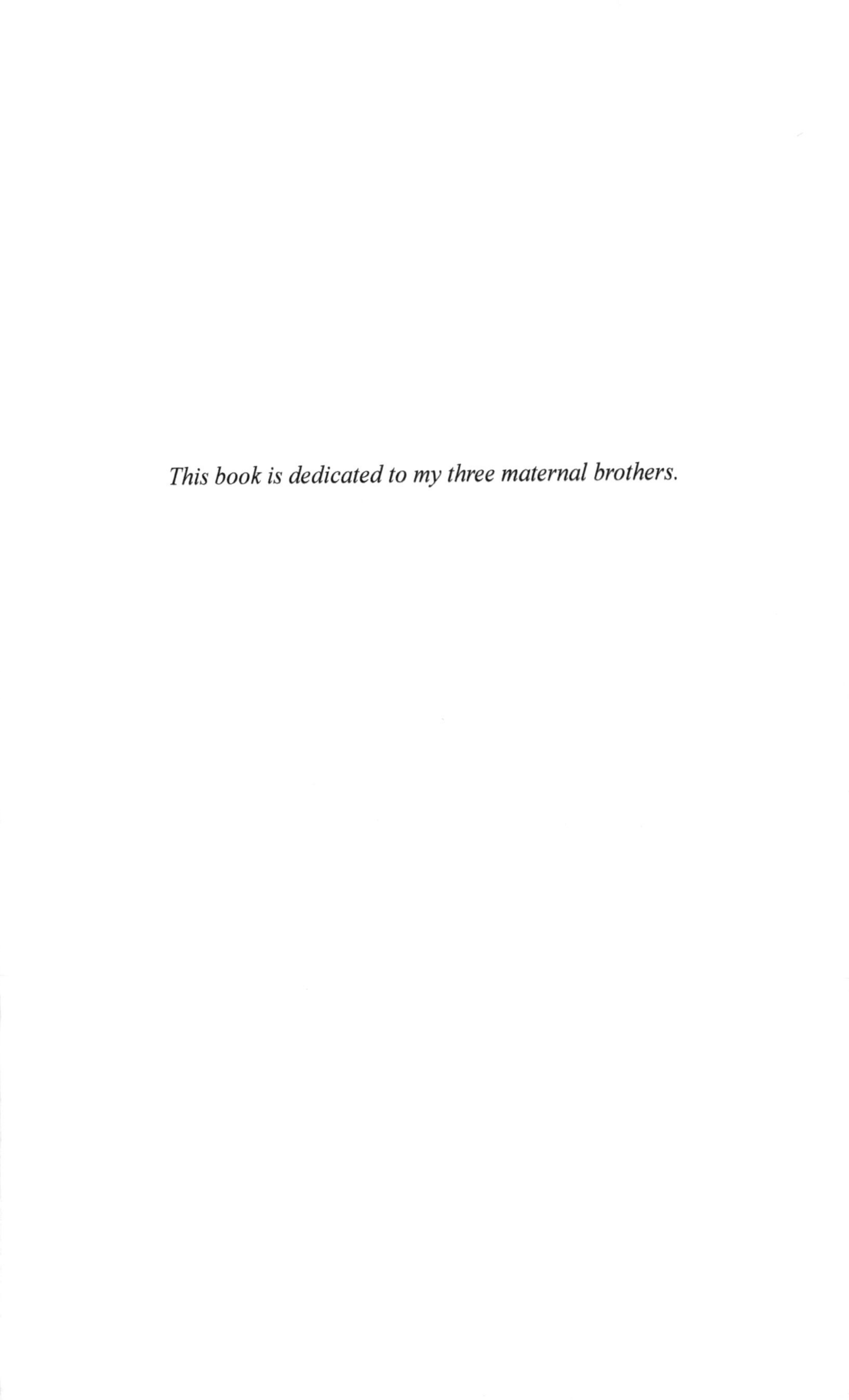

This book is dedicated to my three maternal brothers.

This first dedication message is to my one and only older brother, Jason, who was placed for adoption at birth and later reunited with our family in 2007 after he turned twenty-one.

Jason,

My dear sweet brother, you are the true inspiration behind this book, *Finding Dakota*, which I have been writing since 2005. You are the answer to my greatest childhood wish, and you are the reason that I believe hopes and dreams and prayers can come true. I always hoped and prayed you would turn out to be a sweet, loving, protective older brother, and God surely answered my prayers in July 2007 when you found me on MySpace and reached out to Mama and me. I'm so sorry we missed out on growing up together in our formative years. Words can never convey how great a crushing loss it is to know this pain.

However, I write this message to you with tears of joy in my eyes to say just how much I love you and your wife and her mom and your beautiful children. Thank you for reaching out to Mama and me back in 2007, and thank you for accepting me and loving me as your little sister. Thank you also for allowing me the privilege of watching your beautiful children grow up. You have a special place in my heart that no one could ever replace. I love you so much, Brother Bear.

This second dedication message is for my little "not so little anymore" brother, Michael:

Mike,

I still smile over the countless memories that we made while playing with cars and Hess trucks at Gina and Lenny's, along with building various lego creations. It still feels like yesterday when we were laughing and chasing each other around over at our favorite park called Timbertown and playing Freeze Tag with all our old neighbors on Front Street in Allentown. I don't know how much you remember, but we moved around a lot when we were very young though there's nothing better than family sticking together, no matter how poor we were. It was a joy to see you mature through Cub Scouts and grow up.

Because we knew the painful emptiness of not having our only older brother with us in our childhood, and because we also know the aching loss of our baby brother, I'm incredibly thankful to have you in my life. You've always been there, and you gave my childhood a special meaning. Even now, as we have matured into adults, with both of us doing our own things now, I know you're there. I'm so proud of how far you have come, and I'm incredibly honored to be your big sister. I love you, kiddo.

To the youngest of us, Kristopher, who even in his darkest moments with Neuroblastoma, tried so hard to smile as often as he could:

Kris,

I'm fighting back tears as I type your dedication, though I feel you can already see this from the Heavens above. You never deserved all the pain and suffering you had with Neuroblastoma, and yet you tried to smile through it all until the pain was too unbearable. I remember so much of my early life only because of you. My biggest fear is losing my memories of you, so I've fiercely been holding tight to the yesteryears as if it were all yesterday. No amount of words can ever convey how deeply sorry I am to see you never get the chance to grow up, and if I could've, I would've taken your place instead.

You give my life a special meaning, and I live my life for you. Every sadness, every moment of being down on my luck, every funny moment, every accomplishment, every life experience, it's all for you, except for Prom. Sorry, little brother, that's one rite of passage I never completed, though I've got big plans to check off much more in life, with seeing some of the most beautiful places on this earth and trying out some of the most incredible human experiences, like honoring our Irish heritage by performing at Celticfest as an Irish Step Dancer with the fabulous O'Grady Quinlan Academy of Irish Dance, along with bungee jumping 130 feet in the air at the San Diego County Fair. I'm beyond excited to fill the pages of the story of my life. That way, when we see each other again, we will have an eternity of stories for me to share with you.

You're the reason I believe in life after death, and yours is the first smiling face I cannot wait to see when it's my turn to cross over. I miss you more with every passing moment, and my heart still aches because you're not here with us in the physical realm. Even though I miss you terribly, I know the best kind of peace because I know you're no longer suffering from any type of pain. Until we meet again, may you rest in peace in paradise with Mama. I love you, little brother, and I will forever keep you closest in my heart.

In Loving Memory:
Kristopher Anthony
March 21, 1994 – January 6th, 1997

CHAPTER
ONE

Fifteen-year-old Kaelyn Marie Dalgeau smiled with warmth as she walked into the Denner Family residence for the first time. Before meeting them, California's Child Protective Services had only placed her with one other foster family after her adoption fell through. However, after the authorities discovered the former foster family's link to a massive sex trafficking ring involving a multitude of minors, Social Services removed her from foster care altogether. They felt that she was safer as a ward of the state of California in a group home for young girls they deemed unadoptable or mentally unfit for foster care. Kaelyn prayed fervently for a family to truly love her and care for her as one of their own, though she was more prepared for the real-world expectations of a hard life once she aged out of the system.

She carefully studied the Denner residence upon entrance. After walking through the front door, she immediately faced an ascending staircase to the second floor. On the stairwell's left side was a big, open-spaced living room, and on the opposite side was a dining room with an unusually long but beautifully ornate dining table. In her first meeting with Mr. and Mrs. Denner, she learned that Mr. Denner was a doctor—a cardiothoracic surgeon, to be specific, and he was the best in his field on the west coast. She knew this meant they had money, so she expected that she would be living in a mansion, but this house took her by surprise. Sure, it was immaculate, but the Denners seemed to prefer living a comfortable lifestyle rather than a lavish one. There was a huge family portrait in the living room above the sofa, the first object that caught her attention. Kaelyn knew from the initial meeting that she wasn't the first foster child they've brought into their home, but the picture hanging above the couch was of all of them together, and she felt all the love and pride they had in being a part of this family.

She was rather fond of this new house because it was filled with various family-oriented items, which gave her a vibe of warmth, love, and acceptance. Her nose detected a faint scent of lemon and Windex, though she also smelled salt in the air, which she knew came from the beach of Novis Bay that was just a few blocks away. Considering she was the last person to walk through the front door, Dr. and Mrs. Denner and their two youngest children turned to her. She realized that the expressions painted on their faces told her they were seeking her approval.

"You have a beautiful home here."

"Well, thank you, Kaelyn, and this is your home now, too," Mrs. Alice Denner replied as her lips curled into a smile.

Kaelyn couldn't be happier when she heard those words. Could this family finally be the one to take her in permanently? She'd waited for this for a few years, so she hoped this journey was at its end. She'd taken a long, good look at the family's matriarch. Alice's upturned, almond-shaped, honey brown eyes glistened back into Kaelyn's with a kindness Kaelyn hadn't seen in years. She reminded Kaelyn of her adopted mother before she passed away, as she too had the same kind of eyes with beautiful long wavy brown hair that seemed to match her eyes' softness and coloring.

As for Dr. Denner, Kaelyn didn't know what to make of him yet.

She couldn't say she had a single positive experience with any father figure, including her adopted father, who was why she'd re-entered the system. Dr. Denner had a short, simple hairstyle which was a little long on the top, though the sides were shaved, which meant he tried to be "a cool dad." It was easy to see that he dyed his hair a chestnut brown to keep up with appearances, but she wondered if he had to do this for his career or if this was a mask. She couldn't be sure, but she intended on keeping her distance from him for a time to determine whether or not she could trust him.

"So, Kaelyn, you and I will be sharing a room," stated seventeen-year-old Vinessa. "Come and see it for yourself, and you can start to unpack your things. Then we could all go out to eat for dinner, or do you want to put your stuff in the room, go out to eat, and then unpack later?"

"Either works for me," Kaelyn answered. "Oh, and if it's not too much trouble, can you please call me Kay? No one calls me Kaelyn, and I've never really felt connected to it. It just doesn't feel like me."

"Of course!" Vinessa acknowledged in a cheerful tone. "And you can call me Vinny, Vin, or V."

When Vinessa beamed a bright and intense, pearly-white smile toward Kaelyn, Kaelyn couldn't help but return the same gesture. She sensed with Vinessa's bubbly personality that she was the positive one of the family, that she was the one who lifted everyone when they were down. She already had quite a positive effect on Kaelyn. Kaelyn knew she'd get along with her just fine, especially since she'd always wanted a sister.

"Alright, well, why don't you go see your new room, and Vinny will show you a quick tour upstairs, and then we can all go to dinner?" Dr. Denner suggested.

"I'll help with the tour!" offered nineteen-year-old Matthew with a raised, enthusiastic hand.

"Awesome! Let's go," Vinessa commanded with excitement as she now led her brother and new sister up the stairs.

Dr. Denner and his wife exchanged looks of love and hope as they held each other close.

"Do you think she'll like it here?" Dr. Denner inquired with a cautious tone.

Alice sensed her husband was worried. Kaelyn's Caseworker, Miss Wayne, summarized Kaelyn's past, and it was a lot rougher than the backgrounds of most children they adopted in the past, except for Meghan. Alice knew Michael was concerned that Kaelyn might not want to connect with him for fear of what she'd already experienced. It would certainly be understandable in their eyes, but Alice was clever, and she already had it in mind to ask Meghan if she could return home soon to meet her new foster sister. She placed her hands on her husband's chest for comfort as she kept his loving gaze.

"Well, did you see the look on her face? She was *relieved* when I said this place was her home as well. Remember we know how it feels to be an orphan, Mike? Or have you forgotten? Like all the other children, all she wants is a family to keep her and love her and vice versa. I can see she's already adjusting, though, so I honestly think she will love it here," Alice answered warmly and pleasantly before kissing him.

"Good," Michael said. "Because I have a good feeling about her. She may not have always had the best luck as Miss Wayne said, but I feel all that's about to change."

As Matthew followed close behind Kaelyn, who in turn followed Vinessa, he couldn't help the eager feeling inside him, which tempted him to bust out some form of movement to show how ecstatic he was right now. He was tired of having older siblings adopted into the family while growing up, even though he still loved them with all his heart. Now that Matthew had a new sister who was younger than him and even younger than Vinessa, he instantly felt territorial of her in that brotherly sort of way. He wanted to make sure she was physically and emotionally safe from harm because, as far as he was concerned, Kaelyn was his new baby sister, even though they didn't adopt her into the family yet. He and his family never had any adoption problems with foster kids, except for Timothy Greene, whose mother returned for him once she went into drug rehab and turned her life around. Even then, the Denners were still in Timothy's life, and they were still family to him. So Matthew had a feeling that Kaelyn would ask to be adopted into the family, just like all the others had done.

They'd foster older children, give them a chance to be part of the family by letting them in on every aspect of their lives, and let the children themselves decide whether they want a permanent home with them or not. They never even brought up the subject of adoption. That was the method the Denners used for their 94% success rate in foster care and adoption. They felt the children needed to be ready for it and bring it up in their own time. They knew that even though all foster children were looking for permanent homes, no child was ever the same, and every child had their own time in discerning when they were ready to claim a family as their own.

Some children never get this chance, and they get kicked out of the system when they become of age, and they rarely have successful futures. Other children who get this chance just lived out regular lives or tried to do as much as possible for them, though some even had very successful stories. The way Alice and Dr. Denner handled their parenting skills with each of their adopted children turned them into the most revered foster and adoptive parents in the county.

Matthew followed the girls into their room and watched from the doorway as Vinessa led Kaelyn to her bed, and he folded his arms in amusement as he leaned against the door frame. Without saying a word and going strictly by their actions alone, Kaelyn knew Vinessa was a leader while Matthew was a follower—even though he was older than Vinessa by two years. Matthew seemed like a cool, laid-back guy, though Kaelyn knew that wasn't all there was to him. She looked forward to getting to know both of her new foster siblings. If all checked out, she knew she'd get along well with these two, but in her mind, it was still too soon to put all her eggs in one basket.

"So this is your side of the room, and since we didn't know what colors you liked, we just bought you blue bedding to go with the decor for now," Vinessa explained as she gestured towards the right half of the room.

"No, no, this is fine. I like blue. Thanks," Kaelyn replied brightly. "In fact, I love it and the different shapes and patterns."

"We figured you would, especially since Miss Wayne told us you were remarkably talented in the art department, and everyone knows a good artist appreciates shapes and patterns of all kinds," Matthew chimed in.

Kaelyn looked over at Matthew as he'd met her gaze. When his milk chocolate brown eyes met hers, she quickly realized he had the same kindness in his eyes that Alice had in hers. It was clear with Vinessa's natural bottle-blonde hair and flawless, porcelain skin in fair coloring that she took after her father in appearance. Matthew, however, favored his mother quite a bit. Both he and Alice looked like they belonged on a surfboard. Their skin was a soft tan, like that of a Hawaiian, and they just looked so beautiful and exotic. Matthew's eyebrows, however, were thicker than his face needed them to be, but Kaelyn knew they were soft, like his wavy, shoulder-length hair that matched his gentle eyes.

"And, by the way, it was my idea to get that bedding," Matthew added.

"No, it wasn't; it was Mom's idea!" Vinessa argued in a playful tone. "Don't listen to him, Kay; he'll do this kind of thing *all* the time. It's his way of joking around, sort of."

Matthew smirked when he stepped into the room and greeted his sisters up close.

"She's right, but I don't tolerate anyone else messing around with our family."

"Uh-oh, here comes one of those annoying, older brother antics of his," Vinessa stated as she rolled her eyes toward Kaelyn. "Just ignore him as I do."

"Very funny, Vin," Matthew said as he now looped his right arm over Kaelyn's shoulders.

"Now, listen up, sis. This Brother Bear'll be on the lookout 24/7 for bad boys. And if anyone says or does anything mean to you, let me know, and I'll go round up my boys, and we'll whoop some sense into the idiot that messes with you. Nobody will touch my new baby sister, and I *do* mean nobody."

Kaelyn couldn't help but smile wide at Matthew's protectiveness, though she loved how casual he was in his posture. She didn't have to worry about him. His eyes gave him away, and she somehow knew she'd be safe around him.

"It's true," Vinessa added. "He *does* mean that literally. He won't let me date a guy without a long, stern interrogation. He'll badger the hell out of your potential boyfriends, just so you know, but I've got your back. Everybody in this community knows each other, so it's not like it'll be hard picking out the bad seeds."

"And if you don't follow through with that sensibly, I'll kick *your* ass," Matthew half-jokingly but half-seriously stated toward Vinessa.

All Vinessa did in response was stick her tongue out at Matthew, and during this little spat between the siblings, Kaelyn just stood there and laughed in amusement. She had a feeling she was going to have a great time here in Novis Bay with them. Then suddenly, her stomach started growling, which caused Vinessa and Matthew to turn toward her. It wasn't a second later that all three of them found themselves in a fit of laughter.

"Maybe we should hold off the tour until we've eaten," Matthew suggested once he calmed down and had the girls follow suit. "I think you're going to love The Clam. They've got the *best* surf 'n' turf!"

"Ooh, I can't wait! I haven't eaten since breakfast. I would have eaten lunch, but I didn't have an appetite because I was too nervous," Kaelyn responded.

"Aw, what were you nervous for?" Matthew asked as he looped an arm over Kaelyn's shoulders again. "Oh, wait, I think I know. You were nervous because you were about to be moving in with the most awesome people ever, right?"

Vinessa rolled her eyes, and Kaelyn laughed.

"If you say so," Kaelyn answered.

"Well, since you're hungry, let's just go out to eat. We can give you the rest of the tour later," Vinessa said.

"That works for me," Kaelyn replied.

And with that, all three teenagers were off to join their parents downstairs, and then they all went out to eat. During dinner, though, Alice received an emergency phone call from one of her older adopted sons, Daniel. He'd found himself in jail and needed bail money.

CHAPTER
TWO

After dinner, Dr. Denner dropped the family off and then drove down to the police station.

"We're so sorry about all of this, sweetie," Alice apologized to Kaelyn as they walked through the front door.

Matthew and Vinessa followed suit.

"Yeah, Daniel finds himself in all kinds of trouble a lot, so don't pay any attention to the yelling toward Daniel whatsoever when Dad brings him home," Vinessa explained.

"Yeah … he's kind of had a very troubled past," Matthew added carefully. "So, helping him has been pretty challenging. He's what we call a work in progress. We know that we can still save him. It'll take some time and patience, but most of all, dedication and cooperation."

Kaelyn listened to everyone's explanations, and she almost felt compelled to talk to this 'Daniel' character, though he was a stranger to her because she hadn't met him yet.

"It's okay," she replied. "I don't mind. I've already had a pretty exciting first day, anyway. So, is it okay if I retire to my room?"

"Does that mean you don't want a tour?" Vinessa asked.

Kaelyn sensed that she was about to upset Vinessa, and she didn't want to do that.

"Of course, we can do the tour. After all, I don't know where the bathroom or anything is," she spoke.

Alice smiled at the fact that Kaelyn was a sweetheart. She knew that Kaelyn just wanted to end her night, but because she knew she would've hurt Vinessa's feelings had she declined the tour around the house, she decided against going straight to her room from here.

"I'd tag along, but Mom and I have important issues to talk about right now," Matthew spoke kindly with open arms and a bright smile. "But I'm not letting you out of my sight until I get a hug from my new little sis."

Kaelyn smiled while she pulled herself into Matthew's brotherly embrace, and she wrapped her arms around him, just as he did with her.

"I'm so thankful that you're here," Matthew whispered. Then his voice returned to normal. "Goodnight, Kay."

Kaelyn strongly sensed in Matthew's hug that he meant what he said about her now being a part of their lives. The glistening eyes also proved his joy in her welcome to their family. She smiled at her new brother as she pulled away, and then she responded.

"Goodnight."

Kaelyn turned to Vinessa already waiting near the staircase, and together they went upstairs. Matthew then led his mother into the kitchen, and they began discussing Daniel's current issues.

"So, this is the guest bedroom," Vinessa stated as she opened the first door and showed Kaelyn the room. "It used to be a bedroom for Jessie, Larissa, and Alex. Larissa and Alex are twins, but they're in college together with Jessie. Alex has Muscular Dystrophy, but that doesn't stop him from being a really versatile and brilliant guy. Now,

Larissa … well, Lissy is actually quite hard to describe in a nutshell. Jess is an amazing sister and person, and she's very close to Lissy and Alex. In fact, they all have an apartment together near their college campus. This summer, you'll meet them when we have our annual, weeklong Denner Family Reunion. However, this remains a guest room for when we have friends or other siblings sleep over."

Kaelyn could hardly wait to meet the rest of the family.

"How many brothers and sisters do you have?" Kaelyn asked.

"Sixteen," Vinessa answered, which then caused a shocked, bug-eyed reaction from Kaelyn. "Though Matthew and I are the only ones genetically related to one another. All the others are adopted."

This answer took Kaelyn by surprise.

"I would've thought you would've had more blood siblings than adopted. If I may ask, how come your parents didn't have more kids of their own?"

"My mother was born unwanted in Hawaii, and she spent most of her childhood in orphanages, and my dad spent the first half of his childhood in an abusive home until they were both adopted by two *very* loving families. Mom and Dad are *incredibly* grateful for the second chances in life they were given, and they wanted to give back to the community by taking in children without families or real homes. Take Jacob, for example. He was born HIV positive, and no one wanted him, so he was left without anyone good to care for him.

Mom and Dad came upon him when he was eleven, and once they heard about his story, they immediately took him in. They took their precautions and taught all of us how to prevent any possible spread of his disease while still being able to love and support him in any way he needed it. You would've *loved* Jacob, honestly, because he was one of those guys who would take you by surprise. No matter what, you couldn't predict his next move, and he was just *amazing* all around. Unfortunately, his HIV progressed to full-blown AIDS, and it stripped him of his life last year at the age of nineteen. It was a horrible time for all of us."

Kaelyn felt the hot tears threatening to fall from her eyes. But, unfortunately, she also saw the same thing happening with Vinessa.

"Aw, I'm so sorry," Kaelyn replied in sympathy. "He's in a better place now, though, right? Having AIDS must've been *awful.*"

"It was. Please don't tell Matthew this, but Jacob was my favorite brother. He always had a smile on his face, and he thrived on making people laugh, even if it was at his own expense. He had this uncanny ability to see people for who they were. He also believed that there was good in everyone. Sometimes, I swear, he had super ninja powers because he was *insanely* good at being invisible and sneaking up on people."

Kaelyn laughed as Vinessa whispered in a joking manner. Then Vinessa got serious again.

"And you're right. He's in a better place. And he's watching over all of us. I know you'll meet him someday," Vinessa continued with a bright smile. "Alright, let's continue with the tour, shall we?"

Vinessa led Kaelyn to the next room over to the right, which was similar to a living room, except it was more of a lounge area for all teenagers.

"We call this room the 'Chiller.' It sounds lame, I know, but we call it this because this is where Matthew and I hang out with our friends or other siblings. Sometimes we'll hang back on our own in here, too, usually to get away from everything overwhelming us, and we reflect on life or think about whatever's on our minds. This is where we 'chill.'"

Kaelyn laughed as Vinessa made a funny face in her last few words. Then Vinessa went on with her statement.

"As you can see, we've got a sofa and a loveseat, two reclining chairs and three bean bag chairs, two big-screen TVs, and the biggest movie, show, and game selection you could possibly ask for," Vinessa explained as she pointed to each of the luxuries. "And over here, we have a little music station set up, consisting of a drum set, two electric and acoustic guitars, a bass guitar, keyboard, and a saxophone. Don't ask. One of Matthew's friends, Jazzy, is a Jazz and Blues freak, and he leaves his sax here *all* the time—partly because it's one of his extras that he doesn't need very often.

Everything here was contributed either by Mom and Dad, Matt or myself, our other siblings, or our friends. Oh, and, honey, we have a *lot* of friends in this community. So, as you've guessed by now, this is a popular spot for us. Even Mom and Dad will hang out here with us occasionally, usually on Denner Family Fun Nights, if we're not playing board games down in the den. Also, we have a bathroom here, which means this room was initially meant to be the master bedroom. But, fortunately, Mom and Dad always felt each of us needed a special place to call our own when we needed it."

Kaelyn felt happy on the inside. Alice and Michael were a very intuitive and intelligent set of parents. She felt excited enough that she ran into the room and purposely unbalanced her body so she could fall onto a cerulean blue bean bag chair with white five-point stars. She couldn't help the squeal that escaped her throat. This new world was paradise. She was finally home.

As she looked up at the high ceiling, the only thing she could say was, "Thank you, God!"

By the time Vinessa showed Kaelyn around the entire house, Dr. Denner was back with Daniel, so Kaelyn knew nothing good would come of this. Judging by Dr. Denner's pissed-off facial expression, Kaelyn knew she wouldn't be getting any sleep—at least not anytime soon. However, she knew she had no part of this, so she stayed quiet and out of the way. Still, though, she was curious to know what Daniel had done so wrong, and Kaelyn needed to see how Dr. Denner reacted and handled a challenging situation, though she stayed far enough up the stairs that Dr. Denner couldn't see her. However, Kaelyn caught a glimpse of Daniel before she darted for the stairs, and when she did, she saw something in him, so she wanted to do a double-take.

Daniel was dressed from head to toe in black. His hair was short, layered, and pretty much all black, except for a streak of bangs of a caramel coloring and some soft caramel highlights in his hair. He also wore a studded belt and spiked wristbands.

"Did Kaelyn go to bed?" Michael asked toward Alice as he let go of Daniel's neck, seeing as he missed Kaelyn when he got home with Daniel.

"Yes, she went to bed," Vinessa answered sweetly to her father as she followed him and Daniel into the dining room.

When all three of them disappeared from her sight, Kaelyn then tiptoed down the stairs and listened to the conversation.

"So, Daniel, what happened this time? How did you land yourself in jail tonight?" Alice asked sternly with her arms folded across her chest.

When Daniel refused to speak up and refused to look at anything but a wall, Michael spoke up for him.

"He defaced school property, he had alcohol on the premises, and he was also leading to the delinquency of a minor. I paid for his three thousand dollar fine that the police gave him. He's damn near lucky he's not going to court and that Andy was the one who arrested him; otherwise, I wouldn't have bailed him out. In fact, this is the *last* time, Daniel. Do you hear me?"

Kaelyn peeked out from behind the stair wall and saw that Daniel just shrugged in response. That only angered Michael even more, so Michael placed his hand on the back of Daniel's neck again and made the twenty-three-year-old look him in the eyes. Kaelyn didn't like Dr. Denner's actions, but had Daniel deserved it, or had Daniel been so stubborn that Dr. Denner didn't have any other choice to get through to him like this? She didn't know. She watched in silence and took in everything Dr. Denner said and did.

"I said, 'Do you hear me?'" he asked more sternly this time.

"Yes, sir," Daniel replied as he met Michael's fiery gaze. "Now get your fucking hands off me before I report you for crossing my boundaries."

"Oh, don't push it, Daniel," Michael warned as he shoved Daniel away in disgust. "You're drunk and in no shape to argue with us. Now sit down."

"Fuck you!" Daniel spat at Michael.

Kaelyn was surprised by this, but at the same time, she wasn't. It was easy to see that Daniel emotionally guarded himself. In the way he carried himself and pushed the Denner family away, Kaelyn knew he was scared to get close to them. She wondered why he pushed them away, though. She knew she had to figure out what he feared.

"Dan, will you please just sit?" Matthew pleaded while he walked over to him and urged him to sit down at the dining room table.

Daniel did what Matthew asked, but he never stopped glaring up at Michael.

"You need to stop all this," Matthew continued as he sat next to his older brother, who decided to meet his brown-eyed gaze at the last second. "This is getting too juvenile, and like Dad just said, this is the last time. We weren't kidding from the last time when we said you had one more chance. You need to take us seriously on this. You don't have any more chances or choices left."

"Does it look like I give a rats' ass one way or the other?" Daniel asked in his famous sarcastic tone.

"Believe it or not, but you do care," Vinessa answered as she sat down across from Daniel. "Everyone's right; the acting out needs to stop now; I don't want to see something horrible happening to you. I don't even want to see you out on the streets the way you are now, even if you're rooming with Max. And Max really cares about you too. He's done a lot for you. So we care too much about you, Dan."

Kaelyn popped her head out just a slight bit more, so she could catch a better glimpse of Daniel's face, and he caught her movement through his peripheral vision. He then looked past Vinessa and stared straight into Kaelyn's eyes, which startled the teenager. She hid her face again for a few moments but then allowed one eye to see past the stair wall to keep studying Daniel's face. He knew she was searching hard for something through his eyes, and he melted deep within hers for some strange reason. Kaelyn sensed he had a hard past, but so did she, so she couldn't understand why Daniel acted the way he did. She wondered if maybe he just hadn't found the right person to share his problems with. She didn't know, but she knew for sure that everyone had something good inside them, and that's what she tried to find in him.

"If you cared so much about me, you would've tried to help me connect with my mother," Daniel answered as he looked down at the table.

Daniel's gentle tone of voice was precisely what she was looking for. It showed her that Daniel did have a sensitive side, and it proved to her that he was hiding behind a mask. Now she knew he was afraid. Kaelyn was determined to find out what he was scared of and why. For now, though, she just remained quiet.

"For goodness' sake, Daniel, how many times do we have to tell you? You don't *want* to reach out to your mother. She's *not* that good of a person. She's the reason you went into the system until we took you out," Alice explained.

"Whatever," was Daniel's answer as he stood up from the table in frustration. "I'll pay you back tomorrow for the bail money, but I don't care if this is the last time any of you will help me. I really don't. You claim to help people out, yet when I asked you to help me reach out to my mother, you decided not to help me—the *one* time I've *ever* asked you for help. So whatever. All of you can go fuck yourselves and go to hell because I'm out of here."

Daniel then moved out of the dining room, though the front door opened, which scared Kaelyn because the door was right there in front of her. In the house came another brown-haired boy, about the same height as Daniel and Matthew, and the first thing that caught his eye saw was the horrified expression on Kaelyn's face. He felt awful for scaring her, but he didn't speak to her immediately because he had to deal with Daniel.

"You're not going anywhere," he commanded toward Daniel as they stood there in front of the stairwell. "I heard the entire thing on Matt's speakerphone."

"What is this shit, a fucking crisis intervention?"

"Yeah, that's exactly what it is," the other young male answered.

Daniel rolled his eyes at this, and he got in the young male's face.

"Just get out of my way, Max," he warned.

Kaelyn's ears perked up at that name. Now she realized who this stranger was. He was another Denner, one of the kindest, with an old and gentle soul. At dinner, she remembered that Vinessa told her that they and some of their other siblings looked up to Max as if he was the eldest, even though he was nowhere near the most aged. Kaelyn smiled as she recognized the only person Daniel was even remotely close to was finally here because she knew he needed Max, and Max was the only one who could even get through to him.

"No, I'm not going anywhere, and neither are you. You need to get some rest, and we'll finish up tomorrow. It's either that, or you can go back to that table, sit down, and we can all talk about this until your ears bleed. Take your pick."

Kaelyn watched as Daniel glared at Max.

"I've had enough."

Max grabbed the back of his brother's neck and brought his face close. There was a tender moment between them as Max pressed their foreheads together. She half-expected to see Daniel pull away from Max's grip, but he didn't budge, which told her Daniel trusted Max a lot for him to be in his personal space like this.

"Then go get some rest, and we'll deal with the rest of this in the morning. But I'm *warning* you, Danny, don't be stupid and walk out of here in the middle of the night. At least for me, okay?"

When Daniel refused to say anything else, Max sighed, and then he suggestively pushed Daniel toward the stairs in a gentle manner.

"Go rest up, and I'll see you in the A.M."

Rather than saying another word, Daniel stormed off and passed by Kaelyn while she made way for him by leaning against the wall, though he made eye contact with her and glared at her as he continued his ascent. Max smiled briefly but tenderly toward Kaelyn when she caught his gaze. She knew he was telling her she needn't worry about what she witnessed, but then he marched into the dining room where everyone else was.

"We weren't finished," said the patriarch in a stern tone.

"I know, Dad, but he's drunk, remember? There's no use talking to him when he's like this. You're better off doing it in the morning. And, by the way, you need to let him see his mother for himself. Do yourselves a favor and give him the information he needs to see her. In fact, you should probably go with him. He *needs* the closure," Max explained. "Oh, and I'll talk to him first in the morning."

Dr. Denner took a deep breath and exhaled in frustration.

"If you truly believe that's going to help, then fine. You talk to him first," he replied.

"No, no, hon. Max has a good point. There's no sense in talking to Daniel when he's drunk," Alice stated. "You talk to him first in the morning, sweetie, and then we'll all talk at the breakfast table, okay?"

Max nodded, and Kaelyn knew the conversation about Daniel was now over, so she turned around and headed upstairs. However, she was confused once she saw her bedroom light was on. The door closed behind her when she got in, and Daniel came out from behind the door. Kaelyn gasped in shock as she turned around, as she hadn't expected him to be in here. She braced herself as she wondered if he was trustworthy enough to be alone in a room with him like this.

CHAPTER
THREE

The silence between Daniel and Kaelyn was deafening. Daniel sensed the fear in her, and he wasn't in the best mood, as he was drunk off his ass, so he knew he could be a total jerk. He just had to check out the new foster girl, though. In his eyes, she seemed cute and mousy. He wondered if she was a bratty teenager like Vinessa or more mature like one of his other sisters, Brienna or Meghan.

"Well, well, well," Daniel started as he paced back and forth in front of the young girl with his arms folded across his chest. His left eye looked straight at her while his right eye hid behind his caramel-colored bangs. "A naughty little girl has been up and out of bed."

"I'm not little. I'm fifteen," Kaelyn fired back in defense as she stepped back. "I live here now, and I told everyone I was retiring to my room for the night. That doesn't mean that I'm in trouble."

"Of course it doesn't," Daniel sneered with a step forward. "You must be Kaelyn."

She wasn't comfortable with this tone. She wondered who Daniel thought he was, being rude and disrespectful like this. She knew that he needed a lesson in manners.

"And judging by what happened downstairs, you're Daniel."

Daniel smirked as he slightly cocked his head backward with his bangs now thrown to the side to reveal his beautiful, intense blue eyes.

"Did you enjoy that little show?" he asked.

"Actually, no, I found you to be quite rude."

"Oh?" He wasn't surprised at all to hear this from her. "Why do you say that?"

"Because that's what you are. You're a jerk, and you're rude and disrespectful. From what I've gathered downstairs, the Denners have been nothing but good to you, yet you refuse to see what amazing people they are as a family."

Daniel sighed as he looked away for a few moments.

"Oh, great, another spoiled princess."

Kaelyn took great offense to this.

"Excuse me!" she fired back. "How dare you call me spoiled or princess ... *y*? Meeting the Denners might be a dream come true, but I'm pretty positive that I will live happily ever after with this family."

"Oh, God, you are a spoiled princess!" Daniel retorted in disgust as he turned to her and then looked her up and down while he stepped forward again.

"Get away from me," Kaelyn warned as she stepped back further. "And get out of my room."

This outburst took Daniel by complete surprise. He sensed now that she had trust issues. He wondered if he would dare find out and be this much of an asshole.

"Make me," he challenged as he stepped forward once more.

Kaelyn knew there was a baseball bat in the room because she carefully studied Vinessa's possessions earlier when she first came into this room. When Daniel stepped closer, though this time slower, Kaelyn immediately reached out for the baseball bat. Stunned by the sudden martial arts-like movements that she made with the bat,

Daniel watched as she confidently held the bat as if she was ready to hit him with it.

"Guys like you need a major lesson in treating other people the right way," Kaelyn cautioned. "Now, get away from me before I hurt you."

Daniel chuckled.

"You can't touch me, princess," he taunted. "You're liable to get hurt in the process."

"And what the hell is that supposed to mean?" Kaelyn asked in a low voice as she stood her ground.

"Just that I'm stronger than you … and could take you down if I wanted to, but I can promise you your trust issues aren't with me."

Kaelyn scoffed as she adjusted her hands more firmly on the bat.

"Yeah, right."

Daniel snickered, and though he didn't step closer this time, he sure as hell walked back and forth in front of her again.

"Go ahead then, swing that bat, I *dare* you," he tested with arms folded across his chest. "See what happens."

Kaelyn stepped back once more.

"You don't want to force my hand," Kaelyn cautioned. "I'm not a fighter, but I *will* fight if I have to."

Daniel took a long look into Kaelyn's beautiful chestnut brown eyes. He saw fear, and behind her anxiety, he recognized strength. He thought at first that she was the mousy personality type, but he sensed she'd already been through enough that forced her to use her power in situations that called for a fight or flight response from her. She'd braced herself in this situation, so she was ready to fight. He wanted to prove that she didn't have anything to be scared about and that he wouldn't do anything terrible to her.

He took a big step towards her, and then she swung the bat. When she did, he quickly stopped it in its path with a firm grip now on the bat, and Kaelyn froze in her actions. Their eyes locked in a penetrating gaze, and he saw her strength disappear. Daniel's eyebrows furrowed in bitterness as he swiftly snatched the bat from her hands. Then, with her chestnut-brown eyes still locked with his eyes of blue intensity, Kaelyn backed up, and Daniel watched as she stood there like a deer in headlights. Finally, he threw the baseball bat onto her bed, though their eyes never left each other's gaze, and he backed Kaelyn into the wall behind her.

"I may be a total dickhead," he spoke in a serious, unapologetic tone as his face was now inches from hers. "But I would rather die a thousand deaths than lay a hand on a woman. Of course, you'd also find my ass in prison so Goddamned fast that your head would spin because I'd kill a man who would dare lay a hand on a woman."

Kaelyn didn't know what to say to this. Daniel stunned her with this statement, and the passion in his voice and on his face threw her off. It seems he had a moral compass, after all.

"*Never* judge a book by its cover," he told her as he now stepped away from her. However, he brought both hands up and pointed his index fingers in her direction. "You should go back to the family from which you came. Oh, and thanks to Vinessa, the position of 'spoiled, bratty hypocrite' has already been filled."

When Kaelyn said nothing and became solemn, Daniel decided to leave her alone.

"Later, princess."

Just as Daniel opened the door and turned his back to Kaelyn, she spoke up.

"How can I go back to the family I came from if they're dead?"

Daniel froze as he momentarily felt sympathetic toward the girl, though he had nothing else to say. "And as far as never judging a book by its cover goes, you should do well to take your own advice. You don't know me. So *don't* call me a princess."

Daniel still said nothing, but instead, he just shut the door behind him and left for the guest room.

Later that night, Kaelyn cried alone on the porch. Once Matthew opened his bedroom window due to the stuffiness, he heard her sobs. He knew it wasn't Vinessa because she wasn't a crier, and she'd talk to him if anything ever bothered her. So, he put on a t-shirt, slipped into his sandals, and headed downstairs to the front door. He opened it slowly so that he couldn't scare the poor girl, and then he found her with her face buried in her knees on the porch swing. He walked over to her and gently touched her bare-skinned shoulder.

"Hey," he spoke softly. "What's wrong?"

When Kaelyn looked up at Matthew, she sniffled and then spoke up.

"Do you think I'm a spoiled princess?"

"What? No way!" Matthew exclaimed. "Who told you, you were a spoiled princess?"

"It doesn't matter," Kaelyn replied, looking down at her bunny-slippered feet.

"Can I sit down?" Matthew asked.

Kaelyn brought her legs down off the swing and gave way for Matthew to sit down, and he did. Unbeknownst to them, another pair of ears listened in on their conversation. Daniel couldn't sleep, so he'd been sitting in the nook in front of his guest room windows, which he preferred open so he could smell the salty air from the ocean. He had nothing better to do except roll his eyes at Matthew's answers to Kaelyn.

"My birth parents and brother were killed in a car accident when I was just a baby, and if my adopted mother hadn't gotten cancer and died, my adopted dad wouldn't have done the horrible things that he did to me. I also wouldn't have ended up with the awful Johnsons. You probably already know this, but they got caught with their sex-trafficking ring. They couldn't exactly sell me to someone else since they were just my fosters, but—"

Matthew's heart broke for her.

"I know. Your caseworker told Mom and Dad the basics of what they were putting you through, and of course, they told Vin and me."

Daniel suspected she had a background of significant abuse, and now he knew he was right. He looked up at the moon as a sigh escaped his lips. Then he gently pressed the back of his head against the wall. He didn't know her well enough, but he knew that no child deserved to go through the hell she went through. He had a huge thing against abusers and pedophiles, and he'd kill them with his bare hands.

"I can't tell you how long I've been praying for a second chance with a family like yours. I was beginning to lose my faith."

Daniel knew that feeling all too well, as he'd been in her position once upon a time. Matthew gulped softly when Kaelyn met his gaze. He felt the emotions rising from the deepest parts of his soul. He tried to shake it by keeping his focus on Kaelyn's story.

"But then you guys came out of nowhere, and I know it wasn't a coincidence. But if I've left you with the impression that I'm a spoiled princess, tell me now because that's not what I want to be. I'd rather show my appreciation for what you've all done and for whatever your family will do in the future for me."

Matthew's heart broke even more over this. His face flushed with sadness, anger, and happiness rolled into one ball of emotions. He had difficulty maintaining his composure, though he did manage to keep it. Daniel, on the other hand, was surprised by her response. However, his eyes rolled once more when Matthew spoke up again.

"You're not spoiled, Kay. You're everything but. Though I have to ask, is there something wrong with being a princess? Princesses are known to be good girls who get what they deserve, and you're a super sweet girl. You honestly deserve the best."

"I don't want to be a princess," Kaelyn replied as she never broke Matthew's gaze. "I just want to be loved."

It was lucky it was dark out, or Kaelyn would've seen Matthew's eyes watering, though he held back those tears. His heart was wholly broken for her, and he pulled her into his arms for comfort. Kaelyn's words also tugged at Daniel's heart.

"Aw, Kay, you are loved. We couldn't even begin to express how pleased we are to have you here. But, can I be honest with you? I was the one that picked you out the day we visited your group home. You were sitting alone in a corner, reading A Midsummer Night's Dream, and smiling as if you didn't have a care in the world. But, once I saw you, I knew that was it and that we had to have you.

When I pointed you out to my family, we fell in love with you. Then my parents had to fight for you over another couple interested in fostering you. Mom and Dad almost gave up because it seemed like the other couple had *so* much more to offer than we did, though I begged them not to give up. And I was right for them not to. You're meant to be here with us, and you're not going anywhere anytime soon."

Kaelyn pulled from Matthew's hug and wiped her snotty nose.

"I know who you're talking about. I'm glad I went with you guys. I told Miss Wayne I didn't want to go with them. They seemed like they had a lot to offer, but the husband was *too* friendly, and the vibe coming off him just made me … *so* uncomfortable."

Matthew had a pretty good understanding of what Kaelyn was trying to say without actually saying it. He pressed his head against hers in sweet tenderness and closed his eyes for a few moments before he spoke up again.

"Nothing bad will happen to you here, Kay," Matthew answered in a caring voice. "Our family isn't perfect, though our imperfections bring us together. Every one of us has something in our past that we regret, or we've seen disturbing things we wish we could un-see, or we've been through something dark that we wish we could forget. You know, a year ago, we lost a brother to an illness he was born with. It was a really dark time for all of us."

Kaelyn turned her head and looked at Matthew as he looked at the wooded deck beneath their feet.

"Weirdly enough, what came first was the anger and the fighting. Oh, there was constant bickering between Mom and Dad. I thought they'd get divorced because they never fought in front of us kids until then. Vinessa tried turning to me for comfort after the period of anger and fighting, though I was distant and depressed … and then came the guilt and the shame. Mom kept herself pretty busy with work, and I pushed everyone away. Dad was … Dad was suicidal. I wasn't far from that edge either."

Daniel had tears in his eyes when he heard this. Kaelyn saw that Matthew had fallen into a gloomy trance. Nevertheless, she continued to listen carefully to his words.

"For a while, I … I'd cut myself. The physical pain was easier to handle than the emotional pain. I guess I couldn't deal with all of the overwhelming emotions."

Kaelyn was astonished to hear this. From Vinessa's explanation earlier in the evening, she knew Jacob's death had deeply affected the entire Denner family, but she didn't realize it was this bad.

"Vinessa, with the help of her best friend, eventually snapped out of her shock. She first convinced me that we couldn't get out of that dark time without each other. Once *I* pulled out of my depression, though, Vinessa and I helped Mom, and then all of us, we'd gotten to Dad just in time. Dad felt *so* much guilt about Jacob succumbing to his illness. He's a doctor, but he felt like he didn't do everything for Jacob … like he still could've done something more for him. I felt the same way, but Dad … we found him in the attic … with his nine-millimeter Smith and Wesson pistol in his mouth, and it was fully loaded … with his finger on the trigger …"

Daniel hadn't known how bad things were at the house until now. It bothered him more than he thought it would. When Matthew started talking about Jacob, a tear had slipped from Daniel's eyes. However, he quickly wiped it away and left his fingers over the inside corners of his eyes to better control his emotions. He didn't accept Jacob as his brother until the end, and now one of the last conversations they had, had come to mind.

———

"I SEE YOU, DANIEL," JACOB SPOKE WHILE DANIEL OPENED A SECOND beer for himself. "Just like I've seen Max on a date in the next town over, I've also seen you at AA and NA meetings in the same town. I see you struggling in so many ways that it's hard to keep it all in one neat line."

Jacob approached his older brother as Daniel scoffed at him.

"You leave Max out of this," Daniel warned with a pointed index finger toward Jacob before he chugged some of his beer.

"I'm just saying I'm good at reading people. You go to meetings, yet you're here drinking beer with a blunt on your coffee table waiting for you to smoke up. Hell, I've also seen you beat up men for looking at you the wrong damn way. You have abandonment issues stemming from your childhood, and you've kept your true self hidden from the entire family for fear of being abandoned again. You hate who you are, and you're constantly at war with yourself. Even though Max is always there for you, sometimes you feel utterly alone, and all you want to do is drown out your emotions and low self-esteem with drugs, alcohol, and parties."

Daniel threw his beer across the living room as he now got in his younger brother's face. They both heard the bottle shatter against the wall behind the sofa. Neither brother flinched, and neither had broken each other's intense gaze. Jacob had expected more rage in Daniel's voice but was surprised when Daniel remained calm.

"Who the hell do you think you are, coming over to my house and reading me like a fucking therapist? I didn't ask you for help, and I certainly don't need you psychoanalyzing me."

"No, you didn't ask, but you need it. I can see you losing yourself, but you're still trying everything in hell to stay afloat."

Jacob caught a flicker of water that welled up in Daniel's eyes, but it dissipated as quickly as it came. Daniel started to turn his back, but Jacob grabbed his shoulder.

"I want to be a lifeline for you, Dan. I know who you are, and I accept you as you are."

The room's silence was deafening, as Daniel didn't know what to say to Jacob at first. He wondered how his younger brother picked up on his secret when he was barely around the Denners. He knew Jacob was a good guy and that he'd keep his secret, but still, the thought of coming out of the closet petrified Daniel. Max was the only person who knew this part of him until now. A big knot formed at the back of his throat.

"How'd you know?" he inquired as he met Jacob's eyes again. "What gave me away?"

"I just ... know," Jacob answered. "We're kindred spirits."

Jacob's response brought tears to Daniel's eyes, and he knew it was difficult for his older brother to keep his composure. Jacob pulled Daniel into his arms and held him there to provide safety and comfort.

"I know how close you and Max are, and I know Max is the only person you've ever trusted because you feel he's the only one who's never abandoned you. I need you to know, Daniel, that Max isn't your only option for a lifeline. I'm in your corner too, and I will always be someone you can trust. I promise you can lean on me when the going gets tough because you're my brother. I accept you for who you are, and I would never abandon you because I love you."

DANIEL'S HEAD FELL TO HIS KNEES WHEN HIS MIND HAD RETURNED TO the present, and he ran both of his hands through his hair as a means of comfort as he still listened to Matthew and Kaelyn's conversation in silence. Kaelyn sensed Matthew's emotions as they continued their conversation. His feelings washed over her, and they weighed heavily on her heart and soul. She had tears in her eyes once she saw Matthew bring his hand up to his face to dry his eyes. Kaelyn knew this was hard for him to talk about. She, however, was glad he felt comfortable enough in sharing it with her.

"Vinessa reminded Dad, she reminded all of us, that we needed each other to get through that dark time, or it would've destroyed the dynamics of our family that we'd worked so hard for. Ever since we came out of that period, we've been determined to encourage and lift one another, and coping with Jacob's fate brought all of us closer. Our bonds grew stronger with each other, not just in this house but with *everyone* in our family. Mom and Dad wanted to stop fostering kids after we lost Jacob, but Vin and I ... we knew that's not what Jacob would've wanted."

"He would've wanted your family to continue their work in foster care," Kaelyn whispered. "He knew what a blessing your family was to him. You gave him everything he ever wanted and needed."

Matthew pulled his hand away from his face and sniffled. This proved to Kaelyn that he was quite a sensitive guy.

"Vinessa said I would've loved him," she whispered as Matthew turned to gaze into her eyes with warmth.

"You definitely would've," Matthew replied with a soft, genuine smile. "And he would've *loooved* you. Jacob loved everybody. There was no such thing as hatred or being spiteful in his vocabulary. Even Daniel showed kindness and respect towards him. Jacob didn't judge anyone for their actions or their words. He wasn't the best at giving advice, but people sure could lean on him for comfort. He liked to listen to what people had to say. If people wronged him, he'd just turn the other cheek, and then he'd turn right around and forgive them in the process. He just ... loved."

Kaelyn immensely enjoyed hearing this description of Jacob. Vinessa defined Jacob pretty well, but Matthew described him with such a passionate tone. Kaelyn knew that Matthew was just as close to Jacob as Vinessa was.

"Hey, you want some ice cream? I know a secret place," Matthew inquired as he tried to change the subject now.

Kaelyn's eyes glistened back into Matthew's. Kaelyn knew he didn't want to talk about this discussion anymore. She was content with him changing the subject.

"Oh, yes, I've worked up an appetite," she answered. "Wait, it's like two in the morning. Where are we going to get ice cream this late?"

"Relax," Matthew said as he grabbed her hand to pull her off the porch swing. "Brother Bear's got your back."

Once Matthew grabbed his keys and locked the front door, the two teenagers went to the Arctic Zone ice cream shop where Matthew worked.

CHAPTER
FOUR

When Matthew and Kaelyn arrived at the ice cream parlor, he unlocked the back door, and he first allowed Kaelyn to enter. After he followed her into the shop and locked the door behind him, he switched on all the lights.

"How do you have the keys for this place?" Kaelyn asked. "Do you work here or something?"

"Yeah, I'm the manager. Since I was fourteen, I've been working here, so naturally, I moved up into power. I could even hire people if I want to. However, someone did just resign two days ago because his family was unexpectedly moving to Japan.

So, I should be on the lookout for a new employee, but I haven't found anyone yet. We have an excellent team around here. We trust each other, rely on each other, and we help each other out. Sometimes, Jen can be a bitch, but we all generally get along pretty well. So, what kind of ice cream do you want? We've got all kinds, and we have both regular and soft serve. We even do ice cream sodas and milkshakes."

"Hm. I'm in the mood to experiment. Is that okay?"

"Of course; what ice creams have you had in the past?"

"Rocky Road, Chocolate Marshmallow, Chocolate Chip Cookie Dough, Rainbow Sherbert, Vanilla, Strawberry, and Chocolate."

"Have you ever tried Mint Chocolate Chip?" Matthew inquired.

When Kaelyn shook her head no, Matthew went to the front, and then Kaelyn followed. He opened one of the front counter freezers, grabbed a scooper, ran it quickly under hot water, and opened a new Mint Chocolate Chip ice cream tub. He scooped some out and put it in a little dish for Kaelyn. After closing the tub and the glass door, he turned to Kaelyn and handed her ice cream and a spoon. He didn't leave any moment to spare, though, when he went over to the record machine to plug it in.

"Wow!" Kaelyn exclaimed as she followed him and set her sights on the old jukebox. "I've never seen one of those in real life! So you have one here?"

Matthew turned to her and smiled.

"Yep, and it only plays old music, too. At first, nobody liked it, but then we started a promotional campaign called 'Friday Nights in Time.' Everything was twenty-five percent cheaper on Fridays, and we set this place up like an old-fashioned diner, even though it's an ice cream shop and soda bar, and each Friday was a different decade —décor and all. That got popular, which became the mainstream here at the Zone. Now people love the jukebox, and it pulls in a nice chunk of change for the business, so even if people have to put a quarter in to play a song, it's worth it to them. What would you like to hear?"

"Um, Elvis Presley's *Hound Dog*, if you could?"

"Elvis is one of our populars, and I believe I've heard it on here before."

Matthew put his hand behind the jukebox to push a button. He struggled because of how the jukebox was positioned, though he eventually got it, and the machine then made a clicking noise.

"What did you just do?" Kaelyn asked.

"I just did a super-naughty thing," Matthew answered with an evil smirk as he fixed his posture. "Ol' jukey here is only supposed to be playing with quarters put into him. There's a special switch back here that allows you to turn that off and play any song you want at any time you want. It's used for private non-commercial owners, but it's never supposed to be turned off for businesses. Businesses have them to make money off 'em."

"You're going to switch it back on before we leave, though, right?" Kaelyn asked.

"Oh, yeah, of course; I'm not stupid," Matthew answered with a laugh.

"Oh, okay, good. By the way, this Mint Chocolate Chip ice cream is *so* good," Kaelyn said.

"I know, right? It's my *favo*rite flavor here. All our ice cream is homemade, did you know that?"

Kaelyn shook her head no.

"Would you like to make some ice cream?"

"Can we make Mint Chocolate Chip?" Kaelyn asked.

Matthew's face lit up in excitement when Kaelyn said that.

"Of course! Just let me hit *Hound Dog,* and we can get right on it!" Matthew exclaimed.

Once Matthew blasted the song on the jukebox, he was amazed to find Kaelyn dancing in excitement. He was even more surprised to learn that she knew how to dance like Elvis Presley. He remembered Vinessa's best friend taught him and his sister to dance to some classic songs, including *Hound Dog*, so he jumped beside Kaelyn and pulled off the same moves. After the song ended, Kaelyn couldn't help but laugh, and Matthew was thoroughly pleased.

"Where did you learn to dance like Elvis?" he had to ask.

"My childhood best friend's two dads taught us, which was great because my adopted parents couldn't stand Presley's music while it speaks to me. Where did *you* learn to dance? I've never seen a straight guy dance remotely like Elvis."

"Ah, Vinessa's best friend is a straight guy, and *he* taught us. For him, though, Elvis's music reminds him of his birth parents because they all had an Elvis thing together as a family—that is, *before* his birth parents passed away."

"Aw, when did they pass away?"

"I don't know; maybe when he was around four? You'd have to ask him when he comes back to town, and I'm sure you'll have plenty of chances to get to know him because he's Vinessa's best friend and kind of like a brother to us. He can be crazy sometimes, but he's pretty laid-back and chill."

"That's pretty cool, holding onto his parents like that, keeping the spirit of his family alive," Kaelyn replied with a smile as she got excited again.

She approached the jukebox and hit another classic favorite song of hers, *Jailhouse Rock*, and this told Matthew that Elvis Presley was one of Kaelyn's favorite musicians—which didn't bother him. She was adorable and entertaining when she danced like Elvis and lip-synced to the music. Kaelyn then followed him back into the kitchen. Before long, they were making the ice cream and having a good old time doing so. After putting the new tub in and replacing the one Matthew scooped out of, they took the old one and just overate. Again, they laughed and continued to dance like Elvis, only this time on top of the bar counters. They sang along to all the jukebox classics and laughed like crazy when making a mess. They didn't get any sleep because seven o'clock came much too fast for them. They eventually shut off the jukebox, cleaned up their mess, and locked it up by seven-thirty. And Kaelyn officially dubbed Matthew as her brother—he was just that cool.

They decided to head back to bed when they returned home, but not before saying goodnight. Kaelyn spoke up once Matthew placed his keys on the key rack next to the front door.

"Thanks for everything, Matt. You really made my night."

"Of course! That's what brothers are for, right?" Matthew asked.

Kaelyn smiled up at Matthew and nodded. She wanted to say

something, but she decided not to. Matthew caught this, though, and he knew he couldn't ignore it.

"What?" he inquired.

"Nothing, just something I was thinking."

"And what might that be? You looked like you really wanted to say it," Matthew noted.

"I was just wondering why your family just didn't adopt me," she replied.

Matthew took a serious pause as he looked deep into Kaelyn's eyes. Then he sighed softly.

"We never adopt kids right out of the system. Mom and Dad like to build a relationship with them first. Then they wait until the kids are ready to be adopted, usually when the kids go up to them and ask to be officially part of the family," Matthew explained. "Why do you ask?"

"Oh, no reason, really; I was just curious because you have all these brothers and sisters, and not one of them went back into the system," Kaelyn replied. "I'm actually quite surprised Daniel didn't go back in, considering he seems like he wants no part of our family, am I right?"

"Mom and Dad got him and Max when they were twelve. Max wasn't about to let Mom and Dad let him go, and neither were Vinessa or me. We were determined to get him to turn his ways around, and Max was just really close to him. They practically grew up together before we met them. Wait, did you say *'our'* family?"

Kaelyn smiled softly as she nodded.

"Well … as far as I'm concerned, I've found my family. The only problem is I'm not adopted …"

Now Matthew understood why she asked what she asked.

"Ohhhh, *that's* why you asked about the adoption because you want to be adopted, don't you?" Matthew inquired.

Kaelyn just looked down. Her silence gave him the answer that he knew he needed. Matthew looped an arm around her shoulders and brought his face close to hers.

"Don't worry, Kay. We're not giving you up. But we *do* have all the time in the world for adoption. Just get to know Mom and Dad better first, especially Dad, okay? They'll appreciate that. However, they won't appreciate the fact that we just came home at eight in the morning, and we're still in our pajamas, and you're still in your bunny slippers. So let's hurry up and get back into our beds before the house wakes up," Matthew continued, but then he kissed her forehead in a brotherly manner. "And sweet dreams."

Kaelyn smiled as she began to walk away.

"Goodnight," she replied.

Matthew followed her up the stairs, and then she headed to her room, and he went his own way. They both climbed back into their beds and slipped quickly into their slumbers. Max woke Matthew up when ten o'clock came around, and Vinessa tried to do the same with her new sister. Matthew woke up soon because he had taken nightly trips out before, but Kaelyn was a heavy sleeper, and she couldn't be woken up for anything. Matthew explained everything to his mom when she was concerned about Kaelyn not waking up.

"We were up late last night and had some serious talks. Just let her alone and make her breakfast later. She needs her sleep."

"Oh, and what *were* you talking about?" Alice asked curiously.

"Just, you know … the usual junk on our raging teenage minds," Matthew answered while he stuck his tongue out in a playful manner.

Alice chuckled as she rolled her eyes in response.

"Will you please go set the breakfast table?" she asked. "We'll leave Kay alone for now and make her something when she wakes up later."

Matthew nodded and did as he was told. Vinessa caught up with him in the dining room, and she spoke to him while they were alone.

"What did you *really* do last night with Kay?" she whispered in curiosity.

"Took her to Arctic Zone," Matthew answered lowly so their dad couldn't hear him from the living room. "We only got back a couple of hours ago."

"Dang, *that* late, really?" Vinessa whispered.

Matthew nodded.

"She had fun, and I think I found Andy's replacement. I asked Kay if she'd like a job there since we're looking for somebody, and she said she'd love to. So later on, whenever she wakes up and gets ready, I'm taking her back in to fill out the paperwork. Then we'll go from there with training. She's a quick learner, you know."

"What have you taught her?" Vinessa had to ask.

Matthew looked into the living room and then brought his face close to his sister's.

"I taught her how to make the ice cream."

Vinessa's eyes went wide in shock.

"Oh, you're *sooo* lucky Dave wasn't there to catch you in the act, or you would've been fired on the spot! Are you *crazy*?"

"It was two A.M., and judging by the fact that the ice cream was practically hard, Dave left early in the evening before. So chill and keep this between us. Once I take over the business, Kay will be my most trusted ice cream maker."

"You're going to make it a real position?"

"Yep. You know, the manager and the owner can't be there all the time. The ice cream making should be taken care of by someone who's available anytime. I'll have to throw in some extra cash in the register to pay for what we ate. Oh, by the way, Kay said something to me this morning ..."

Vinessa looked up at Matthew's face and found he was glowing in excitement.

"What did she say? What's it about?"

"It's about us. As a family. And her being part of our family."

Vinessa knew that it must have been something good that Kaelyn said because Matthew was practically jumping up and down as it was.

"Go on …" Vinessa continued. "Give me her direct words."

"'Well … as far as I'm concerned, I've found my family. The only problem is I'm not adopted.' Dot, dot, dot."

Vinessa gasped at this.

"Really? She said that?" she asked as excitement filled every fiber of her being.

Matthew could only nod.

"What did you tell her?" Vinessa continued.

"I told her not to worry, that we weren't giving her up and that we have all the time in the world for the adoption to happen. I told her just to get to know Mom and Dad better. She loves us, Vin; she really does."

"Dude, do you know how awesome this is? Oh, Matt, this makes me so happy!"

"What makes you so happy?" Alice inquired as she walked into the dining room. "And why aren't all the plates and silverware on the table yet?"

"Nothing," Vinessa replied to her mother. "Sorry, I distracted him. I'll help you set the table, Matt."

"Sure, I could use the help, thanks," Matthew said.

Alice watched as her two children grabbed what was needed for the dining room table. She knew something was up with them, but she knew it couldn't have been anything wrong, so she decided to leave it alone.

CHAPTER
FIVE

Denver James Knight sighed in frustration while he put a hand through his hair, the hair he was glad to have back at the length he missed. This meant no more wigs for a while, at least for now. He looked down at his Frankie Winters handkerchief, his all-time favorite bandana that he owned. Denver was so used to wearing them over his head after his Leukemia treatments that he felt awkward and naked if he didn't wear one. Frankie was his favorite musician, and she had personally autographed his bandana, so he'll never forget that day. Frankie had visited the Oncology ward at his hospital when he was twelve, and he just so happened to have that specific bandana with him when he was there, so this was one of his favorite days.

Denver looked up at the large, tall building in front of him that he was approaching on the ferry, and then he sighed. A part of him didn't want to be here because it was *the* prison that held the one man he never wanted anything to do with. But, another big part of him was desperate to get this all over. Denver also needed to get the answers to the questions he'd had for so many years. He felt he deserved some of them. He was robbed of his parents fifteen years earlier and then of his only surviving sister a few months later through the foster system. It was his worst nightmare come true.

Now here he was at the age of nineteen. He was filled with rage for Davis Anderson. This criminal was the evil man who destroyed his perfect, little family life. Denver was a good kid, respectful, and a total sweetheart, though he could flip his psycho switch if and when someone chose to mess with him. He was in a mood where he could easily be irritated, and that's not a mood he or anybody else liked to see him in. However, Denver had a feeling he'd get pissed off today anyway. He also sensed he'd leave this island with more unanswered questions than when he got here. At this very moment, he was starting to wonder if this trip was worth it until he remembered it was because he needed to see the face again of the man who ruined his life—even if his conscience was screaming, *'NO!'*

"Just *do* it, Den," he told himself.

At that moment, the ferry driver looked over his shoulder at him and gave him a look that had crazy written all over it. Denver realized he must have looked peculiar to the guy right now. When he sighed, that's when the man spoke up to him.

"May God protect your soul in there. It's like a man-made Hell. That's why it's dubbed Hell's Island, you know."

Denver found it odd that the ferryman would say this. Overall, the man appeared skinny and awkward, and he had gray, balding hair. What stood out was the man's unnaturally large ears, which made his face seem a little small. In truth, the ferry driver gave Denver the creeps. He tried not to judge the man's appearance any longer by clearing his throat to focus his mind on the subject at hand.

"I don't believe in God," he replied.

This statement surprised the man, though he spoke up again more passionately.

"Then may God have mercy on your soul."

The ferryman's tiny gold cross necklace caught the sun and had glistened into his eyes. Had Denver believed in God, he'd have found that to be a sign. Maybe. But what was certain was that had he not lost his family, he would've still believed in God and continued his walk with the Lord. When the boat docked, Denver thanked the man, and without getting a response from him, he walked off the ferry and stepped foot onto this cursed island. Denver turned around to find the ferry driver standing guard of his boat with a rifle in hand, so Denver spoke up.

"Will you be here long?"

The man looked down at him and nodded.

"Unless I get a call to bring over an inmate or some other visitor, I don't have any other appointments. So Hell's Island never gets many visitors, and most people never come out."

Denver knew the man now referred to the prisoners. Hell's Island was the west coast version of Riker's Island, which was on the eastern seaboard. It secured and cared for some of the most dangerous men in the region.

"I could never understand why anyone other than authorities and lawyers would want to visit this place anyhow," he continued. "But may God have mercy on *their* souls is all *I* have to say."

"I came to set the record straight," Denver said. "A record that should've been straightened out fifteen years ago."

The ferryman knew Denver was built up of hatred for the prisoner he was visiting, fifteen years of hate, so he knew this couldn't lead to anything good.

"As I said, may God have mercy on your soul," he repeated now as he looked away from Denver.

This told Denver he was done talking with him. Once again, the ferryman's tiny cross caught the sun and sparkled in Denver's eyes. Denver wondered if that was a sign, but then he shook that out of his thoughts. He didn't believe in God. Denver cleared his head and then turned around again to face the large building in front of him.

The image of Davis smiling and laughing popped into his head. Oh, how he hated that man. He hated how the night of the murder was one of his sharpest memories from many years ago over all his joyous family's memories that started to fade. The night of the murder was a nightmare Denver repeated every night in his sleep if he forgot to take his medication for Post-Traumatic Stress Disorder.

Denver shook this image out of his head as he tied his Frankie Winters bandana back onto his head and walked on. Once he walked into the prison, he went up to the visitor desk and signed in while giving the male receptionist a prisoner's name. Next, they took away his keys, his metal spiked belt, and anything else he might have had on him that would be sharp or may be used as a weapon. Afterward, they led him to an open communication center where seven stalls of four-inch-thick glass were between the prisoner and his visitor.

He turned to the guard standing in front of the only exit, and he knew this guard was there for his safety. Denver then turned back to find two guards bringing in the man he hated with every fiber of his being. Denver walked over to it when they sat him in stall number six and sat down. The man looked at him as if he saw a ghost. He smiled his famous evil smirk, though. The prisoner picked up the phone and waited patiently for Denver to pick his own up, which he did after he stared at the man for a good minute.

"Hello, Denver."

Denver somehow knew the prisoner would recognize him. By his tone, the criminal seemed pleased to get a visit from the young man. Davis looked pretty much like he did fifteen years ago except for a few wrinkles on his face and a more muscular tone to his body build. He had short brown hair with a natural reddish tint to it, though the expression on his face freaked Denver out. He made the same facial expression Denver had last seen him in, the same insane, twisted face that proved he'd never change from his psychotic ways.

"It's been … what, fifteen years? I knew I'd get a visit from you sooner or later. You're about … nineteen now, right?"

Denver didn't know what to say to the man, though he glared at him. He wondered why this man expected him and why had he kept tabs on his age? What was it he knew that Denver hadn't? Why was he so calm? Denver didn't like the way the man was acting.

"How are you?" asked the prisoner.

"Fuck you," Denver replied. "I didn't come here to catch up on each other's lives. I came here to set a fucking record straight."

Davis knew this was coming.

"Then set it," he said.

"Why the *fuck* would you kill my parents?"

"Your beautiful mother was supposed to fall in love with me and marry me. However, James took my woman and children away from me. If I couldn't have them, nobody could."

Denver's eyes burned with hatred.

"You're one sick, twisted motherfucker," Denver stated. "They were my fucking parents! And you also tried to go after my sister and me!"

"It figures you would've thought I'd want to kill you two kids. I wouldn't lay a damn hand on you *or* Dakota. I was trying to take back the children that were rightfully mine. You're my son, and Dakota is my daughter."

"Fuck you!" Denver spat with rage. "Tell me the fucking truth!"

Davis smiled as he just sat back and watched Denver turn furious.

"I just did. It's not my fault you refuse to see the truth. I wouldn't lie to my son. I would've thought you would've turned out to look so much more like your mother, but I was wrong. You look a lot like me from when I was a teenager, except you got the better genes. Or have you gotten Leukemia before?"

Denver couldn't believe what had just come out of this man's mouth.

"You *have* gotten Leukemia before, haven't you?"

When Denver didn't respond, Davis just smiled bigger.

"So, then my genes *are* stronger than your mother's. Hm. Well, just know that if you ever get Leukemia again, which you probably will, I'm willing to be a bone marrow donor for you—*if* you can get me out of here."

Denver wanted to kill this prisoner. His hatred for the man grew stronger. In fact, what was a four-inch-thick glass wall going to do if he went after this man?

"Fuck you!" he shouted as he stood up now and slammed on the glass. "If you *ever* get out of here, I'll fucking kill you! Do you *hear* me? They should've given you that goddamned death penalty, you sick, twisted bastard!"

The guard who once stood in front of Denver's only exit came rushing over to him. Davis just sat in silence as he sinisterly smirked toward the nineteen-year-old boy.

"You fucking killed my parents, and you've been stalking me! I *hate* you! I fucking *hate* you!"

The guard then dragged Denver out of the communication center.

"Alright, pal, you're time is up," the guard said, though Denver's arms flailed as he tried to get out of the guard's arms.

"I'M GOING TO FUCKING KILL YOU, DAVIS; YOU HEAR ME? I FUCKING HATE YOU! I'LL KILL YOU IF YOU EVER GET OUT, YOU CRAZY MOTHERFUCKER! YOU DESERVE TO GO TO FUCKING HELL!"

Davis watched and listened as Denver kept screaming in the hall before the door to the communication center closed.

"Oh, Denver, you shouldn't have done that," he whispered as he mentally accepted Denver's challenge. "Eh, but then again, I do *love* a good challenge."

Denver snarled as the authorities escorted him outside the prison. He knew he would've had more questions unanswered than when he went in.

"Take my advice, kid," warned the one guard as he returned the items they took at the desk. "Don't ever come back here. Coming here won't change anything."

Denver said nothing to the guard and watched as they returned to their post inside.

"FUCK!" he shouted as he took off his bandana.

The ferryman saw his display of frustration. He figured the young fellow hadn't gotten what he needed. He hadn't heard what the angry young man shouted, though he was thankful he couldn't make out the words. When Denver's eyes fell upon the ferry, he realized there was no use staying another second on Hell's Island. He then put his belt back on, and with his bandana in one hand and his car keys in the other, he headed toward the ferry. The moment he stepped foot onto the boat was when the driver prepared them to leave. When Denver refused to say a word to the ferryman as he passed by him, the man knew not to say anything back, but he did pray silently for the Hell's Island visitor. Danger was written all over Denver and in his aura, and the man could sense it a mile away. Then, when he was well on his way back to the mainland and had a moment to spare, he turned to Denver and found him deep in thought.

"You didn't get what you came for, did you, boy?"

Denver looked up at him, almost solemn yet still frustrated.

"No," he answered.

The ferry driver gazed deep into the young man's eyes and found something he hoped he wouldn't—persistence.

"Then you best press forward from here on out, son. If you didn't get what you came for now, you never will."

Denver wondered why the man said that.

"Excuse me, no offense, but I think you need to mind your own business," Denver replied to him nicely.

"Then may God *really* have mercy on your soul, young friend, because if you don't look ahead now, the danger will hit you *hard* at home. You may not believe in God now, but you better start soon, or all will be lost for you."

Denver rolled his eyes at this one. He didn't believe in God, and he certainly wasn't about to accept the words of a religious lunatic.

"Piss off," he warned.

Once the man realized he couldn't get through to Denver, he just turned his back and focused on returning to the mainland. Denver then looked out at the waters and thought about his past. He thought about the moment he was taken away from his one-year-old sister when he was four years old because the Knight Family wanted to adopt a little boy for their one-year-old daughter, Rori. He remembered not having anything to do with Rori for the first two weeks with the Knights. Then one day, out of the blue, the babysitter hit Rori, all because Rori was a colicky baby. The Knights fired the woman once Denver proved she was abusive, but after that first hit, he never separated from Rori again—not even when C.J. was born and came into the picture. Rori became his new sister, but he'd never stopped thinking about Dakota. To this day, he still thought about her, and he intended on keeping it that way until he found her.

As he continued to look at the waters, an old memory came to mind, and it was one of his last few summer memories with Dakota and their parents. They were all swimming at a local community pool and introducing the pool water to baby Dakota for the first time. He remembered she had a look of confusion on her face, especially after Denver splashed her with water. Then he remembered that she made a sour face as if she didn't like the water. This caused Mommy and Daddy to laugh.

His parents' laughter echoed throughout Denver's mind but soon faded when he now focused on reality. He still couldn't believe he'd never hear their laugh again, not for real anyway. Tears stung his eyes, but he refused to let them fall. He looked to the horizon now and decided to renew his vow. He vowed again to find Dakota, even if it meant he was on his death bed. Denver brought himself to a more stable mental state when the ferry soon docked.

He thanked the ferry driver for the ride, but the ferryman only told him, "Please consider what I've said. Don't allow danger in."

"I can take care of myself," Denver replied.

This man was seriously getting on his last nerve.

"Then God bless your blind soul, son."

Denver felt like telling him to go to hell, but he bit his tongue because it would've been like telling his Catholic best friend to go to hell, and he wasn't about to disrespect her. *'Shit, how has Vin been?'* he thought. It'd been a month and a half since he last saw her, but it'd been a month since he had last talked to her over the phone and three weeks since he got a text message from her. Last he heard, her family considered fostering another orphaned teenager for old times' sake. Knowing Dr. and Mrs. Denner and how they can't refuse the puppy faces Vinessa, and her brother would likely give them, they probably took in another child.

CHAPTER
SIX

When Denver returned to his vehicle, he then opened his glove compartment and took out his emergency pack of cigarettes. He only ever smoked when he was highly stressed out, and right now, he was, all thanks to the wicked man he just visited on Hell's Island. Denver thought back to the face that he saw of Davis. He couldn't believe the man hadn't aged a day and that he still looked the same, except for his graying seven-inch goatee. The nerve of the man calling him kin and calling him out on his Leukemia!

"Fuck!" he shouted as he relaxed back into his seat.

What to do, what to do. He wondered if he should continue his merry way with finding Dakota since he had a few more days left to spare? Or should he just go home and earn a few paychecks before taking off again for another search for his sister? Denver scratched his left itchy eyebrow with the thumb of the same left hand holding his cigarette. He looked at the ferry and saw the man had parked his boat and had taken off somewhere in a hurry. He thought about what the man said about pressing forward and realized he should go home. He started his engine up and rolled down his windows. The car felt like an oven on the inside.

"For now," he mumbled as he put his seatbelt on.

He'd return home, and for now, he'd go back to a normal life, but only because he knew he really needed a break. So he backed out of the near-empty parking lot and returned home. After Denver finished his cigarette, he took his cell phone out and speed-dialed Vinessa. When he found that her cell phone was off, he decided to call her landline. Vinessa was in her closet, picking out something to wear for the day, when her phone started ringing. She quickly ran over to it, careful not to trip over her mess of clothing on the floor from her closet, when she tried to find something to wear and picked the phone up on the third ring.

"Hello?" she said into the phone without even bothering to check her caller ID.

"Hey, Vin, what's up?" Denver replied.

"Denver!" she exclaimed, now sitting down on her bed to give her best friend her undivided attention. "Man, I missed hearing your voice. How *are* you?"

"I've been better," Denver answered. "And I miss seeing your face."

Vinessa smiled big at this.

"How's the search going?" she asked as she tucked a few strands of her sunny blonde locks behind her free ear.

"No such luck. I'm right back where I started. The group home we were placed in is no longer in business. The few kids that were left had been transferred to other group homes. I tried finding the names of the new places to see which one has mine and my sister's files, but I had no success there. I think it's in the court's hands, so I might need to hire a private investigator. Either way, though, I'm coming home for a while."

"Aw, I'm sorry you haven't had any luck. I've got a *big* surprise for you, though, when you get home," Vinessa responded. "Where are you? We need to hang out soon! We have *so* much to catch up on!"

"I'm just two hours north of Novis Bay, near Hell's Island."

Vinessa was surprised to hear this.

"What are you doing there? The group home you were in isn't even a half-hour away."

"I needed to see Davis and try and get some answers out of him. Didn't I tell you that before?"

"Actually, no, you didn't," Vinessa said. "Well, you talked about it a long time ago, but you weren't serious at the time."

"Oh. Well … I saw him, and I thought I'd try to get some answers from him, but it turns out he *is* more sick and twisted than I thought. So, that was a waste of my time. I hope the fucking bastard rots in Hell."

Vinessa knew that Denver was furious right now.

"But enough of that and how I've been. How are *you*? It's been a while since we last exchanged words."

"Yeah, it has. Matt and I convinced Mom and Dad to take in another girl. You've *got* to meet her, Den. She's *such* a sweetheart! She's actually one of the subjects I *really* need to talk to you about. She's only been with us for a day, and Matt said she already wants to be adopted."

"Does she have any family?" Denver inquired as he merged onto I-5 south. "It would really suck if they came back for her when she's happy with *your* family."

"She *had* adopted parents, but her adopted mother passed away, and her adopted father had his parental rights taken away from him permanently. So, Mom and Dad are free to adopt her any time they want. Unfortunately, Daniel decided to get himself into more trouble again, so we're doing one last major crisis intervention. He picked a horrible time for this because Mom and Dad want to establish a good relationship with Kay."

Denver rolled his eyes and shook his head as if Vinessa saw him.

"What did he do this time?" he asked.

"Vandalized the high school, had alcohol on the premises and led to the delinquency of a minor."

"Seriously? What is his problem? He really needs to get his act together," Denver stated.

"I know," Vinessa replied. "This is why we're putting extra effort into this intervention today. Matt decided he'd take Kay to the Zone later to get her a job there, which she's thrilled about. Apparently, she's a quick learner and already knows how to make the ice cream."

This statement took Denver by surprise.

"How did he ever manage to pull *that* off when he could get fired for that?" Denver asked with a chuckle.

"He took her to Arctic Zone in the middle of the night," Vinessa answered.

Again, Denver rolled his eyes, more playful this time.

"Yep, that's Matt for ya. How's Jen, by the way?"

"Oh, Matt broke up with her right after you left town. The last time I saw her was at the Zone, and she wasn't happy. She could've had an off day, though."

"Or she's bitter because she now has to listen to everything Matt tells her to since he's her boss. Why'd he break up with her anyway? I thought he was in love with her?"

"He was, but she was beginning to be too much for him to handle, according to him. In his own words, 'she's too bitchy for me.'"

Denver laughed at this and then nodded.

"Yeah, she *was* a bit much for him."

"So, what are your plans when you come back to town then?"

Denver sighed as he drove and randomly looked in his rearview mirror.

"I don't know how long I'll be staying, but I know I need to take a break and get back to a normal lifestyle. Maybe I'll find a girl to date or something too. I don't know."

"Alright, no problem, but call me once you've got both your work schedules. We need to plan an evening of fun very soon."

"Will do. Hey, guess what? My hair is completely back now."

"Awesome. You're back to being a grade-A hottie then. I know you'll be dating someone."

Vinessa felt Denver blushing on the other end of the phone.

"Don't hide it," she added. "I know you too well, Den."

A light laugh escaped Denver's lips.

"Whatever lands in front of me, I'll give it a try."

"Awesome," Vinessa said. "Well, hey, I have to go. Olivia asked me to cover her shift today because she had a family emergency, so I agreed I'd do it for her. It was nice to hear from you. Thanks for letting me know you haven't dropped off the face of the earth yet."

"Ha, ha, very funny, Vin," Denver replied sarcastically, getting a laugh from Vinessa in return. "Alright, I'll catch ya later."

"Love ya, Boo-Boo."

Denver grinned at the fact that his best friend was still calling him 'Boo-Boo.'

"Right back at ya, Ba-Ba."

Now it was Vinessa's turn to smirk.

"Bye," she said and then hung up.

Denver shook his head while he also ended the call. Even though they were nineteen and seventeen, they still called each other by their favorite childhood nicknames that they gave each other. Denver now focused back on the road and continued homeward.

CHAPTER
SEVEN

After Kaelyn woke up, she realized it was three in the afternoon and that nobody had woken her up earlier. She shrugged it off, though, and she got ready for the day. Once she stepped out into the hallway, she found Matthew pacing with his face practically buried in a three-inch-thick book about business ownership.

"Doing some light reading?" she asked as he walked closer to her in the hallway, which distracted him and caused him to look up from his book.

"Yeah," he answered with a chuckle as he approached her. "I'm just working on my summer reading list for school."

"Wow. That's quite a big book to be on a summer reading list," Kaelyn noted as Matthew now stood a foot away.

"This is true," he agreed. "But I'd already finished my reading list for school three weeks ago. I always make up my own list when I finish the school's list. Besides, I'm an avid reader, and I need to keep learning, or I'm going to be brain-dead when school starts back up in August."

Kaelyn laughed when Matthew made a silly, cross-eyed face and joked around toward the end of his statement.

"So, did you sleep well?" he inquired as he turned serious again. "Vinny says you were sleeping with a smile on earlier."

"Yeah, I slept very well. Thanks for asking," she answered. "By the way, what's going on? How comes I wasn't woken up earlier?"

"Oh, I told everyone to leave you alone since you needed sleep because we were up late talking," Matthew explained.

"So they don't know … ?" Kaelyn started to ask. Matthew knew where she was going with this question.

"Oh! No, they don't," he answered with a laugh. "Arctic Zone is still our secret. Well, Vinny knows, but she won't tell anyone."

Matthew knew her face went from curious to relief pretty quick.

"Speaking of which, are we still going in today?" she asked as she referred to Matthew giving her a job at Arctic Zone.

"Definitely," Matthew affirmed. "After you get something to eat. Are you ready to go?"

"Mhm," was Kaelyn's response with a nod. "What kind of cereal do you have?"

"Cereal? We're not much of a cereal kind of family, Kay. We eat hot breakfast foods. Around here, breakfast can be as simple as pop-tarts and a packet of oatmeal or a big meal like eggs, sausage, bacon, and home fries."

"Oh," Kaelyn replied with a pause, as she was a little surprised. "Okay, then what's for breakfast?"

"Waffles," Matthew answered with a smile. "Why don't you go on downstairs and let Mom know you're awake so that she can make them? By the way, Dad's at the hardware store, and Vinny left to cover the second half of one of her co-worker's shifts at the Seaside Surf Shop. So it's just you, me, and Mom. Oh, and Daniel and Max are here too. Max, I believe, is in the kitchen with Mom. I don't know where Daniel is, but whoever does? I know Max is excited to meet you, though. I'll be downstairs in a minute. Oh, and there's a special surprise waiting for you in the kitchen."

Kaelyn smiled up at Matthew as he playfully nudged her toward the stairs.

"Okay, see you in a bit," she replied as she now went downstairs.

Kaelyn was curious to see her special surprise as she walked toward the kitchen, but she froze in her steps when she heard a very familiar voice talking to her foster mother.

"I can't believe she's *actually* here!" exclaimed an excited voice.

That voice sounded just like her youth mentor's, Brienna. It was strange because she hadn't heard from Brienna in a few weeks. She started walking through the dining room, though slowly, to continue to eavesdrop without being seen.

"It's amazing how you know her through your youth mentor ministry," said a voice that she knew belonged to Max, and he'd just confirmed her suspicion.

Suddenly, Kaelyn remembered her youth mentor having the last name of Denner. When Kaelyn neared the kitchen entrance and saw Alice washing dishes with Brienna standing next to her and leaning against the counter while Max sat at the bills table, she squealed in excitement. Everyone turned in her direction, and Brienna's face lit up when she saw Kaelyn.

"Brie!" Kaelyn exclaimed as she ran to her.

Brienna opened her arms wide for Kaelyn and engulfed her with a big bear hug.

"Kay!" Brienna called in return.

Max and Alice smiled at their reunion.

"Oh, my goodness; I haven't seen you for three weeks!" Kaelyn said as she pulled away.

"I know, and I apologize about that, but my fiancé was in the hospital," Brienna replied.

"Oh, that's okay, but what happened? Is he okay?" Kaelyn asked with worry.

"Oh, he's fine now. He just had pneumonia. But goodness, girl, how have you *been*?" Brienna inquired.

"I'm fine," Kaelyn replied. "I'm better than fine, actually."

"So I see," Brienna answered with a big, toothy grin. "I told you to keep your chin up and pray for a family to take you home forever, and look what happened!"

Max and Alice were stunned, especially with Kaelyn's following statement.

"I know, right? Praise the Lord!" Kaelyn exclaimed.

Max chuckled softly as he knew Kaelyn and their family were becoming a very compatible match. It was like a perfect match, and Kaelyn fit in well with this family. He was happy for her and everybody all around.

"Yeah, you've definitely found the right place to call home," Max said as he stood up and walked toward all three women. "I'm one of your older brothers, Max."

"It's nice to meet you, Max," Kaelyn said. "I'm Kay."

"What, I don't get a hug?" Max asked as he pouted now in a playful manner.

Kaelyn rolled her eyes jokingly in return and let out a happy sigh.

"Of course, you get one," she said as she entered his arms and hugged him.

Max hugged her close and kept her in his arms for a few moments longer than she expected.

"Welcome to the family, Kay. All your troubles are over."

Kaelyn momentarily closed her eyes as she hugged Max even tighter and laid her head on his chest. She was so happy to have the Denners in her life. And she couldn't wait for the day she became a Denner too. All she could do at this point was smile in relief. She was definitely home now.

"You know what's so funny about all this?" Brienna asked. "I had no part of the whole fostering process with you. Normally, I go with

Mom and Dad to pick out foster kids, but I was too busy taking care of Nathan."

"Really?" Kaelyn asked, somewhat surprised.

"Yeah," Brienna replied. "And there's actually something I've wanted to talk to you about. I thought I would need to ask Miss Wayne, but since you're with us now, I don't have to."

Kaelyn was confused by her statement.

"What?" she asked.

"I thought it would be a good experience for you to be a *part* of my wedding, instead of just being invited," Brienna said. "I'd like you to be my Maid of Honor."

Kaelyn's eyes bugged out at this in excitement.

"*Really?*" she asked, almost squealing. "You *really* want me to be your Maid of Honor?"

Brienna laughed at Kaelyn's excitement and nodded in response.

"I mean, Nathan and I still have a long engagement ahead of us, but I wouldn't want anyone else to be my Maid of Honor over you. So will you?"

"Absolutely!" Kaelyn exclaimed in excitement as she wrapped her arms around her sister. "It would be my honor, Brie."

A little while later, after four waffles and a long conversation of catching up with her youth mentor and new foster sister, Kaelyn spoke up towards Alice.

"May I have two more?" Kaelyn asked.

"Goodness, Kay, you already ate four. Haven't you had enough?" Alice asked with a laugh.

"I usually stop at three, but you make them so delicious, I can't get enough."

Everyone laughed at Kaelyn's statement, including Matthew, as he walked into the kitchen.

"You just wait until you've had Mom's fresh blueberry muffins straight from the oven. They're a little taste of heaven. They're to *die* for."

Alice rolled her eyes while she put down the last two chocolate chip waffles she made on Kaelyn's plate.

"Alright, sweetie, if you're still hungry after this, then have a banana. What you have here is the last of the waffle batch."

"Okay, thanks," Kaelyn said as she buttered her waffles and then poured syrup lightly on afterward.

"Oh, Kay, since you're going down to the Zone with Matthew for a job, why don't I take you to the bank tomorrow to open up your own savings account? So you have a safe place for your money?"

Kaelyn very much liked this idea.

"Sure!" she exclaimed before digging into her waffles.

"I'll make sure she's not on the schedule tomorrow unless you're going to the bank early?" Matthew inquired.

Alice thought about this for a few moments. Keeping Kaelyn off the Arctic Zone schedule tomorrow would give her the whole day to get to know the fifteen-year-old better and vice versa.

"Maybe you should keep her off," Alice replied as she smirked at Kaelyn and then winked. "I'd like to take Kay to get some new clothes."

Kaelyn looked up in response and swallowed her food.

"Oh, it's okay. I'm satisfied with what I have."

Alice sensed it really wouldn't take much to make this girl happy.

"No, it's okay," Alice reassured her. "It's what I want. Besides, you *do* need new clothes. If you don't mind me saying, the ones you have look like hand-me-downs."

"Well, *that's* true, they are," Kaelyn admitted.

"Nobody gets hand-me-downs in *our* family," Brienna said. "So, go get some hot, new clothes, girl. Look good for them beach boys!"

Kaelyn giggled at Brienna as Brienna nudged elbows with her.

"Uh, no, don't," Matthew interrupted with his left hand raised slightly above his head and with his index finger now erect. "You can get some cute stuff, but nothing in which *'them beach boys'* will drool over. You don't want their attention. Trust me."

Everyone laughed at Matthew's protectiveness over Kaelyn as a brother.

"Oh, relax, Matt. Brienna's just messing with you," Alice said.

"Yeah," Max added. "Besides, we all know *'them beach boys'* will be drooling over Kay anyways. If you haven't noticed, she's a real looker, so good luck fending off the rotten eggs."

"I sincerely hope you're joking," Matthew spoke as he playfully shoved Max's head down sideways onto the table. "Fending off the bad seeds isn't just a one-brother job."

Max laughed as he brought his head back up and finished the last of his buttered and cinnamon sprinkled toast.

"Yes, I know, but I somehow get the feeling we should be giving Kay here a chance to fend them off herself. Something tells me she'll know who's naughty or nice."

Kaelyn smiled at Max as he returned her smile and threw in a wink.

"You *have* to say that," Matthew said. "You're a J.P.O."

"Actually, no, I *don't* have to say that," Max replied. "What you just said doesn't even make sense. Besides, I believe Kay will know how to pick a good guy. Stick to the sidelines and see for yourself."

Kaelyn, however, was confused at the terminology Matthew was using toward Max in their discussion, so she looked over at Max again.

"What's a J.P.O.?" she asked.

"Juvenile Probation Officer," Max answered.

"You're a probation officer?" Kaelyn further inquired in surprise as she looked straight into Max's eyes. "Isn't that a job that's hard and demanding?"

Max nodded softly.

"It can be," he answered with a pause. "But it has its perks too. It only gets challenging when dealing with stubborn, hard-headed repeat offenders. You have to have a lot of energy and patience for it, or it'll wear you out fast."

"Wow. See, I don't think I could do that kind of thing. I don't think I have that kind of patience."

"Not a lot of people do. Even *I* let my frustrations get the best of me sometimes, but the trick is to know how to remain *professional* about it, which is my favorite part of the challenge," Max explained.

"Well, kudos to you then," was Kaelyn's response. "I'm curious; what motivated you to pursue that profession?"

Max smirked toward Kaelyn as she was curious to know what his answer was.

"Actually, Daniel convinced me, but we'll save that for a later discussion," he said as he now got up from the bills table. "Right now, I have to go, or I'll be late for work. I have a court appearance I need to make."

Alice whipped her body around after momentarily taking a break from washing the dishes.

"You *are* coming over for dinner tomorrow night, right?" Alice asked.

"Absolutely," Max replied as he grabbed his keys lying just inches from Kaelyn's plate.

"Okay, good," Alice replied. "And where's my goodbye kiss?"

Kaelyn watched as Alice made it clear she wanted a cheek kiss. Then she watched as Max leaned over and kissed the sweet woman on her right cheek.

"I'll see you tomorrow then," Brienna added as she hugged Max.

"Of course," Max said as he hugged Brienna and at the same time gave Matthew their signature pound fist.

When Brienna pulled from Max's arms, Max turned to Kaelyn and smiled big toward her.

"Do I get a hug?" Kaelyn asked.

"You know you don't have to ask, right?" Max answered as he stepped toward her.

Kaelyn returned his smile and nodded.

"I guess I do now," she spoke as she stood up from her food for a few moments to hug him.

"See you tomorrow," Max said as he hugged his new baby sister. She was so tiny in his arms he had to bend over a little bit. "And again, welcome to the family. We're glad to have you here."

"Thanks," Kaelyn said as she pulled from Max's embrace and sat back down. "Have fun at work!"

"Oh, I will, ha," Max said as he now walked over to the doorway to the family room. "See y'all tomorrow night!"

When everyone said goodbye simultaneously, Max walked off, and Matthew turned to Kaelyn when the front door could be heard as Max closed it behind him.

"So, are you almost done?" Matthew asked.

"Oddly enough, yes," Kaelyn replied as she grabbed her fork. "I think I *over*ate for once. I'm not even sure I can eat the rest of this."

"Then don't," Alice said as she stepped forward and attempted to grab the plate.

"But … you made it for me. I don't want to let it go to waste," Kaelyn replied.

Before Alice had a chance to respond, Brienna stepped into the conversation.

"Oh, I'll finish it for you! It'll be my brunch," she said happily as she now sat down where Max sat, across from Kaelyn. "Have fun at work with Matt."

"Oh, she will," Matthew said as he looked to Kaelyn again. "You ready?"

Kaelyn wiped her mouth with her napkin, gave up her fork and plate to Brienna, and then stood up.

"I am now," replied the fifteen-year-old.

Once Kaelyn stood in the doorway to the family room, Matthew turned toward his mother and spoke up.

"Oh, Mom, we're probably going to kick back at the cove with the crew when we're done at the Zone. So odds are we won't be home until maybe midnight or so."

"Okay, you two have fun then," Alice said. "Stay out of trouble and *no* surfing after sunset!"

"Alright, see ya," Matthew said as he walked into the living room with Kaelyn following him.

"Later!" Kaelyn shouted to Brienna and Alice.

And, of course, Brienna and Alice had to say the same. Before long, Matthew and Kaelyn were in his car, and they took off.

CHAPTER
EIGHT

Along the drive to Arctic Zone, Kaelyn marveled at the sights of Novis Bay through her window, and Matthew had blasted the House and Trance music of her favorite band, Cosmic Obsession.

"Novis Bay is *so* amazing!" Kaelyn exclaimed as she noted how laid back the locals seemed to be.

Matthew couldn't hear what she said, so he turned his music down a little bit because he didn't want to shout over it and vice versa.

"I'm sorry, what did you say?" he asked.

Kaelyn turned to him with a smile for a few moments.

"Novis Bay is *amazing*. I can't wait to do some exploring," she answered.

"Oh, yeah, you'll love this town. Everyone here is real chill and laid back. Sometimes it feels like a village when you run into one person right after another that you know. But once everyone finds out you're a Denner, even people you *don't* know will address you by name as if they've known you all along. Novis Bay is pretty awesome, though. I never want to move away from here. Hey, do you surf?"

"Oh, no, I'm too afraid to," Kaelyn responded.

"Are you serious?" Matthew asked as he momentarily glanced at her and received only a nod before turning her focus back on the locals that zoomed by. "If you're going to be a Denner, Kay, you *have* to learn how to surf. That's actually how Mom and Dad met."

Kaelyn was surprised to hear this.

"Really?" she asked as she turned to Matthew once more.

"Yep," he answered. "They met when Mom vacationed here with her friends during her senior year spring break. Mom was surfing some gnarly waves when Dad arrived with his brother and best friend at the cove. Because Dad knew all the surfers in the county, Mom naturally stuck out like a sore thumb, especially with her *amazing* surfing skills. He immediately fell in love with her, and he was compelled to approach her on the main beach when she touched sand. They clicked right away, and the rest, as everyone always says, is history."

"Aw, that's so cute, but if your Mom wasn't a local, where was she from?" Kaelyn asked.

"Washington State," Matthew answered simply.

This took Kaelyn by surprise.

"Wow. People surf up there? Isn't it cold?" she asked.

"The waters up there are freezing, yes, but only those who have the surf in them will ride the waves there, whether they're natives or not. Mom was born in Hawaii and spent most of her childhood there. Hawaii is where she learned her surf skills and learned from the best. It would be amazing if I could have the same kind of love story with my future wife. I love this story so much, about how they fell in love. Mom and Dad used to tell it to Vin and me every night before bedtime when we were kids."

As Matthew drove into Arctic Zone's employee parking lot, it grew silent for a few moments.

"It's amazing how you know about your parents' history. It's the little things like that I wish I had of my parents. I can't even recall a *single* memory of them *or* my brother."

Matthew solemnly met her sad gaze as he turned off his engine.

"If it weren't for this old family photo I have of them, I'd have *no* idea what they looked like," she said as she was almost in tears. "It's the only visual that I have of them, and it's my most treasured possession. I carry it with me everywhere I go."

"May I see it?" Matthew asked kindly.

Kaelyn took out her wallet and took the picture out of her front credit card pocket. Matthew inspected the picture closely and noted how happy they seemed when she gave it to him. Even baby Kaelyn seemed to smile for the precious Kodak moment.

"Wow, Kay!" Matthew said in shock once he realized how alike she and her mother looked. "You and your mom are like twins. Do you know that? Like, *damn*, you're going to age better than the rest of us."

Kaelyn smirked at Matthew's comment as she stared down at the picture in his hands.

"Your Mom is *so* beautiful!"

"I know," Kaelyn replied softly with a warm smile. "Our similar looks and faith help me feel closer to her. At one time, I didn't know her necklace was a rosary until I asked Miss Wayne where somebody could find a necklace like the one my mom's wearing in this picture. That's when Miss Wayne told me it was a rosary and what it was used for. After that, I did my own research and discovered God in my own way. I've been a believer since."

Matthew listened to Kaelyn's words and even the tone of voice, and he watched her eyes stay sadly focused on the picture, on her mother.

"I bet you wish you had that rosary," he whispered as his eyes momentarily glazed over her dark chocolate hair.

"I *do,* actually," she replied as she slowly met his eyes again. "To have my mother's rosary, I think, would mean something more than this picture. It would be more special. Even a replica would beat this picture."

Matthew took a closer look at the rosary in the picture, and he realized it was familiar.

"Oh, hey, I think Vin has a similar rosary," he said. "Same color and all; she collects rosaries, you know."

"Really?" Kaelyn asked as Matthew gave the picture back, and she put it back in her wallet.

"Yep, ask, and she'll show you her collection. I'm sorry you lost your biological family, though. I hope we're an excellent alternate? I mean, *a* family is better than *no* family, right?"

Kaelyn smiled with warmth toward Matthew and nodded softly.

"*Not* quite. *No* family is better than an *abusive* family. But you're an excellent alternative, actually," she answered. "So, which one of you is teaching me how to surf, or, rather, which one will be pushing me to stop being so chicken and *try* to learn?"

"Oh, if you're going to learn, you've got to learn from the best, and that would be Mom. And I'll be doing the pushing," Matthew said with a big grin.

"Figures it would be you doing the pushing," Kaelyn replied.

Matthew just gave her a dorkier grin.

"Yep!"

Kaelyn rolled her eyes and got out of the car, which signaled for Matthew to do the same, and then he locked his vehicle with his keyless entry remote.

"So, are you ready for your first day of work?" Matthew asked.

"Totally!" Kaelyn exclaimed with excitement. "Now I can start saving up for college!"

"You mean you can start saving up for your first *car*?" Matthew corrected in question. "If you maintain your grades well, which I have no doubt you will, Mom and Dad will pay the whole tuition for the school of your choice."

"*Seriously?*" Kaelyn asked as she turned to him. "No way!"

"Yes, way," Matthew answered with a laugh. "Dad's a doctor, remember? Our family is for real, Kay. With us, nothing is so difficult to believe. Your troubles really *are* over. So, don't worry about the future and just focus on the present. Just kick back and have fun!"

Kaelyn knew he was right, but everyone knows that old habits die hard, right?

"I'm trying," she said more reservedly as she followed Matthew to the employee entrance.

Matthew stopped in front of her and turned to face her.

"Stop worrying," he said as he now poked her in the left arm and continued to do so. "Stop worrying. Stop worrying. Stop worrying."

"Stop poking me," Kaelyn replied as she grinned.

"Are you carefree yet? Have you stopped worrying?" Matthew tested as he kept poking her in the arm. "I'll stop poking when you stop worrying."

Kaelyn rolled her eyes as she saw this was one of those annoying, older brother antics of his that Vinessa had previously mentioned.

"Stop worrying. Stop worrying. Stop worrying. Stop worrying," Matthew continued in a playful monotone as he still poked her.

"Alright, fine!" Kaelyn said with a wild laugh. "Just stop poking me already."

Matthew stopped for a moment and stared into her gorgeous milk chocolate brown eyes. He loved how her wavy dark chocolate brown hair framed her face in such a perfect way. Like her mother, she was really, *very* beautiful. Compared to the focused girl he first saw in the group home reading William Shakespeare, this girl seemed lighter and happier, as if some massive burden had been lifted off her shoulders. But he knew that most foster children and those orphaned children couldn't help but worry about where their futures will lead them. So Matthew was here to make sure Kaelyn knew everything was secured for her now and that heavy load of worries once carried on her shoulders disappeared permanently.

"Can I trust that you've stopped worrying?" he asked.

Kaelyn sighed for a moment and then nodded.

"Yes, now open the door, you dork!" she answered with a playful shove in Matthew's chest.

And now, as Matthew already knew, this was the beginning of some fundamental internal changes for his new sister.

CHAPTER
NINE

Kaelyn followed Matthew inside the ice cream parlor, but before Matthew went to the front counters, he stopped near the freezer and turned around to face Kaelyn, which also caused her to pause in her tracks.

"Oh, shoot, I forgot you can't do training until Mom or Dad sign your paperwork," he said as he slapped himself on his forehead.

"Oh, because I'm underage?" Kaelyn asked knowingly.

"Yeah, exactly, um," Matthew answered as he tried to think on his feet with what to do. "Oh, I got it! Dad's at the hardware store. He can stop in on his way home. Hold on a sec."

Kaelyn stood still as she watched Matthew take out his cell phone and call Dr. Denner.

"Yeah, son, what's up?" Michael asked once he saw who was calling his phone.

"Hey, can you stop in at the Zone on your way home?" Matthew requested. "I need you to fill out some paperwork for Kay."

"Sure, I'm leaving the hardware store as we speak. I'll be there in a few minutes or so."

"Alright, cool, see ya," Matthew replied as he hung up and turned to Kaelyn. "Dad's on his way."

Kaelyn nodded as she didn't know what to say at this point.

"In the meantime, why don't you start filling out what you can of the paperwork, and I'll introduce you to some of the crew?" Matthew suggested.

"Okay," Kaelyn said as she eagerly followed Matthew to the front of the store.

"Hey, guys, how's it going?" Matthew asked toward the crew as they were now in sight.

"Oh, hey, Matt!" Jordan exclaimed. "What are you doing here on your day off?"

"Bringing in Andy's replacement," Matthew stated as he came to the counters and stood next to Jen at the register. "Jen, can you please move? I need a hiring packet."

If Jen hadn't been in the middle of ringing up a customer's order, and no other customers were in the shop, she would have challenged Matthew to make her move. But, instead, she'd moved aside without saying a word. Matthew then noticed he was missing a particular third employee.

"Where's Marcus?" he asked as he turned to Jordan and Jen. "I'm pretty sure I put him on the schedule for today."

Kaelyn stood in the doorway to the back of the store where she and Matthew came from and leaned on the door frame in silence as she watched Matthew making conversation with their co-workers.

"He had a family emergency," Jordan replied as he cleaned up Jen's mess from making her customer's order.

Kaelyn observed how Jordan and Jen worked, and she watched as Matthew took out her hiring packet from the cabinet underneath the register. She then studied Matthew's face and watched as his expression turned annoyed.

"So who's replacing Andy?" Jordan asked as he now washed the tools Jen had just used. Jordan hadn't yet noticed Kaelyn was even there, considering his back was to her the entire time, but Kaelyn knew it wouldn't last. "Customers are already complaining he's not here anymore."

"Oh, they'll survive," Matthew answered as he rolled his eyes but quickly turned to Kaelyn with a smile. "Kay, c'mere, will ya?"

"Sure, what's up?" Kaelyn asked as she walked passed Jordan and stopped in front of Matthew when he stood up straight again with a hiring packet now in his hands.

After Jen was done with her customer, and because nobody else was in line at the time, she turned to find out who Matthew was hiring. It surprised Jordan that Matthew had found a gorgeous girl to replace Andy.

"Kaelyn, this is Jennifer Molina," Matthew stated with a gesture toward the dark brunette girl at the register. "But everyone knows her best by Jen."

"Hi!" Kaelyn greeted in a charming tone.

Jen just studied Kaelyn from head to toe, and with an expression of disgust that was quickly painted on her face, she ignored Kaelyn by turning her head away in silence.

"And this is Jordan Powell, Dad's best friend's brother's son. He'll be a senior with you in the fall," Matthew continued.

"Well, hello there," Jordan said to Kaelyn in a flirty tone as he stepped forward and put out his hand.

Kaelyn found this dirty-blonde boy about 5'11" to be super cute.

"Hi," she replied as she took his hand for a proper shake.

Matthew watched the two and noticed how quickly Jordan made Kaelyn blush.

"Don't even think about it, J.P.," Matthew warned as he knew Jordan already liked this new girl. "Guys, this is my new foster sister, Kay."

"Oh, damn, man; that's not fair!" Jordan exclaimed as he pulled away from Kaelyn. "Why do you get all the hot sisters?"

Both Matthew and Kaelyn laughed, and Jen was jealous beyond anyone's imagination.

"C'mon, Kay, follow me," Matthew ordered as he lifted the side countertop so they could get out from behind the counters.

"Okay," Kaelyn replied as she followed him to the nearest table.

"Just scan briefly through the employee manual and then fill out what you can of the paperwork. Dad will help you out with the rest when he comes in," Matthew added as he allowed her to sit down and placed the hiring packet in front of her.

"Okay," was Kaelyn's simple reply as Matthew handed her a pen from the register.

Once Kaelyn started looking through the hiring packet, Matthew turned to his employees and folded his arms in annoyance.

"Alright, you two, why didn't you call me when Marcus called off? I don't think I need to tell you that we need at *least* three people per shift."

Both Jen and Jordan knew Matthew was angry with them, but they also knew he tried to remain calm in front of his new foster sister.

"I was going to call you, but Jen wouldn't let me. Luckily Dave came in to drop off some stuff," Jordan answered. "He went to the bank real quick, but he told us to do what we can until he comes back or Arielle comes in."

"When does Arielle come in again?" Matthew inquired as he looked at his watch.

"Five," Jordan answered again.

"Well, that's forty-five minutes away, and you know it doesn't matter if Dave came in. You're lucky he let this slide. You *know* you're still supposed to call me and tell me when we're short-staffed. Don't make me treat you like babies, okay? And I'm not blaming you entirely, J.P.; I know you were following orders, but I'm just stressing this out. And, Jen, I don't care if you're the supervisor when I'm not here. If we're short-staffed, you *need* to let me know whether I'm busy or not as soon as possible. Don't *force* me to demote you or, worse, fire you when I take over this business," Matthew said first toward Jordan but then toward Jen.

"It's not that big of a deal, Matt; relax," Jen replied. "Thursdays are never busy."

"That doesn't *matter*, Jen, and it is a big deal!"

Kaelyn couldn't help but look up from her paperwork to see Matthew yelling at his employees. In the two days she'd known him, she didn't think he'd be the type to yell.

"You can't *always* count on Thursdays being laid-back. You both know that Novis Bay is a popular tourist spot, and it's *summer*. It could get busy at *any* moment," Matthew continued as Jen squinted back at him. "What you did was *completely* irresponsible, but since Dave already let this go, I'll do the same *just* this once. You better not let it happen again because I'll write you up if you do! And don't be expecting me to be leaving anytime soon today because once Kay is done with her paperwork, I'm giving her hands-on training. So guess what; your supervising duties are *done*."

This pissed Jen off, Kaelyn knew, and she knew Matthew and Jen have some kind of history together outside the work environment. She focused on her paperwork, though, and she could fill out almost everything except her street address. She knew the street's name, but she was unsure of the house number.

"Hey, Matt, what's our house number? Is it 2462 or 2426?" she asked as she looked up again from her hiring packet.

Matthew looked over his shoulders at her and smiled sweetly.

"It's 2462," he answered.

"Thought so," she replied. "Thanks."

"No prob," Matthew said as he turned back to Jordan and Jen.

Just as Kaelyn had finished her paperwork, everything she could anyways, Dr. Denner entered the shop.

"Hey, Dad," Matthew hailed as his father caught his attention by the ringing of the overhead doorbell.

"Hey!" was Michael's greeting. "While I'm here, why don't you get me a banana cream shake? I'll take a medium. You know how I like it."

"You got it," said the young manager as he got to work.

As if on cue, a crowd of customers walked into the store after Dr. Denner.

"Alright, Kay, what have we got here?" Michael asked.

"Just a bunch of papers," Kaelyn answered as the man sat down next to her. "Everything's filled out, except for the part where you need to sign your permission for me to work here."

"Oh, right, because you're a minor. Got it," Michael replied as he borrowed Kaelyn's pen and took what she gave him of the hiring packet.

"Also, I wasn't sure if I should put you and Mrs. Denner or Miss Wayne down for the emergency contact," Kaelyn added.

"Oh, sweetie, you should *never* put Miss Wayne down. She is our case manager, though we're your caretakers and guardians now. So we'd go down on any paperwork as your primary contacts. If anything happened to you here at work while Matt was here, he would be your primary contact, though, for the most part, Alice and I go down as the primary. Regarding the secondary emergency contact for any other situation, Matthew and Max would be the third. If Alice or I can't be reached for some reason, Matthew and Max are *always* available. Here, I'll fill that out for you."

"Okay, good to know," Kaelyn replied.

"So, are you excited?" Michael asked as he continued filling out the paperwork.

"Oh, yeah, definitely!" Kaelyn exclaimed. "This is my first real job! Alice said she'll take me down to the bank tomorrow to open my own savings account."

Michael smiled with warmth toward her as he remembered Miss Wayne telling him and Alice that Kaelyn was very eager to try new things and soar to new heights in her life.

"Here you go, Dad," Matthew intervened as his father finished his part of the paperwork. "Extra banana, extra thick, just like you like it."

"Thank you, son," Michael answered as he took his banana cream shake. "Everything's filled out now, so I'll see you two back at the house later."

Dr. Denner got up and took a long sip from his shake.

"Oh, and make sure you teach your sister first to make my shake. And, Kay, you let me know if he doesn't do that, and I'll go ground him," Michael winked toward Kaelyn.

Kaelyn giggled and nodded as Matthew just rolled his eyes.

"Yeah, yeah, yeah," Matthew replied as he now shooed his father away with a hand gesture. "Now, get out of here before I make you pay for your shake."

Dr. Denner just laughed as he walked toward the entrance of the shop.

"Alright, you two have fun!" he said as he now turned his back to them and left the ice cream shop.

The teenagers watched as he left, and then Matthew turned back toward Kaelyn.

"So!" he said with a bright smile as he now had her undivided attention. "Now that all the paperwork is finished, are you ready?"

Kaelyn sighed heavily before nodding.

"Yes, I'm ready," she answered.

Matthew laughed lightly at how nervous she was. He knew this was her first job.

"Don't worry, Kay, you'll do fine," he added as he led her to the back room. "Here's your apron and visor. What size t-shirt do you wear?"

"Medium," Kaelyn replied.

"Ooh, I believe Dave might be out of that size. I'll check on that with him. Worst case scenario, would you be willing to wear a large?"

"Sure," Kaelyn said.

"Cool. I'm gonna make your tag real quick, and then I'll see you out front."

Kaelyn nodded again, and she once more sighed in nervousness.

"If you need help, don't be afraid to ask somebody. The crew will be more than willing to help you out, and most of our customers will probably go easy on you anyways because they'll know you're new. Just relax and have fun. Go to the front and have J.P. show you all the equipment. I'll be back in a bit."

"Okay," Kaelyn replied as she did what he said.

Jordan found himself smiling ear to ear when Kaelyn made an appearance again.

"Hey, um, Matt suggested you show me where everything is and whatnot."

"Not a problem," Jordan replied. "So, how goes living life with the Denners?"

Kaelyn smiled with warmth in response to Jordan's question.

"The Denners are wonderful. The best family I've ever met."

"That's awesome," Jordan stated. "Social Services couldn't have placed you with a better family. The Denners are awesome."

Jen glared her down because she was jealous that Kaelyn was another girl new in her man's life. They were broken up right now, but she planned to get back with Matthew, even if it killed her. Jordan showed Kaelyn where everything was, and once Matthew came back from the manager's office, he gave Kaelyn an Arctic Zone uniform shirt. After she went to the bathroom to change, Matthew officially started training her, and he put her to a real test later in the evening once Kaelyn thought she knew everything. A tall, handsome young man with brown, surfer-boy hair entered the ice cream parlor, and he went right up to Kaelyn. Matthew couldn't help but smirk as he knew he asked the guy to come in to put Kaelyn up to a customer test.

"Hi, I'm Kaelyn; welcome to Arctic Zone. How can I take your order?" Kaelyn asked.

"Yeah, I'd like my regular, please?" he requested.

Mesmerized by this tall fellow's sharp bluish-gray eyes, Kaelyn was surprised. She didn't know who were regular customers yet, and she didn't know each customer's orders. She almost didn't know what to say. But, then, the young man rolled his eyes with impatience, and he stomped his foot on the floor while he parted his lips again.

"Chunky monkey with bananas, strawberry and raspberry syrup, and a pinch of cinnamon."

Kaelyn was disgusted about this request. It left an image in her head to which she wanted to puke. Matthew and Jordan couldn't help but laugh in silence to themselves. Jen was smirking as if this was the most incredible scene she'd ever seen from a movie or something. Kaelyn's crew stood behind her, so she missed their reactions, but she knew they watched and judged her.

"Would you like that in a cone or a bowl?" Kaelyn asked kindly.

"Are you insane or something?" the guy replied. "I asked for a chunky monkey *smoothie* with bananas, and strawberry and raspberry syrup, with a touch of cinnamon."

Kaelyn was shocked by his rudeness, and she could've sworn he didn't mention 'smoothie' before, and she wondered what a 'touch' of cinnamon was. Wasn't it a 'pinch' that he said the first time?

"Would that be a small, medium, or large?"

"Oh, um, I'll take a large," he said kindly this time.

"Coming right up, sir," was Kaelyn's response as she maintained her cheerful expression and enthusiasm.

The tall customer immediately took out his phone and texted Matthew. When Matthew got the text, he smiled as he read: *OMG, she's the cutest girl I think I've ever seen. I'm not even in the same league as her. She'd never go for this.* Matthew smiled and, in reply, wrote: *Trust me, you two would be perfect.* As Kaelyn nervously blended Alex's drink, Matthew smirked at Alex and gave him a very approving nod. Alex just rolled his eyes and texted: *I'm going to have to undo this first meeting, thanks to you.* Matthew's response was: *Yeah, I know, I'm sorry, man. I couldn't get anyone else for Kay's test on such short notice. I'll make it up to you by inviting you to the bay with us tonight. Huge party.* Alex nodded approvingly and soon got his drink.

"Here you go, sir. That'll be three dollars and seventy-five cents," Kaelyn said as Alex took a sip.

"Oh, my God! This is disgusting! What did you put in this?" he barked.

When Kaelyn grew scared of Alex, he instantly felt guilty, but he had to act like a demanding customer.

"I put in chunky monkey ice cream, milk, bananas, strawberry and raspberry syrup, and a touch of cinnamon," Kaelyn replied.

"This isn't what I asked for. I asked for a *pinch* of cinnamon, not a touch. Don't you know the difference? Learn to listen, would you? Just get me a large banana smoothie, if you can make that right."

Kaelyn kept her cool and brought back her smile.

"Of course, sir. Coming right up. I promise it will be the best banana smoothie you've ever tasted."

When Kaelyn turned around again to make another smoothie, Alex texted Matthew again. *Oh, you SOOO owe me. I feel so horrible! I hate being mean. I hope she'll forgive me when I explain that this was all your doing.* Matthew's response to that was: *Don't worry, she'll know once you leave the store that it was a test.* After Kaelyn finished making her first customer's smoothie, she put it in a large cup, put the lid on, and then handed it to her customer.

"Here you go, sir. To make up for my not knowing the difference between a pinch and a touch, I'll give this to you for three dollars. I promise next time you come in. I'll know the proper terminology."

"Thank you," Alex sneered as he handed her the money. "You better know, or I'll tell everyone I know that Arctic Zone just hired a new, incompetent employee."

Alex took a straw from the straw dispenser and soon left the store. Almost immediately after, Matthew got another text: *Holy shit! Yo, this is the most amazing banana smoothie I've ever had! You couldn't have found a better person to replace Andy. See ya tonight!* Matthew applauded Kaelyn and cheered on for her.

"Go, Kay! You handled that very nicely. By the way, I asked Alex to come in and be a tough customer so that you know what to expect. What did you learn from this experience?"

Kaelyn was quite surprised to hear this from Matthew, but she thought his question through carefully.

"Uh, never argue with the customer about what they ordered?" Matthew nodded in approval. "And, of course, listen to the customer very carefully."

"Bravo," Jordan applauded.

"And you also need to be more competent because Alex is right. You aren't."

Everyone turned their eyes on Jen.

"Why do you always have to be such a bitch?" Matthew asked her in a nasty tone as he defended Kaelyn. "Kay's a really nice girl, and she's doing the best for her first day, so quit it with the attitude!"

Matthew then turned around to face his new foster sister.

"I really did ask Alex to be a tough customer. Everything he said when he was rude was my doing. Alex is a great guy. I'm sorry if I took the test too far."

"I believe you," Kaelyn replied as Matthew looped an arm over her shoulders. "And I'm glad you tested me the way you did. I never had a job, so I didn't know where I was in my customer service skills. Now I know, thanks to you."

Matthew smiled wide for a few moments before he spoke up.

"What are brothers for?"

CHAPTER
TEN

Denver aggressively slammed his apartment door behind him in frustration. He was sick and tired of coming home to an empty, barely furnished apartment, and yet, he couldn't surrender himself to the love and kindness of the Knights, his adopted family. They'd adopted him when he was just four years old, and he was grateful for having been raised by such a wonderful family, but he couldn't call them his own. Ever since Denver graduated high school at seventeen, he hadn't spent more than a month or so in Novis Bay because he was always searching for his only long, lost biological sister.

He'd tried his hardest to find her and even had a few leads at one point, though they all brought him back to square one. He was wise enough to understand that *California's Children and Family Services Division* separated him and his one-year-old baby sister just fifteen years ago for a reason. He knew it had something to do with the man who murdered their parents. Still, he refused to let that factor stop him. Even Mr. and Mrs. Knight warned him not to dig into his past for the same reason, but he knew they couldn't understand. Oh, they'd *never* be able to understand.

He remembered the very day Dakota was born, which still felt as if it was yesterday, and it was because his parents included him in the decision for a name for his new baby sister. His mother was raised in North Dakota all her life, and since she had her own family in California, she missed North Dakota a lot. So brilliant little Denver suggested Dakota for his sister's first name, and his parents took well to it, and they suggested Skye for her middle name. And since Denver loved it, that's what her name came to be, Dakota Skye Malone. She was a precious little thing, and Denver adored her very much.

He loved her so much he thanked his parents for bringing her into the world. He promised them he'd be 'the bestest big brother' there ever would be. And he was an excellent older brother until the day Social Services separated them, which was the second most awful day of his life. Since then, Denver never stopped dreaming about their reunion, and he vowed he'd never stop searching for her. At one time, the Knights thought it was an unhealthy obsession, so they'd taken him to a psychologist and psychiatrist, but both reassured the Knights he was just like many other adopted children that longed to know their biological family.

Denver flipped on the light switch in the kitchen, and once he set his two bags of groceries on the island and his keys, he sighed. On his way home, he went to the grocery store to pick up a few things he knew he would need for the rest of the week, and now he was home with his necessities. He also went to both of his jobs for his new work schedules. Since he was home early, he had the rest of the week off and didn't start work until Monday. Then, out of nowhere, came a disturbing memory.

"No! No!" were his parents' screams as their blood splattered everywhere, even all over Denver's face as he stayed hidden in the distance.

His eyes widened in horror as he knew he'd be next if he didn't find a better place to hide. He ran back upstairs quietly as his parents still screamed for their lives. He ran into Dakota's room and picked up his baby sister from her crib. Seeing that she was still peacefully asleep, he carried her closely and tightly to her chest.

"Denverrrrrrrrrrrrrr!" screamed his father.

Denver looked at the entrance to Dakota's room. Suddenly his parents stopped screaming, and he heard Davis coming up the stairs.

DENVER ANGRILY SLAMMED HIS HANDS ON THE ISLAND AS HE BEGAN to cry. He couldn't help but wonder why? Why did he have to be the one whose parents were murdered? Why did he have to be separated from his only sister? He hated not having his biological family in his life. He wanted nothing more in this world than to have them back. As he turned his back to the island, he leaned against it and couldn't help but slide down it, and soon his head was in his hands.

"Dakota," he whispered between sobs.

About fifteen seconds after he was on the floor, he heard a loud knocking at his door, but he didn't care about who it could've been.

"Denver? I know you're home. I saw your car in the parking lot."

Her voice gave her identity away. It was Vinessa, his best friend. Then he heard his doorknob rattling until the door opened.

"Dude, I'm coming in, whether you like it or not!" Vinessa added in a playful tone.

Denver never cared if she came in or not. Right now, he didn't want to get up from the floor. He was expecting Vinessa anyways since he called her when he got into town and was in line to buy his groceries at the store.

"Okay, I know by the fact that your door's unlocked that you're here, but why isn't your living room light on?" Vinessa asked from the living room as she flipped the living room switch.

When she saw the kitchen light was on, she walked toward it and found a vulnerable Denver sitting on the floor and leaning his back against the island. She knew something was wrong.

"Denver!" She called as she hurried over to him and reached his level. "What's wrong?"

She knew he was distraught when she saw his tear-stained face, which was a rarity with him. If anything, he'd get angry, but she'd seen him cry once before. Instead, Denver met her gaze and sighed before he spoke up.

"Fucking life," he answered in a soft tone. "I should've found her by now."

Now Vinessa knew what was wrong. She placed her right hand on his knee, and her left hand grabbed his right hand.

"She's actually one of the things I wanted to talk to you about the most. Your Scoop handle is still deactivated, right?"

"Yeah, you know I'm not crazy about social media. What does this have to do with—"

"You need to go on Scoop. *Now*. Here, *I'll* open it up," Vinessa replied as she now turned on the Scoop social media app and went to her latest post, which was the first night they got Kaelyn. "I took this photo last night of us at the restaurant. I wasn't sure you'd believe me without a picture."

When Vinessa handed her phone to Denver, he didn't know what to say. He read the post, *"Please give a warm welcome to Kaelyn, the newest addition to our Family."* Denver looked up at Vinessa, and with fresh tears in his eyes, she read his mind.

"Please, before you say anything, there are a few things you need to hear first."

He still didn't know what to say, though he had a feeling she had a lot to share with him, a lot to explain, so he remained quiet.

"Just a few months after you were adopted, Dakota was adopted by a couple named Meri and Dennis Dalgeau. They changed her name to Kaelyn. She lived a good life with them until her adopted mother passed away from cancer. She was eight when that happened. After a year passed, the courts took away Mr. Dalgeau's parental rights, and he's now sitting in prison for fifteen years for child abuse. So, Kaelyn went into foster care, and then later, she was moved to a group home. Matt saw her first when we visited the group home, and he pointed me in her direction, and my mouth practically hit the floor in shock."

Denver was stunned by this explanation.

"I know Matt's never seen the picture of your family, but he told me that there was just something about her that caught his attention. When I saw her, I knew what I had to do. We were both determined to have Mom and Dad take her home with us. It took a little bit of convincing once she met us because she didn't want to leave the group home."

"Why didn't she want to leave?" Denver had to ask.

"She loved the group home she was in because it was meant for girls who were severely traumatized by abuse, so she felt safe there. Kaelyn was being groomed for a big sex-trafficking ring. Thankfully, though, she was able to reach out to her caseworker for help and report the foster family they placed her with, and that's when Social Services rescued her and all the other girls in that last home, and obviously, they busted everyone involved in the sex-trafficking ring."

Denver was shocked by what she said. He was about to speak up, but Vinessa continued with her statement.

"It wasn't until Kaelyn saw our track record with adoptions that she decided to try us out. Mom even showed her some pictures from her phone. She's getting along *really* well with Matt, me, and even Max. Mom's taking her shopping tomorrow, like a girl's day out, to buy all new clothes and stuff. She's standoffish with Dad, and I think she will be for a while, but she told Matt last night that she already considers us family. It surprised me to see how fast she went from not wanting to leave the group home to wanting to be adopted by us."

Denver was once more at a loss for words.

"There's something else you should know. I overheard Mom and

Dad talking the last couple of weeks about her. Before we all went to get her and bring her home, I mean. Social Services told them they'd have to sign some special papers. They told Mom and Dad about your parents' murders, how it was all over the news. Social Services felt it was in Kaelyn's best interest to stick to the story they told Kaelyn about how her brother and parents died in a car crash. They said that to foster Kaelyn, they'd have to sign papers that said if they ever told Kaelyn the truth about what happened to her real family, Mom and Dad would permanently lose their license to foster. I only know she's your sister because I'm the only one that's ever seen that photo of your family, but I can't tell any of them what I know."

Denver looked again at the photo Vinessa took of her and Kaelyn sitting together at the restaurant. Of course, Vinessa and the Denners were a notable family in the community, and everyone wanted to be friends with Vinessa, so hundreds of comments were on the post. He could hardly believe that after all this time, he finally found her. Well, Matthew and Vinessa did, but that may as well have been a needle in a haystack. Denver took a sharp, deep breath as he studied his sister.

"Is her birthday September 21st, 2005?"

Vinessa knew why her best friend was asking this. He wanted to be sure Kaelyn was his sister. She only nodded.

"So … I've been looking for her all this time under the name of Dakota Malone, but … her name changed to Kaelyn Dalgeau when she was adopted." Vinessa knew by the tone of his voice that he felt defeated. An exasperated sigh escaped his lips as he now leaned his head against the wall of the island. "And if they lied to her about what happened to our parents and me, they probably changed her social security number. Now I understand why there's been *no* activity on the original one she was assigned at birth."

Denver banged his head against the cabinets now.

"God, I've been so *stupid*."

"You're not stupid, Den," Vinessa reassured as she now sat next to him. "I know what she means to you. I'm sorry it took nearly fifteen years to find her."

"It still feels as if that only happened yesterday. It's the second-worst day of my life."

"I'm so sorry, Den," Vinessa replied as she cuddled with her best friend. "You know how we are with fosters, though."

She'd hope that would make him feel better, but her statement made him even sadder.

"You're welcome to see her anytime you want."

"What's the point if she doesn't even know I exist?" he asked as he met her gaze. "She thinks I'm dead."

"Did you forget, Den? You're not the only one to inherit money from your parents. She's going to find out when she's eighteen. You said that would be the failsafe end of your search for her."

Denver forgot all about the settlement. Vinessa was right, though he wondered if he could stomach being around Kaelyn while keeping the truth from her.

"I don't want to ruin things for you and your family. What they're doing with fosters, it's a beautiful thing. I don't want to tell her who I am and that I'm still alive, only to lose her all over again and cost your parents their license to foster. That's too much chaos. I just want her to be happy and safe. I *know* she's got that with you guys."

"She's really cool, Den. I think you should meet her and get to know her, but I also support your decision to leave her alone for now. Mom, Dad, and Matt haven't connected the dots between you and Kaelyn. So, just know, it *is* still safe to meet her. She can be our little secret."

Denver looked down at the photo again and felt a sense of relief to know that he finally found Dakota with his best friend's help. He looked to Vinessa and spoke up.

"Can you please send me a copy of this photo?"

"Of course!" Vinessa replied as she took back her phone. Denver watched as she shared the photo into a text message, and then she sent it to him. "You know … now that we've found her, I think it's time for you to kick back and relax. Have you considered going back to school for computer programming and graphic design?"

"Maybe, I don't know. I just know it's time to get back to being normal."

Vinessa placed her chin on Denver's shoulder.

"Oh, Den. You're normal. You just haven't been living a normal lifestyle, that's all."

Denver gazed deeply into Vinessa's eyes, and then she stood up before him and lent a hand. Denver grabbed it, stood up, and smiled toward his best friend.

"Thanks, Vin. Seriously. You found Dakota," he said as he pulled her into his arms for a long-overdue hug. "I don't even know how I can ever repay you for that."

"No problem, babe. That's what best friends are for," Vinessa replied as she pulled from the hug and took out some of his groceries from one of his bags. "Ooh, popcorn, yay! Movie time! Oh, wait, did you get your schedules?"

Denver forgot about that until now.

"Yeah, and I don't start work until Sunday in the P.M. at *Luna's* and Monday in the A.M. at *Partridge*, so I've got about four days of peace before going back to anything."

"Sweet! I'll text Mom and let her know we're having a slumber party!" Vinessa exclaimed. "Oh, and *please* tell me you bought some cheese curls?"

Denver playfully rolled his eyes as he'd pulled out a bag of her favorite snack from the other grocery bag.

"Do I know you or what?" he answered in question.

Vinessa smiled wide as she grabbed them from Denver.

"Ah, we'll call that even. You're the best! Thank you!"

"And, of course, I also bought white cheddar cheese powder for the popcorn," Denver added as he took it out of the same bag the cheese curls were in.

Vinessa grew even more excited.

"Awesome! So what are we watching tonight? And should we invite anyone?"

"No, let's just keep tonight between us, please. I just want some peace and quiet tonight. I'm sure that word will spread by tomorrow afternoon that I'm back, considering everyone at the store saw me. But not even the Knights know I'm back yet."

"Really? Okay, well, what do you want to watch?"

"Why don't you pick something out? I'll make the popcorn and put the rest of the groceries away. Do you want a *Bud Light*?"

"Okay, and sure, I'll have one; how did you get away with buying any tonight anyways?"

"I still have three left from before I hit the road. They're all sitting at the bottom shelf in the fridge," Denver replied.

"Oh, duh, silly me. Why didn't I think of that?" Vinessa replied as she laughed. "Alright, yeah, bring one out when you're done here."

Vinessa went into the living room, but before she picked out a movie, she called her parents to let them know she was spending the night at Denver's. When Denver came into the living room with a bowl of popcorn and their drinks, Vinessa grabbed her beer, and they walked over to the couch.

"So, what have we decided on?" Denver asked.

"That's for me to know and you to find out," Vinessa answered as she hogged the DVD remote and the bowl of popcorn.

"Alright, cool," was Denver's response. "Oh, hey, how's Dale? I haven't heard from him in forever. I think he changed his number or something because his cell isn't in service."

"How should I know?" Vinessa answered as she popped a piece of popcorn into her mouth in a carefree manner. "I haven't seen him since the night you left. I think Matt and Ace scared him out of town."

Denver quickly realized Dale must have done something terrible for Matthew and Ace to scare him out of town.

"Why, what did he do?" he asked. "Oh, please tell me he didn't touch you or something? I'll kill him if I ever see him again!"

"No, he didn't touch me," Vinessa replied. "I don't think he ever would've. Women aren't his type."

Denver's eyes bulged.

"No way! He's *gay*?" Denver asked loudly in shock.

"I haven't seen anything, but Ace sure did," Vinessa answered. "You remember Preston was hosting a party at his place the night you left, right?" Denver nodded. "Well, Dale and I had plans for dinner and a movie, and he called me last minute saying he wasn't feeling good. I insisted on coming to his place to make him some soup, but he insisted I should just stay home and not worry about him. So, I did, and I found out later through Matt and Ace that he lied to me. They found him at Preston's party, and Ace noticed something peculiar about him and some mystery guy standing a little too close together, so Ace followed them while Matt was in an argument with Jen.

He didn't give me details, but I heard him and Matt talking about it the next day, how Dale and the other guy flirted while nobody else caught it. So ace started to follow them when the other guy led Dale upstairs. Dale then closed the door behind him, and Ace stood outside the door and listened in on them. He heard them giggling and immediately knew they were more than just friends, so he went and got Matt, and they busted Dale already half-naked with the other guy and in a very heated make-out session."

Denver couldn't believe he'd heard this. He never expected such a thing as this to happen. Not to his best friend.

"That's what they said, but that night, Matt and Ace brought him to our place and made him apologize to me *in front* of our parents. I'm telling you, Den, they *really* beat the crap out of him. I know from Ace that he chased the other guy out of the party, but he let him run scared because the guy was too fast. He then helped Matt beat Dale, even though Matt didn't need the help because he already beat him up badly. Mom and Dad were quite upset with Matt for a few days, and they continuously lectured him for letting his anger out through violence, even though Dale cheated on me with another guy.

Since that night, though, nobody's seen Dale *or* the other guy around. I already had a feeling that Dale lost his attraction to me from about a month before, but I couldn't confirm it, and I wasn't about to make any accusations, so I just left it alone until that night. You'll be twisting Matt and Ace's insides if you ever bring Dale up around them again, that's for *damn* sure. They hate him more than anybody else."

"Oh, that boy better pray he never runs into me because I'll kill him. I can't believe he cheated on you, and with another guy, too! That's just *insane*!" Denver exclaimed.

Vinessa now stared at the floor, thinking about Ace as she zoned out, but she still spoke up.

"You know, I never thought Ace would be so protective of me. He admitted he'd never been more furious than when he caught Dale sucking face with someone else because he thought it would've hurt me, even though nobody knew I had already detached from Dale and was preparing to dump him. Ace thought I was in love with Dale and was pleasantly surprised when I said that I wasn't even close to being in love.

He said that was good because I deserved someone better, much better. He even put a winking smiley at the end of his text about me deserving better to top it all off. Since then, he's been flirting with me, behind Matt's back and through our cell phones—whether it's by having an actual phone conversation or texting each other."

"Ooh, sounds like the boy is crushing on you," Denver noted as he nudged her in the arm.

Vinessa looked up at Denver and began to blush.

"Oh, I know he is," Vinessa replied shyly. "And do you want to know something? I really like him. Like, I mean, I *really* like him."

"Ask him out," Denver suggested while throwing some popcorn into his mouth. "He's a good guy. I don't think he'd hurt you, and if you two ever broke up, I don't think it would be bad. I see it being a mutual break-up, if anything. I think you two would be cute together, too adorable."

Vinessa smirked at Denver and then nudged him back.

"You know Matt would kill him if he even *saw* Ace send a wink my way, right?" she asked.

"He wouldn't. They're best friends," Denver assured her as he took another piece of popcorn and popped it into his mouth.

"Best friends or not, he'd kill him. Matt refuses to let such a thing happen with any of his friends. His sisters are especially off-limits to them."

"How often do you talk on the phone or text?" Denver asked with curiosity.

Vinessa paused and remained silent until she got a text message. Denver watched as she glowed in excitement when she took out her phone. He peeked over her shoulder and smirked when he saw the incoming text message was from Ace. They both read, *'So wuts my cutie ^ 2 2nite?'*

"Oh, you are *so* dating him!" Denver exclaimed as he took her phone away from her to reply to Ace's text with, *'Sleepover at my Boo-boo's.'*

Vinessa gasped as she realized what Denver was trying to do, and she tried to take her phone back before he could send the message, but she accidentally pressed the send button herself. Both Vinessa and Denver started to laugh.

"He's *so* going to be jealous!" she said.

After a minute passed, another text message then came from Ace. Vinessa and Denver looked down at the phone as Vinessa hit the read button. *'Oh ... when did you get a man?'*

"Aw, Den, he's upset now," Vinessa replied with a pout. "He's using full words. It's the only time he'll use them."

"Tell him to relax, that you're just joking," Denver stated as he sat back further into the couch now.

Vinessa texted away and explained in further detail that boo-boo was just her nickname for Denver. Before she knew it, she got another text back, which put a smile on her face this time. As usual, Denver peeked over to see what Ace said. *'Oh! Srry thght u meant sum1 else. D's back in Novis?'* Denver watched as she texted Ace back with, *'Yep, and we're just chilling. You thought I had a new man? Would you be jealous?'* Once more, Vinessa got a text, but this time it was final. *'Duh. Ur my cutie! Have fun w/ D. Gnite, sweetie :-*.'*

"Aw!" Denver exclaimed. "He called you a cutie and a sweetie! Wait, scratch that. He called you *his* cutie. Are you sure you're not already dating him?"

Vinessa smirked toward Denver.

"C'mon, Den. Do you really think I'd keep something like that from you?" she asked.

"No," Denver replied. "No, I suppose not."

Vinessa sighed now as her smile faded.

"I wish we didn't have to sneak around," she continued. "I mean, we're not *really* sneaking around. Honestly, we technically run into each other when we're out doing errands or something. We don't plan these things because we know it would get back to Matt and cause trouble if we did. Well, in a way, we're still sneaking around because we're still texting and calling each other and flirting with each other all the time. *And* he snuck a kiss on my cheek one time when Matt wasn't looking. I wish Matt would give us a chance. I think … I feel like … okay, you're going to think I'm crazy."

"Um, Vin, you're talking to somebody who's done some pretty psycho shit back in the day."

Vinessa laughed for a moment before she spoke up.

"True," she agreed. "Okay, well, this whole conversation about Ace and me can't go anywhere."

"Girl, you know you can trust me."

"I know; I was just reiterating it," Vinessa said. "I feel like with Ace, this is it, as in I think we're meant to be."

"Don't you think it wouldn't be such a big deal with Matt if you and Ace were meant to be? It really shouldn't be this complicated to get together."

"I think the timing is off. I don't think we're meant to be together just yet. I do know, though, that the time is getting closer. We make each other happy, Den, and we always seem to know when something is wrong and how to cheer one another up."

Denver gave her words a few moments to sink in while he threw more pieces of popcorn into his mouth. Once he swallowed the last one, he parted his lips to say something, but Vinessa spoke up first.

"Denver?"

He looked straight into her eyes as her voice got quiet.

"I think I'm in love."

CHAPTER
ELEVEN

Kaelyn smiled warmly as she and her co-workers got to the beach. Her first day was finally over, and she could enjoy herself. The beach party was already filled with teenagers laughing, drinking, dancing, or roasting marshmallows and hotdogs around several metal garbage cans being used for bonfires. Jordan went off to meet a couple of his buddies, but Matthew stayed behind with Kaelyn, and so did Jen.

"Matt, can I talk to you alone, please?" Jen asked as she tugged at Matthew's hand.

Kaelyn watched as Matthew irritatingly rolled his eyes and pulled his hand away.

"If this is about what I think it's about, the answer is 'no,'" was Matthew's answer as he looked straight at Jen now.

Kaelyn knew at this point that Jen and Matthew had a history. By watching how Jen was all over him, she knew they dated at one point and were maybe even a real couple. Jen sighed in frustration.

"We need to talk," she said firmly, annoyance written all over her face.

"Fine," Matthew replied, raising his voice slightly above hers, but then he softened it when he looked toward Kaelyn. "Kay, I'll be right back. You'll be fine for a few minutes, won't you?"

Kaelyn nodded with a smile.

"Of course; I might have me a s'more or two," she said, keeping her smile.

"Alright, I'll see you in a bit," Matthew spoke. "Knowing Vin, she's probably around here somewhere. See if you can find her. If not, I'll see you at one of the bonfire pits."

Before Matthew or Kay could say anything else, Jen grabbed Matthew's hand and led him somewhere they could be alone. Kaelyn sighed softly in content as she studied her surroundings. At the same time, she looked around for people she met, but she couldn't even pin down Jordan. When she went to turn around and find a bathroom, she knocked right into somebody, and that somebody happened to be the customer from Arctic Zone that gave her a hard time.

"Oh, I'm so sorry," she apologized.

When she met his bluish-gray-eyed gaze, he smiled kindly at her and spoke up.

"No, it's okay," he said. "It's Kay, right?"

She returned his smile and realized he had a more pleasant side to him. Then she nodded in response.

"I'm Alex, and I wanted to apologize for how I acted earlier at the Zone. I was sure that the moment I walked in and saw your pretty face, I didn't want to be rude, but Matt asked me to come in as a tough customer to test your customer service skills. Speaking of which, you handled my situation really well. Oh, and for future reference, my regular order is Rocky Road in a medium bowl, extra crunchy."

Kaelyn laughed at how silly Alex turned toward the end of his statement.

"Okay, I'll keep that in mind, and I get it. I'm honestly glad you were tough because now I know where I stand in serving customers."

Alex smiled at Kaelyn's statement.

"I'm glad to hear that, though, for the record, I'm actually a really nice guy. The guy you met today at the Zone is *so* not me."

"Thanks for letting me know," Kaelyn said.

"So, how old are you?" Alex asked. "Matt told me you're new to his family, but he didn't tell me your age."

"I'm sixteen," Kaelyn answered, which surprised Alex slightly. "How old are you?"

"Oh, Matt and I graduated together," he replied. "I hope you're not freaked out by talking to some nineteen-year-old."

Kaelyn laughed at Alex and shook her head.

"No, you're fine. So, who did you come here with?" she asked.

"I came here by myself, hoping to find my friends, but I haven't spotted anyone yet."

Kaelyn nodded with Alex as she looked around again.

"I came with everyone from Arctic Zone, but they've somehow managed to disappear, and Matt took off with Jen because she wanted to talk to him privately. He didn't seem happy about it either."

"Oh, they'll probably get back together again before the night is up."

Kaelyn knew it.

"So they *do* have a history then?" she asked.

"Oh, yeah; they're one of those on-again, off-again couples. It's crazy, really. They should either stick together or forget about it altogether."

"What makes them fight so much?" Kaelyn asked.

"Jen gets jealous easily if Matt doesn't give her enough attention. She gets jealous of his friends, other girls he talks to and even his own family. She's very demanding, and he tries his hardest to tend to her needs, but when she's jealous of him spending too much time with his family instead of with her, the major fights break out. I imagine she's jealous of you because you're new to the family, and she knows that he'll be putting all his energy and time toward the family during a time like this. If I were you, I wouldn't expect Matt to return anytime soon tonight because Jen will make sure to get his attention now that she's got him alone."

Kaelyn sighed sadly at this. She was hoping to spend some time with her new brother.

"Well, that kind of sucks because I don't know anyone here," she admitted, looking around her at the large crowd of teenagers mingling everywhere on the beach.

"Well, since you're alone, and I can't find anyone, why don't we stick together for a while and get to know each other?"

Kaelyn looked up at Alex and smiled warmly at his words.

"Okay," was all Kaelyn could say.

"Are you hungry or thirsty?" Alex asked. "Because I sure am; a hotdog or two sounds good right now."

"I'd like to try a real s'more," Kaelyn answered, which surprised Alex.

"Wait, are you telling me you've never had a s'more before?" he asked.

"Well, I've had s'mores, but never by fire. The marshmallows were always warmed up in a microwave."

Alex shook his head.

"Oh, I sure pity all you foster kids. You haven't tasted life until you've had a real s'more with some fire-roasted marshmallows. What a shame."

Kaelyn laughed at Alex and followed him to the nearest fire pit once he grabbed her hand and asked her to follow him.

"Are you a fan of burnt crispy or crispy golden?" Alex asked as he grabbed a stick and a marshmallow.

"Hm. I don't know. I could try one of each," Kaelyn answered.

Alex turned to Kaelyn and smiled very warmly at her. Kaelyn just melted, not because of the fire she was standing near, but because of Alex's gorgeous smile. She couldn't help but mirror it.

"You know, you have a gorgeous smile," Alex complimented as he now stuck the marshmallow into the fire.

Kaelyn blushed as she turned her face shyly away from his. She also grabbed a graham cracker and some chocolate and broke the graham cracker in half.

"So, how long have you known the Denner family?" she asked as she avoided answering Alex's compliment.

"I've been going to school with Matt since kindergarten, but we were never really friends until high school when kids started picking on me because I was a geek."

"You were a geek?" Kaelyn asked.

"Yeah, I had the glasses, I was valedictorian, and I beat everyone in the local science fair *every* year. I also brought the debate and mathematics teams to victory four years in a row in high school. We sucked before then as a team, and the debate team is where Matt and I became good friends. I'm also a computer whiz kid. I've only ever had one girlfriend, but she was too much for me to handle, she was way too high maintenance, and she broke up with me because I wasn't ready to become sexually active. Matt's a very cool guy. He stuck up for me in high school and applauded me on my intelligence, and he's the only person outside my family that has supported my choice of celibacy."

Kaelyn listened contently to what Alex was saying. She couldn't picture him with glasses and being super skinny. He wasn't wearing them now, and he had a nice build.

"You're lucky that Social Services placed you with the Denners. They're pretty awesome and wholesome. The Denners may be a huge family but they're all incredibly loving and supportive, and they're super close to one another."

"I know," Kaelyn replied as she stared softly into the flickering flames. "I'm already in love with them. God came to my rescue."

Alex pulled the marshmallow out of the fire, wiggled it into the air a little to get rid of the flames, and then he placed the marshmallow right onto the chocolate. Kaelyn put the lone graham cracker on top of the marshmallow and squished it down carefully as she pulled the marshmallow off the stick it was roasted on. Alex watched as Kaelyn took a bite out of her s'more, and he smiled wide when she nodded in approval. After she swallowed, she parted her lips.

"This is definitely a little bit of heaven. You were right," she said.

"And you're very, very beautiful."

Kaelyn's smile softened a little. She was flattered he was flirting with her.

"I'm sorry if I'm coming on too strong. I took one look at you when I walked into the Zone, and my breath got caught in my throat."

Kaelyn didn't know what to think.

"I bet if I kissed you, you would taste just like that s'more."

Kaelyn's eyebrows lifted in surprise. Alex blushed and averted her gaze into his eyes by putting down the marshmallow roasting stick.

"I'm sorry, that sounded like a line," he apologized.

"What will you bet if you're right?" Kaelyn asked to avoid any further awkwardness.

Alex was surprised to hear this from her, though he knew she was now returning his flirting, so he went with the flow and smiled again.

"I would like a bite out of your s'more," he said. "And if you win, what do you want?"

"I'll let you know when I can think of something," Kaelyn said with a wink.

Alex laughed, and Kaelyn loved hearing it. He couldn't believe she was challenging him. He knew he was going to be correct. At that exact moment, someone accidentally pushed Kaelyn towards Alex as they tried to catch a football, and Alex quickly caught Kaelyn in his arms.

"Oh, dudes, I'm so sorry," said the guy who turned around.

"It's okay," Alex replied as he smiled down at Kaelyn. "Are you alright, Kay?"

Kaelyn laughed awkwardly, but she nodded. Finally, the random guy ran away with the ball he caught, and Kaelyn and Alex were left alone with their faces just inches apart. Then Kaelyn quickly pulled apart with shock and guilt written on her face.

"Oh, my goodness; I'm so sorry!" she exclaimed while they both looked down at the s'more now smashed into his shirt.

Alex just laughed and slipped his shirt off.

"It's okay. I hated this shirt anyways. Now I have an excuse to throw it away," he answered as he threw it into the fire pit.

"Why do you hate that shirt? I thought it looked fantastic on you," was Kaelyn's response.

"My ex bought it for me when we were going steady," Alex said sheepishly. "I promise she means nothing to me. She's Jen's sister, and she acts a lot like Jen, except she's more fashionable."

Kaelyn couldn't help but eye up Alex. He knew she was studying him too, and he knew she approved what she saw.

"Go ahead, you can say it; I'm beautiful too," he said playfully.

Kaelyn couldn't help but laugh at his words. Alex instantly fell in love with it, and he stepped closer to her.

"You are pretty handsome," she admitted as she now just smiled at him.

Alex slowly and delicately placed the fingers of his right hand in between Kaelyn's left-hand fingers. Kaelyn caught this and looked up at Alex as he kept inching towards her.

"Your hand is soft and tiny, and I love it. What shall a kiss from you be like?"

As Alex inched even closer, Kaelyn felt her head clouding. Her soul was melting in his gaze. He was so unbelievably handsome.

"Soft … and tender … like my heart," responded Kaelyn.

As their lips brushed delicately upon each other's, their eyes had involuntarily closed, and their hearts lept for joy. Kaelyn took her free hand and placed it gracefully upon the left side of Alex's waist, and Alex took his free left hand and cupped it around Kaelyn's face to keep her lips as close as possible. The chemistry ignited between them, and together they felt as if they were one.

CHAPTER
TWELVE

Matthew saw Kaelyn and Alex kissing, and he instantly felt territorial and, believe it or not, jealous. He wanted to keep them from kissing, but Jen wouldn't let him.

"Matthew, what are you doing?"

"He has his shirt off!" Matthew exclaimed.

"She doesn't need rescuing. You're the one who hooked them up, remember? Besides, it's Alex. He's a fucking prude."

"Well, I told Kay I'd be right back," Matthew replied. "So I'm going back."

Jen sighed in exasperation, and then she grabbed Matthew by the collar of his shirt, and she fiercely pulled him back to face her.

"Matthew Kristopher James Denner, I'm horny as hell right now, and I want you to fuck my brains out."

Those words, used in that intense tone, turned Matthew on right then and there. After an argument, he never turned away sex if it was an option, so Matthew ferociously attacked Jen's lips with his own, and Jen knew he was hers for the night. When Matthew turned his lips away for a few moments, he went to the nearest cooler and grabbed two beers. Jen also grabbed a couple for herself. Matthew looked back at Alex and Kaelyn and saw them standing in front of the bonfire, hands interlinked, and they were now only smiling at each other.

"I have to ask him if he can take her home," Matthew said.

"I'm sure he'll be glad to take her home, Matt. They're fine on their own. Now let's go, stupid."

Matthew instantly turned back and glared Jen in the eyes.

"You're such a bitch!" he exclaimed.

"You're damn right I am," Jen said after pushing her body against his, grabbing his balls, and kissing him on his neck.

Matthew's eyes closed automatically, and his heart picked up a few paces. He knew he'd regret this, though he wanted it just as bad as Jen did, and he was unsure how much longer he could go without sex. When Jen started driving him crazy, he couldn't control himself any longer, and he took her up on her offer.

———

KAELYN HAD BUTTERFLIES IN HER STOMACH, AND HER HEART HAD jumped into her throat for joy. She was impressed with the way Alex kissed her.

"So, did I taste like a s'more?" she asked.

"No, but you did taste sweet … and intoxicating," was Alex's response. "Besides, there's no s'more for me to bite from if I won."

"This is true, thanks to that footballer," Kaelyn replied.

"So, what shall the winner ask for?" Alex asked while he took his free left hand and entangled it with Kaelyn's free right hand. "She can have whatever she wants."

Kaelyn thought about this, but not for too long, because she was very interested in Alex.

"How about a breakfast date?" she answered curiously.

"Okay, I can go for that, but why not a dinner date?" Alex further inquired.

"Eh, dinner dates are becoming too overrated. I like being a little different."

Alex smirked at this.

"So different is what you want, eh? Just say when you want to get breakfast together, and I'm down. Then afterward, I'll take you to meet my very best friend."

"Your best friend?" Kaelyn asked in confusion.

"Her name is Delilah. She's a beautiful ten-year-old gingerbread mare with black legs, a black tail, and a black mane, and she also has a beautiful white diamond patch between her eyes."

Now Kaelyn was surprised.

"Your best friend is a horse?"

"Yep, she's an American quarter horse, and she's *sooo* gorgeous. I've had her since middle school. I work on a horse farm fifteen miles inland, and she was bred to be a champion racehorse, but they just couldn't get her to train right for racing, and she and I grew attached before she became of age to be sold, so her owner kept her and gave her to me. She just stays on his farm. She loves running when nobody pressures her to—unless she has someone like me on her back, she doesn't mind running. She knows I won't race her. She's very, very sweet. If you give her even one sugar cube or carrot, she's like your best friend for life. Oh, and she *loves* being brushed and bathed. She will actually nicker and shake her head in excitement if she sees you grabbing for a brush."

Kaelyn loved to watch how Alex gushed about his horse.

"She loves being touched and talked to; I swear, sometimes it's like she can understand what you're saying. She's an amazing therapy animal. This one time I was agitated because my parents were getting divorced, and I legit had no friends in middle school, so Delilah was all I had to talk to. I cried because I couldn't understand how one's love for someone could just fade and disappear from the heart. After I told her how I felt about my parents, she nickered and rubbed her face against mine as if she was trying to comfort me. It worked, too, because she made me feel better."

Kaelyn knew when a guy was a major animal lover, especially a lover of horses, they were usually a good guy. She was so happy that she met Alex, and she had a feeling he would treat her right if things continued the way they were going.

"I'd *love* to meet your best friend. I'd even go tomorrow, but I can't. I'm spending the day with my … Mrs. Denner." Alex picked up real fast on the sudden change in Kaelyn's words. Kaelyn knew where his thoughts went, so she further explained. "I want to call her Mom, but this is all happening so fast, and I feel like I shouldn't let my guard down."

Alex let go of her right hand and led her to a more private part of the beach, so they could sit down and relax without having anyone listen in to their conversation.

"Is keeping your guard up a way of surviving in the system?" Alex asked.

Kaelyn nodded as she kept her eyes on the sand.

"You get placed with a family, and you think you'll have a good family, but they turn out to be … *Hell.* So, you get put right back into a group home, waiting for another family to come by. When I'd given up hope, though, when I was sure God didn't exist, the Denner family came to my rescue. They're like the perfect family I always dreamed of and prayed for. It's like they just fell right into my lap."

Kaelyn looked into Alex's eyes now, but with tears in her own, she held onto those tears for fear of losing her strength.

"It seems like it's almost too good to be true, doesn't it?" Alex asked.

He only got a nod from Kaelyn. Alex kindly moved Kaelyn's hair away from her face, and he tucked it behind her left ear.

"Good things come to those who wait, especially those who are good people. And it's not just the Denner family that found their way into your life. You have a friend in me, a forever kind of friend."

Kaelyn couldn't help but smile up at Alex.

"The Denners aren't perfect, nobody is, but they don't give up on family. They took you in for a reason. They took one look at you at the group home, and they fell in love, at least that's what Matt told me. They always will. They've never given up a foster child, and they won't start with you. God heard your prayers, and He's given you what He wants you to have, what you whole-heartedly deserve. He won't take this away from you."

"Thank you," Kaelyn said. "That means a lot to me."

"Hopefully, it will become something more down the line after we get to know each other," Alex said as he nudged Kaelyn.

Kaelyn couldn't help but blush. Alex was already in love with her at first sight. He knew that he couldn't give up on making her his girlfriend, though he'd wait until the timing was right. Unbeknownst to the two new friends, Daniel had made an entrance to the party, only because he heard there was booze. He grabbed a few near the bonfire and then walked towards the ocean water.

"So, Kay, tell me something about you," Alex replied with a wide smile as he wanted to know more about Kaelyn.

Daniel wondered if he heard that name right. He looked around in response to Kaelyn's name being spoken, and then he found her in a conversation with Matthew's good friend Alex just a few feet away. He sat in the sand in silence and carefully listened to their discussion.

"I love Shakespeare's works. I can understand his language."

"Very nice; will you be a sophomore or a junior?" Alex asked.

"Actually, I'm going to be a senior, though I'm considering just skipping it and going straight for a GED," Kaelyn stated. "I might be young, but I've already taken the SAT and the MCAT exams. I got very high scores on both tests, and I took them because I wanted to have some options. I'd like to take my time on my college decisions because I honestly don't know what I want to do with my life yet. All I knew these past few years of living in a group home was that I didn't want to be kicked out on the street at eighteen with no place to go. That was, like, my worst nightmare."

Alex listened carefully to the tone of Kaelyn's voice. He sensed she left herself vulnerable to some strong emotions, specifically fear. He understood full well what her reasoning behind her college prep testing was. Daniel was impressed with Kaelyn. He had a newfound respect for her. He smiled to himself as he almost couldn't believe he started to like her. Maybe she wasn't the spoiled princess he thought she was.

"I promise your worst fear is over, Kay. I'm sure the Denners will let you take as long as you need to figure out what you want to go to school for after high school."

Kaelyn was pleased that Alex was here. He knew exactly how to ease her mind off her troubles. She never met anyone who could do this.

"So are you into any of the arts, like dancing, singing, acting? Or are you more into sports?" Alex asked as he changed the subject.

"I've never danced or acted, but singing is fun. I'm a *huge* hockey fan, though. Go, Ottawa Senators!"

Daniel knew he was now wrong to judge Kaelyn for something she wasn't. He thought she was a total girly girl, but he didn't know a single girl even remotely interested in Hockey.

"You've really never danced?" Alex inquired, surprised to hear this. "C'mon, everyone's danced at one point or other."

"I've never, like, gone to school or anything like that for dance," Kaelyn admitted with embarrassment.

Alex stood up, and he pulled Kaelyn onto her feet.

"You don't have to be educated or trained to know how to dance. Why don't we get closer to the music? We should dance."

"N-no, that's okay. I don't want to dance. I'm fine not doing it," Kaelyn said with a friendly smile.

Daniel stood up and watched the two of them now in curiosity.

"Oh, c'mon, dance!" Alex exclaimed. "It's fun!"

Daniel saw how Kaelyn felt uncomfortable with Alex's pleading at this point. So he started walking toward them.

"No, really, that's okay," Kaelyn continued as she then let go of Alex's hand.

"Please?" Alex begged as he tried to grab hold of Kaelyn's hand again.

"No is no, Parker, and I do believe the pretty lady said no," Daniel cautioned as he now stepped beside Kaelyn.

Kaelyn and Alex were surprised to find Daniel trying to protect her.

"Um, what are you doing?" Kaelyn inquired. "I can take care of myself."

"I believe you can. This guy, however, apparently needs a lesson in respecting women when the answer is no," Daniel said as he now glared over at Alex.

"You, moralistic? *There's* a shock," Kaelyn replied with sarcasm.

Daniel was offended by this, and Alex figured these two hadn't gotten off on the right foot, so he was silent for a moment.

"You know, I'm not *all* asshole. I *do* know when it's necessary to respect a woman's wishes, and I *certainly* know when to quit after hearing the word 'no.'"

Before things could get out of hand, Alex decided now was the moment to speak up, especially for himself.

"Relax, Daniel, it's not like I'm trying to have sex with her. I just wanted to show her how much fun dancing can be."

"Are you not listening? She said she didn't want to dance. You know what, just get out of here before you *really* piss me off," Daniel warned as his face was now just a few inches from Alex.

"Watch what you say to my friends, Daniel, or you'll discover my mean right hook real fast."

Alex couldn't believe that Kaelyn could be feisty. She seemed so dainty and shy. He definitely couldn't wait until their first date.

"Um, I'm sorry. I didn't mean to upset anyone. I think I'll let you two work this out for yourselves. I'll catch you later, Kay. I'll pick you up around eight in the morning on Wednesday for breakfast if you're still down?"

Kaelyn smiled warmly up at Alex and nodded.

"Of course. Good night, Alex," Kaelyn answered.

"Good night," was Alex's only response as he now walked away and left the beach.

"Great job, Daniel. You had to go and ruin my night, didn't you?" Kaelyn inquired toward Daniel. "And what are you doing 'sticking up for me' anyways; whatever happened to me being a spoiled princess?"

"Oh, you're still a princess, but you're a princess who's acutely aware of her reality," Daniel responded with a smirk.

Kaelyn squinted in anger and shook her head in annoyance.

"You need to stop calling me princess," she advised.

"Or what, you'll give me your mean right hook?"

Kaelyn balled her left fist and attempted to punch Daniel in the face, but Daniel quickly grabbed her fist before it could get anywhere near his face.

"Better women have tried to hit me," Daniel continued.

However, Kaelyn punched him in his side with her free right fist as soon as he finished his statement. This punch took Daniel by total surprise. She did have a mean right hook, after all. He released her left fist, dropped his beer, and held the left side of his abdomen.

"Okay, you just won some major brownie points. I'll stop calling you princess," Daniel replied as he winced. "Damn, woman, you sure know how to pack a fucking punch."

Kaelyn smirked.

"Good. Now leave me alone," she demanded as she now turned around and started to walk away.

Daniel quickly followed after her.

"What's in a name? That which we call a rose by any other name would smell as sweet!" he exclaimed as he continued to walk beside her.

Kaelyn stopped in her tracks and looked over at Daniel in shock.

"You know Shakespeare?" she asked.

"Shakespeare's the shit. But what I'm trying to say is that it doesn't matter what anyone calls you. You are you, and you make a pretty fucking awesome you," Daniel explained. "Besides, I can be full of surprises. Like I said before, I'm not all asshole."

Kaelyn gazed into her foster brother's eyes. She found it hard to believe that he read Shakespeare. She wondered if that was part of the side of him he hid so well from everyone else.

"Then why don't you let it show?" Kaelyn asked.

"That's what I'm doing."

For once, Kaelyn couldn't argue. He was actually pretty nice to her. At that moment, Kaelyn realized Daniel seemed to let his guard down, and she knew it was rare to see with a guy who was as much of an asshole as Daniel made himself to be. In thinking that, Kaelyn also realized she was like him with keeping walls up and not letting anyone get close. She smiled as she learned she now shared something in common with him.

"What?" Daniel asked.

Kaelyn shook her head no.

"Nothing," she answered. "Can you tell me which way it is to the house from here?"

"Why, leaving the party so soon?"

"Yeah, Matt kind of ditched me for his ex, and now Alex left, so I kind of just want to turn in for the night."

"Wait, *Matt, our* Matt? He ditched you for *Jen*?" Kaelyn saw the shock on Daniel's face, though she nodded. "That's not like him at all, and it's *so* uncool. C'mon, I'll take you home."

"You just had a beer in your hand," Kaelyn noted.

"The first beer that I was *about* to drink from until I heard you and Alex arguing," Daniel explained.

"We weren't arguing," Kaelyn replied.

"Call it what you will. If it makes you feel any better, I plan on coming right back here because I'm getting drunk tonight."

Kaelyn rolled her eyes at Daniel's "bad boy" image and sighed.

"Well, we better hurry back to the house then if you want to get your drink on," she said.

Kaelyn followed Daniel off the beach, and she saw him hop onto a motorcycle as he put on a helmet. He then gave her his extra helmet.

"Um, I don't do motorcycles," she said.

"What, you don't trust me?" Daniel asked.

"I don't trust motorcycles, *period*. There's no protection between you and the gravel or whatever you might hit," Kaelyn explained.

"Then you may not want to date Alex Parker because he's got a motorcycle." Kaelyn didn't know this. "Look, I promise I'll take it slow and easy, and I promise the house isn't far from here. It's just a few blocks away. I also promise not to take any sharp turns, either. Please just get on and hold me tight. I'm not comfortable with the idea of you walking the streets alone. It's not safe when there's a beach party. You never know what kind of drunken idiots you might come across or even when."

Kaelyn knew Daniel was serious, but she also knew he was right. She took him up on his offer and put on the helmet. She loved seeing this side of him. Then she hopped on the bike and hugged him.

"By the way, I was just kidding about suggesting that you don't date Alex because of his bike. He's a cool guy."

"Please, Mr. Nice Guy, don't stop now," Kaelyn replied with a warm laugh, which brought a smile to Daniel's face as they left the boardwalk.

CHAPTER
THIRTEEN

When they pulled into the driveway, Daniel parked his bike. Kaelyn then hopped off.

"Thank you for bringing me home," she stated as she took off the helmet and handed it back to him.

"You're welcome," he replied as he turned off the ignition and removed his helmet from his head, which confused Kaelyn. "Um, can I talk to you for a sec?"

"Sure. What's on your mind?" she questioned in response.

Kaelyn allowed him some room to get off the bike, and when he did so, he placed both helmets on the seat. Then he leaned against the bike and ran a hand through his black hair. She couldn't help but take notice of his caramel-colored bangs, though. She thought they were cool and wanted to do the same thing if she could find the courage. She shook these thoughts out of her head, though, and she paid close attention to what he had to say.

"Listen," he began as he looked down before he looked back into her eyes. "I'm sorry for how I treated you. I was angry, drunk, and itching for a fight. I'm not making excuses for my behavior, as that's all on me, but … you're new to the family, and I know you didn't deserve what I did and said to you."

Kaelyn had tears in her eyes when she heard this apology. Maybe there was something for Daniel, after all, some hope. She sensed it was hard for him to own up to his mistakes like this. It was written all over his face. She remained quiet, though, and kept her ears open for him.

"We got off on the wrong foot last night, and … I don't want my actions to reflect poorly on your view of our family." His breath shook as he looked down again and leaned against his bike. He waited until he could regain control of his emotions. When he looked up, though, Kaelyn swore that she saw a flicker of water from his intense blue eyes under the driveway lamp. "If you can forgive me, and if you're willing, I'd like a do-over."

Kaelyn wanted to say something, though Daniel looked down at the ground again and shook his head.

"I'm sorry, it's hard for me to talk like this," he continued as he now brought his fingers up to his eyes as if he was trying to stop the tears. "I don't know why, but you remind me so much of Jacob when I look you in the eyes."

Based on what Matthew and Vinessa already said about their late brother, Kaelyn took this to be a compliment, and she somehow knew that Daniel needed a hug. So she wrapped her arms around him, which stunned him at first. After a few moments, though, he slowly wrapped his arms around her.

"You're right. We did get off on the wrong foot. I judged you too harshly, and I'm so sorry for my part in last night too."

"I can't blame you for that, though, not after the hell you've been through before you came to us."

Kaelyn pulled away and looked up into Daniel's eyes.

"Yeah, I kind of overheard you talking to Matt last night. I didn't mean to. I just couldn't sleep, and I was kind of already sitting by the open windows when you two started chatting the night away." Kaelyn was at a loss for words. "Trust doesn't come easy for people like us."

She knew where this conversation was headed, so she knew what to say now.

"No, it doesn't, but I know I can trust you. You've got a heart of gold, Daniel, or you wouldn't have done what you did for me tonight, making sure I was safe." Now it was Daniel who became speechless. "May I ask why you don't show your true authentic side more often?"

Daniel remained silent for a good minute, though Kaelyn seemed patient while waiting for his response. Then he spoke up.

"You may, but I'm not sure I'm comfortable with answering that right now."

Kaelyn nodded before she replied.

"*Trust*. I get it. I'm new here, and you still have to see for yourself if I'm worthy of yours. I'll do whatever I can to earn it, though."

"Why?" Daniel inquired.

Kaelyn stepped even closer to Daniel now, and their faces were mere inches from one another.

"Because I can see you for who you are, Daniel, in *here*." Kaelyn then placed her hand over his heart. "I want to get to know *this* person. Forgive me if I'm stepping out of line here, but ... I can see that you're struggling with something. I don't know what it is, but you don't have to hide from me. I understand if it's too complicated and messy to talk about at a time like this. We can talk about it when you're ready, and if you want, we can keep it between us. I promise I won't judge you for it because I'm in your corner."

Daniel could barely handle her words. He stepped away from her and the bike as he tried to look away from her.

"My God. You even talk like him."

Kaelyn knew he referred to his brother. Daniel's voice changed on him, though. She heard the tears.

"Is that ... good ... o-or bad?" Kaelyn inquired with caution.

"I don't know," Daniel said as he crouched down to the ground and buried his face in his hand.

Kaelyn knew by the way he reacted that she'd unsettled him.

"I'm sorry if I've upset you," she apologized.

"You didn't." Daniel stood up again, though he stood frozen for a few moments before he sighed and turned around to face her. "It's just that Jacob once told me pretty much the same thing you're telling me now. It's like you're tapped into … I don't even know what to call it. All I know is it's freaking me out."

Kaelyn didn't know what to say to this.

"Something … tells me that I can trust you. I can't shake it, and I can't ignore it, but the thing is … I'm just …"

Daniel folded his arms across his chest as it grew silent between them for a good minute. He studied his new foster sister while their eyes remained locked in an intense gaze. Kaelyn felt awkward, but Daniel couldn't pull his eyes away from her.

"Not ready?" she interjected.

Her question distracted him from his internal thoughts, though he gave a simple nod as his response.

"No worries," she continued as she approached him and smiled once more. "It'll be a conversation for another day. Just know that I promise I won't judge you when you're ready to talk, and I know a promise means something to you, or you wouldn't have brought it up so many times as you did on the beach. Promises mean something to me too. My word is my honor."

"Yeah?"

Kaelyn nodded, and this made Daniel feel better. Even as freaky as it was, hearing her words brought him comfort, and the world felt like it wasn't as heavy on his shoulders tonight. Daniel hated how he didn't get to take his chances on growing his bond with Jacob before Jacob succumbed to his disease. He had to wonder, though, if perhaps Kaelyn was his second chance. She was very much like Jacob, where she had a magnetic personality that Daniel knew would be hard for him to escape, though he wasn't sure he wanted to—not this time. She took him by complete surprise tonight in her words and actions.

"In that case, allow me to promise you that you have nothing to be afraid of when it comes to Doc." Kaelyn knew he referred to Dr. Denner, though she remained quiet. "He's one of the greatest doctors in his field, but he's an even better man … and the best father any of us could ask for."

Just as she could see through him, she realized Daniel could see through her as well. Fresh tears had formed in her eyes as she heard this statement of reassurance.

"I say that because I know you saw him get physical with me last night," Daniel continued. "And based on what I've heard from your conversation with Matt, I can see how Doc's interaction with me may cause further trust issues. As I said before, I don't want my behavior to negatively influence your opinion of our family. I hope that you'll believe me when I say that the Denners are all good people. We truly hit the lottery with them."

"Thank you, Daniel," Kaelyn replied with a smile of appreciation as she wiped away her tears before they fell. "That means a lot to me."

Daniel mirrored her smile with a nod, though he now looped an arm around her shoulders.

"C'mon. We should get you inside."

Alice was in the middle of putting her long soft brown hair into a bun when she saw the front door open. She was confused when Kaelyn walked in with Daniel by her side.

"Aren't you supposed to be at the beach with Matt?" she inquired toward Kaelyn.

"He ditched her for Jen, so I brought her home."

"You brought her home on your *bike*?" Alice asked, almost in an angry tone.

"Yes, but I could've just left her to walk back here alone with a bunch of drunken idiots prowling the streets …"

When the brown eyes of her foster mother gazed hard at Daniel, Kaelyn sensed Alice wasn't pleased with Daniel, and when Daniel started trailing his statement, she added something of her own to say.

"I wanted to leave, and he promised that he'd be safe on his bike."

Alice's eyes lifted at her new foster daughter's words. Then she turned her eyes back to her adopted son.

"You can relax, Alice. I know you know I wouldn't *really* let her walk the streets alone on a party night."

Alice glared up at Daniel for a moment before she then softened her gaze.

"Well, thank you for bringing her home."

"You're welcome," Daniel said with respect as he looked over at Kaelyn. "Hey, do you want to see a movie tomorrow night? We could also catch the sunset after. I promise I'll drive a real vehicle this time."

Kaelyn was glad to know Daniel was still so sweet with her and that he actually seemed interested in hanging out with her instead of just being her bodyguard. On the other hand, Alice was in pure shock at Daniel's actions and words tonight. He was kind and respectful for a change!

"Sure," Kaelyn replied with a soft smile.

"Alright, cool. You ladies have a good night then, and I'll see you tomorrow, princess," Daniel answered. "Oh, and I know that I haven't officially said this before, but uh … welcome to the family. It's been a pleasure getting to know you."

Kaelyn now knew Daniel wouldn't stop calling her that. After the way things turned out between the pair, she had a feeling that it turned into a friendly nickname.

"The pleasure's mine. Good night."

"'Night."

Both women watched as Daniel left, and then Alice turned to her new foster daughter.

"*Princess?*"

"Inside joke," was Kaelyn's simple response as she ran a hand through her long chocolate brown hair in nervousness.

"So you two are getting along rather well then?"

"I guess so," Kaelyn replied. "He was nice to me on the beach. I can tell he guards his heart well, though."

Alice knew this to be true. Daniel very rarely showed a soft side, like tonight.

"If he continues to act like this with you around, maybe you'll be the one who turns those walls into bridges," she said. "Oh, and about Matthew—"

"Don't punish him for ditching me. I have a feeling he was trying to match me up with Alex. So far, I like Alex, and we have a breakfast date on Wednesday."

"Ooh, Alex is quite the catch! Good choice, sweetheart!" Alice replied. "Oh, how was work?"

"Work was great! Matt said that I'd be making a dollar more than everyone else."

Alice instantly nodded.

"That's great, honey! Keep that to yourself, though, or your other co-workers will be jealous." Kaelyn nodded in acknowledgment. "So, what are you up to for the rest of the night?"

Kaelyn knew Alice wanted to spend some time with her.

"I'm up for a movie," she answered.

"Alright, well, why don't you select a movie, and I'll go make the popcorn?" Alice suggested.

Kaelyn did as Alice asked, and then when Alice returned with the popcorn, both ladies sat down on the couch in the den and watched a romance-comedy. When the movie ended, Matthew rushed in through the front door, turned on the lights, and both ladies saw the sheer panic in his dark brown eyes until he saw that Kaelyn was home.

"Oh, thank God you're here, Kay!" he exclaimed with relief as he shut the door behind him and stepped into the den. "I couldn't get a hold of Alex, and I couldn't find you! I'm so, so sorry I ditched you! I swear I'll make it up to you!"

"That's okay, and I forgive you, though you *can* make it up to me by keeping me off the schedule for Wednesday morning. I have a date with Alex," Kaelyn replied with a smile.

"Not a problem, not a problem at all," Matthew said, but then he turned toward his mother. "Mom, can you please make sure that you get Kay a cell phone tomorrow when you two go shopping?"

"Oh, don't you worry, I will. As for *you*, Matthew, I better not hear about you ditching your sister again—regardless of the reason behind it, or your college funds are being cut off for a semester, whether you remain on the Dean's List or not."

Matthew knew not to mess with his mother, so he nodded his head in acknowledgment rather than saying a word.

CHAPTER
FOURTEEN

Denver watched as his best friend laughed hard at *Mrs. Doubtfire*. They'd seen this movie a thousand times, and for Vinessa, it just got funnier and funnier, especially when she was drunk. Denver rolled his eyes at his best friend. She never failed to amuse him. He couldn't wait to see her start dating Ace because he knew Ace made her happier than Denver himself ever did when they dated at one time. He loved her so much then that he was devastated when she told him she only thought of him as a friend. However, Vinessa's heart spoke differently when she was drunk. The last time Viness got drunk in his presence, she just couldn't keep her hands off him.

"You know, there's a party on the beach. We can get more booze there," she suggested with a giggle.

"No, that's okay. You already drank two beers and half of mine. I think you've had enough."

"Why did you only drink half of yours anyway?" Vinessa asked curiously.

"I'm just not really in the mood to drink tonight, I guess," was all Denver could think to say.

Vinessa turned her back to Denver and then freely fell backward onto his lap.

"You know, Den, I'm thrilled that you're home. I've missed you so much."

And her affectionate ways were a-go. Denver tried to ignore it by responding to her statement.

"Yeah, me too. Thanks to you, I can just kick back and relax."

"I'd be happy to help you relax even more."

Vinessa traced his facial features now, and she couldn't help but giggle.

"Vin," Denver called as he pulled her hand away from his face and looked into her eyes. "What are you doing?"

"I'm studying your handsome face and thinking about how much I want to kiss you."

"What about Ace?" Denver asked.

"Matt will never let me date him," she answered. "Besides, I'm horny as hell right now, and I want to have hot, drunk sex with you."

"Well, unfortunately for you, I'm not drunk," Denver stated. "So, it's not happening."

"Please, Den?" Vinessa begged with puppy dog eyes while she sat upright and rubbed his groin area with her hands.

"If you really wanted me, we'd still be together."

Denver's words took Vinessa by surprise. Denver also realized his words were harsh.

"I'm sorry," he apologized. "I was out of line. Here, I'll make it up to you. Give me your phone."

"Why?" Vinessa asked.

"Because I asked for it," Denver said.

Vinessa gave him her phone, and he dialed up Ace.

"Hey, 'Ness," Ace said as he picked up.

Denver quickly realized Ace had read his caller ID.

"Hey, no, it's Denver," he corrected. "I was wondering if you'd be able to get me two cases of beer."

"Yeah, why?"

"Because you'll *sooo* owe me for what I'm about to do for you. Get over here as quickly as you can."

"Alright, will do," Ace said as he disconnected.

When Denver also hung up, Vinessa squealed in excitement and hugged her best friend.

"Thank you, thank you, thank you!" she exclaimed.

Denver smiled as he knew this would make her happy.

"You're welcome."

Denver cared a lot about Vinessa, so he always found a way to turn her drunk attraction toward him into something else. He knew her well enough that she'd regret drunken sex with him once she sobered up. The duo remained silent at this point, though Vinessa still cuddled with Denver. Before either of them knew it, the doorbell rang. Vinessa squealed as she sat upright.

"Who is it?" Denver shouted in curiosity.

"Ace!"

"Door's open!" Denver shouted again as Vinessa now jumped off the couch in pure joy.

Ace came into the apartment with Denver's request, two packs of beer. He lived in the same apartment complex, and there was a liquor store right across the street, so Denver knew it wouldn't have taken Ace very long to get here. He sensed Vinessa couldn't be happier now that Ace was here, and Ace knew what was happening.

"Dude, you're the *best*!" he exclaimed as he approached Denver and handed him the beer. "Here's your beer."

Denver took the beer and watched as Vinessa pounced on Ace.

"Glad I called, aren't you?" Denver inquired with a smirk as he watched Vinessa attack Ace's lips.

Ace gave Denver a thumbs up while he deepened Vinessa's kiss.

"Your secret's safe with me," Denver added. "You can have my room, by the way. Real nice bed, last door on the right."

"Are you sure?" Ace asked after pulling his lips from Vinessa's.

"Absolutely, I never use it anyways," Denver replied. "I'm fine out here, *trust* me."

"Good night, Den," Vinessa said.

"Good night," Ace added.

"'Night," Denver replied.

He watched as the two lovebirds headed off for some privacy. Denver somehow knew, deep down inside, that those two were made for each other. Denver got off the sofa to put his two packs of beer in the fridge. Before he knew it, his mind brought him back to the night of his parents' murders. He hated when the memories returned, and right now, he fisted his freezer, but not so hard that it would put a dent into the freezer door, and then he pressed his forehead against the door. He hated himself for not being able to help his parents, for calling the police too late, but he knew he did what his parents wanted him to do—to get him and Dakota into hiding until the police had arrived on the scene.

Denver shook this image from his head, then he snatched a bottle of beer out of the pack closest to him, and he kicked the fridge door shut. He wished he could forget that night, but it was burned into the back of his mind. Denver took his medication as soon as possible, and then he downed his hatred of himself and his sorrow for his lost family with some beer. He put the movie back where it belonged on the DVD rack. Finally, he grabbed his phone and headphones, lied down on the sofa, and listened to Cosmic Obsession until he fell asleep.

THE FOLLOWING DAY, THE ENTICING AROMA OF HOMEMADE FRENCH toast and bacon woke Denver. He heard giggles and laughter coming from the kitchen, which he knew was from Vinessa and Ace. He'd noticed that the beer bottles on the coffee table were missing, which meant Vinessa had recycled them. He then got off the sofa and went into the bathroom. Afterward, he noticed Ace was setting the dining room table with plates and silverware. Glasses of orange juice were already taken care of too.

"Hey!" Ace acknowledged. "Sleep well?"

"Actually, yeah; how was your night?" Denver answered.

"It was amazing," Ace said. "I really can't thank you enough for keeping our secret. We've been waiting to tell someone for a while, but we were worried the news of our getting together would get back to Matt."

"You *do* realize you have to tell him at one point or other, right?" Denver asked. "You don't want to hide this forever. It'll get annoying after a while. *Trust* me, I'd know."

"Yeah, we don't really know how to break it to Matt without Matt killing us both, me more than 'Ness, but still."

Vinessa came out of the kitchen carrying a plate with a few layers of steaming hot French toast sprinkled with powdered sugar, and the other plate she held had a medium-sized pile of bacon, enough for the three of them, that is.

"We'll break it to him the night before our wedding," Vinessa joked as she set the food down in the center of the table.

"She's such a kidder, isn't she?" Ace said with a few laughs.

"Good morning, Denver!" Vinessa spoke in a cheerful tone as she now looked at her best friend. "You have impeccable timing!"

Denver smiled at how his best friend was always chipper in the morning. She was always so cheerful, *period*. She was so popular and was always the first to be invited to parties or small get-togethers. Her attitude always rubbed off on people or made them feel better, like in Denver's case.

"Awesome; hey, Vin, thanks for cleaning up my mess in the living room. You didn't have to do that."

"Oh, that was Ace. I thought you weren't in the mood to drink last night, though?"

Ace smirked over at Denver, and Denver caught his expression.

"I wasn't at first, but then after you and Ace went off to do your thing, I couldn't stop thinking about Dakota."

Vinessa lost her smile.

"I'm sorry, Den. Maybe we should've stayed out here last night. We should've—"

"It's okay, Vin, *really*. I *wanted* to be alone."

"Okay, well … speaking of sisters, do you want to meet Kaelyn today?" Vinessa asked.

Denver loved how she kept 'Dakota' a secret from Ace. Neither of them needed anyone to find out about this news. They couldn't risk the spread of the information getting back to Alice and Michael. He thought about Vinessa's question for a moment as the three of them sat down at the table. The more he thought about it, the more he knew he couldn't stay away from his sister.

"Actually, yes, I'd love to meet the newest addition to the Denner family," he answered.

"I wish I could meet her with you, but I've gotta head out to work after we finish up here. Raincheck, though?" Ace inquired.

"Of course," Vinessa replied. "You know where we live."

The trio chowed down on breakfast. They all enjoyed themselves, continued their conversation, and they pitched in together to clean up afterward. Vinessa and Ace parted ways when they finished cleanup, and Denver drove Vinessa home. Unfortunately, the house was empty with a note that Alice left for everyone on the family's bills table.

"I guess Mom and Kay aren't here yet. Want to hang out in the Chiller for now?" Vinessa asked, which only got a nod from Denver.

He was a nervous wreck, anxiously waiting to see his sister after all these years. Vinessa tried to keep him occupied throughout the afternoon. It was three o'clock before they knew it, and Vinessa got a text message from an unknown number. She quickly realized who it was, though, when the text message read: *Hey, it's Kay texting you from my new cell phone. We're pulling up to the house now.*

"Mom and Kay are back!" she exclaimed as she shut down the video game console they were playing. "C'mon. Let's go downstairs."

Denver stayed quiet as he didn't know what to say. Instead, he just followed Vinessa downstairs. When Denver touched the bottom of the stairs, the front door opened, and in came Alice with arms full of shopping bags. Vinessa was the first person to reach for those bags, and Alice acknowledged Denver's presence.

"Well, hi there, Denver!" Alice exclaimed with excitement as she looked towards Vinessa and Denver. "Welcome back! How are you?"

"I'm doing great, Mrs. Denner. How are you?"

"I'm doing well! Hey, could you please be a dear and help Kay out at the car? There are a *ton* more shopping bags to bring in."

"I'd love to help."

"How was shopping?" Vinessa asked as she helped her Mom unload.

Denver now walked out the door, and he saw Kaelyn half-inside the trunk of the SUV. He approached her, though he couldn't see her face because of her large, floppy, straw-striped sun hat and because she was trying to reach for the bags in the back. He noticed she wore a long, flowery summer dress. He was suddenly overwhelmed with anxiety. He didn't want to startle her, so he spoke up softly.

"Hi there. I'm Denver. Alice said you needed help?"

"Thank you!" Kaelyn replied with enthusiasm, but then she stood straight up and looked straight into Denver's eyes. "Wait, what did you just say your name was?"

Denver took the rest of the bags out of the trunk. Then he looked down at Kaelyn's face. She had oversized aviator sunglasses that gave her face a bit of mystery, but he already knew what she looked like from her photo at dinner with the Denners.

"Denver," he repeated for her.

He wondered if she recognized his name.

"Wow, I haven't heard *that* name in a long time. I'm Kay!"

Like their mother, Kaelyn's smile made Denver feel warm inside.

"Let's get inside with the rest of your bags. Knowing Vin, she's excited to see everything you and Alice bought," Denver replied.

"Okay!" Kaelyn replied while she followed Denver back into the Denner house.

When they were inside, Vinessa called out to Kay.

"Hey, Kay, how was shopping?" Vinessa asked enthusiastically. "I see Mom went overboard!"

"I had lots of fun! Alice insisted on buying me whatever I wanted, so I let loose for the first time in my life. A lot was actually on sale! Everything came out to three hundred and seventy-eight dollars!"

"If not for sales, it'd all be close to around eight hundred," Alice added.

"Somebody's a real good bargain hunter," Denver stated with a smirk as he put the bags on the table. Then he turned to Kaelyn. "So, Kay, what do you think of Novis Bay?"

Kaelyn smiled toward Denver after she loaded her shopping bags on the table.

"I *love* it! It's like a dream," she answered with a warm laugh that followed. "I *totally* can't wait to catch the sunset later. I've never seen a real one that wasn't on a television screen."

"You'll love the sunsets here," Denver replied. "I wouldn't live anywhere else."

Kaelyn met Denver's eyes, and he suddenly felt familiar to her. She couldn't explain it. Denver could hardly believe that she was his sister. She was a baby the last time he saw her, which felt like it was only yesterday. Today, she was practically all grown up, and she was identical to their mother, Elena.

"Alright, show me what you got, girl!" Vinessa spoke excitedly.

"I'll let you ladies to it," Denver replied.

All three women looked up at Denver in response.

"Are you sure?" Vinessa asked as she approached Denver.

She sensed that Denver felt awkward and out of place. He nodded and spoke up.

"Yeah, I'm sure. You ladies have a lot of unbagging to do here," Denver answered. "But, hey, I need to borrow something of yours. Is it alright if I just go grab it from your room?"

"Of course," Vinessa replied, though she was curious about what he wanted.

"Thanks," Denver replied. "I'll catch up with you later?"

Vinessa nodded with a smile as Denver kissed her on the temple before he turned for the stairs. When he got to her room, he went over to her rosary box on her dresser. He opened the box and went through the collection she had until he found the one that belonged to his mother. It had a pretty, dainty stainless steel chain with tiny simple black onyx beads, a simple crucifix, along with a sterling silver Virgin Mary centerpiece that had the phrase: *Our Lady of Perpetual Help*. Denver studied it as he picked it up, and as he judged it by the shape it was still in, he knew Vinessa took special care of it. He put it in his pockets and then closed Vinessa's rosary box. Then he left the room and headed downstairs. Before leaving, though, he spoke once more to the ladies of the house.

"Have a good evening, ladies!"

"It was a pleasure seeing you, Denver. Stop by anytime," Alice stated.

"It was nice to meet you!" Kaelyn exclaimed.

"Text me later, Boo!" was Vinessa's parting statement.

"It was nice meeting you too," he said towards Kaelyn, and then he looked to Alice and Vinessa. "I'll catch you, ladies, later."

Denver then left the house and returned home to his apartment. He headed to his room, approached his cherry oakwood armoire, and pulled open the bottom drawer. A cherry oakwood box with a glass display lay in the far right corner. It was his mother's rosary box that he rediscovered in the house he inherited from their will. However, by the time he found this box, he'd already given his mother's rosary to Vinessa.

He'd planned on giving this box to Vinessa but could never find a way to part with it once it came into his possession. His mother wore this rosary every day of her life. She'd put it in the box at the end of the day, and when the next day came, she'd take it out of the box and wear it again. He was angry with God, but this rosary symbolized how her faith played a huge role in who she was. He turned to his dresser and decided he'd display it there. He carefully placed the delicate rosary inside its true home with tender loving care and closed the display. Then he set the box down on top of his dresser, right next to a framed picture of his parents. Tears filled his eyes as he gazed at his mother in the photo.

"I don't know if you can hear me," he whispered. "But I finally found her."

CHAPTER
FIFTEEN

Vinessa began to help Kay and her mom with unbagging Kay's new clothes.

"Oh, my *goodness*!" Kaelyn exclaimed, which caught both Alice and Vinessa's attention. "He's *so* cute for you!"

Vinessa was a little surprised at Kaelyn's outburst.

"Who is?" she asked as she hoped that Kaelyn wasn't referring to Denver.

"Denver!"

Alice smirked but remained silent as she took out some of Kay's clothes from the bags she had on her side of the table.

"Oh, you're so funny, Kay. My romantic history with Denver is *ancient*!" Vinessa exclaimed with a hearty laugh. "Denver and I are *way* better as friends. Besides, I've got my eyes on someone else."

"Would that be Ace?" Alice asked.

Both girls looked over at her, and Vinessa was shocked.

"Who's Ace?" Kaelyn asked.

"He's Matt's best friend," Vinessa replied. "How'd you know?"

"Matt may be blind, honey, but I've seen how you and Ace look at each other when he's over here. You *know* how Matt feels about his friends dating his *precious* sisters."

"Well, Alex is his friend, and he's matching Alex with Kay, so why can't I date Ace?"

"Because Ace is Matt's best and oldest friend. When he finds out about your feelings for each other, he'll blow a head gasket."

Vinessa had a guilty expression on her face as she knew where her mother was headed with this conversation.

"I can't help this one, Mom. I care about Ace in more ways than I've cared about anyone else," Vinessa stated as she stepped forward.

Alice was unsure of what to say to her daughter at this point. It was clear to her that Vinessa was in love with Ace.

"Please don't tell Matt yet!" Vinessa begged. "There's a certain way that Ace wants to do it. *He* wants to be the one to tell him since he fell for me first and made the first approach."

"I'm not the one you should be concerned with. People in town will talk, you *know* that, so whatever Ace has in mind, he'd better do it fast. This is between you and Matt, and I am *not* getting involved," Alice replied.

"Are you *sure*?" Vinessa asked tentatively. "Because Matt might kill him!"

Alice smirked again as she stole a glance at her daughter.

"You've known your brother your whole life, and you know how this will play out once he finds out about you two. You and Ace are welcome to tell him in this house, as Matt will be less likely to punch Ace with your father or me around, but you can't tell me you didn't know what you were getting into when you decided to get involved with Ace."

"Yeah …" Vinessa whispered, though she turned her attention to Kay. "So, what are we up to tonight?"

"*We* are waiting until Brienna comes over, and then *we'll* be wedding planning," Kay answered with a squeal. "But I was thinking, if you're cool with it, about seeing your rosary collection? Matt told me all about it yesterday."

"Oh, yay! I *love* wedding planning!" Vinessa squealed. "And yes, I'd be happy to show you my collection."

Alice just chuckled. She loved how these two were getting along so well.

"She'll be here soon, so let's get all these beautiful clothes and accessories put away, huh?" she suggested to the teenage girls.

"Yes, ma'am," Kaelyn replied as she gathered a pile of clothing.

"Oh, Kay, you don't have to call me that. Besides, it makes me feel so *old*. You can call me Alice until you're comfortable enough with calling me Mom."

Kaelyn felt warm and fuzzy when she heard this, and Vinessa saw the excitement in her eyes.

"I haven't had a mother in so long," Kaelyn replied. "It would be nice to be able to have a mom again and call her that."

Vinessa knew what Kaelyn was getting at, and she saw on her mother's face that her mother was happy to hear those words, and she knew that Kaelyn was starting to accept her.

"You just wait until you meet the rest of this family. Then, you may decide *not* to be part of us crazy Denners," Vinessa stated in a playful tone.

"On the contrary, the more family you introduce me to, the more I love being involved," Kaelyn replied.

"Isn't that the truth? Vin, did you know that *Daniel* brought Kay back here safely from the beach party last night? He was pleasant, and he even smiled!"

Vinessa was shocked to hear this from her mother.

"Wow, *really*?" she asked towards Kaelyn. "That's *completely* out of character for him!"

"They're going out tonight to see a movie!" Alice added.

"I don't mean to sound rude or anything, but is this really a big deal?" Kaelyn asked curiously.

Vinessa could hardly believe Kaelyn was so calm right now.

"It's a *huge* deal. C'mon! This is *Daniel* we're talking about. He *hates* hanging out with any of us, except for Max," Vinessa explained. "He'd rather pour acid into his eyes than be around any of us, his words exactly."

Alice hated the fact that Vinessa brought up those words.

"Vinessa!" Alice scolded.

"What? You know it's true!" Vinessa replied as she met her mother's stern gaze. "You were there when he said it!"

"I'd appreciate it if you didn't repeat those hurtful, hateful words, please."

Vinessa knew her mother hated it when Daniel was cruel, and in a sense, she realized she was being harsh by reminding her mother of something mean Daniel said in the past.

"Okay, I won't. I'm sorry," Vinessa apologized, though she then turned to Kaelyn again. "I don't know what your method is, but keep it up because we *need* something to work on him."

"Oh, it's *working* alright," Alice answered. "He's already taken to calling her 'princess.'"

Vinessa's eyes went wide toward Kaelyn, but Kaelyn spoke up before Vinessa could.

"Inside joke!" she explained. "He kind of heard some things that Matt and I were talking about on the porch a couple of nights ago, and I think he felt obligated to talk to me about what he heard. So it was a nice little chat last night, a real heart to heart."

Alice was pleased to hear this, and Vinessa just smirked. Before either of them could say anything, Vinessa's phone buzzed at her, and she pulled it out from her jeans pocket.

"Oh, Brie's on her way!" she exclaimed.

"Sweet!" Kaelyn added.

"Okay, let's finish untagging, and then we can all go upstairs and put this stuff away," Alice suggested. "We'll need the table for Brie's wedding planning."

As excited as she could be, Kaelyn grabbed two armfuls of her new untagged stuff and darted for the stairs. Vinessa did the same, as did Alice.

LATER ON, WHILE THE LADIES WERE A FEW HOURS INTO FINISHING UP some of the wedding plan details, Max walked through the front door.

"Ladies, I'm home!" he announced. "I heard that Matt and Dad wouldn't be joining us for dinner?"

"That's correct. Your father's in surgery, and Matt's closing the Zone tonight. So, it's just us for dinner. What do you think of pizza?" Alice suggested. "Everybody seems to be in the mood for it."

"You *know* I'm down for Gio's pizza anytime!" Max exclaimed. "I'll order. Do we know what we want?"

"Yes, three large, hand-tossed pies. Make them one meat lover's, one Hawaiian, and one with pineapple and anchovies."

Max couldn't help but raise an eyebrow at how quickly Kaelyn responded to his question.

"Did you just say pineapple and anchovies?" he asked in surprise.

Brienna, Vinessa, and Alice all smirked over at Max.

"Yes, I did," Kaelyn confirmed.

"Wait, I'm sorry," Max apologized. "I'm not sure if I'm missing something here. Is *Daniel* joining us for dinner?"

"No, not for dinner, but he and I'll be catching a movie over at the promenade," Kaelyn replied.

"Oh, so then the pizza is for later?"

Kaelyn quickly looked up at him in confusion.

"No," she said slowly. "It's for me. Oh, and don't forget to add hot Buffalo wings to that order and a family order of breadsticks."

Max was thoroughly surprised.

"Wait, hold up," Max said with a pause. "*You* like pineapple and anchovy pizza?"

Max was curious, surprised, and disgusted all at once.

Vinessa and Brienna broke out in laughter at Max's reaction. He stole a glance at them before he met Kaelyn's eyes again.

"That was my initial reaction too!" Vinessa added.

"Yeah, do you remember when I told you that I knew someone from my youth mentor program who loved pineapple and anchovy pizza?" Brienna asked.

Max now put two and two together.

"Ahhh, that person was *Kay*," he stated as he pointed to Kaelyn. "*Well* then … I guess you and Daniel *will* get along well."

"Don't forget that Denver was the one who introduced pineapple and anchovy pizza to Daniel in the first place," Vinessa added.

This threw Kaelyn off track. She turned her attention toward her foster sister.

"Denver likes pineapple and anchovy pizza, too?" she asked with a serious expression now painted across her face.

"Yeah, that's a no-brainer. Denver's quite an unusual guy," Max explained, which now grabbed Kaelyn's attention. "So, you have any ideas on what movie you and Dan will be catching tonight?"

"No, not yet. I figured we'd check out what's in when we get to the theatre," Kaelyn answered.

"Speaking of Daniel," Alice said as she captured Max's attention. "*Please* tell me he's borrowing your car?"

Everyone knew Alice hated motorcycles.

"Don't worry, Mom, he already talked to me about it last night. I told him we'd do the key switch once he gets here. I promise it's all taken care of."

Max took out his phone and speed-dialed *Gio Peep's* pizzeria. After he placed the order, he then texted Daniel to let him know there would be pineapple and anchovy pizza at the house. After putting his phone away, he sat between Kaelyn and Brienna at the dining table.

"So, ladies, what have we been up to this afternoon?" he asked as he looked down to see wedding-related stuff spread all across the table. "Ooh, wedding planning! How's it coming?"

"It's almost finished," Brienna confirmed. "We're waiting on a few guests who haven't replied to the invitations yet. One of them is Meghan, by the way. I know her work back east with special victims is pretty important to her, but I'm *really* hoping she can make it to the wedding."

"I'd say reserve some plates and seats and leave one for Meg. Her work is important, though knowing her, she'll be there. You know, as well as I do, that she *always* shows up for the important family stuff. And you never know who else may show up at the last minute," Max suggested.

Alice knew Brienna was worried. Like Matt, she was pretty close with Meghan, and Meghan was one of the people she wanted most to be there for her on her special day.

"I'll be calling Meghan in a little while. I need to speak with her about a few things, anyway," Alice replied as she then met Brienna's concerned gaze. "I'll talk with her for you, honey."

"Thanks, Mom," Brienna replied with a smile of relief.

CHAPTER
SIXTEEN

When Denver found himself on the boardwalk, and people had realized he was back in town, he received many eager hellos. Instead of staying out in the sun, though, Denver stepped inside the Sunshine Smoothies shop. He stood still in the doorway and examined how busy the place was. Once he saw a few tables were available, he then headed up to the empty counter and waited to be served. A pretty redheaded girl sanitizing the counters inside the employee zone had noticed him and quickly stopped what she was doing. She then walked over to the cash register and beamed a new, enthusiastic smile towards Denver.

"Hi, I'm Amber! How may I serve you today, sir?"

Denver didn't used to believe in love at first sight. Now, he wasn't so sure about that.

"Amber, huh? I've never seen you before. Are you new around here?" he asked.

Amber was pleasantly surprised by how observant Denver was.

"Actually, I am! I moved here two weeks ago!" she exclaimed.

"What do you think of Novis Bay so far?" Denver asked with excitement.

"I'm a big town girl, so I'm still getting used to living in a small town. I love that it's sunny and warm here, though," Amber said with what appeared to be an expression of peace.

"Yeah, sometimes the small population gets to me. All the locals around here know each other. Sometimes I just want my privacy, you know?" Denver explained.

"I know! I'm from Manhattan, so I'm used to everyone minding their own business. My father makes business trips all over the world. He thought that this place would bring me humility," she replied.

Denver understood the feeling behind what she was saying.

"Yeah, this place tends to do that. Even though everybody knows everybody, everyone here is pretty laid back. This place is beautiful and *so* serene. Except for a few mischievous drunken idiots, our crime rate is pretty low compared to other towns around us."

"That's what my father said," Amber said.

Denver couldn't help but mirror her gorgeous smile.

"Has anyone had the luxury of showing you around town yet?" he asked.

"Actually, no. My father assumes that all I am is a shopaholic, like my sister, so he has his chauffeur drop me off at the mall after I get out of here, and he expects me to be standing outside the mall by a certain time for my chauffeur to pick me up."

"Tell him you want to hang around the boardwalk," Denver replied. "I'll do the honors of showing you around town."

Amber's smile changed.

"I can do that. I'll text him on my break, which is actually coming up in a few minutes."

Denver loved the smile on her face. He couldn't help but fall head over heels for her. Her straight blunt-cut bangs hung down to her eyelashes, and every time she blinked over her chocolate brown eyes, the tips of her bangs would move with the fluttering of her top lashes. To Denver, her eyes twinkled with pure joy and added with her lips curling into the most prominent, whitest smile; Denver sensed she was just as much into him as he was her. He could hardly wait to show her around town.

Denver then gave Amber his order for a blueberries and cream supreme smoothie, and after he gave her the money for it, their hands accidentally touched. Neither of them had moved for a moment, and Amber couldn't help but mirror Denver's cheeky smile. Denver was the first to pull away when his cell phone rang. After seeing the caller ID, he knew it was Mrs. Knight, his adopted mother. He tapped the 'Ignore' button while he put his phone back in the left front pocket of his tan cargo shorts.

"My mother always calls at the worst moments," he said with an awkward smile. "I apologize."

"Oh, you're fine," Amber replied.

"So, uh, can I wait for you outside?" Denver asked.

"Absolutely. I'll see you in a bit," she spoke as she put his money in her cash register and turned around to finish what she was doing before serving him.

When he saw she went back to cleaning the counters, he turned around and walked outside with his smoothie. He then returned Mrs. Knight's call, and she immediately answered on the first ring.

"Denver, honey, where are you, and why did you ignore my call? I know you're back in town, and I haven't seen you in *forever*!"

"Sorry, I was in the middle of something. I was going to call you right back." Denver replied. "What's up?"

"'What's up?' I want to see you! Where are you?"

"I'm on the boardwalk outside of S 'n S," Denver answered as he now took a sip of his smoothie.

"Okay, great, I'll be there in twenty minutes. I'll call you when I'm there."

Denver knew she wouldn't be satisfied until she saw him, but she could be so nosy sometimes, though Denver supposed it could be her motherly instinct to be so concerned about him.

"Okay," he replied. "I'll be here. I might end up sitting in the sand if you don't see me over by the shop."

"Alright, honey. I'll see you soon!" Mrs. Knight stated.

Before Denver could say anything else, she disconnected the call, and so did he.

"Hey there, handsome!" exclaimed a voice from behind.

Denver turned around to find Amber now standing before him, smiling wide, and he couldn't help but mirror her smile.

"Hey, there!"

"I've cleared things up with my father. My shift will end in two hours once I go back inside. Then *you're* my tour guide and chauffeur for the evening," she said.

"Where do you live, if I may ask?" Denver asked with curiosity.

"Over on Sunset Boulevard," she answered. "You?"

Denver immediately realized this chick came from money, as do all the residents living on Sunset Boulevard. It was part of Novis Bay's wealthy neighborhood, and it also wasn't a two-block walk, either.

"Oh, um, you'll find out. My car's parked at home, and we'll need it to get you home tonight. I have my own place in the Seaside Condominiums complex."

"Oh, so then you're just a few blocks away," Amber replied. "My chauffeur, Reynaldo, drives me by that place every day when he picks me up or drops me off. I think it's a very nice place."

"Yes, it is," Denver agreed. "Oh, before I forget, let me give you my cell phone number."

"Oh, yes!" Amber said as she now handed Denver her phone. "Here."

Denver also gave his phone to Amber, and they each put their cell numbers on each other's phones. When they handed each other's phones back, they couldn't help but feel giddy inside.

"Can I be honest?" Amber asked, which only got a nod from

Denver as he stared into her eyes. "This is the first time I've been truly excited since before I found out I was moving here."

"Really?" Denver replied. "Well, I promise you'll love this place. I'll start you off with dinner at Luna's. You can be casual or fancy in your attire, so what you're wearing will be perfect. Luna's is the best restaurant in town."

"Cool! The only place you *don't* have to show me around is the Seaside Shopping District. I've spent enough time there to be bored with it. Don't get me wrong, I love shopping as most women do, but it's not on my list of priorities and interests."

Both Denver and Amber laughed softly.

"You know, now that I think of it, with all the things to do around here, I might just spread them out so that I have an excuse to see you on other days …"

Amber smirked at Denver and then spoke up as she put her left hand on her waist.

"Am I to assume that I'm *not* taking valuable time with you *away* from some girlfriend?" she asked.

Denver liked where Amber went with this, and he also smirked at her.

"If I had a girlfriend, I wouldn't have been so quick to give you my number, and I would've just told you that I'd see you around," Denver answered.

"Ah, how very respectable of you!"

Denver couldn't stop smiling. He even started to blush.

"Thank you!" Denver replied. "Am I also to assume I have no competition?"

"It *is* safe to assume that, especially since I've never really been involved with anyone on a serious level of commitment."

Denver was pleased to hear this. It meant there were no real jealous ex-boyfriends that would mysteriously appear at any one given moment.

"Are you *looking* for any commitments?" Denver asked with curiosity.

"Well, I haven't *intentionally* been looking, but uh ...I wouldn't be opposed to one, so long as the right person came along," Amber answered. "How about you?"

"Well, since I'm settling down from my travels for a while, I wouldn't mind finding a nice, steady commitment, but I don't go for just anyone. She *has* to be worth my time."

Amber liked Denver's response.

"Nice! I must agree with you on that! I *loathe* wasting my time and energy with people who aren't worth it."

"Then, if that's the case, I'll try not to waste yours," Denver replied.

When Denver said that as he bowed before her, all Amber could do was blush and bring out her pearly white smile.

"Denver?"

Both Amber and Denver turned to the voice that had just called his name. A girl nearly as tall as him stood before them. Her long fiery red hair glistened under the sun, and her intense green eyes twinkled in joy. When Denver realized who stood before him, his face lit up, and he spoke out in excitement.

"Rori!" Denver exclaimed in excitement as he pulled his sixteen-year-old adopted sister into a big bear hug.

"Hey, why didn't you call me when you got back into town? I had to hear the news from Mom, who in turn heard it from Gabe at the grocery store."

Amber was silent as she now watched Denver pull away from the young redhead that stood before them.

"I'm sorry," Denver apologized as he pulled from his hug but kept his eyes locked on Rori. "I just wanted a low-key return until I settled back in."

"Well, next time, you better speed dial me, huh? You know I miss you like crazy when you're gone!" Rori then caught a glimpse of his newly grown soft brown hair. She couldn't help but run her hand through it quickly. "Hey, I see your hair's back!"

He couldn't help but chuckle at her side comment about his hair. However, he avoided the topic because he didn't want to scare Amber away by mentioning his health so soon.

"I know, but I'm finished with my search, so that won't happen again," Denver replied. "Oh, Rori, I'd like you to meet Amber. Amber, this is my adopted sister, Rori."

Now that Amber knew who this was, her smile returned. She even extended her hand for a warm introduction.

"Hi, I'm Amber!"

Rori mirrored her expression and then she welcomed Amber's handshake.

"It's always a pleasure to meet a friend of my brother's, Amber. I'm Rori," she replied before she turned to Denver again. "So, did I hear you right? Is your search for Dakota over? Did you find her, or are you giving up?"

"Uh, who's Dakota?" Amber had to ask.

"She's my biological sister. We were separated in Social Services before Rori and her parents adopted me," Denver explained as he looked Amber in the eyes sincerely.

"*Our* parents," Rori corrected.

"Sorry, *our* parents," Denver repeated as he turned to Rori. "And, to answer your question, it's ... complicated."

Rori almost couldn't believe this.

"I've never known you to quit."

"Do you mean you're taking a break or quitting altogether or is the search over because you found her?" Amber asked.

"It's ... complicated," Denver answered as he smiled over at Amber when he met her gaze. "A story for another time, perhaps?"

"Ah, well, I can't wait to hear more!" Amber exclaimed. "I, however, need to get back to work. I'll see you back here at six?"

"Can't wait," Denver replied. "Have fun."

"I'll try, but the real fun doesn't start 'til six," Amber replied with a wink before heading back inside *Sunshine Smoothies*.

When Amber disappeared inside the smoothie shop, Rori spoke up.

"Wooow!" she exclaimed as she looked up at her big brother. "She's a little much, a little too high maintenance for you, don't you think?"

"No, she's perfect," Denver answered with a goofy grin.

Rori saw that Denver fell hard for Amber a little too fast for her liking, but she knew he could take care of himself. Before she could say anything else, Denver snapped out of his trance and looked to Rori with a serious expression on his face.

"So, what's up?" he asked.

"Nothing much, just waiting for Mom to call me back. She wants the four of us to spend some time together, us and CJ."

Denver rolled his eyes in annoyance.

"I know she's very needy sometimes, but she says she has something important to tell us, and based on the way she said it, it kind of makes me uncomfortable," Rori added.

Before Denver could say or think anything else, his cell phone rang again. When he took out his cell phone, he saw that it was Mrs. Knight calling, and he answered this time without tapping the 'Ignore' button.

"Hey, sweetie, change of plans. Something came up at work," she stated before he could get a word in.

"Do you want me to let Rori know? She ran into me, and now she's standing right outside of S 'n S," Denver replied.

"Yes, please, thank you! Let's talk tomorrow, okay? Will you be home then?"

"I don't have any plans for tomorrow, so you can come by around noon," Denver answered.

"Alright, I'll. I'll see you then. I love you!"

"Love you too, Mom. See you tomorrow," Denver said as he hung up and looked over at Rori. "Plans are canceled. Something came up at work."

"I figured that. It's been happening a lot lately. Well, then, I will turn my plans with Nathan back on. I'll see you later, big brother."

Rori began to walk away, but Denver extended his left arm straight out in front of her.

"Who's Nathan?" Denver interrogated as he caught his sister's green-eyed gaze.

"He's my boyfriend. Why? Oh, wait, you weren't here when he and I made it official and got Mom and Dad's approval. He moved in next door to us. He's very respectable and responsible. He'll be my study buddy in math and science when September comes. He's *super* smart and is currently taking college math and science courses. Like, I'm *seriously* jealous that it comes to him so easily, but at the same time, I'm happy that I now have a free tutor."

Denver knew Rori wouldn't lie to him to make a boyfriend of hers more likable to him, and he sensed that the boy was a total nerd.

"Okay, I better be meeting him soon," Denver replied.

"Mom and Dad are having this big barbeque picnic tomorrow for dinner. Nathan and his entire family will be there. You're welcome to join us if you want to meet him tomorrow."

"You know what? Count me in!" Denver exclaimed.

Rori's face lit up in total surprise and excitement.

"*Really*? I'll tell Dad to thaw out a couple of steaks for ya then!" she exclaimed.

Denver didn't join many Knight Family events because he never felt like he belonged with them, and that feeling of not belonging somewhere always made him feel uncomfortable. So when Denver *did* join the Knights for even a little fun, Rori would go crazy in her eagerness, and the energy she'd put out always put Denver at ease. He was closer to Rori than anyone else in the family, and he knew Rori loved him and looked up to him as if he was her true blood brother.

"Excellent, I'll see you tomorrow. Have fun with your man. Oh, but don't have *too* much fun!"

Rori only rolled her eyes at what Denver had hinted.

"Later, gator," was her only response as she now attempted to walk off.

"Hey, wait," he called as he brought her into his arms again. This time, though, he placed his head on top of hers. "I know I don't say this enough, but I hope you know that I love you, kiddo. I'm *incredibly* thankful to have you in my life and to call you my little sister."

Rori enjoyed this extra special hug, and Denver's words meant a lot to her.

"I love you too, big brother," she replied as she gave him an extra squeeze. "Keep Saturday open. Let's do something special with CJ over the weekend, just the three of us."

"Sure, we'll coordinate with Mom and have you guys spend the night at my place, and then we can take it from there and do whatever you two want to do."

"Excellent," Rori answered as she pulled from the hug and met her brother's gaze for one last time. "See ya tomorrow, Den."

"See ya."

Denver watched as she walked passed him and quickly minded her business when she pulled out her cell phone. Denver also decided to head off to the beach for some downtime. Naturally, people recognized him, welcomed him back to town, and they had short but enjoyable conversations with him. When six o'clock came around, though, Denver waited patiently for Amber, and he lit up when he finally saw her walk out of the smoothie shop.

"Hey there, beautiful!" he exclaimed when she approached him.

"Hi there, handsome! I don't know about you, but I'm *so* ready for dinner!"

Denver looped Amber's right arm around his left, and he smiled over at her.

"How was work?" Denver asked.

"Boring to the end."

"Well, it's a good thing we're about to have a good evening, huh?" Denver inquired.

"You know it!"

"Alright, let's get going!" Denver suggested as he led the way to Luna's Restaurant.

CHAPTER
SEVENTEEN

The Denner ladies were quite stunned when Daniel hummed and waltzed into the house. The extra pep in his step had also thrown Max off. It was unusual for Daniel to be so cheery and joyful like this. He smiled toward everyone as he closed the front door behind him.

"Hello, Denners!" he exclaimed with excitement. "I hear there's pineapple and anchovy pizza!"

Alice gave Max a knowing look, though he just shrugged. Daniel then made his way to the dining room table and picked up a slice of his favorite pizza.

"I thought you were coming over later?" Alice asked.

"I was going to, but I can't turn down a slice of this good mood food," he replied as he noisily chomped down on a bite with his mouth wide open.

"Gah!" Vinessa exclaimed while she winced and turned away in disgust. "I *hate* when you *do* that! Chew with your mouth closed, and try not to be so noisy!"

"Mmm!" was Daniel's response with his lips closed.

"Jerk," Vinessa called as she looked up at Daniel with a glare.

After Daniel swallowed his bite, he parted his lips again.

"Tell me something I don't know," he stated as he looked toward Kaelyn. "I hear you're the one who ordered this pie of Heaven."

"What can I say? I've been hooked on it since I was seven. If it doesn't have pineapple and anchovies on it, it's not pizza."

Daniel was delighted to hear this.

"You're officially the coolest girl in my book!"

Vinessa scoffed at those words.

"What about Brie and me?"

Kaelyn and Daniel both looked over at Vinessa and Brienna.

"You're the Denner brat, and Brie's the Denner angel."

"Daniel," Max warned softly as his smile now left his face. "Be nice."

Daniel's arms spread out in feigned innocence, with the slice of pizza still in his right hand.

"What?" he asked as he looked back and forth between Max and Vinessa. "Have you not heard of a little harmless fun? You know I'm teasing you, right?"

"Do I?" Vinessa inquired as she raised her eyebrows and folded her arms across her chest.

Daniel was silent for a few moments before he spoke up again.

"See, this is why I'm never around. You don't know how to take a joke," he explained. "You need to lighten up!"

Then Daniel turned toward Max and flashed his bike keys. Max dug out his car keys from his pockets, and then they traded.

"Ready whenever you are, princess!" Daniel finished.

Everyone watched as Daniel walked out of the house and closed the front door behind him.

"Kay, are you *sure* you want to chill with Daniel?" Vinessa asked as everyone now looked over at her. "He's such an—"

"Vinessa," Alice warned.

Vinessa obeyed her mother and shut up, but Kaelyn spoke up.

"I'm sure," Kay answered. "He was nice to me last night."

"I have to ask," Max intervened. "What's up with the 'princess' moniker?"

Kaelyn wondered how many times people would ask her what the deal was with Daniel's pet name for her. She was tempted to roll her eyes at this, though she didn't want to be rude, so she just smiled instead.

"Inside joke," she replied. She knew it wasn't an inside joke, but it was easier to say than to explain the story behind it. "Save me some pizza? It's the best breakfast or midnight snack ever!"

"Trust me when I say your pizza's safe here," Brienna assured her. "Nobody else in this family likes anchovies."

"Thank you!" Kaelyn got up and walked towards the front door. "It was nice to see you again, Max. Brie, I'll see you Saturday, right?"

"You know it, sister!"

"Have fun!" Max replied.

"Don't stay out too late!" Alice added.

Vinessa just waved and smiled. When Kaelyn closed the front door behind her, she saw Daniel sitting on the porch swing, swinging, and finishing his slice of pizza.

"What was *that* about?" she asked as she pointed behind her and referred to what happened inside the house.

"*That* was Vinessa being a brat," Daniel answered.

"Actually, I think she was trying to get along with you," Kaelyn said as she sat down next to Daniel on the swing. "She seems upset that she's known you longer, yet you seem to like me better than her."

When Daniel finished his pizza, he then spoke up.

"Okay … Vinessa is always so full of life and laughs. She's the carefree kind of person because she knows she doesn't have to worry much about anything. When it comes to me, she automatically stiffens up and suddenly becomes serious about everything. It happens *every* single time I come around. *She's* the one who hates *me*."

"I somehow don't think so," Kaelyn replied. "I just don't think she likes your attitude about certain things. She told me you could do anything if you put your mind to it, which tells you she's optimistic about your future, but I don't think she feels like she has any respect from you."

Daniel sighed when he heard Kaelyn's words.

"She *does* have my respect. I understand that everyone is looking out for me, but nobody can change overnight, you know? I know that I have a bad attitude, but I *do* care about the Denners, *especially* her. Vinessa doesn't know this, but I've already protected her from harm on several occasions throughout the years."

This seemed to catch Kaelyn's attention.

"Really? Like what?" Kaelyn questioned with further interest.

"You don't want to know," Daniel answered.

"Actually, I do."

Daniel stared at her for a moment before he spoke up.

"Let me just put it this way. You know from last night that I'm a firm believer in respecting a woman's decision when it comes to a lot of things, mainly sexual and related activities. Well, not too long ago, Vinessa went on a date with someone from my class. He was a Mr. Goody-two-shoes prep-boy in school, but he was a fucking monster off school grounds. There was no way in fucking Hell I would let him anywhere near my baby sister after I saw him slip a roofie in her drink when she went to the bathroom."

Kaelyn was quite surprised by the passion in Daniel's voice. It was easy for her to understand that he was very protective of Vinessa. However, she remained quiet because she knew there was much more to this story.

"I wasn't her waiter, though I was working when they decided to have their date in my restaurant, and when he slipped that roofie in her drink, I told him to walk out, or I'd beat the living shit out of him, right then and there. I told him that I didn't care if I'd lose my job over him because Vinessa was more important to me. I *love* that girl, Kay, and I'd do *anything* for her safety. Needless to say, though, when she returned to the table, he was already gone. To this day, she likes to think of him as the jerk that stood her up, but she doesn't know how lucky she is that he left."

Kaelyn couldn't be more proud of her foster brother.

"Right, because she would have been a date rape victim," Kaelyn replied. "So, you *do* care."

"Yes, I do," he affirmed. "As I said, I know I'm a dickhead and that the Denners want to see much, *much* less of that, but I've been this way for years, and it isn't going to change overnight. I'm working on it."

Kaelyn couldn't help but smile at this.

"See? I was right. You *do* have a heart of gold."

"Yeah, yeah, yeah," Daniel said as he stood up but still kept his gaze on her. "Can we not talk about me anymore? I don't even talk like this to Max."

Kaelyn knew Daniel was ready for this conversation to be over.

"I'm ready to go when you are," she said as she stood up.

"Great. Now, let's go check out what's playing in theatres."

They headed toward Max's car, got in the vehicle, and then left for their destination.

———

"So, do you have any nicknames?" Amber asked in curiosity as she opened her menu but kept her eyes on Denver.

"Actually, yes. Some people call me D, but most people prefer to call me Den. It started with my best friend when we were little, and then everybody started doing it."

"That's a nice nickname. I like it," Amber replied, now looking at the menu.

"Hello, welcome to—" a waitress began as she stepped up to the table but stopped as she realized Denver was here. "Hey, D!"

Denver smiled at Amber while Amber chuckled to herself.

"Hi, Alexa, how are you?" Denver asked as he looked up at the tall brunette.

"I'm great, but how are you? You can't stay away from us for too long, can ya? I heard your first shift back is on Monday?"

Amber sat and listened to the pair make small talk.

"Yeah, from open to close," Denver replied. "And I'm doing alright. Listen, I'd like you to meet my date, Amber. She's pretty new to town."

Denver looked over at Amber now and smiled.

"Amber, I'd like you to meet my co-worker, Alexa."

Alexa quickly smiled wider toward Amber, and Amber returned the smile.

"*Amber*, I *love* that name! I want to name one of my girls that someday … if I ever have any girls," Alexa said with a laugh.

"Thank you!" Amber stated. "It's a pleasure to meet you, Alexa."

"What do you think of Novis Bay so far?" Alexa continued with interest.

"I love it," Amber answered as she stole a glance over at Denver. "It's really growing on me."

Denver knew what she was saying between her lines, and he couldn't help but smile.

"That's great!" Alexa exclaimed. "So, sunshine, what can I get you?"

"I'll have a …" Amber started to say as she looked down at her menu. "You know what? It's been a *long* time since I've had a root beer. Why don't you get me one of those?"

"That goes for me too," Denver added. "A root beer sounds amazing right about now."

"Alright, two root beers coming right up! Will you have any appetizers to start your dinner off with?"

"Yes, I'll be getting an order of the fried shrimp with our famous sauce, please?" Denver asked.

Amber looked up at Denver with a huge smile on her face.

"I *love* shrimp!"

Denver looked back over at Denver, a little surprised but happier at the same time.

"Yeah? Well, we've got the *best* fried shrimp around town," he exclaimed, then he looked up at Alexa. "Make that two with an order of fried mozzarella sticks, please."

Alexa was stunned by each of their little outbursts of excitement, and she knew they were hitting it off well.

"Alright, I'll let Jay know yours is priority," she stated.

"No, please, don't," Denver replied with a serious expression on his face now, which confused Amber. "You know everybody in the kitchen will want to see me if they know I'm here and, as you can see, I'm on a date. *Please* keep my visit on the DL? I'd appreciate it *so* much."

"No problem, your secret is safe with me. I'll put in your order, and I'll be back with your drinks," Alexa said.

Denver smiled again with appreciation but looked back to Amber as Alexa walked away.

"You're sure popular around here, aren't you?" she asked.

"Yeah, my best friend's a Denner, and the Denner Family is very well known here. Then, of course, my best friend also did *a lot* for me by getting the community involved in raising awareness of Leukemia when I had it."

Amber was shocked to hear this, and her mouth was wide open.

"Wait, you had Leukemia?" she continued in shock.

"Three times," Denver said. "So, the community around here was very supportive and helpful during that tough time. I'd finally gone into remission just before Christmas."

Denver saw the look of horror written on Amber's face now.

"I'm sorry, is this conversation turning you off?" he asked.

Right before Amber could say anything, Alexa was back with their drinks.

"Here you two go," she announced as she placed their drinks right in front of them. "Are you two lovebirds ready to order yet, or do you still need more time?"

Denver, almost ignoring Alexa, kept his eyes on Amber as she quickly took her drink, ignored the straw, and gulped down about half of her root beer.

"Somebody's thirsty today," Alexa stated with a soft smile meant for Amber.

Amber just looked down at her menu.

"I-I …" Amber started, but she couldn't get her statement out, nor could she look up at Denver.

"Can you come back in about ten minutes, Alexa? There are just *so* many delicious dishes to choose from. We both know it's hard to decide in only a couple of minutes."

"Sure," Alexa said.

Denver was thankful she was oblivious to what was going on here. He watched as his co-worker walked away, and then he looked back at Amber. He grabbed her left hand with his right hand, and this caught Amber's attention. She met Denver's concerned gaze.

"Are you okay?"

In response, Amber let go of her menu with her left hand and gently put down the menu with her right hand.

"I'm sorry," she apologized. "My mother passed away ten years ago to cancer …"

Now Denver understood why she was upset. The L-word brought back painful memories of her mother.

"I'm so sorry, Amber. Had I known, I wouldn't have mentioned it—"

"It's fine," Amber interjected as she looked down at Denver's hand that held hers. "You didn't know."

"No, it's not fine," Denver replied. "I don't want to ruin our date. I really am sorry. I'm sorry to hear about your mother, and I'm so sorry for bringing back your pain."

Amber once again met Denver's gaze but smiled softly.

"Thank you, and it *is* fine. I was just shocked. Thinking of my mother will still hurt for years to come because I just miss her so much, but that's not going to stop me from having a good time with you. You're not ruining our date. Actually, by calling it a date, you're making me feel a little better."

Denver mirrored Amber's smile.

"Good, because I'm hoping this will be the first of many." Amber's smile got more expansive, and her pearly whites even came out briefly. "And if you ever want to talk about your mother, I'm here for you. I'm here to listen."

"You are so sweet. I'm so glad you came into the shop today," Amber replied.

CHAPTER
EIGHTEEN

When Kaelyn and Daniel got out of the movie theatre after their movie ended, Kaelyn jumped in excitement.

"Oh, my goodness!" she exclaimed. "That movie was incredible!"

"I know!" Daniel added in just the same enthusiasm.

"Bruce Dunbar's my favorite action actor!" Kaelyn replied.

"Mine too!" Daniel gushed as he got even more animated. "He's so hot!"

"Yes, he is!" Kaelyn agreed, but then she froze when she realized what Daniel had just said. "Wait, what?"

When Daniel also realized he had just revealed himself, he froze in his shoes and suddenly felt embarrassed.

"Oh, God, I'm sorry," he quickly apologized. "*Please* don't tell anyone!"

Kaelyn couldn't help but raise her eyebrows at his statement. The puppy dog expression on his face with worry in his eyes was all she needed to understand that he was scared of how she'd react.

"Wait, are you telling me th—"

"That I'm bisexual?" Daniel interrupted. Kaelyn watched how he stiffened his posture as if he was now under threat. "I'll deny this if anyone finds out about this. Max is the only other living person who knows about me, so I'll know who blew the whistle. Please, please, *please* don't make me regret telling you this."

Kaelyn was surprised to find Daniel's eyes turning glassy. Now that it was broad daylight, it was easy to see that this was an early warning sign of tears for Daniel. He kept his composure, though, and she suspected it was because they were out in public, and he refused to be seen as so emotional.

"Daniel," she whispered as she kept his eyes on her. "I *promise* I won't tell anyone. Despite my faith, I don't care about who you may be attracted to. I'm a firm believer in love, acceptance, and equality."

Daniel's posture loosened up slightly, and Kaelyn knew this to mean he felt a little more relaxed. The worry in his eyes dissipated as well, though tears now threatened to escape his hold. He tried like hell to fight them by closing his eyes and allowing his head to fall.

"Is this why you're not around the Denners as much?"

Daniel was quiet, though she caught the subtle nod he gave as his answer. She knew he was trying to keep his emotions in check. She stepped as close to him as she could and wrapped her arms around him. He also placed his arms around her without hesitation, though he rested them comfortably on her shoulders. Then Kaelyn put her head under his chin and rested it against his chest. He knew she tried to make this interaction look as natural as possible in the public's eye, but he was also aware she did this to show she cared about him.

"Is it crazy for me to say that even though it's only been a couple of days, I've already come to fall in love with all the Denners I've met so far? *All* of them?"

Kaelyn then felt his grip tighten quite a bit around her shoulders, but she wasn't bothered by it. She sensed he was mentally processing her words. It meant a lot to Daniel to know that he could be his true authentic self in front of her without being judged. In truth, the older he grew, the more exhausted he was with staying hidden in the closet.

Hearing her say that she already loved him almost threw his emotions out of balance. Her embrace brought him the comfort he needed, and it helped to keep his composure. He was incredibly thankful to have someone else in his corner. He inhaled and exhaled steadily for a few moments before he answered her question.

"No," he whispered.

Once Amber and Denver both finished their dinner, they enjoyed a nice, long walk on the boardwalk. They then went from the one end of it, consisting of restaurants and bars, to the other end with hotels, a movie theatre, and the Novis Bay Casino. Specialty stores and novelty dessert shops were all placed in-between. Denver saw that Dakota, or Kaelyn as people knew her by now, was nearby when they stopped to get in line for frozen yogurt. She hadn't noticed him, as she was with Daniel, and they seemed to be in the middle of what looked like an embrace that was a little too long for Denver's comfort.

In Denver's eyes, Daniel was an ungrateful bastard who wanted nothing to do with any of the Denners, and most of the locals shared the same viewpoint about Daniel. Who Denver saw in Kaelyn's arms at this moment seemed like a completely different person. The more he studied Daniel's face, the more he realized something was wrong with Daniel, and Kaelyn was trying to comfort him. He couldn't help but wonder how those two had gotten so close so fast, though Denver knew not to interrupt them. He concluded that maybe, just maybe, Kaelyn was the right person Daniel needed to help him turn his life around.

When Daniel was ready, he headed toward an empty bench cemented in the sand along the edge of the boardwalk. Kaelyn also sat down on the bench, except she allowed Daniel some space. Silence filled the air between them as they kept their gaze on the horizon for some time. Daniel propped his right arm on top of the bench and allowed his posture to loosen up so he could relax. The gap between him and Kaelyn was only an arm's length, so Kaelyn knew she had plenty of space to bring her legs up to her chest, though she positioned herself to face him for when he was ready for the next phase of their conversation about the Denners.

"Thank you for inviting me out," she stated. "It means a lot to me to finally see my first sunset at the beach. Of course, I'd always hoped my first one would be romantic, but I realize you don't have to be on a date with someone to enjoy its beauty. You just need good company that you care about, and it won't matter if they're friends or family or otherwise. I'm thankful it's with you."

Daniel turned his head toward her, and she saw this movement in her peripheral vision, so she also turned and met his gaze.

"How do you keep pulling at all the right heartstrings?"

"I don't know, but I'll take that as a compliment," Kaelyn replied with a huge grin now plastered to her face.

Daniel chuckled at her response and shook his head. Kaelyn then looked back at the sun. Daniel couldn't stop staring at her, though. He found her to be one of the most beautiful people he'd ever met, but by beautiful, he didn't mean in the romantic or sexual sense. The beauty of her soul was refreshing, and in the short amount of time he'd gotten to know her, he'd already felt so close to her.

"Would you be willing to come a little closer?" he asked. "I don't want to talk so loudly that others might hear what I have to say."

He had a valid point, which she agreed with, so she scooted much closer to him. While she still had her legs up, he didn't mind her knees touching his chest. He looked around to make sure no one was within earshot before he began his story.

"The Denners are nice, but they're Catholic, *very* Catholic. Alice, I think, suspects that Max and I are attracted to men, but ... I guess it's something she'd rather not face. Max and I can't figure out where Vinessa is in her beliefs, as it's not something she seems interested in discussing." Daniel paused when his mind had turned to Matthew and Dr. Denner. "Based on what I've learned over the years about their backgrounds, it comes as no surprise to me that Doc and Matt are the most conservative when it comes to religion, and they're *no* friends of the LGBTQIA+ community. They're *very* vocal about how they're so disturbed by this group. They believe the community is immoral, and a greater sin against God, and they want absolutely *no* affiliation with *anyone* who identifies themselves as part of this community."

Kaelyn met Daniel's gaze, and then she saw a sadness in his eyes.

"I don't need their judgment to ruin my life, head, and heart. It's bad enough I struggle with my sexuality on a daily basis. I believe in God, and I believe with my whole heart that Jesus died for my sins, and I believe Jesus will come back someday to call all His followers back home. I may not attend church like the rest of the family does, but I pray regularly. I even read the Bible every night before I go to bed and every morning when I wake up—and I'm *not* just referring to short little passages either."

Kaelyn was at a total loss for words.

"Max already knew he was gay at eight years old, but I've been struggling since I was eleven. When we were eight, we met in a foster family we were both placed with, and we grew close. After we were taken away from them, when we were twelve, I confessed to Max the beginning of my … I guess at that time, you could call it confusion."

Kaelyn was blown away by Daniel's admission. He once again looked out at the horizon. She wholeheartedly appreciated his honesty and was thankful that he confided in her, so she remained quiet as she listened.

"Max even kissed me once to see if that would clear things up. Keep in mind that this *was*, of course, two months *before* we met the Denners, so we weren't brothers then, foster or otherwise."

Kaelyn was stunned by this revelation.

"Wow," she said as she caught herself losing her breath.

"Naturally, the kiss only made things worse for me. By the time the Denners found us, I'd discovered what it'd meant to be bisexual. I've only ever made out and had sex with women, and it all brings me such great pleasure, but I find men to be just as attractive as women. After Alice and Doc introduced me to Christianity, my struggle then became based on morality versus immorality. Now I'm just …"

Kaelyn sensed that Daniel thought carefully about how to explain further what he felt about his struggle.

"I guess you could say afraid," he continued as he looked out at the ocean. "Afraid to act on the other half of my sexuality. It makes me feel trapped, stupid, hopeless and lost. Sometimes I feel so lost that I feel like there's no coming back, and sometimes I just let myself stay lost through drugs and alcohol because then I don't have to face it. I've never known what to do about my sexuality. It's why I've distanced myself from love and relationships. Aside from you and Max and Jacob, this is definitely not something I'll *ever* confess to the Denners … or anyone else in this town."

Kaelyn felt sorry for Daniel. She knew he shouldn't have to hide his heart, his soul, and who he really was. She was about to look out at the ocean, but then she caught Daniel looking at her again. He spoke once more when she met his soft yet glossy and heartbroken gaze.

"This is going with me to my grave."

Kaelyn now had tears in her eyes.

"As much as I love the Denners, they're wrong to criticize those whose sexualities don't conform to what is right in God's eyes. God knows your heart, Daniel. He knows your heart better than *you* do. Judgment Day will come for all of us, and God will judge every one of us by our actions, hearts, minds, and souls. None of the Denners have the right to condemn people for any reason. Everyone is a sinner, and everyone sins differently. God says to love all equally, no matter what."

Kaelyn saw the pain in Daniel's eyes flicker, but he didn't say anything.

"I'm glad you're talking to me about this. You shouldn't have to keep all this bottled up inside, and nobody should. Something tells me that even though Max knows, it's not something you two *really* talk about. Daniel, I want you to know that you can talk to me about this or anything else because I think you're extraordinary, and I like you. You're a good person, and I'm here for you whenever you need me as a friend … *or* as a sister."

"Thank you, Kay." He was both relieved and in awe. "You have *no* idea how much that means to me."

CHAPTER
NINETEEN

O nce Amber and Denver got their frozen yogurt, they turned to each other and smiled. Denver couldn't help but look past her to see what Daniel and Kaelyn were up to now. This time, he saw them on a bench, and they seemed to be having a conversation. He was too far away to hear what it was about, and he wasn't about to invade their privacy. He saw how Kaelyn sat close to Daniel on the bench, though neither seemed interested in cuddling, which made Denver feel better about their situation.

"Mmm, this pomegranate fro-yo is *sooo* delicious!" exclaimed a voice that brought Denver out of his thoughts.

"I know," he agreed as he then returned Amber's gaze. "It's my favorite."

"So, Den, what do you want to do after this?" Amber asked.

"I don't know. Is there anything *you* want to do?"

"Yes, catch the end of the sunset," Amber replied. "It's one thing on my bucket list I'd like to accomplish with a guy who's worth it."

Denver was pleased, very pleased, to hear this.

"Well, then let's go relax on the beach. I guarantee you there will be a party after sunset anyway."

"Okay," Amber replied before taking another bite of her frozen yogurt. "I'm down with that!"

The couple walked into the sand and soon stopped about halfway between the water and the boardwalk.

"I don't know about you, but I'm having a wonderful time with you tonight," Amber confessed as she flashed a smile toward him.

"Strangely, I am too. I haven't been able to relax like this in quite a long time," Denver answered.

As both of them sat down in the sand, Denver took off his shoes and socks. Amber did the same as well.

"This is such a beautiful place to sit down and relax," Amber stated. "I can't believe I almost didn't give this place a chance, but at the same time, I'm a Daddy's girl, so I'll follow my dad wherever he moves."

"That's cool. Do you have any brothers or sisters?" Denver asked after taking another bite of his frozen treat.

"I do. I have an older sister, and her name is McKenzie, but she stayed behind in New York with her fiance. She and I haven't gotten along well since our mother passed away. She's a *major* shopaholic, and she's *super* materialistic. She also believes she doesn't have to work. She's got the typical blonde stereotype down to a T."

Denver just nodded in silence until Amber looked over at him.

"How about you? I know you have one biological sister and one adopted, but do you have any other siblings?"

"Yes, I have an adopted brother. His name is Carter, but he goes by CJ, and he's ten years old. He's quite shy, but he *loves* airplanes," Denver answered. "He's always got his eyes in a book about planes, and he *loves* building and painting airplane models. His entire room is a display of them sitting on shelves or hanging from the ceiling. He wants to be a pilot when he grows up."

Amber enjoyed hearing this description of his little brother.

"Aw, he sounds adorable!" Amber commented. "I take it the J in CJ has something to do with his middle name?"

"Yeah, it's short for James. After Rori was born, the doctors told my adopted parents that they couldn't have any more kids. So, when CJ came along, he turned out to be a special surprise. He's a little on the small side, but he's really the best kid you'd ever want to meet."

"That's a cool name, and I'd love to meet him sometime!"

Denver couldn't help but smile wider at this.

"And some time you shall!" he exclaimed.

The couple sat in silence for a few moments as they had a few more frozen yogurt bites.

"So, can I ask you something personal?" Amber then inquired as she looked back over at Denver.

Denver looked up at her, though her smile faded as her eyes fell upon his own curious gaze.

"Anything," he said.

"You don't have to answer it if you don't want to ... but I'm curious about something. If I may ask, how did you and Dakota end up in the system, and how did you two get separated?"

Denver's smile now faded, and his curious gaze left his face as he now thought about his birth parents. He then looked down at his small cup of pomegranate frozen yogurt because he could never look anyone in the eyes when he told his story.

"Our parents were murdered."

Amber put her spoon back into her frozen yogurt dish.

"Oh, my God!" she exclaimed. "I'm so, so, *so* sorry! I shouldn't have asked!"

"It's okay," Denver said as he met Amber's gaze for a moment, and when he saw her eyes, they already had tears of horror. "Dakota was just a little under one at the time, and I was four. We had paternal grandparents, but they refused to take us, so we went into the system. I was adopted first by Mr. and Mrs. Knight, and then a few months later, another couple adopted Dakota."

When Denver looked back down at his cup of frozen yogurt, he sighed.

"When Dakota was adopted, her adopted parents had changed her name to Kaelyn, though the adoption fell through some years later, so she ended up in foster care. I'm not supposed to know this, but foster care was bad for her, so when they rescued her, they placed her in a group home for young girls with similar backgrounds."

"Why aren't you supposed to know?"

Denver looked back into Amber's eyes.

"Social Services lied to Kaelyn about our parents and me. They told her we were killed in a car crash."

"What? That's insane!" Amber exclaimed though she spoke in a volume that caught looks from people around them.

"Shhh," Denver whispered in a low voice. "She's sitting on the bench to our right. She's a little ways off, but I don't want her hearing this."

Amber wanted to look in the direction that Denver said, but she knew that would be a bad idea. Rather than looking past Denver, she placed her chin on her shoulder and gazed deeply into his eyes.

"Don't you think she has a right to know?"

"I do, but it's a complicated situation. I'll tell you more about it later when she's not sitting so close."

"No problem," Amber replied in acknowledgment. "Well, since you've been so honest with me about a lot of stuff tonight, I feel it's only fair that I'm equally honest with you."

Denver watched as she removed her chin from his shoulder, and he saw how she placed her frozen yogurt cup into her lap.

"I'm, uh … I don't want you to think I have any ulterior motives in getting to know you because I really like you, Denver. I also don't want you to see me as a victim of something that happened to me three months ago, back in Manhatten."

"No judgment here," Denver said as she met his gaze again. "I'm all ears."

"A stranger attacked me … "

Denver knew where this conversation was headed.

"He violated you, didn't he?" Denver asked in a soft tone. Amber nodded, though tears formed in her eyes. "I'll go find the bastard and kill him. What's his name? Were the authorities able to identify him?"

Amber appreciated the protective side of Denver that just came out, and she loved how he placed his hand on hers.

"I appreciate the offer, handsome, but the universe already took care of him for me. You'll be happy to know that a truck hit him the next day after he robbed a convenience store. He had a long criminal history, though, so the authorities were able to identify him when they processed his DNA from the evidence the hospital gave them."

"I would've made him suffer," Denver replied. "I'm sorry about what he did to you."

"Thank you, Denver. I really appreciate it," she stated. "I hate to say this, but there's more …"

Denver knew where she was headed with this statement too. He looked out upon the waters for a moment. Then he returned her gaze.

"He got you pregnant," he finished for her.

Again, Amber nodded, though this time she remained silent. She didn't know what to say to him. He saw the shame on her face as her head dropped.

"Hey," he called in a soft tone as he removed his hand from hers and lifted her chin to meet his loving gaze. "I'm not judging you. I'm sorry to see you sitting here with all this hanging over your head."

"So … "

"I'm not going to write you off for something like this … if that's what you're worried about. What happened to you wasn't your fault, and it's certainly not the baby's fault either. I appreciate your honesty, and although I don't know what you've decided to do about the baby yet, I want you to know that I'll stand by you in whatever you decide is best for you. I think you're beautiful and incredible and brave and strong. I also enjoy spending time with you, Amber, and … if you're still interested … I'd like to continue seeing you."

Amber's smile returned, and Denver wiped her tears away.

"I'd love that," she answered.

They remained silent for a few moments as they gazed tenderly into one another's eyes. Denver felt sparks with her throughout the evening, though now they'd intensified. He couldn't help but look at her lips with a new desire to kiss her, though he didn't know if she'd welcome it yet.

"May I?" he asked as he slowly brought his face closer to hers.

She knew what he wanted, as she had the desire to kiss him too. She gave him a nod, and she also leaned forward. From the moment that she met him, she somehow knew she could trust him. Denver's heart pounded against the walls of his chest. The closer he got to her face, the faster his heart seemed to beat.

The closer he got to Amber, the better she could catch a whiff of his intoxicating cologne. He smelled like rain in the spring mixed with a perfect yet light and creamy blend of earth, oak, and cedar. Had they not been out in public, she suspected that with how much this scent affected her mind and body, she wouldn't be able to resist taking him into herself. When his gentle fingers brushed against her soft cheeks, she stunned him in a bold move with a sweet and delicate kiss. From the moment their lips met, their minds turned hazy, and all they knew was that they needed this and each other.

CHAPTER
TWENTY

K aelyn couldn't help but notice a familiar person on the beach not too far from where she and Daniel were. She realized it was Denver, the guy Vinessa introduced her to earlier this afternoon. She saw that he was with a beautiful girl, a redhead, and they were in the middle of a slow romantic kiss.

"Hey, how long have the Denners known Denver?" Kaelyn asked as her eyes were still locked on Denver and his date.

Daniel looked in the direction she was focused on, and once he saw Denver, he turned to look at Kaelyn again.

"Since the Knight Family adopted him. Mr. and Mrs. Knight are old family friends of the Denners. Why do you ask?"

"I got this funny feeling when he introduced himself to me earlier today. Social Services once told me that my parents and brother all died in a car accident, and my brother's name is … *was* Denver."

Daniel now understood what Kaelyn was getting at.

"That's … a little weird," he stated as he looked back to Denver for a brief moment. "How old were you and your brother at the time of this 'accident.'"

Kaelyn saw how Daniel had quoted the word 'accident' with his hands.

"I was just a little under one, and he was four," Kay replied. "And I'll be sixteen in a couple of months."

"Denver, I know for a *fact*, is two years older than Vinessa, and Vinessa's seventeen," Daniel replied. "So, that makes him nineteen."

Both were silent as they simultaneously looked over at Denver again.

"How many people do you know have the name of Denver? In all my life, I've never seen or met or heard of anyone with that name until now."

"That's because it's a very unusual name," Daniel said. "Denver is the only person I know of with that name. It's interesting to me that he's the same age your brother would've been. I have to say, though, I don't see any family or physical resemblance. Maybe it's a freaky coincidence?"

"Yeah … those *do* exist," Kaelyn agreed. "And I don't see why Social Services would lie about my family's death."

Daniel thought about that for a moment, and then he chuckled.

"Maybe your parents were murdered by the mob or a sociopath, and CPS split you and your brother up and lied to protect you both," Daniel joked.

When Kaelyn's face got serious in half a split second, he realized his comical statement didn't amuse her at all.

"That's not funny," she scolded.

Daniel's smile left his face.

"I'm sorry," he apologized. "I didn't mean to upset you."

"It's okay, just don't mess around with me like that, especially when it comes to my biological family."

"Okay, I won't," Daniel replied. "Can you forgive me?"

"Of course."

It grew quiet as both looked out at the horizon. The sun was three-quarters gone now.

"If it makes you feel any better, my biological father actually *is* a psychopath."

"It doesn't make me feel better," Kaelyn replied as they met each other's gaze again. "What happened with him?"

"Well, when I had just turned four, he left my mom and me for some married woman he became obsessed with. She refused to leave her marriage, and not having her to himself drove him mad to the point that he ended up killing her and her husband. He's locked up in Hell's Island for life. Serves him right, though. That motherfucker can rot in Hell for all I care."

Kaelyn had tears in her eyes when she heard this.

"That's sad."

"That he killed a couple?" Kaelyn nodded. "I agree. At least the system did right by the victims and got justice for them. By the way, did Alice tell you when she wanted you back home?"

"No, she didn't," Kaelyn answered as she met Daniel's curious blue eyes.

"Alright, then that means she's waiting to see if she can trust me to bring you home at a decent hour," Daniel replied as he now stood up from the bench.

When he extended his hand, she took it, and he helped her onto her feet. "

"Do you play video games?"

"If I'm in the mood, sure," Kaelyn answered.

"Are you in the mood to have your ass kicked?" Daniel asked with a smirk as he poked her sides.

Kaelyn squealed for a brief moment, and when Daniel realized how ticklish she was, he took full advantage of it. Kaelyn couldn't believe Daniel just assumed he'd beat her at video games.

"Name your game, Daniel, and you can kiss *my* ass," she dared as she escaped his grip.

"We should head back to the house," Daniel suggested.

"Only if you promise not to cry when I bury your ass in the ground," Kaelyn taunted.

Daniel couldn't help but laugh at Kaelyn.

"That's bold of you to assume. You're dealing with the master of gaming."

"Oh, really?" Kaelyn inquired. "I think it's time I show you up!"

"*Now* you've done it!" Daniel replied as he chased after her. "Get back here, girl!"

———

When Amber and denver both pulled from their kiss, they couldn't help but smile toward one another. Before they could say anything, they heard a scream not too far from them. They both turned to find that Kaelyn had playfully squirmed out of Daniel's arms, and she started to run around him in circles. Kaelyn glowed with her huge smile. Denver smiled as he realized she was more like their mother than he realized. She managed to get Daniel to loosen up around her in two days when the Denners have tried to do so for years now. She was *definitely* like their mother. She seemed to bring out the best in everyone, including Daniel, and Denver was glad for this.

"She's beautiful," Amber commented as she placed her chin on Denver's shoulder again.

"Yeah, she looks just like our mother," he replied in a soft tone as he turned to Amber again.

"Is that her date?"

"I should hope not. He's her foster brother."

"Gotcha," Amber acknowledged. "She looks so happy."

"Yeah," Denver replied in the same soft tone as before. He turned to his sister again to see that smile of hers. "She is."

"Last one to the car's a rotten egg!" Kaelyn exclaimed as she playfully nudged Daniel out of her way.

"Oh, you said it, not me!" Daniel shouted back at her.

Kaelyn and Daniel now raced each other to the car in the sand. Both of them were excited to win their spontaneous sprint.

Denver looked back into Amber's eyes, and he sent her another smile. Before he knew it, she'd grabbed his face and planted her lips on his. He took her kiss into himself, and he deepened the kiss with every bit of passion he could give her.

"Bonfire party!" shouted a voice that ran right by the couple.

It was clear the young guy shouted to a group of his friends, but it was distracting enough that they both pulled away from the kiss.

"Wow," Amber said softly, blown away.

"*I'll* say," Denver added in the same soft tone.

"The sun might be ready to say goodbye to this date, but *I'm* not," Amber stated with a smirk.

Denver knew where she was headed with this.

"That makes two of us," he replied as he stood up and lent her a helping hand.

Amber took Denver's hand, and then she stood up as well. The sun now disappeared behind the horizon, though there was still a little daylight left. Amber went to pick up her shoes, but before she could bend over, Denver had pulled her into himself, and once again, their lips met, and Denver had cupped Amber's face into the palms of his hands. He surprised her, though she enjoyed this bold yet spontaneous and passionate move.

"Take me back to your place," she whispered once the kiss ended.

"Are you sure?"

Amber firmly grabbed Denver by the collar with both hands, and then she pulled his body as close to her as possible.

"*Damn* sure," she affirmed with another passionate kiss.

When Denver and Amber got back to his apartment, Amber was surprised to see how plain his apartment was.

"Do you live alone or with a roommate?" she asked as she turned to look at him when he closed the front door behind them.

"I've had this place to myself for a little over a year," he replied.

Amber liked his answer.

"So … we can be alone here?"

"Yes."

Amber couldn't help but smirk as she studied the living room and the dining room before looking back to Denver.

"If you don't mind me saying, this place needs a woman's touch," she observed.

"You're right. It does," Denver replied as he approached her and gazed into her eyes. "I'd leave it to you to bring this place to life."

Amber's phone rang, and she answered it after reading the caller ID.

"Hi, Dad!" Denver placed his car keys on the hook right next to his front door. "Aw, really?"

Denver saw she had a look of disappointment written on her face.

"But we were supposed to go up north tomorrow," she continued, then allowed her father to talk for a few moments before she replied. "Alright, thanks for letting me know. Have a safe trip! I love you too. See you on Monday!"

Amber disconnected her call and then put her phone back in her handbag.

"I guess it's just Reynaldo and me for the rest of this week," she stated as she looked up at Denver. "My dad has business to take care of in Tokyo."

Denver was surprised to hear this.

"Big businessman, huh?" he asked.

"Absolutely!" Amber answered as she set her handbag on top of the sofa. "Now, where were we?"

She softly wrapped her hands around the back of Denver's neck.

"Oh, right, we were talking about bringing life to this place," she continued. "You know, I could bring it to life right now if you wanted me to."

Denver couldn't be sure how she meant that. He could have taken it several different ways.

"Care to tell me or show me how?" he asked as he gently placed his hands on her hips to pull her closer to his face.

Their noses were just inches apart now, and the sexual tension sky-rocketed. Amber parted her lips to say something, though she was mesmerized by his blue eyes. Denver felt a shiver travel up his spine when Amber's fingers started twirling around with the hair at the nape of his neck. Her touch was warm and invigorating. Instead of saying anything, she slowly pressed her body against Denver's, and his grip on her hips tightened just enough for her to bring her lips to his. They both remained silent, as neither needed to say a word. How they felt about one another did a fine job of filling the air on its own. Denver didn't know why, but he felt so drawn to her.

"I trust you, Denver," she spoke. "I don't know why, but there's just something in the way you look at me, the way you touch me, the way you hold my face and kiss me, that makes me feel like you're the only one I ever want to trust."

Denver couldn't be more pleased when he heard this. There was something special about her too. When he brought his hand up to her face, he tenderly caressed her cheek with his thumb and kept his gaze locked with hers.

"I know what you mean," he whispered as he tilted his head and then brushed his lips with hers for a moment. "You're so beautiful."

Amber couldn't help but smile as he kissed her again. This time, his lips remained sealed with hers. The slow and steady rhythm was his signature move, but the way Amber mirrored him so effortlessly drove his mind into a fog where all thoughts ceased to exist. She tasted warm and sweet, and he couldn't get enough of it. This was the kind of kiss he could keep going for hours, though he'd let Amber take the reigns on what she wanted to do.

While his lips remained locked with hers in the most romantic and synchronized kiss that she had ever come to know, Amber fought to keep it together. Her mind also turned hazy, and the scent of his cologne made it a challenge to resist stripping him of his clothes. She wanted him so bad, but she couldn't bring herself to escape from this perfectly perfect kiss. She'd kissed a few guys before Denver, but man, oh, man. None of them came close to this keeper.

WHEN KAELYN AND DANIEL HAD RETURNED TO THE HOUSE, THEY couldn't help but laugh about their race from the beach to the car. Michael, Alice, Matthew, and Vinessa were sitting in the living room when Kaelyn and Daniel walked in. They were pretty shocked to see Daniel laughing, let alone smiling. Dr. Denner had to admit that it was nice to see this soft, carefree, bright side of Daniel. Matthew sensed by how they interacted with one another that Daniel had grown close to Kaelyn, and it was a good thing to see Kaelyn bring Daniel out of his shell.

"I take it you two had a nice evening?" Alice asked. "And thank you, Daniel, for bringing Kay home at a decent hour."

Daniel smiled knowingly at Kaelyn, and Kaelyn nodded as they looked back at Alice.

"Oh, it's my pleasure," Daniel answered. "Especially since the night isn't over yet."

"It isn't?" Michael inquired as he then lay the sports section of his newspaper down on his lap.

"Kay here may be able to beat me in a sprint, but—"

"Not only did I *beat* you, but I *buried* you!" she exclaimed.

"Don't push it, princess. That was pure luck, and your luck is just about to run out."

Everyone was confused with where this conversation between them was headed. When Matthew heard Daniel's pet name for her, he couldn't help but wonder why Daniel called her that.

"Name the game, pal, and I'll *show* you up!" Kaelyn replied.

"Wait, you're going upstairs to play a game?" Vinessa asked.

"Yeah. You're welcome to join us," Daniel invited as he looked over at his adopted sister.

"Yeah, c'mon, let's team up against him!" Kaelyn added.

"Oh, c'mon, now *that's* just not fair!" Daniel argued as he turned his attention briefly to Kaelyn before looking at Matthew. "Matt, my man, I need your help with this one!"

Both Vinessa and Matthew looked at each other, surprised that Daniel wanted them to hang out with him.

"Ladies versus men? Are you *sure* that's wise?" Matthew asked as he now looked back and forth between Daniel and Kaelyn.

"Excuse me?" Vinessa answered, which then caught everyone's attention. "Who says a lady can't whoop a man's tush in a game?"

Alice and Michael smiled at the entertainment their children gave them by playfully messing with each other. Matthew gave out a little laugh before he spoke up again.

"Oh, you're *on*, sis, and Daniel and I'll *smoke* you both!"

"First one up to the Chiller calls first dibs on the game!" Daniel exclaimed, now heading towards the stairs.

Alice and Michael watched as all four of their children now raced each other up the stairs.

"Looks like Daniel is warming up to Kay quite nicely," Michael observed.

"*Just* Kay? This is the first time Daniel has ever invited Matthew and Vinessa to hang around him! Maybe we finally broke through to him the other day?" Alice wondered out loud.

"Maybe, but something tells me it has something to do with Kay. Daniel's formed some kind of close bond with her. She seems to *really* be bringing him out of his shell. Maybe she understands him better than we can, or maybe that's the way Daniel feels about her," Michael said.

"You know, I have to agree with you, honey. I think you're on to something, and Lord *knows* Daniel needs someone that can be a good influence on him, and Kay *might* just be that person," Alice added in agreement.

CHAPTER
TWENTY-ONE

Amber and Denver lay next to each other in bed as they tried to catch their breaths. They were exhausted, in shock, and utterly amazed as they looked up at the ceiling.

"Wow," Amber commented. "Just …"

"Wow," Denver added as he grinned from ear to ear.

Amber just smirked and turned to her right as she met Denver's eyes, and he looked over at her as well.

"Copycat," she stated. "Do you like to cuddle?"

"Do I like to—" Denver started to ask, but rather than finishing his question, he pulled Amber into his arms and snuggled her instead. "Not *only* do I like to cuddle, but I snuggle, and I nuzzle!"

"Nuzzle?" Amber asked in confusion.

"Yes, like burying your face into one another's neck or any other body part," Denver explained.

"Ah," Amber replied. "And I take it there's a difference between cuddling and snuggling too?"

"Absolutely," Denver affirmed as he looked Amber in the eyes. "Hey, I don't mean to interrupt this *amazing* snuggle-fest, but are you hungry? I know I am!"

Amber giggled a little and got out of bed with Denver. The first article of clothing she saw and was nearest her was Denver's t-shirt. Denver smiled with warmth as she put his t-shirt on over her own head, and he realized it was way oversized for her, but he didn't mind.

"Already wearing my clothing, huh?"

"Damn straight! Besides, it smells like you!" she answered with a wink. "God, this cologne is *amazing*!"

Denver put on his boxers, and then he followed Amber out of the room. Knowing that she wasn't wearing underwear, he gave her butt a nice, firm squeeze, which elicited a short squeal from Amber as she jumped up slightly in surprise. Amber then stepped up her pace, and once she cleared the hallway, she turned to face Denver.

"I'm going to get you back for that!" she exclaimed.

"Oh, really?" Denver asked as he now made a left turn into his kitchen.

"Mhm! I'll get you when you least expect it!"

"Fine by me," Denver continued as he headed over to the bread drawer. "It'll show you're still interested."

Amber just giggled as she followed Denver into his kitchen. She headed first to the fridge for something to drink, and when she opened the door, she lit up in surprise.

"Ooh, beer!" she said as she now grabbed one.

"Ah, ah, ah!" Denver interjected as he approached her and gently took it from her. "Not in your present condition. If you decide to have an abortion, then that's a different story. You're not getting this beer, though, if you decide to carry to full-term."

"Ooh, did I hit a sore spot?" Amber asked with a pout.

Denver chuckled as he pulled her from the fridge, and the fridge door closed on its own. He set the beer down on his kitchen island.

"No, but if you're cool, let's talk about it for a minute. Hop up?"

Amber listened to his request and hopped onto the island. Denver placed himself between her legs and wrapped his arms around her. He looked up into her gorgeous brown eyes for a few moments before he spoke up.

"Okay, so being that I'm a Leukemia survivor," he began. "Life kind of means something to me. I've gone through hell and back with quite a few rounds of treatment. I'm as sterile as a man can get. I'll *never* be able to have any kids of my own."

"Do you *want* to have kids?"

A loaded question, he knew, but he wanted her to know where he stood on the matter.

"I always thought I'd adopt later in life," Denver answered. "But in short, *yes*. I *do* want kids. That's why I said what I said back on the beach about not writing you off, that and the fact that what you went through *really* wasn't your fault."

Amber saw how Denver's eyes turned glassy. He then sighed as he looked down. She lovingly ran both of her hands through his hair to comfort him, though he still kept his head down for a little longer.

"I don't know where you are in your belief on this, and it's none of my business unless you want to tell me, but … I'm on both sides of the fence with abortion." Now Denver looked up into her eyes. "In my opinion, it's wrong for a woman to kill a baby if she finds it to be an inconvenience for her. She could place the baby for adoption where it won't be an inconvenience but rather a blessing. On the other hand, I can understand if a medical abortion is necessary or if a woman got pregnant by rape."

Amber was at a loss for words. He kept his gaze on her, though.

"This is *your* body. I don't have the right to decide for you. If you want to have an abortion, I'll stand by you. If you decide to place it for adoption, I'll support you. If you decide to keep it, I'll be here to help you raise it." Denver took her hands from his hair, and then he kissed both of them before he met her gaze again. "Ride or die, baby. That's how I roll."

Amber had tears in her eyes now. Denver knew this was because she was relieved to hear that he was on her side. She grabbed his face and smiled.

"I want you to know what I believe too. I don't know yet if I can raise this baby or if I should give it up for adoption. I also don't have the right to speak for any other woman when it comes to abortion, but what I *can* tell you … is that *for me* … I'm pro-life. *All* the way."

Denver was quite pleased to hear this. She leaned in to kiss him, and he wrapped his arms around her again. He sensed she was a strong person, and he was glad they met. When she pulled her lips away, she grinned and looked towards the beer sitting on the island. Then she spoke up.

"You're right. I shouldn't drink, and I won't, *buuut* I just realized something."

"Yeah, what's that?"

"In all the conversations we've had today so far, not once did we ever discuss how old we were."

Denver chuckled as he pulled away from her and then opened the beer.

"Yeah, I wondered when we'd get around to that," he said as he took a sip while he leaned against the island. "I was raised not to ask a woman her age, as it's considered rude and disrespectful."

"Your mama taught you right," she replied with a laugh. "I bet I can guess how old you are, based on whatever answer you give me to the question I have for you."

Denver chuckled again.

"This should be good. Alright, shoot."

"Are you drinking this legally or *ill*egally?" she inquired as she watched him take another sip of his beer.

"Illegally, of course," Denver replied.

"Ooh, I was *right*! Okay, so then, based on what you said earlier about having this apartment all to yourself for a little over a year, I'm thinking that you're nineteen."

"Beauty *and* brains," he replied.

Amber whooped in joy at this, and he couldn't help but laugh at her.

"Your turn," she dared.

"Oh, hell no. That's a slippery slope for us men, my dear lady."

Amber had to laugh when she heard this.

"Okay, okay, you don't have to play. I'll tell you," she stated as he took another sip of his beer. "I'm sixteen, though I'll be seventeen in October."

In the exact moment he sipped his beer as she gave her age, he also spat his drink out in surprise. Denver instantly froze in his spot. Denver's inside voice was panicking because now he realized what he'd just done. He'd just committed statutory rape. She looked into Denver's eyes and realized that he wasn't happy with her answer, and it suddenly dawned on her that Denver was stunned by her response.

"Wait, how old did you think I was?" she asked with curiosity.

"I thought you were eighteen or nineteen," Denver answered.

"Aww, I'm flattered, but nope." Denver grew silent as he leaned forward on the island, set the beer down, and buried his face into his hands. "It's no big deal, honestly."

"It is in the eyes of the law," Denver replied as he now looked at her. "Your father could have me arrested, and I could go to prison for this."

It was written all over his face that he was too uncomfortable with her being as young as she was.

"As long as you're under the age of twenty-one, and you treat me well, my father doesn't care. My sister was fifteen when she met her fiancé, and he was twenty at that time. Daddy will want to meet you when he returns to the states, of course, but those are his only dating requirements for his daughters."

"Mmm," was Denver's tentative response as he remained unsure of how to handle this.

"Well, that's just perfect," Amber replied with a sarcastic tone as she hopped off the island. "You'll date me if I'm pregnant, but you'll write me off if I'm a minor. So much for that ride-or-die crap. I'll go get dressed and be out of your hair."

Denver was silent as his hands now rested softly on the edge of the kitchen island counter. He suddenly got a nagging feeling in his gut. He knew being with her was wrong, but he couldn't overlook this gut feeling. He ended up listening to it and immediately chased after Amber. Before Amber could enter the bedroom, Denver pinned her against the wall in the hall. Her body now stood still between both his arms that he pressed against the wall behind her. He saw on her face that Amber was upset with him.

"What are you doing?" she asked in an angry tone as tears now threatened to fall.

"I'm sorry!" Denver apologized. "I can't … *just* have sex with you, and call it a night, and let you walk out of my life. I'm not a one-night-stand kind of guy. At the same time, I haven't had sex since I was a minor myself. This is new territory for me."

Amber raised her eyebrows at this statement. For a moment, he couldn't look her in the eyes. He looked down at the floor in shame.

"What we had tonight … today was …" Denver began as he now looked back into Amber's eyes. "The *best* thing that's happened to me in a *long* time. I'm sorry for upsetting you. I really am. I'm just in shock. I honestly don't want this to end, but *we* could get into a lot of trouble if we decide to continue with this."

"'Decide' to?" Amber asked. She straightened her posture as if she was ready to break Denver's hold with her against the wall. "No, I'm not playing this game."

Before Amber could move, though, he said her name softly.

"I *really* like you. I'd be the *biggest* idiot in the world if I let you walk out of here, only never to see you again. I'm so sorry I hurt your feelings. I *want* you, Amber, and I want to be with you. I just need to know that you're *sure* your father will be okay with us being together, despite our age difference."

Amber knew Denver was fighting the anxiety he had about their age difference. She knew he wanted to be with her, but he also wanted to do right by her too.

"I *promise*, Denver," she affirmed as she grabbed his face. "I've no reason to lie to you about this. He might badger the hell out of you in your first meeting with him, but he will see what I see, and I *know* he'll like you."

Amber then removed her hands from his face, but he immediately grabbed her right hand and placed it back where it was because he loved her touch and didn't want her to stop touching him. He closed his eyes as he sighed and leaned his face into her right hand.

"Then I'm with you," he replied. "*All* the way."

"Ride or die?"

He smiled at her question and nodded.

"Ride or die, baby," he affirmed as he lovingly grabbed her face and brushed his lips with hers for another one of their favorite tender kisses.

CHAPTER
TWENTY-TWO

It was two a.m., and all four Denner siblings were still at a playful video game war. Alice opened the door to the Chiller and made her presence known. She was thrilled to see Daniel getting along with everyone, but she was tired, and she couldn't sleep with all the noise they made.

"Okay, ladies and gentlemen, it's time to call it a night or take it somewhere else. Your father and I *do* work tomorrow."

"Sorry, Mom," Matthew apologized.

"All in favor of continuing this at my place?" Daniel suggested.

"Aye!" Kaelyn replied with a raised hand in excitement.

"I second that!" Vinessa added.

"I'm down with that!" Matthew responded.

Alice was pleased to see Daniel was actively seeking to connect with his adopted and foster siblings.

"Alright. Keep it quiet on your way out, and *please* don't forget to lock the front door," Alice said. "Good night."

"Night!" everybody shouted back in unison.

When the Denner siblings got to Max and Daniel's house, Daniel went to see if Max was home and soon confirmed Max wasn't there.

"Alright, it appears to be just us tonight. Why don't we grab some snacks and beer?" Daniel suggested. "It's going to be a *long* night."

Everyone was surprised that Daniel was now sharing his beer with them.

"Thanks, man!" Matthew exclaimed as he went to the fridge now and grabbed himself a beer. "Vin, beer?"

"You *know* it!"

"Kay, beer?" Matthew asked as he gave Vinessa her beer.

"Absolutely!"

"You can grab me one too," Daniel replied.

Matthew did as he was asked, and everyone opened their drinks.

"You got some grass?" Vinessa asked Daniel.

Daniel, Matthew, and Kaelyn were shocked when they heard this question pass from Vinessa's lips.

"I do," Daniel answered, which surprised Kaelyn. "But I didn't know you smoked."

"Yea, me either," Matthew added.

"Well, I do ... occasionally," Vinessa replied.

"Well, alright then. Would you prefer the bong, bowl, or blunt?" Daniel inquired. "Or, dare I ask, the mask?"

"Mask? *Nooo*!" Vinessa replied quickly. "No, I'm good with any of the other choices, so surprise me."

Daniel disappeared into his room for a minute.

"How long have you been smoking?" Matthew asked.

"For a couple of years," Vinessa confessed. "And, before you say anything, you can't tell me you haven't done it yourself."

"I'm not saying I haven't," Matthew replied. "As long as you're staying away from the hard stuff, I'm cool with you and Mary Jane. Just be safe about it, okay?"

Vinessa nodded in acknowledgment.

"I, for one, have never tried the stuff," Kaelyn confessed as she added herself to the conversation after she took a sip of her beer. "Oh, my God. This is disgusting."

"I assume this is your first beer?" Matthew asked with a smirk. Kaelyn nodded in response, though she continued to drink it anyways. "That somehow doesn't surprise me. I hope you don't take offense to this, but your presence comes off as innocent with a high set of morals that you stick by."

When Daniel returned with his weed and bong, Kaelyn spoke up first.

"I call first hit!"

Daniel instantly smiled and cheered.

"Alright!"

"Second!" Vinessa quickly added as she now had all the chips and pretzels on the island counter.

"*Yaaas*!" Daniel exclaimed as he prepared the bong. "Ladies first tonight!"

"While you get all this ready, I'll set up the Wii," Matthew stated as he grabbed his beer and headed to the living room.

Vinessa put the salt and vinegar chips in a big brown bowl, then she put nacho cheese Dorito chips in a tan bowl just as big as the first, and the pretzels went into a smaller light blue bowl.

"I *so* can't wait to see you stoned," Daniel said towards Vinessa as she ate a Dorito.

"Why?" Kaelyn inquired as Vinessa met Daniel's blue eyes.

"Because she's always so uptight around me," he answered as he kept his eyes on Vinessa. "Ganja will relax her to the max."

Vinessa smirked at Daniel and then spoke up when she finished her chip.

"I am *not* uptight," she argued.

"You are when *I'm* around," Daniel stated as he finished his bong preparation.

Vinessa was silent for a few moments. Kaelyn also stayed quiet as she knew not to interfere. She'd referee for them, though, if a fight broke out.

"Okay, you're right," Vinessa admitted. "But that's because you seem like you hate being around me and everyone else in the family."

"Is that all?" Daniel inquired as he opened the drawer nearest him and pulled out one of his trusty lighters. "Well, I'm sorry for all the times I appeared to hate you guys. I compensate in attitude for all my personal problems. My life was never and still isn't as simple as this family rescuing me from a life of hell in the system and adopting me. I know I often let my frustrations get the best of me. Just know that I don't *actually* hate or dislike you. I'm just not the easiest person to be around. I'm working on it."

Matthew was out of sight, though he couldn't help but overhear what Daniel said to Vinessa. This was the first time Daniel was candid with her, and Matthew had no words.

"You know you can come and talk to any of us, right?" Vinessa asked. "Even if you just need someone to listen?"

"Trust me when I say that I'm complicated," Daniel replied. "But thank you for letting me know, and despite me being an asshole most of the time, I still love you."

Kaelyn was shocked to hear the last part of his statement towards Vinessa, and so was Matthew. Kaelyn turned her attention to Vinessa, who now had tears in her eyes. She was just as surprised.

"Really?" she asked quietly.

Daniel stared at her for a moment and realized that she did think he hated her, after all. He then put everything in his hands down on the kitchen island. He smiled as he wrapped Vinessa into his arms for a brotherly hug of comfort.

"Of course I do," he said softly. "Everyone's always telling you how much they love you. I didn't think you needed to hear it from me too."

"Well, I did," Vinessa replied with tears as she pressed her head against Daniel's chest. "I really thought you hated me."

Kaelyn saw the tears form in Daniel's eyes, and then she saw how he tightened his grip around Vinessa. Matthew stood up from his spot in the living room, and he looked over at the pair. He had never seen tears in Daniel's eyes, so he knew Daniel's actions and words were genuine.

"I could never hate you," Daniel declared in a tender voice as he kissed her on the crown of her head. "Please forgive me for not having said it sooner. You're my sweet little sister, and I *really do* love you. You're one of the biggest reasons why I chose to become a Denner. You're special to me, Vinessa, and I'd kill anybody who'd touch you or cause you harm. Your life, and safety, and happiness mean more to me than my own. I'd even take a bullet for you."

Kaelyn saw a smile spread wide across Vinessa's face as her eyes closed for a brief moment.

"I love you too, Daniel, and I forgive you."

Kaelyn's heart melted when she witnessed this raw and genuine communication between Vinessa and Daniel. She knew Daniel would still never tell Vinessa about his bisexuality, though.

"Mario's up and running!" Matthew exclaimed from the living room.

Everyone joined Matthew in the living room and sat down on the sofa and sectional connected perpendicularly. Daniel placed the bong on the coffee table corner, where everyone could reach it, and then he put the lighter right next to it.

"Alright, y'all, let's get lit! Video games are *much* more fun when you're stoned," Daniel said.

"I can't believe you guys are about to do this," Matthew stated. "I've never seen any of you get high."

"Oh, don't be counting yourself out of this one, li'l bro," Daniel replied as Matthew took a swig of his beer. "I'm hitting this only after all of you are stoned."

"Who says I'm getting high?" Matthew asked.

"C'mon, Matt, I'm not stupid. You smoke every chance you get when you drink. Don't you think I know that from attending some of the same parties? You may not see me, but I certainly see you."

Matthew turned silent as he knew Daniel was right in this matter. Everyone watched as Kaelyn fired up the bong and took her first hit like a pro. She hadn't coughed or anything. She just inhaled for a few moments and then released the smoke.

"Are you sure you've never smoked?" Vinessa asked. "I coughed a lot on my first few hits."

"Oh, trust me. I felt the urge," Kaelyn answered. "I've smoked cigarettes before, though."

Daniel grinned when he heard this.

"Nice," he replied as he now looked to Vinessa. "Your turn, and I dare you to take a deep one."

"Done deal!" Vinessa stated as she now took her first hit.

Matthew had watched his sister closely, as did the other two, and Vinessa inhaled for a few moments longer than Kaelyn had. Daniel was impressed, and Vinessa quickly released the smoke as she gave a slight cough.

"Nice!" Matthew replied.

"I concur," Daniel agreed as he now met Matthew's gaze.

It grew silent as everyone waited to see what Matthew would do.

"Don't stop talking on my account, people," he finally spoke as he grabbed the bong. "No need for silence."

"I could cheer you on?" Daniel suggested, arms wide open now.

"Please," Matthew replied sarcastically. "If I agree to hit this up, that means you and I are sleeping on the couches while the ladies take over your bed."

"Fine by me," Daniel replied as he now leaned back into his part of the sofa. "One of them can have Max's bed because he won't be home tonight, or he would've been home hours ago."

"Where would he be this late?" Vinessa asked in curiosity.

"Good question. He's in a relationship, and sometimes he prefers his privacy," Daniel answered as he gave Kaelyn a knowing look that only she'd understand.

Matthew caught the expression between Daniel and Kaelyn, and though he couldn't interpret it yet, he knew they knew something that he and Vinessa didn't know about Max.

"How comes we haven't met his woman?" Vinessa asked.

"In case you haven't noticed, Vin, Max has always been pretty secretive about his love life," Matthew answered. "We've never met anyone he dated."

"Come to think of it, you're right," Vinessa noted.

Matthew then took a good hit at the bong, which was even longer than Vinessa's. Daniel knew he was a master at this, as Matthew was a regular smoker, and weed was how Matthew blew off steam. Daniel knew that Matthew was instantly relaxed after he released the smoke.

"I guess you needed this more than 'Ness here," Daniel observed.

Matthew handed the bong to Daniel.

"You have *nooo* idea," he answered as he stole a glance at Kaelyn for a brief moment. "Your turn."

"I told you, bro, I'm not taking a hit until everyone here is stoned first," Daniel replied as he then handed his bong to Kaelyn.

"Won't take me long," Kay stated.

"Same here," Vinessa added. "Wait, did you just call me 'Ness?"

Daniel met Vinessa's curious gaze before he spoke up.

"That a problem?" he asked as Kaelyn took another hit.

"Uh, no! No, not at all!" Vinessa replied quickly. "It's better than being called a brat."

"If I'm calling you a brat, it's because I'm playing around with you, honestly," Daniel explained. "I have pet names for everyone."

Matthew decided to butt into this conversation.

"You mean like how you called Kay 'princess' on the first night with us?" Matthew asked as Kaelyn gave the bong to Vinessa. "You know, she was—"

"It's fine, Matt," Kaelyn interjected before Matthew had a chance to jump down Daniel's throat.

Daniel knew Matthew had figured out why he first called Kaelyn 'princess' to begin with, but he was a bit surprised by how defensive Matthew was when it came to their new foster sister.

"No, you're right," Daniel said towards Matthew as Vinessa took her second hit. "I judged Kay too harshly, but then we connected and cleared the air, and now here we are. She's got a knack for tugging at the heartstrings, just like Jacob."

"Don't you dare say his name," Matthew warned in a threatening tone, which caught everyone off guard.

The room turned silent as Matthew glared at Daniel with daggers in his eyes. Neither of the girls knew what to say. Daniel did, though.

"Why? Because I wasn't there for the funeral?"

"Damn straight!" Matthew exclaimed as he then stood up from his spot on the sofa. "You were probably too busy getting drunk in God only knows where. I mean, hell, the night he died, you'd gotten arrested for drunken disorderly *and* assault and battery! So, *you* don't get to speak Jacob's name, not in front of me!"

Daniel scoffed at this and stood up as well.

"You know what? I'm not doing this with you. I don't know what you want from me, but I'm not biting. Feel free to smoke up my stash, raid my kitchen, and stay the night, but this conversation is over."

Daniel now headed for his bedroom, though Matthew pulled him back by the shoulders.

"I'm not done talking to you," he said.

"Oh, my God!" Daniel exclaimed in annoyance as he turned and looked at his brother again. "Fine! Then tell me what the hell it is that you want from me!"

"I want to know why you weren't there that night he died when we all came together, and you got yourself drunk and arrested instead? I want to know why you weren't there at our brother's funeral to pay your respects to him? I want to know why you weren't there for any of us like *we've* always been there for *you*?"

Kaelyn and Vinessa exchanged looks before Vinessa now stood up from her spot on the couch.

"Matt, that's enough!" she exclaimed.

"No, wait," Daniel said as he kept his gaze on their brother. "Sit down, 'Ness. You *really* want to know why?"

"Yeah, I do!"

The room was silent again, though this time, Daniel looked into Vinessa's eyes and nodded to let her know he'd handle this situation. So, she gave in to his request and sat down again. Then Daniel turned his attention back onto Matthew.

"Think about what you said to Kay on the porch on the first night she came to us." Matthew was surprised by this. "Yeah, I heard your entire conversation with her that night. You already have your answer to the first question you just asked me, and you *still* don't have a clue because you don't *see* me."

Daniel saw Matthew was now confused by what he had just said.

"What the hell are you talking about? Of *course,* I do!" Matthew argued.

"No, you fucking *don't*, Matt!" Daniel yelled. "You don't see *me*. You see *through* me!"

Matthew didn't know what to say to this.

"What did you say to Kay about the five stages of grief?" Daniel hinted to jog his brother's memory. "Which of the five stages of grief came first for us after Jacob died?"

"Anger," Matthew whispered.

"Ding, ding, ding!" Daniel hollered. "Ladies and gentleman, we *have* a winner! Is any of this clicking for you yet, little brother?"

Matthew was at a loss for words, though Daniel approached him.

"If you want the answers to the rest of the questions, you have to *swear* to me that what I'm about to tell you *doesn't* leave this room. This can't get back to Alice and Doc. It stays between *all* of us." Then he turned to Kaelyn and Vinessa. "That goes for you too."

"I promise I won't tell anyone," Kaelyn stated.

"I promise too," Vinessa added.

Then he gazed back into Matt's eyes.

"*Swear* to me, Matt, or if you don't, I'll tell Alice and Doc about your little warehouse escapades."

Matthew's jaw dropped when he figured out that Daniel knew his darkest secret.

"What warehouse?" Vinessa asked.

"None of your business!" Matthew growled as he looked over at her for a moment before he turned back to Daniel. "Fine, you asshole, I swear it, but this *better* be good!"

Daniel was content with this, and he gave Mattew some space.

"I'll have you know that I had *every* intention of going to Jacob's funeral. It just so happened that as Max and I were getting ready, I got a call from my little sister."

This answer threw off everyone in the room.

"What little sister?" Matthew inquired. "You mean Vinessa?"

"No, I mean my biological sister," Daniel further explained. "My mother was pregnant with her when CPS put me in foster care. I met her at a party two years ago, and when I realized who she was, I knew I had to help get her back on the right track, but I didn't know how to at first. She was thirteen years old and drinking heavily and partying harder than even *I* ever have. Our mom was pulling the same bullshit with her that she pulled with me, and it kept me up all hours of every goddamn night until I *had* to get involved."

Matthew was still speechless; only now he felt like a total ass. He watched as Daniel walked away from him and then folded his arms across his chest as he turned toward him. This time, Matthew saw how Daniel's eyes had teared up.

"Jacob had this uncanny ability to be invisible whenever people least expected it. He was following me and watching my activities in the next town over. He figured out what I was doing and confronted me about it. He knew that I couldn't help my sister when I also needed help too. I'm not perfect, and I'll never claim to be, but my sister is a *far* better person than I will *ever* be."

Matthew remained quiet, and the girls couldn't help but exchange expressions of shock with one another.

"Just like with these two over here," Daniel pointed out. "I love her, and I'd do *anything* for her. Jacob tried to get me to talk to Derek, Alana, and Andy, but I was petrified of my sister ending up in an even worse situation than Max and I were before we met you guys. Jacob saw me struggling, and he wanted to be my lifeline like *I* was trying to be for my sister. In our last conversation, he begged me to keep helping her but told me I needed to come forward to Alice and Doc with this … but then after he passed away, Alice and Doc said they didn't want to take in any more kids."

Matthew couldn't help but mirror the tears in Daniel's eyes when he heard this explanation.

"And then Mom and Dad brought Kay home," Matthew thought out loud. "Is that why you were so angry the other night?"

Everyone knew he referred to the night Kay arrived while Daniel got arrested. Daniel nodded in silence, but then he realized maybe this would upset Kaelyn.

"No offense, Kay," he said as he met her gaze.

"None taken," she answered as they looked back to Matthew.

"When my sister called me on the day of Jacob's funeral, she was in tears. She tried to stop our mom from committing suicide, but our mom locked herself in her room with a whole lot of pills."

Now the girls had tears in their eyes, though they too stayed quiet.

"I went over to help, and I had to use my whole body weight to get that damn door open. I slapped the pill bottle from her as fast as I could. The pills flew everywhere, but then my mother collapsed into her depression. I had to call the police and have her admitted. She was in the psych unit for a month, and someone needed to take care of my little sister, so *I* stayed with her. Max knew too, but he promised me that he'd keep it between us. So, *now* you know why I wasn't around. I *did* love Jacob, *honestly*, though I also knew he'd understand that my sister needed me more that day."

Matthew saw that it was hard for Daniel to keep his composure. He approached his older brother and wrapped his arms around him.

"I'm sorry," he apologized with tears that were also difficult for him to hold back. "I didn't know. I feel like such an asshole, and you don't deserve it. Please forgive me, Daniel. I'm so sorry."

Daniel remained silent for a minute as his brother kept his arms wrapped around him. Then he brought his arms around Matthew and hugged him as well.

"I forgive you."

The girls both decided they wanted to join this hug, so they stood up and approached their brothers.

"Group hug!" Vinessa shouted as they swarmed both Daniel and Matthew.

Daniel and Matthew smiled and let this be for a good minute, but then Daniel had had enough.

"Alright, alright," he stated as the hug broke up, and he wiped his tears from his eyes. "That's enough loving and hugging for one night. I've got a reputation to protect here."

Everyone knew he was joking when a smirk appeared on his face, though deep down, Daniel loved the togetherness they all experienced tonight. He was also happy to have the heart-to-heart he just had with his brother.

"Heart of gold, Daniel," Kaelyn reminded him as she threw him a grin before she returned to her spot on the sofa.

"Yeah, yeah," he replied as he followed her back and reclaimed his spot.

Vinessa and Matthew both followed suit, though Kaelyn was the first to take another hit at the bong.

"Does anyone else have any other grievances they want to share before we proceed?" Daniel asked.

Everyone exchanged looks, and they all shook their head no.

"No, but I have one question," Kaelyn said, catching everyone's attention. "Since Alice and Michael took me in, they may be willing to take in another foster. Maybe we could have a talk with them about your sister?"

"They'll wait until you're all settled in and doing well and stuff first before they take anyone else in," Daniel replied. "She's okay for now, though. I have her checking in with me every day."

Matthew was next for his hit on the bong, though a question had also popped up in his mind.

"So, that whole thing the other night with having Mom and Dad connect you with your mom, it all has to do with your sister?"

"Yes, I want them to come with me to meet Dylan and have a talk with my mom to let her come and stay with us."

"Gotcha," Matthew spoke as he gazed into Daniel's eyes. "Now everything's starting to make sense. You're right, Daniel. I didn't see you before, but I do now. And you know what? We're going to find a way for all of us to help you save your sister."

Daniel became speechless while tears welled up in his eyes again, though he was quick to wipe them away. Those words meant more to him than Matthew knew. They all felt a change in the dynamics of the bonds they had with each other.

"We'll figure something out," Kaelyn replied.

Daniel felt relieved, and for what was the first time ever, he felt like he genuinely belonged. When everyone started spacing out from their highs, Daniel took some hits too, and when he became high, he gave everyone a controller.

"Alright, ladies and gentleman! Here we go! It's time for a good old-fashioned Mario party!" Daniel exclaimed. "And we'll kick this up a notch by getting rid of teams. It's everyone for themselves now."

No one seemed to mind, and they had a lot of fun playing against each other. They'd grown fond of each other, and they became close. It only took Kaelyn a few days to get to know them. She had already considered them family. Now, she only had one other bond she knew she needed to work on before they'd legally adopt her: Dr. Denner.

CHAPTER
TWENTY-THREE

When Amber woke up the following morning, and she saw that Denver was already awake, she smiled up at him. He had one arm around her stomach while the other one had his head propped up. He was smiling down on her, taking in her beauty.

"Good morning, sunshine," Amber greeted.

"Good morning, beautiful," he replied.

"How long have you been awake?" she asked.

Denver thought about her question and debated whether he was ready to share the whole story about what happened the night he lost his mother and father.

"Since five o'clock this morning. I have PTSD from the night I lost my parents. I usually take meds before bed to prevent the night terrors, but … forgot to take the meds last night." Amber watched as Denver repositioned his head to rest it on his pillow now, though his eyes remained locked with hers while his other hand stayed on her stomach. "You already know they were brutally murdered. When the killer was caught and prosecuted, he told the courts he didn't want anyone else to have my mother if he couldn't have her."

Amber was in complete shock. She didn't know what to say. She was indeed at a loss for words.

"He would've killed Dakota and me if I hadn't done what my dad told me to do," Denver added.

Denver's thoughts went back to the day his father completed his home add-on project as Denver continued to tell his story.

"Denver, my son, would you come over here, please?"

Four-year-old Denver did as his father had asked, and he walked over to his father, who was kneeling before him at Denver's closet door. The man smiled lovingly down at his son as he opened a brand new compartment added to Denver's closet.

"I want to show you something."

Denver continued to remain quiet as his father urged him to step into the closet.

"This, my son, is where Mommy and I want you to take Dakota if we ever tell you to do so. We want you to go here, okay? I want to run a practice drill with you, just like we've done with fire drills, okay?"

Four-year-old Denver nodded to show he understood.

"Okay, an intruder has entered the house, and Mommy and I tell you to run. What do you do?" his father asked.

"I grab Kota and climb in here?" Denver answered.

"Yes, that's correct, son. Why don't you give it a try and climb in?"

Denver did as his father had suggested, and he crawled into the rectangular closet compartment.

"It's dark!" Denver exclaimed as fear overcame every fiber of his being. "I can't see!"

"Just relax, Denver. I promise nothing is going to hurt you in here. You're very safe in here. Nothing and no one can get in here but you and Kota. Just feel your way around, son. Your safety is the focus

point. Just take your time and feel your surroundings, son," his father explained. "If you look down the crawlspace to your right, you will see a large, glowing red button.

"I see it!" Denver exclaimed in excitement.

"Good! Now don't hit the button. Only hit it if you really need to call the police," his father explained, but if you feel around beneath the red button, you will find a light switch. Go ahead and flip it."

Denver did as he was told, and then suddenly there was light, and Denver realized how big the room was. Now he stood up in eagerness.

"Wow!"

Denver felt like he had his own secret place, like nobody in the world could reach him or find him.

"If you look behind you, you will see a large, shiny, metal square on the wall above where you just crawled through. I want you to hit the red button next to the shiny metal square. It will open and close the crawl space. Why don't you give it a try?"

Denver obeyed his father and hit the button. Instantly, the metal plate came down, and Denver grew even more excited. He hit the red button once more to open it, and it did.

"Cool!" he exclaimed.

"Take a look around, son. You should see a green button. Let me know when you see it," said his father.

Denver looked around the small room for a good minute and then found the green button a few spaces above the glowing red emergency button.

"I see it!" Denver shouted to his father, who wasn't in sight, but within earshot.

"Great, now push it, and then turn the light off."

Once again, Denver did as his father asked of him. A half-sized human door opened up on Denver's right. He was small enough that he didn't have to bend himself to walk through it. He turned off the light and walked out of the new secret room. When he realized he was stepping back into his bedroom from the new secret place within the walls, he looked over at his father, who now smiled back at him. When Denver walked towards him, he heard a noise and turned to find the secret room's door was closing itself.

"What do you think, son?"

Denver turned around and smiled wide toward his father.

"I like it!"

"Good, because this is where you will need to hide with Dakota if anything bad happens. If you have to push that big red button, make sure it blinks, okay? When it blinks, it means the police know there is trouble, and they'll come as fast as they can to help us. Before you push the button, though, make sure you close all the doors. Come here for a second."

Denver walked back over to his father.

"Get down on your knees," instructed his father.

As Denver did so, his father took his left hand and showed him a big circle in the crawlspace's darkness on Denver's left.

"Do you feel that?" his father asked.

"Yes."

"If you have to come in here, make sure this door and the door in front of you that is coming from Kota's room are both closed. Then you push this button. It's fail-safe, and it will keep out anybody trying to hurt you, okay? If Mommy and I tell you to run, you run, Denver. Don't stop for anything. You only get your sister. Do you understand me, Denver?"

Denver nodded in complete understanding.

"You push this button first, then the red circle button until it blinks, and then you push the button that closes the shiny metal door, and you wait until the police show up, or if Mommy and I say it's safe to come out. It's very, very important that you understand this 100%, son. This secret room I made for you and your sister could mean a difference between life and death for you two. If you're confused by anything I've just shown you, now's the time to ask about it. Do you have any questions for me?"

"No, Daddy," Denver replied. "It's like a fire drill, except there wouldn't be a fire, and I crawl in here with Kota when you or Mommy tell me to run."

Denver's father smiled wide at his son and kissed him on top of his head.

"You're growing into such a big boy. I'm so proud of you, son. I love you."

"I love you too, Daddy."

"They knew," Amber whispered after Denver told her his memory while he thought about it. "They knew they were in danger."

When Denver looked up at Amber, he just nodded, though he had tears in his eyes at this point.

"That's so creepy! Ugh, it gave me the chills," Amber noted. "He must've been stalking them, threatening them, *something*."

"He was. Court records indicate a violation of a restraining order they had against him. He stalked them like crazy at the hospital where my dad worked as a doctor and my mom worked as a nurse. He got thirty years to life for what he did. He's at Hell's Island Penitentiary."

Once again, Amber was speechless.

"I think Social Services split Dakota and me up in case he ever got out of prison. That's why her name isn't Dakota anymore. Even though Kay was adopted as a baby, she still ended up going back into the system, though my best friend's family loves foster care. My best friend, Vinessa, she's seen the photo I have of my family, and since Kay looks exactly like our mother, it was easy for Vinessa to spot her in the group home they'd visited. Vinessa's parents haven't seen the photo, and they haven't connected the dots between Kay and me. It's best that they don't, though, because they signed an agreement with the state that if they tell Kay the truth about what happened with our family, they'd have to forfeit their foster license permanently."

Amber was disheartened when she heard this, though she knew Denver had more to say, so she remained silent.

"As much as I would love for her to know who I am, I can see how happy she really is with Vinessa's family. They're a great family, and after the abuse that she's been through with another foster family, she deserves to have one that loves her as much as I do. Vinessa had me meet her yesterday, though, and Kay seemed to recognize my name. I'm not sure if she's going to figure it out."

"That's not surprising. You don't exactly have a common name," Amber replied. "Are you going to tell her who you are?"

Denver was silent for a moment, as he knew that was the million-dollar question and one he kept asking himself.

"I haven't decided. She'll find out eventually, though. She's got a big inheritance waiting for her when she turns eighteen. Our parents gave us their house, and I can't sell it until she's eighteen, so if she doesn't figure it out between now and then, she'll know then. I hope the Denners adopt her first."

"Well, at least you know she's safe where she is, and you get to see her anytime you want. There won't be any more missing out on her life," Amber replied. "But I'm so sorry about what happened to your family."

Denver's lips curled into a small smile as he met Amber's gaze.

"Thanks," he replied. "Hey, can I ask what your schedule is for the day?"

"Well, today's my day off, and I haven't made any plans yet. So, I'm free. Why do you ask? Did you have something in mind?"

"Yes, I do. How would you like to meet CJ and our parents?"

Amber smiled wider.

"I'd love to," Amber answered.

"Great. Do you have a bathing suit?"

"Yes."

"Okay, so we'll hit the shower, and after brunch, we can swing by your place to get your stuff. Then we'll head over to my parents' place. They're having a barbeque, and we've got a big inground pool. Fair warning, though, my family *loves* water sports, and they're *huge* on playing aqua volleyball in the pool, so they get quite competitive."

Amber couldn't help but smirk at this.

"Well, then you'll be happy to know that volleyball's my game. I was captain of my team back east, and we won the state tournament last year."

"Wow," Denver replied as he sat upright in bed. "You'll fit right in then."

CHAPTER
TWENTY-FOUR

Once Amber and Denver showered and ate brunch, they went to Amber's place to grab a fresh change of clothes and swimming gear. Then they drove to the Knights' house. When they had arrived, Denver walked in through the front door with Amber's hand in his. Mr. Knight was sitting on his armchair reading the stocks in the paper, but he'd looked up when he heard Denver enter.

"Hey, Dad," Denver greeted with a big smile as his father set the paper down.

"Denver!" he called as he approached the young couple while he opened his arms for a hug. "Rori said you might be joining us for the barbeque."

Denver let go of Amber's hand for a moment to hug his father.

"Yep, and I've brought company," Denver replied as he pulled from the hug and turned to Amber. "Dad, I'd like you to meet my new girlfriend."

Denver's father was quite pleased to see this beautiful young lady standing before him. The lean, ruggedly handsome, dark-haired man towered over them, which must have meant he was about six foot and four inches or so, but he had the kindest gray eyes Amber ever saw.

"Well, hello there, Miss … ?"

"Storm," Amber answered as she put a hand out for a handshake. "It's Amber Storm."

"We don't do handshakes in this family. Come on over here and give me a big ol' hug," Mr. Knight said as he pulled her right in for a friendly hug.

"Oh, okay," she replied with a smile as she looked to Denver.

"I'm sorry," he apologized with an awkward smile. "Did I forget to mention we're big huggers?"

Amber laughed.

"It's fine," she replied as the hug broke up, and she looked to Mr. Knight again. "Hugs are the best."

Mr. Knight chuckled as he met Denver's gaze.

"I like her, son. She's a keeper," he spoke as he patted Denver on the back. Then he looked toward the stairs on the left side of the living room. "Rori! CJ! Your brother's here!"

Denver leaned over into Amber's ear and whispered, "And now comes a roaring stampede with high-pitched squeals of excitement."

Amber couldn't help but giggle when she suddenly heard a rush of feet pattering, which seemed to pound through the ceiling from the second floor. When she saw his brother and sister race down the stairs, with only pure joy painted on their faces, it was easy to see how much they loved their big brother.

"Denver!" CJ shrieked as he ran into Denver's arms.

"Hey there, little man!" Denver greeted as he picked him up and spun him around for a few seconds before he set him down again.

"Did you find her? Did you find Dakota?" the little guy asked.

Before he could answer, Rori threw herself into Denver's arms.

"Hey, Den!" she greeted when the hug broke up. Then she turned toward Amber and hugged her as well. "Hi, Amber. It's so nice to see you again."

"Oh, you too!" Amber replied as she returned Rori's hug.

Denver kept his focus on CJ.

"As a matter of fact, I did. She's happy and safe, right where she is. Hey, did you grow on me?" Denver inquired as he made a playful height measurement gesture with his chest and CJ's head. "I seem to remember you being a *liiiiiiittle* shorter."

"I grew two inches! Mom says I'm growing like a beanstalk! I'm eating green veggies now!"

Then he noticed the redheaded girl Denver brought home, and he hid behind his big brother.

"Who's this?" he asked in a small voice.

"Don't be shy, CJ. This is Amber. She's my girlfriend," Denver replied as he stepped aside and tenderly pushed CJ towards Amber. "Amber, this is my little brother, CJ."

"Hi, CJ," Amber acknowledged as she bent over to become eye level with him. "Your big brother's told me so much about you!"

CJ tugged on Denver's shirt, so Denver bent over in response. CJ then met his gaze.

"She's really pretty," he commented.

Denver couldn't help but break out into an enormous smile with his dimples.

"Yeah, she is," he agreed as he looked at Amber.

"Awww, you're so sweet," Amber replied to CJ. "Hey, I heard you love airplanes."

"I *do*! Would you want to see my newest airplane project?"

Before Amber could respond, Mrs. Knight walked into the house from the lanai connected to the open kitchen. She was pleased when she saw the family gathered with Denver and a friend at the front door.

"Denver!" she called as she now approached him and pulled him in for a long-overdue hug.

"Hey, Mom," he greeted as he hugged her for a few moments.

"I sent you a text message about not being able to come over to your place earlier. Did you get it?"

"Yeah," Denver replied to his mother as he pulled from the hug and met her gaze. "I sent one back. Did you get mine?"

"Probably. I've been a bit busy this afternoon, so I haven't had a chance to look at my phone."

Then she turned to his guest.

"Mom, this is—"

"Amber Storm!" Mrs. Knight finished as she pulled Amber into her arms for a hug. "Hi, there! I'm your father's accountant. He told me so much about you, and he's showed me pictures of you. Actually, Denver, this is what I wanted to talk to you and Rori about. How did you two meet?"

"We met yesterday at S 'n S," Denver answered.

Amber carefully studied Mrs. Knight's face. She had a flawless glass complexion with no makeup on, though she didn't need it, as she had a beautiful, youthful glow. She also had gorgeous blue eyes, as well as long, curly fire-red hair. She didn't detect any kind of Irish accent, though she suspected that Mrs. Knight had Irish ancestry in her heritage. She also stood about five foot and eight inches, though she was slim in her figure with well-toned arms and legs, which was an indication to Amber that she also worked out.

"Oh, that's wonderful!" Mrs. Knight exclaimed as she looked to Amber now. "Your father asked if my children could give you a grand tour of our beautiful beach town. Has Denver given you the tour yet?"

"Yes, he has," Amber replied. "There's so much to do, but it's *so* beautiful here."

"Denver, may I please borrow your pretty new girlfriend?" CJ asked as he grabbed Amber by her hand. "I wanna show her my cool new airplane project."

Amber exchanged looks with Denver, and he nodded.

"Go for it, little man," he replied.

"Alright! Come with me, Amber," CJ commanded as he led her away by the hand.

Everyone watched as he took her upstairs. Then Denver turned back to his mother.

"Did he say *girlfriend*? Honey, *please* tell me you're not dating a sixteen-year-old," Mrs. Knight replied.

"She'll be seventeen in October, and she'll be a senior in the fall," Denver argued.

"Yeah, and she's pregnant," his mother added.

"Yeah, I know the full story," Denver replied. "And I don't care about that. I really like her, Mom. You should know that if everything works out with her, I'm more than willing to accept her child as my own."

Mrs. Knight stood stunned for a minute.

"Um … Darling, this isn't the young girl you wanted to talk to me about, is she?" Mr. Knight asked his wife.

She turned to her husband, and so did Rori and Denver.

"Actually, yes, she is. She's the one I was telling you about that might be giving her child up for adoption."

"Wait. Wait a minute here. *Please* tell me you're not considering adopting Amber's child?" Denver had to ask.

The room was silent for a few moments before Mr. Knight spoke up.

"Well … your mother and I *have* been in the talks with going into another adoption—"

"No," Denver interjected. "You're not adopting Amber's child. She's *my* girlfriend."

"Is she going to keep the baby?" Rori asked.

"I don't know," Denver replied towards Rori before he looked back to their parents. "She hasn't decided what she's going to do yet, though I already told her I'd support her in whatever decision she makes."

Denver watched as his parents exchanged looks, though he knew his adopted mother all too well.

"I know what you're thinking, Mom. If she decides to place it for adoption, then maybe I'll bring her to you about this, but until she *does* make that decision, don't you *dare* approach her about it. You leave her alone on this." Mrs. Knight remained silent as she looked at her son. "*Promise* me, Mom. *Promise* me you'll wait until she makes her decision."

A heavy sigh escaped Mrs. Knight's lips.

"Oh, alright. I promise. I really don't think you should be going out with a girl who's sixteen, though."

"Well, that's not your decision to make. Will you please just give her a chance? She might surprise you, you know."

"I like her," Rori replied. "I think she's cool."

Denver smiled and brought her into another hug.

"Yeah, she is."

"I like her too," Mr. Knight added, though his wife glared at him. "*What*? C'mon! You didn't see our son's face when he walked in here and introduced her to me. She makes him happy!"

"Thanks, Dad," Denver replied. "And, yes, she does."

CHAPTER
TWENTY-FIVE

Everyone noticed a significant change in Daniel's behavior over the next month. Alice and Michael's eldest, Derek, who was Chief of Police for Novis Bay, saw Daniel hadn't been arrested or been caught doing any illegal activity around town since Kaelyn came into the picture, and the rest of the Denners were made aware of this as well. Alana and Andrew, who were also Denners and were both on the police force with Derek, met Kaelyn at a small family picnic. They immediately suggested to Alice and Michael that Daniel had fallen in love with Kaelyn.

"No way," Michael stated when he knew their conversation was private. "Do you really think that little of Daniel?"

"Have you seen the way he looks at her, Dad?" Alana asked.

"I've been starting to wonder about this myself," Alice stated, which threw off her husband and her two older children.

"No, that is *out* of the question, Alice," Michael stated. "That is *completely* against—"

Before Michael could finish what he was saying, fifteen-year-old Timothy Greene ran up to them and gave both Alice and Michael a huge hug.

"Hi, Denner 'rents!"

Alana and Andrew knew this was now over.

"This conversation stays between us," Alice whispered quickly to Alana and Andrew as she returned the big hug Timothy gave her. "How are you, Timmy? Wow, you've *grown!*"

Alice took note of how Timothy went from 4'11" when he was nine years old to being 5'10" at fifteen years old.

"I know!" Timothy replied, then he smiled over at Alana and Andrew. "Wow, it's been forever since I've seen you two!"

Both Alana and Andrew gave Timothy a big hug.

"How are you, Timmy?" Alana asked. "Staying out of trouble, I hope?"

"Oh, you know it," Timothy answered.

"Are you still thinking of joining the force?" Andrew asked.

"Oh, I'm not interested in criminal justice anymore. I want to be a Marine when I graduate."

Everyone was quite surprised to hear this.

"Hey, guys, Timmy's here!" Vinessa shouted to the other kids in the field.

Before Alice and Michael could respond to Timothy's statement, Timothy was swarmed with all the young Denner teenagers and kids, and then he went off to play with them.

"I wonder what made him change his mind?" Alana inquired. "I thought he was dead set on becoming a police officer?"

"Well, he's a teenager, and it's not uncommon for this to happen. He'll probably change his mind again and again before he graduates," Alice added in a logical tone.

All four of them watched as Timmy played with the Denner kids.

***

KAELYN GIGGLED AS SHE TRIED TO KICK THE SOCCER BALL OUT FROM Daniel's ankles.

"Cheater!" she exclaimed as she nudged into him, which caused him to laugh.

"What? Can't handle a little challenge?" Daniel asked. "I know you're smarter than that."

Suddenly Kaelyn stopped in her tracks and put a hand on her hip.

"Your shoe's untied," she said as a matter-of-factly.

Daniel looked down at his shoes in response, and before he knew it, Kaelyn kicked the ball out into the field.

"See? I knew you were smart!" he exclaimed as they both ran for the ball.

***

ALICE AND MICHAEL, AND ALANA AND ANDREW, ALL STOOD AND watched in amusement as Alice thought about Kaelyn while Michael thought about Daniel.

"Kaelyn *really* does bring out the best in him," Andrew noted.

"Andy, honey, she brings out the best in everybody. That's the thing with Kaelyn. She just somehow has this uncanny ability to see the best in people and revitalize their spirits. She's grown so close to Daniel, Max, Matt, Vinny, and Brienna, and they all just … *love* her. I heard her talking to Matthew last night. She's so happy here." Alice now looked at her husband as he returned her gaze. "She said she'd rather die than be taken away from us."

"Do you think she's going to ask us to adopt her anytime soon?" Michael asked.

"I'm almost certain she will," came a voice from behind.

All four adults turned to find Erika, Timothy's birth mother, now coming between them with her arms folded.

"She's a lovely girl, and like all the rest of the children you've adopted, she's very blessed to have you two in her life," Erika said.

"We're so glad to see you came," Alice replied as she wrapped an arm around Erika for a partial hug as all three parents looked out toward the field to see their children having fun under the sun.

"I'm sorry I hadn't been in town all week when I dropped Timmy off. I've just had a lot of running around to do, a lot of things to take care of, that I had to do without Timmy being present," Erika stated.

Alice and Michael turned to her now in curiosity. Her tone gave them the impression there was something wrong. Alana and Andrew both sensed a very private conversation was about to happen, so they both went off to join the soccer game the Denner kids and teens had going on.

"What kind of things?" Alice asked.

"I've been going back and forth all week between my lawyers and my oncologist," she answered softly. "I updated my will, and I'm giving you custody of Timmy. I hate to do this because I love my son, and I've been trying my hardest to be his mother, but I need you to take him back. I don't have much time left, and I have no one to care for my son for me after I'm gone, and I'd love to see you both adopt him before I leave this earth."

When Erika was in tears, Alice and Michael hugged the poor woman.

"Oh, sweetie, of course, we'll take him. It's not fair this has to happen to you because you've made such a turnaround in your life," Alice said as Alice and Michael pulled away. "Does he know?"

"Yes," Erika answered. "He's been trying to fight for me. He's refusing to accept the fact that I'm d—"

"You don't have to say it," Alice replied in a tender tone. "And, of course, he's going to fight for your survival. He's your son, and you're his mother. He loves you."

Erika looked out toward the field again to find her son laughing and having a good time with all the Denner children.

"He seems brave right now, and he's always trying to stay strong for the both of us, but he breaks down at the end of each night. He's been praying *so* hard for me, but I know it in my heart that my time is almost up, and he just cries himself to sleep over this because I know that deep down, he too knows my time is up. He's terrified, and it's because he doesn't know what to do, which is why I want you to take him now. I don't want him to see me in my last days. I don't want his last memory of me looking like death warmed over."

Alice rubbed a hand on Erika's shoulder in comfort.

"Have you told him what you're doing?" Michael asked.

"As I said, he's been trying to fight for me. He won't let me go, won't accept any other options other than staying with me. He broke up with his girlfriend to spend as much time with me as possible. He knows, though, that he has you two."

OVER THE FOLLOWING MONTH, AN EMERGENCY ADOPTION WAS PUT IN order, as Erika Greene's health deteriorated quite fast. It got to the point where Erika was hospitalized, and the adoption judge had to show up at the hospital to finalize the paperwork. In Erika's hospital room stood Alice and Michael and Timothy, Matthew, Vinessa, Kaelyn, and even Daniel. Everyone, except for Dr. Denner and the judge, was in tears. Timothy was the most upset and couldn't stop crying and holding his mother's hands. Once the paperwork was signed, the judge proudly looked to everyone in the room and parted his final words for the evening.

"By the powers vested in me, and with God as my witness, I now pronounce the official adoption of Timothy Greene, who now holds the name of Timothy Denner."

The family was quiet, and the judge knew this was now a private family matter, so he got up and patted Michael on the back before he left. Timmy knew by the expression on his mother's face that she was making her peace. He held his mother's hands tighter and buried his face into her neck.

"This doesn't mean I don't love you any less," he whispered. "I love you more than yesterday, but never more than tomorrow. I love you so much!"

"I know, Timmy," Erika said as she now took off the silky floral bandana she had wrapped around her head. Then she handed it to him. "I love you too, and I want you to have this. When you see the sun shining in the sky, please think of me smiling down on you. When you feel the wind overwhelming you, think of me hugging you."

Erika tenderly pulled her son's face away from her neck so that she could meet his eyes, and she softly ran her hands through his hair to comfort her one and only child as he took her bandana.

"When you see the moon at night, think of me as a beacon of light in your darkest times. When you feel alone, just think of me standing beside you, for you will never be alone. For as long as you hold me in your heart, you can never lose me, never really."

Timothy broke down as he held his mother's hands tighter.

"I don't have much time, Timmy, and I don't want you to see me at my worst," Erika said as she pulled her son's face away from her neck and made him look into her eyes. "I want you only to remember me as I was before this happened."

Everyone in the room stayed quiet as Timothy had his last few moments with his mother.

"I need you to let me go," she said softly. "Can you do that? For me?"

Timothy couldn't say anything for a minute. He just buried his face into his mother's stomach now. Seeing Timothy like this only tore her and everyone in the room apart.

"My son," she whispered, but she paused as Timmy now pulled his face away from her body.

Timothy nodded in complete understanding, though tears still fell down his cheeks.

"I don't want you to suffer any more than you have," he stated.

"I have my peace, knowing you've made yourself a family with the Denners. Nothing can hurt me anymore. I promise, my darling."

Again, Timothy nodded, and he now stared passionately into his mother's eyes.

"Okay," he said as he brought her hands up to his lips so he could kiss them. "I don't want to do this, but I will."

Erika shed a few more tears.

"I'll see you again, but next time it'll be in Heaven. I want you to *promise* me you'll be the one to take me into the light when it's my turn. Can you do that for me? Yours is the first face I want to see when that time comes."

Everyone knew, including Timothy, that this may or may not be possible, but for now, Timothy needed this closure.

"I promise," Erika whispered as her voice broke up now.

It was silent for another minute as Timothy gave his mother's hands a few tiny, soft kisses, and he then leaned into his mother's ears to whisper something only she heard.

"You can let go now, Mama," he whispered. "You needn't worry about me. I'll be fine. I will love you 'til the end of time."

Erika closed her eyes when Timothy gave her a very tender kiss on her forehead. When Timothy stood up, Erika smiled up at her son, and she met his eyes for one last time.

"Thank you," Erika replied in relief. "I will love you 'til the end of time."

It was easy for everyone to see that whatever he whispered to his mother seemed to lift whatever worries she had left on her shoulders because her face changed to show how at peace she finally was.

"Anything for you, Mama," he whispered while he squeezed her hands one last time before he moved away from her bedside.

Alice stepped forward and kissed Erika on her forehead.

"I promise we'll take good care of him. We'll give him *so* many wonderful memories, so many stories to last you an eternity when you two meet again."

Timothy couldn't stand being in this room anymore. He ran out into the hall and collapsed to the floor. Daniel was the first to run after him, and Matthew and Vinessa followed them. Kaelyn also stepped into the hall, and she saw Daniel already on the floor with Timothy in his arms to provide him comfort. Daniel cried along with Timothy as he lovingly rocked him while his younger brother's body only shook in sheer pain. She was surprised by Daniel's empathy, though she also realized those two had their own special bond with one another. To see Timothy as heartbroken as he was had also broken her own heart.

Matthew and Vinessa engulfed their newly adopted little brother with their tender loving embrace as well. Kaelyn saw how Timothy lost himself, and he buried his face into Daniel's neck while he tightly grabbed onto his shirt around his lower back. Kaelyn felt awkward, as she hadn't really had a chance to get to know Timothy better since he'd previously spent the last month with his mother. She wanted to hug Timothy too, but she felt out of place at this moment.

⁂

TWO NIGHTS LATER, TIMOTHY AND THE DENNERS WERE ALERTED THAT Erika had passed on, and a small memorial service was planned in her honor at the northernmost part of the bay. It was Erika's favorite spot, as it was quiet and peaceful, and she wanted Timothy to spread her ashes there. Timothy looked down at her urn, and he tried his best to be strong, for he knew that's what his mother wanted of him. He took the lid off and hugged the urn for a few moments.

"Goodbye, Mama," he said as he kissed the urn before turning it onto its side. "I will love you 'til the end of time."

The Denners stood in silence and prayed Erika made it safely to Heaven, and they only thought good thoughts about her. A breeze had suddenly picked up as if Erika was also saying goodbye to her son. Timothy and the Denners watched as the breeze picked up the ashes and carried them slowly away out to sea. When the urn was empty, Timothy tenderly put the lid back onto the empty jar, and he closed his eyes as he hugged the urn tightly to his chest. Daniel had stepped beside him and put an arm around him for support.

"I'm glad we got to know her," Daniel began. "I know that things with you and your mom started in a rough patch, but then you two had overcome *so* much together, and I'm glad that you got to spend these last few years with your mother in all the ways that are good, positive, supportive, and happy."

Timothy didn't say anything at first, but then he met his adoptive brother's eyes and spoke up.

"Me too," he whispered. "Can we go home?"

Daniel only nodded as he and Timothy turned around to face the rest of the Denners.

"Let's go home," Daniel said toward everyone, and they did.

CHAPTER
TWENTY-SIX

During the next few weeks, Denver had gotten to know Amber, and he also got to meet her father. He even made time to get to know Kaelyn better. In fact, since he didn't work today, he made it a point to go and visit her. First, though, he wanted to see if she'd be working, so he went to Arctic Zone. When he walked into the shop, he caught Matthew arguing with Jen. Denver could never understand how those two could work together, let alone stand each other. He didn't know about anyone else, but Denver noticed Matthew had been under quite a load of stress lately. He had some major mood swings, and he'd seen Matthew pick random fights on the beach at night, and both of these actions were out of character for Matthew.

"Screw you, Matt!" Jen fired back at Matthew.

"Been there, done that, not going back," Matthew replied in an almost carefree but more annoyed tone.

"Yeah, we'll see about that," Jen hissed.

Both of them were lucky no customers were in the shop because they were both acting completely unprofessional at this time.

"Hey, lovebirds," Denver said, announcing his presence.

Denver caught their attention, and Jen flashed him a bright smile. "Hi there, handsome!"

Denver knew she did this on purpose to annoy Matthew, and it seemed to work because he looked pissed at her.

"Really?" Matthew said in a bitter tone. "He's taken."

Jen just stuck her tongue out at Matthew, and Matthew just rolled his eyes and put his attention back on Denver.

"So, what's up? You visiting or buying?"

"Both, actually, but is Kay not here right now?"

"She's not here, but I am," Jen said in a flirtatious tone.

Denver didn't say anything, for he knew Matthew would, and he watched as Matthew turned to her in frustration.

"You're annoying the hell out of me. You know that? It's time for you to go on your lunch break. I don't want to see or hear you for forty-five minutes."

"You can really be a prick sometimes," was her response as she disappeared into the backroom.

"Only when you're a whiny, little bitch," Matthew stated.

"Whatever!" they heard from the back.

Matthew rolled his eyes and sighed.

"Why do you put up with her bullshit?" Denver asked.

"She's a good lay."

Denver's eyebrows instantly lifted in surprise.

"So blunt, but really?" he asked.

"Yes, really, and there's nothing wrong with being blunt. Until I can find myself a good woman, if Jen offers me sex, I'll take it. She doesn't *just* have an aggressive personality."

Denver didn't say anything.

"I'm sorry. What were we talking about?" Matthew asked, but then he remembered. "Oh, yeah, Kay's off today. She's chilling at the house, and what can I get you?"

"A medium mint chocolate chip milkshake," Denver answered. "Wait, do you know what Kay likes? I'll bring one for her."

"Is mint chocolate chip your fave?" Matthew asked.

"Yes, I *love* it, and I haven't had it in a while," Denver said.

"It's funny how you and Kay seem to have so much in common. It's her favorite ice cream too. I'll make that two medium milkshakes with whipped cream on top."

That seemed to answer Denver's question as Matthew prepared the shakes in one big blender.

"So, what are you up to tonight?" Denver asked.

"Closing up shop and then partying on the beach," Matthew said as he now started the blender and dipped the ice cream scooper in a small tub of cool water. "You?"

"I'll be on the beach with Amber," Denver replied. "I'm thinking of inviting Kay, though."

"Don't," Matthew stated as he quickly whipped his body around to face Denver. "It's an open party. You know anything goes during those parties."

Denver knew this kind of party wasn't suited for his sister.

"Oh, yeah, you're right. Yeah, I'm not subjecting her *or* Amber to those parties. I might just invite Kay over to my place for a movie night with Amber instead. It sounds like a *much* better idea."

Matthew was silent for a few moments until he folded his arms across his chest.

"Y'know, Vinessa keeps encouraging Kay to get to know you, yet Kay is dating Alex, and you also have a girlfriend ... so *why* the interest in her since you've been back?"

Denver suddenly realized Matthew thought he was interested in Kay on a romantic level. He knew he had to clear this up as soon as possible before Matthew had any further thoughts about this.

"*Trust* me, Matt, I could *never* date Kota. That would just be *so wrong*," Denver explained, now with a look of complete disgust on his face.

"Kota?" Matthew asked.

"I mean Kay," Denver corrected himself.

"How did you know that was Kay's birth family's pet name for her?" Matthew inquired.

This confused Denver for a bit until he realized Matthew was the confused one.

"You don't know, do you?" Denver asked softly, which surprised Matthew.

"Don't know what?" Matthew continued with curiosity. "Is there something I need to know, something that I'm missing out on?"

"No, Kay and I are just friends, I promise. She told me about her nickname from when she still had her birth name."

Matthew just nodded, knowing that Denver wouldn't lie to him. He grabbed two medium cups as he heard the blender come to a soft, slow hum.

"Wait a sec. Did you just say Kay's dating Alex?" Denver asked as he changed the subject off of him.

The blender had come to a complete stop, and Matthew tended to it, momentarily turning his back to Denver.

"Yeah, why?" Matthew replied as he poured the milkshakes into the two medium cups he now had on the counter in front of him.

"Who paired *them* up? That's genius matchmaking."

Matthew sprayed whipped cream on top of the milkshakes, and then he put the lids over the tops.

"Thank you," Matthew said as he then turned around with both of the milkshakes in his hand. "I don't usually go around boasting my matchmaking skills, but thank you," he said as they both walked over to the counter.

"*You* did that? Good call, man!"

Matthew smiled briefly before he set the milkshakes down on the counter next to the register.

"Thanks," he said. "Yeah, he's a good guy and not one that uses people."

"Yeah, *and* he's a prude, so we don't have to worry about Kay in that regard," Denver added.

"Damn straight," Matthew replied. "That'll be four dollars and ninety-five cents."

Denver pulled out his wallet, and as Denver opened the billfold section, Matthew couldn't help but see a picture of Denver's family in front of all his credit cards and other photos.

"Wait, let me see that," Matthew commanded.

Denver instantly knew Matthew saw this photo. It was too late now. He had no choice but to pull out the picture and hand it to him.

"Is this your biological family?" Matthew inquired as he flipped to the back and saw, *'I luv yoo,'* written in a young child's handwriting that was colored in a red marker.

"Yes, and by seeing this picture, I assume you're now figuring out that—"

"Kay's your sister," Matthew finished as he looked up at Denver. "I mean, she's your *real* sister. *That's* why you called her Kota."

"How'd *you* know about that nickname?" Denver asked.

"I saw it written on the back of her family photo, except hers says *'I luv yoo Kota'* in a purple marker."

Denver was amazed to hear this.

"She still has her picture?" he continued in curiosity. "I thought Social Services would've taken it away from her. They took her away from me."

"That reminds me, did you know she was told you died in a car accident with your parents?" Matthew asked. "After finding this out just now, it's starting to feel like a bald-faced lie."

"That's because it is," Denver said softly. "I think it was for our protection."

"Weren't your parents murdered?" Matthew asked.

Denver didn't feel like talking about this right now.

"Yeah, but I don't really want to talk about it."

"I can respect that, " Matthew said as he looked back down at the photo and sighed.

"Your parents haven't figured it out yet, the connection between

Kay and me, so I'd advise you to keep this from them for now. Kay doesn't know either. Only you, Vin, and my girlfriend know."

Matthew was quite shocked to hear this. He'd heard from Vinessa that Denver spent *so* much of his time and energy into finding Dakota, and now that she was found, he didn't want her to know that he was her long, lost brother.

"I think we should discuss this with my parents and return her to you," Matthew suggested.

"You want to rip her away from her true happiness, take away the family she so desperately wants and so rightfully deserves?"

Matthew thought back to the first night he and Kaelyn talked, on the porch swing in the middle of the night, when she spoke about how all she wanted was to be loved, and then when she told him on their way to bed that she wanted them to adopt her.

"I see your point," Matthew said as he returned the photograph to Denver. "But don't you think Kay has the right to know who you really are and that you're still alive?"

Denver put the photo back in his wallet and sighed.

"She *does* have that right, but I don't know if I want her to know, at least not right now. I'm just trying to get to know her before I decide what to do with her. I may just decide to wait until after you adopt her before I tell Kay and your parents the truth."

"What if she'd rather be with you?" Matthew asked.

"You see why this is so complicated?" Denver said as he only got a nod from Matthew. "*Please* don't tell your parents or *anyone* right now. I don't know how I'm *ever* going to repay Vin for what she did for me, for spotting Kay in that group home, and for fighting to make sure she came home with you guys."

"This explains *so* much," Matthew stated. "By the way, I'm sorry for thinking you had a romantic interest in Kay. I didn't—"

"It's fine," Denver interrupted quickly as he handed Matthew a five-dollar bill, but Matthew refused it.

"No, don't, it's on me," Matthew replied.

Denver then attempted to put the five in the tips jar, but Matthew quickly pulled the jar from Denver's sight before he could do so.

"This is the least I can do for you," Matthew continued.

Denver smiled while putting the money and his picture back in his wallet, and then he parted his lips.

"Thanks, man, and like I said before, *please* don't tell anyone yet about Dakota, *especially* your parents. Besides, Vin said something to me about how your parents signed a contract that if they told Kay, they'd lose their license to foster."

Matthew paused for a moment when he heard this.

"I won't," Matthew acknowledged. "Your secret is safe with me. You have fun with Kay today."

"Thanks. See you later," Denver said as he put away his wallet, grabbed the mint chocolate chip milkshakes, and left the Zone.

CHAPTER
TWENTY-SEVEN

Kaelyn was in the den, smiling as she looked through one of the Denner Family photo albums. She saw so many happy faces and so many wonderful Denner family moments, and Kaelyn couldn't wait to be a part of their photo album. When the doorbell rang, Kaelyn was curious to know who it was. She wasn't expecting Alex because he was at work, and she was alone in the house because everyone else was also working. She carefully set the Denner photo album down on the arm of the sofa, walked over to the door, and peeked through the hole in the door. She was surprised to find Denver was here, and he had two Arctic Zone milkshakes in his hands, though she opened the door for him.

"Hi there," she greeted. "I'm sorry to say this, but no one's home right now, and Vin's at work."

"Oh, I know. I was just wondering if you're interested in hanging out for a while. I'm bored, and I don't work today. I stopped by the Zone to see you, but Matt said you were here. Here, I got this for you. He told me it's your fave, which is surprisingly mine too."

When Denver extended his right hand to give her the milkshake, she took it from him and smiled. Then she opened the door wider for him to come inside.

"Thank you," she said as she stepped aside. "Come on in."

"Thanks," Denver replied as he closed the front door while she reclaimed her spot on the sofa. "So, how are you enjoying life here in Novis Bay with the Denners?"

"I love it," she answered as he approached and sat down next to her. Then she took a sip of her drink before she placed it on the side table. "I wouldn't want to be anywhere else. Though I have to admit, it's been a little difficult trying to get to know Doc. He's always being called away into surgery."

Denver saw how she tried to hide the disappointment in her face by keeping the smile on her face, but he heard it in her voice.

"Don't worry, Kay," he told her. "He'll set some time aside with you soon. I'm surprised you're calling him Doc, though. Daniel and I are the only ones who do that."

Kaelyn chuckled and nodded.

"I guess I've been spending a little too much time with him," she replied. "Though I honestly enjoy hanging out with him."

"I saw you two on the beach the first day I met you. I didn't want to be nosy or anything. He's kind of known around town as an asshole, but it seems like when he's around you, he's not that at all. Does he treat you alright?"

"Yeah, he does. He's kind of like my best friend and the brother I wish I had growing up."

Denver was surprised to learn how close Kaelyn was to Daniel.

"What about Matt and Max?" he asked with curiosity.

"Them too, but they're in relationships, and they're also always working, so I don't see them as often as I'd like," Kaelyn added. "Tim doesn't seem interested in hanging out at all. He prefers to spend most of his time with his girlfriend. He broke up with her for a little while, but I guess they're back together again, so I just leave him be."

Denver nodded in silence while he sipped on his milkshake and thought of what to say next. Then his eyes caught the Denner Family photo album she was going through.

"Are you going to ask them to adopt you?"

"Yes, I want more than anything to become a Denner. It would be a dream come true."

It was hard for Denver to hear her answers. Kaelyn saw the tears in his eyes too.

"Hey, are you okay?" she asked.

He didn't know how to answer this.

"Yes and no, but I'll be fine," he answered. "I have something I wanted to ask you. I hope you don't mind that Vinessa told me this, but she said that Social Services told you that your birth family passed away when you were just a baby?"

Kaelyn paused for a moment when he told her that. She wondered why he brought this up.

"Yes, my brother and parents died in a car accident. Why do you ask?" she inquired.

Denver became quiet as he now put his drink on the floor in front of him.

"Did she tell you my story?"

"No, she didn't. Daniel told me you were adopted, though?"

"Yeah," Denver answered as he looked at the floor for a moment before he looked back into her eyes. "Um, my parents were murdered. I was four at the time, and my baby sister was a little under one. The state split us up and adopted us out to two different families. I couldn't find her for years, but I didn't know until recently that her name had changed. They even changed her social security number, and they lied to her about what happened."

Kaelyn was speechless. She stood up and turned her back to him. He knew she was putting two and two together now.

"Why are you telling me this?" she asked as she turned around to face him again, only this time with tears in her eyes.

"I wasn't sure if I should tell you because I didn't want to scare you, or possibly compromise your safety, or ruin things between you and the Denners," he answered as he stood up from his spot on the couch and approached her. "But as I stand here in front of you, I know that I can't keep this from you. Kota deserves to know the truth, and she deserves to know that I'm still alive."

Kaelyn gasped and covered her mouth in shock when she heard him call her by the nickname written on the back of her family photo. Denver saw in her face how upsetting this news was to her, and all he wanted to do was hold her, but he didn't know if she'd welcome a hug from him just yet. He didn't want to make her feel uncomfortable.

"I can see how happy you are with the Denners," he continued as he felt overwhelmed with tears in his own eyes. "You're happy here, and you're safe, and you deserve to have everything that the Denners can give you. I wouldn't dream of taking that away from you, and I'd kill anybody who would."

Although she still had her mouth covered, he heard her sobbing, and he knew she was devastated.

"I don't know if you'd want to get to know me or if you'd prefer I leave you alone, but I'll respect your wishes either way. I just hope you'll let me be here with you for today because … today marks the fifteenth anniversary of what happened to Mom and Dad. I still have nightmares about seeing what happened to them. So, I *really* don't want to be alone with the darkness of my thoughts right now."

Kaelyn still said nothing. Before Denver knew it, though, she had wrapped her arms around him, and he returned the gesture.

"Vinessa's the only Denner who's seen my family picture. She'd seen it *so* many times. She spotted you right away in that group home. I don't know how this is even possible, but you're the spitting image of Mom."

Kaelyn's only response was a tighter grip around him.

"I've been looking for you for over two years," he added. "Never did I think I'd be standing here, reunited with you in my best friend's living room."

"I knew it," was her response as she looked up into his eyes while she pulled from the hug. "I don't know how I knew it, but I just knew it from the first day you introduced yourself at the car. I'd never felt anything like what I felt that day. The way you looked at me was like you were looking at a ghost, and then when you said your name was Denver, I couldn't help but wonder. I've never met or known anyone with that name, and I knew that my brother's name was Denver J—"

"James Malone," Denver finished for her.

Kaelyn brought her hand over her mouth again as fresh tears now formed in her eyes.

"Oh, my God! It *is* you!"

Kaelyn pounced on him with another hug, but it was one of relief this time. Denver was never more pleased than right now to have his baby sister in his arms. Denver never wanted to let her out of his sight again.

"I'm sorry," Denver apologized.

Kaelyn looked up into Denver's eyes with curiosity.

"For what?" she asked.

"For not being there for you," he answered. "For not being able to protect you from …"

Kaelyn suddenly realized that Vinessa must have spoken to him about her background before coming to the Denners. She had tears in her eyes when she realized he felt guilty for not being able to be her brother during her period of hell.

"It's not your fault," she replied. "*Please* don't blame yourself."

It grew quiet between them for a few minutes until they were able to pull themselves together.

"So … what do we do here?" Kaelyn asked as she finally wiped the tears away.

"Honestly? I don't know," Denver replied. "Technically, you're not supposed to know the truth about the past. Alice and Michael were forced to sign a contract that said if they ever told you the truth about what really happened to Mom and Dad, they'd permanently lose their foster license."

Kaelyn was stunned when she heard this.

"I don't know if there are any other conditions in the contract that they signed, but I don't want to take any chances and lose you to the system all over again."

Kaelyn saw the fear in his eyes.

"You're really scared," she observed. "Aren't you?"

Denver took out his wallet and removed the picture of them and their parents. She looked down at it and realized it was the same photo that she also had.

"I already lost my family once," Denver whispered. "I *can't* lose you again."

When she met his gaze again, she saw the fresh tears in his eyes. Then she nodded in complete understanding.

"May I?" she asked as she referred to the photo.

He handed it to her, and she flipped it to the back. She read the message on his as '*I luv yoo,*' but it was written in red marker.

"I have the same message on the back of my picture, except it's written as—"

"I luv yoo, Kota," Denver finished for her, which stunned her as their eyes met. Tears formed in her eyes again, though she gave him back the photo. "Purple was my favorite color back then. It was also Mom's favorite color."

"What's your favorite color now?"

"Oh, you're *so* going to think I'm lame if I tell you," Denver said as he chuckled while he put the photo back in his wallet and put his wallet back in his jeans pocket.

"Well, now, I *really* have to know."

Kaelyn watched as Denver reclaimed his spot on the couch. She followed and sat down next to him.

"C'mon," she pleaded with a smile. "I need a laugh."

Denver caught her smirk, and he couldn't help but mirror it.

"Oh, alright," he caved. "It's pink."

"*Pink?*"

"Baby pink."

"*Baby pink?*"

Kaelyn couldn't help but laugh at this.

"See? I'm lame," Denver replied in shame as he took another sip of his milkshake.

"Oh, no, you're not lame. I might tease you for it every once in a while, but then again, we have a lifetime of silly sibling squabbles to catch up on," Kaelyn replied with a playful nudge in his arm.

Denver appreciated the fact that she smiled and laughed, even if it was at his own expense.

"You have her laugh and smile."

Kaelyn knew what he meant. She felt the hot tears stinging in her eyes again as the tone in the room became serious.

"Were they really … ?" she started to ask, but she found it hard to finish her question, though Denver knew what the question was.

"Yeah," he whispered as the smile left his face. "It was all over the news, even made national headlines because Dad was a doctor, a well-known neurosurgeon. Dr. Connor James Malone. He preferred to go by James, though. Even my doctor went to medical school with him."

Kaelyn didn't know their father was a doctor. She wanted to reply to his statement, but then she saw blood dripping from his nose.

"Denver, your nose!"

Denver felt a warm trickling, and he touched it and realized he was having a nosebleed when he saw red on his left index and middle fingers. Kaelyn instantly went over to the mantle across the room and grabbed a box of tissues, and she immediately handed him a couple of them.

"Thanks," Denver replied as he placed them underneath his nose and kept a firm grip there for a few minutes. "Fuck, I haven't had one of these since … *no.*"

"How bad is it for you to have a nosebleed?"

Denver sighed as he momentarily closed his eyes.

"It's a symptom of CML."

"CML?"

"Chronic Myeloid Leukemia. A nosebleed in a CML patient like me can mean that I'm no longer in remission … unless something else is wrong."

"Are you *serious*?"

"Yeah, it's bad. God, please don't tell me I've got it again …"

"You should probably call your doctor," Kaelyn said.

Denver took out his phone and dialed his doctor's office.

"Hart's Oncology and Associates, Michelle speaking, how may I help you?"

"Hey, 'Chelle, it's Denver," he replied with his phone on speaker.

"Hi, Denver! How are you?"

"I don't know. I'm having a nosebleed, and I'm concerned about it. I think my follow-up with Dr. Hart needs to be bumped up *now,* if I may add. When's the earliest you can pencil me in?"

"Well, it's lucky that you called. Dr. Hart *just* had a cancellation for a slot that's a half-hour from now. Why don't you take it and come on in?" Michelle suggested.

"Perfect. Thank you so much. I'm on my way," Denver replied.

When Denver hung up the phone, he stood up but looked over at Kaelyn.

"I need you to do me a favor."

"Anything!" Kaelyn replied as she also stood up and walked him to the front door.

"Please promise me you won't tell anyone about my nosebleed, and please don't tell anyone what we talked about today."

A shaky breath then escaped her lips.

"I promise, but you have to promise you'll keep me in the loop."

Denver nodded and gave her his cell phone.

"Can you put your cell phone number in my list?"

"Sure," Kaelyn replied as she took his phone and added her own number to his contacts. "Will you text me after your appointment, no matter what the results are?"

"I promise."

She handed him back his phone, but she also hugged him.

"Thank you for being honest with me," she whispered. "I have so many questions, but I don't know how to process all this yet …"

"One step at a time," he answered as she pulled from the hug and looked up into his eyes. "I'm not going anywhere, and I don't expect you to say this back anytime soon, but I *do* want and need you to know that I love you, Kota. You're my sister, and I'm here in whatever way you need me to be."

Kaelyn smiled when he called her by that nickname. She was also glad he was here and in her life. Denver mirrored her smile briefly as he now headed toward his car.

"I'll text you later!"

"Be safe!"

When his car drove off, she stepped back into the house, closed the front door, and leaned against it. She couldn't help but pull out her phone, turn to the internet, and search her biological father's name. Sure enough, a bunch of news articles from fifteen years ago talked about the brutal murder of her parents and how a little four-year-old boy was witness to it before he grabbed his sister and hid until the police showed up. Even the family photo she had all these years was attached to a couple of the news articles. Everything Denver said was the truth, and now she felt like her entire life was a lie. The burning sting of tears rushed back into her eyes, and before she knew it, she'd slid down to the floor in total devastation. After all the lies and the betrayal, she didn't know how she could handle it, yet keep it all to herself.

CHAPTER
TWENTY-EIGHT

When Dr. Hart came into the patient waiting room, she smiled briefly at Denver as she closed the door behind her.

"Personally, it's nice to see you again, but professionally, not so much. So, I see you're having a nosebleed. Is this the first time since entering remission?" she asked as Denver let out a small 'yes.' "Let me see what we have here."

Dr. Hart put down her clipboard on the counter and then walked over to Denver as she slowly replaced his hands with her own. When she tried to remove the tissues, his nose began trickling again.

"Oh, yes, we have ourselves a good one. Do you have any other symptoms?" Dr. Hart asked.

"I don't know. I, um … kind of haven't been paying attention," Denver confessed. "I've been trying to enjoy life for a change. Oh, by the way, I found Dakota."

Dr. Hart was quite surprised to hear this piece of news.

"Oh, that's wonderful news!" Dr. Hart replied as she let Denver hold the tissues to his nose again. "Your parents would be *so* happy for you. I know *I* am. What's she like? Tell me everything."

Denver smiled as she sat down on her doctor's stool.

"Well, she was adopted as a baby, and since court records were sealed, I couldn't see that her name had changed and that she was also assigned a new social security number. When I came home from the last trip out looking for her, I found out that my best friend's family took her in as a foster. Apparently, her first adoption fell through, so she ended up back in the system. She looks, and sounds, and smiles *just* like our mother. Social Services told her that our parents and I had died in a car crash, but I told her the truth shortly before coming here. I needed her to know that I'm still alive, especially today since it's the fifteenth anniversary of what happened."

Dr. Hart nodded as she listened to Denver, though she forgot that it had already been so long since her fellow medical school classmate and his wife had passed away.

"That's terrible that they hid the truth from her, and it's a shame that it's been so long. I'm *so* happy for you two, though. Did you tell her about your health?"

"Only the basics," Denver answered. "I was with her when this nosebleed started."

"I'd like to meet her. Can you set up a time for her and her foster parents to come in and discuss getting tested to find out if she's a bone marrow match?"

Denver was a little concerned with the fact that Dr. Hart would bring this up before discussing any testing to see if this nosebleed was just a fluke or not.

"Do I have to?" he asked. "Does this nosebleed mean I'm not in remission anymore?"

"I'm not going to lie, Denver. This nosebleed is *really* not a good sign. We're going to do some testing with you today if you have the time, and there have been some treatment changes since you last went into remission, so we'll explore all possible options after we've done all our testing. Still, though, I would feel a whole lot better knowing whether or not your sister is a possible match for bone marrow. She's truly your *best* bet for a match because you have the same parents."

"That's going to be a tough conversation to have, so if it's okay with you, I'd rather wait to discuss that until *after* the tests and after we've discussed all other options first."

Dr. Hart nodded in understanding.

"I take it you want to give her a little time to process what you've already told her today?"

"More or less," Denver replied simply.

Dr. Hart nodded in acknowledgment.

"Alright, then give her a few days, but Denver, *please* don't wait too long."

"Okay."

"Well, I'd like to admit you tonight for a couple of days while we run some tests, or we could just take care of all the testing today and wait out these next few days if that's what you would prefer."

Denver sighed in frustration.

"I don't know … I have dinner plans with my new girlfriend later tonight. See, *this* is why I prefer staying single. Every time I start to like someone, *this* shit happens," Denver answered as he referred to his health. "Oh, never mind on dinner plans. I can't subject Amber to this. She already lost her mother to cancer ten years ago."

Dr. Hart understood where Denver came from. He pushed people away so that they didn't care so much about him if he ultimately succumbed to his disease. When he cared about people, she knew he cared deeply and intensely for them and wanted nothing but the best for all of them.

"Denver, I love that you care so much for the people in your life, but have you ever thought about just being honest with a girl you like and letting *her* decide if she wants to stay with you rather than being pushed away?"

Denver grew quiet as he knew Dr. Hart was right. He was glad to see her today because she was his unofficial psychologist at times like this.

When Amber showed up at his apartment later on in the evening, she had an enormous smile from ear to ear.

"Hey, handsome!" she exclaimed as she kissed him on the lips and walked passed him into the apartment.

"Hey, beautiful, you're just in time. Dinner's ready."

"Sweet! I smell steak, and it smells great!" she responded as she dropped her handbag on the couch, and then the pair walked toward the dining room and sat down to eat. Denver even pulled out her chair for her. "Thank you!"

"Anything for you," Denver replied as he sat in his chair. "Hey, listen, there's something I'd like to discuss with you before we dig in."

"Okay," Amber said as she grew curious about why Denver got serious so quickly. "Is everything all right?"

"Well, that's a good question," Denver answered as he brought his hands together. "It's one I don't have an answer to, not for a few days anyway."

Denver saw a look of confusion now painted on her face.

"Something happened today, and what happened today may be a prelude of things to come, and this is the kind of thing that I don't like to subject a girlfriend to. In the past, I've guarded myself and pushed everyone away, though now I'm looking at this differently. Before I explain it, I want you to be completely aware of the options I put on the table for you."

Amber didn't like where this conversation was headed.

"Okay, you're scaring me. What's going on? Are you breaking up with me?"

"Actually, no, because I care about you enough that I want your say on important matters," Denver answered. "I had two nosebleeds today, back to back."

"Oh," Amber said, shocked to hear this.

Denver knew by her reaction that she didn't understand what this meant.

"As a leukemic patient in remission, random nosebleeds are bad. It's a symptom and a sign that I may no longer be in remission."

Amber finally understood why Denver stressed the seriousness of this matter.

"Oh, my God," she whispered while she rested her elbows on the table and momentarily buried her face into her hands.

"Yes, exactly, so I'm giving you some options," Denver started to say, but Amber interrupted him.

"Denver James Knight, if you're about to tell me you're giving me an out on this relationship, you better not finish that statement." Denver, surprised by the stern tone in Amber's voice, was now silent. Amber, not hearing anything from Denver, looked up at him. "I'm not walking away from you. I'm right here with you, in sickness and in health. I appreciate you being open and upfront with me about this, though," she replied as she grabbed both of his hands.

Denver could hardly believe she was willing to stay with him.

"Did you call your doctor?" she asked.

"Yes, she wanted me to be admitted into the hospital for a couple of days to run some tests, but we did them all today instead. We'll get the results in a few days."

"Here's to hoping for the best, right?" Amber replied as she now kissed Denver on his forehead. "By the way, is now a bad time to say I've decided what I want to do about the baby?"

"No, not at all."

Denver waited patiently to hear what her decision was. She met his tender loving gaze for a few moments with the huge smile that had now returned to her face.

"I've decided I'm keeping it. It doesn't seem right to place it for adoption if we decide to adopt other kids later on down the road, you know?"

Denver couldn't help but smile at this.

"C'mere," he asked of her as he patted his lap.

She did as he requested and sat down on his lap. He wrapped his left arm around her, and then he brought his right hand up to her face, where he tenderly caressed her cheek.

"My mother is going to be *so* disappointed."

"I know. She pulled me aside at the first barbeque you invited me over. When you were in the pool with Rori and CJ, she privately spoke with me and offered to adopt the baby."

Denver rolled his eyes at this.

"I *told* her *not* to approach you on the subject until *after* you've made your decision. She *promised* she'd leave you alone on it. I'm so sorry, Amber."

Amber giggled as she wrapped her arms around him.

"It's fine, Den. If your parents still want to adopt, then they'll just have to look somewhere else because I'm raising this baby with you."

"I can't wait," Denver said as he now leaned in toward Amber's stomach while he now rubbed his hand on it. "*Please* be a girl."

Amber giggled again.

"I know you told me that your adopted parents' names are Maria and Anthony, but what were your bio parents' names?"

"Elena and Connor," Denver answered. "Why do you ask?"

Amber smirked for a moment before she spoke up again.

"What do you think of Kathryn Elena Maria Knight for a girl? Or Connor James Anthony Knight for a boy? I thought it would be cool to honor all our parents."

Denver had tears in his eyes when he heard this.

"You would do that? You would give the child my name *and* my parents' names?"

"Of course," Amber replied. "I love you."

This was the first time she told him this, and he couldn't help but light up. He pulled her face toward his and brushed his lips with hers for a few moments before he returned her passionate gaze. His thumb lingered on her cheek for a few moments longer.

"I love you too."

CHAPTER
TWENTY-NINE

Kaelyn placed the photo album back where she found it, but she still couldn't help her tears. She'd just learned that Denver was her biological brother and that he was still alive, which meant Social Services had lied to her about her past. She wondered how many people lied to her face, and she wondered just how much Alice and Michael, and Vinessa knew. She pulled out her phone and started texting her best friend, Dan: *Are you free? I really need to talk to someone.* She waited for a few minutes, and then when she got a response back, she read: *Sorry, princess, I'm at work until closing. Is something wrong?* She immediately responded as she wiped her tears away: *I'm sorry for bothering you. Nothing's wrong. Just wanted to talk. I'll catch you later.*

She then put her phone away, even after Daniel sent her a reply, but she didn't have to read it to know what he said. She tried to think of someone else who she could talk to, but everyone was working, except Timmy, though he was out with his girlfriend. Later on in the evening, Kaelyn waited patiently as someone, *anyone*, came home. She was ready to confront the Denners. She just sat in the living room, anxiously waiting with her left leg rapidly bouncing up and down. She was nervous, upset, and impatient, but above all, she was angry. She'd thought about what Denver asked of her, to keep this a secret, but she didn't know him all that well yet. She didn't know if she could really keep the news of her biological parents to herself.

"Kay?" said a voice that snapped her out of her thoughts.

Kaelyn looked up at the front door to see Vinessa standing there. When did Vinessa get home, and how did Kay not hear the front door open? Was she that lost in her train of thoughts that she didn't notice anything around her? Just as Kaelyn met her foster sister's eyes, her phone went off, and she pulled out her phone to look at a text message she had just received: *Hey, darling, what are you up to? I'd love to see you if you're not doing anything.* It was from Alex, and boy, was she glad she heard from him because now her anxiety outweighed her anger.

"Hi!" Kay replied as she stood up from the armchair.

She suddenly felt quite energetic. Vinessa was a tad bit confused, though.

"Are you … okay?" she asked as she knew she caught Kaelyn in the middle of a serious train of thoughts when she first walked in.

"Oh, I'm fine. I was just … waiting for Alex to text me, and he *did*, so … I'm leaving."

Vinessa felt a strange vibe from Kaelyn. Kaelyn was sure acting weird, and Vinessa couldn't figure out why.

"Are you *sure* you're okay?" Vinessa asked.

"Absolutely! Now, if you'll excuse me, I have a hot date with Alex," Kaelyn replied as she walked passed Vinessa and walked out the front door.

When the front door closed behind her, Vinessa shook her head and put aside the funny feeling. Kaelyn was already on the phone with calling Alex once she stepped outside.

"Hey, sweetie," he said. "Where are you? I'm at home."

"Oh, good, because I'm on my way over!" Kaelyn replied.

"Sweet. Take your time walking. I have a surprise for you, and I need to set it up real quick. The front door is open, so make yourself at home. Just don't come upstairs until I come down and get you, okay?"

Kaelyn couldn't help but giggle.

"Okay, I'll see you in a little bit," she said.

"Okay, baby."

With that said, they both hung up their phones, and Kaelyn took a stroll down the street. When she saw the Thompson Family's dog barking for her attention, she then crossed the street to greet it behind the Thompson white picket fence that was three feet high.

"Hello, Precious!" she greeted as she now petted the pomeranian.

"Oh, hello, Kaelyn!" said a voice not too far from the Pomeranian named 'Precious.'

Kaelyn looked over to find Mrs. Thompson off to the side, sitting in her garden on her knees and weeding it. She was a sweet, elderly lady.

"Hi, Mrs. Thompson, how are you?"

"I'm doing well, sweetie! How are *you*?" Mrs. Thompson asked in return.

"I'm doing wonderful," Kay replied as she gave Precious a few more pets and some rubs on the head.

"Would you like to come in and have some cookies and milk? I just baked them fresh!" exclaimed Mrs. Thompson.

"Thank you, but I have a date with Alex," Kaelyn replied.

"Oh, he's such a sweetheart. You tell him to come by sometime. I have something for him and his beauty of a horse, and you give him a big hello for me."

"Okay, I will. I'll see you later," Kaelyn replied as she waved goodbye.

"See you later, sweetheart!" Mrs. Thompson responded with her own wave as well.

Kaelyn was then back on her stroll, and before she knew it, she reached Alex's. She was surprised to find he was already on his porch, waiting patiently for her in the front doorway. He smiled passionately with his arms folded across his chest. Kaelyn instantly noticed he was wearing a black, satin button-down shirt with a dark pair of blue jeans. She realized that whatever Alex had planned, it was no simple thing. She sure was glad to be wearing a dress that could be worn casually or for something a little more upscale.

"Hey, beautiful," he greeted as she approached him.

"Hello, *handsome!*" she exclaimed as she eyed him up and down.

"You like?" he inquired as he looked down at his outfit briefly before he met her eyes again.

"Yes, I love it," she answered as she pulled herself into Alex's arms and gave him a big hug.

She hadn't seen him for a couple of days, so she missed him, and he was a sight for sore eyes.

"I missed you," Alex said as he kissed her on the lips.

"I missed you too," Kaelyn replied. "By the way, Mrs. Thompson says she has something special for you and Delilah."

"Okay, cool, I'll check in with her later."

"So, what have you been up to these past couple of days?" Kaelyn asked as she placed her chin on his chest.

"I've been working on something for you, something special for our one-month anniversary."

"Aw, you didn't have to!"

"Aw, but I did because you're special to me," Alex answered as he stepped inside his house and gently pulled Kaelyn by her hands.

Kaelyn followed his lead, and Alex kicked the door shut.

"I'm making dinner for us, but it's going to be in the oven for a couple of hours, so I hope a late dinner is fine with you," Alex added.

"Yeah, that's fine. I'm not hungry right now."

"Alright, let's go upstairs for a while," he suggested as he held her right hand in his own left.

Kaelyn followed him up the stairs slowly, and she smiled up at him every time he looked at her over his shoulder with his own smile.

Kaelyn lost her breath when she reached the top of the steps, as there was a trail of red and white rose petals leading to his room. Alex had something very romantic in store for her, and she knew it. When they reached his room, he stopped and turned around to look at her.

"I hope you don't think any of this is cheesy."

"You are *not* cheesy," Kaelyn said as she placed her free left hand on his face for a few moments.

"Good, because what you're about to see is me stepping up and moving forward. You're very special to me, and I'm *so* invested in you."

Kaelyn was silent as Alex opened the door and allowed Kaelyn to walk through. When she entered the room, she was amazed at how beautiful the room was set up. His canopy bedding was satin red, and the curtains were red but soft and translucent with red, paper-made roses pinned all over them, both inside and outside the curtains. There were red and white rose petals lying on the bed, and there was still a path from the door to surrounding the bed. Sitting on all the desks, side tables, and bookshelves were red and white candlesticks burning. When Alex turned the music on, soft jazz music started to play, and Alex had turned to Kaelyn with a soft, passionate smile.

"Wow, you *really* put yourself into this. This is *amazing*!"

Kaelyn was taken by surprise when Alex grabbed her face and gazed lovingly into her eyes.

"That's because you're the most amazing woman I've *ever* met," he said in the kindest tone. "All this time I have spent with you has been wonderful, and it's shown me that you're the only one I want to spend my time on this earth with, and you're the one I want to give my whole soul to. I'm so irrevocably in love with you, and someday, when we're ready, I want to make you my wife. You're the one for me, Kaelyn Marie Dalgeau, and I love you *so* much."

Kaelyn felt the love and passion radiating off of Alex, and she couldn't help but shed a tear over his words. This was *just* what she wanted and needed to hear.

"I'll be honest, I won't be bothered if you decide you're not ready to take this to the next level because we could still just make out and snuggle, but all of this is to show you I'm ready. With you, I want it all, and I don't want to turn back."

"I love you too, Alex, and for the record, I want to make love to you as well," was Kaelyn's response.

Kaelyn indeed couldn't have found a more romantic boyfriend. Kaelyn allowed herself to fall into Alex's embrace when he wrapped his arms around her. They both slowly headed towards the bed as their lips met one another's. Kaelyn didn't have to put any effort into moving back onto the bed because Alex used all his strength to lay her down with her body in his arms. When they were on the bed, Alex hit a button on his left, foot side bedpost, which closed the canopy curtains and put Alex and Kaelyn into their own private world.

"I want to hear it again," she said as she pulled his face into her hands while she brought his face close to hers.

"I love you, Kaelyn," he replied. "I love you *so* much."

"I love you too, Alex."

They embraced one another and slowly allowed the passion to fill the air.

***

"I UNDERSTAND NOW," ALEX SAID AS HE TRACED HIS RIGHT-HAND fingers all over her back after they finished making love. "Sex is … *really* amazing."

"It is … when it's with the right person," Kaelyn replied as she pulled her face away from his neck and looked into his eyes.

"You're *so* right," Alex whispered. "I'm *so* glad I saved myself for someone I really love. You know … you took me by total surprise. You came into my life *so* unexpectedly. When I met you, all my plans in my near future were just… *thrown in a loop*, you could say, but I don't mind it one bit."

Kaelyn was delighted to hear this.

"It's nice to know that someone genuinely cares for me," she said as she sat upright.

"I'm not the only one that loves you," Alex replied as he also sat upright but kissed her on her shoulder as he tenderly grazed her arm. "You have a *big* family who loves you too. You've even gotten Daniel to care about other people besides Max."

Kaelyn sighed as she got out of bed.

"I don't want to talk about the Denners right now," she said as she avoided eye contact.

Alex was confused by how cold-hearted Kaelyn was right now. This was the first time he'd seen her be truly serious since the first night they met.

"Is there any particular reason why?" Alex asked tentatively.

When Kaelyn didn't respond, Alex also got off the bed. His gut feeling told him not to force her issue out, but he put on his boxers as Kaelyn also put on her undergarments. He then walked around the bed to pull the love of his life into his arms.

"I love you," he spoke as he kissed her on the forehead. "I'll *always* be here for you."

Kaelyn sighed as she held Alex in her arms as well.

"Thanks," she replied. "I needed to hear this from someone who wouldn't betray me."

"*Betray* you?" Alex asked. "Who would betray you?"

Once again, Kaelyn sighed, but now she bent down to pick up her dress off the floor. Alex stood in silence as he watched Kaelyn slip on her dress, and he placed his left hand on his hip, and when he looked down awkwardly towards the floor, she spoke up.

"I've already said too much. I promised Denver I'd keep the truth between him and me. For now, anyway. I'm angry with the Denners for not being honest with me about some things."

"Wait, *what*?" Alex inquired as he met Kaelyn's eyes. "What's going on between you and Denver and the Denners? I'm confused."

Kaelyn sighed in frustration.

"Just … drop it, Alex, okay?"

Kaelyn's snarky attitude surprised him.

"Okay, I get that you're angry, but please don't be snippy with me," he asked.

"I'm not—" Kaelyn started to say, but then she stopped in mid-sentence when she realized Alex was right. "I'm sorry. I'm just *really* upset with everyone right now. I just found out from Denver that my whole life's been a lie, and the Denners knew it!"

Alex saw how Kaelyn turned red in the face as tears surfaced. She looked away for a few moments as she ran through her hair.

"I have *no* clue what you're talking about, but I *really* can't see the Denners hiding any kind of truth from you."

Kaelyn looked at Alex in disbelief.

"Alice and Doc *aren't* as clueless as *I* was. There's *no* way they *didn't* know. They're way overprotective of me, which … now that I think of it, raises a huge red flag!"

"They're overprotective of you because they *love* you!" Alex exclaimed as he stepped towards Kaelyn, but she put her hand out in front of her, which stopped Alex in his tracks. "Are you *serious*?"

Kaelyn knew Alex now referred to her gesture that put him in his place. He was now officially annoyed. He sighed as he folded his arms across his chest and kept his eyes on hers.

"I find it hard to believe that you're taking their side right now!" she exclaimed in a harsh tone. "Y'know, maybe Daniel is right about them. They're way overprotective of us enough to withhold important information from us that we *actually* have a right to know."

"Wait a minute," Alex said as he now put his right hand out in front of him. "Are you telling me you're siding with *Daniel* on this? I don't know if you know this, but Daniel is a drug addict, and he's a drug dealer! I think you've been hanging around him just a little too much."

Kaelyn couldn't believe Alex was this bold. She stepped closer to him, now with an expression of anger on her face, though her face was still red with tears in her eyes.

"*Nobody* tells me who I can and can't hang out with. Daniel is my best friend, got it?"

Alex sighed as Kaelyn now slipped on her flip-flops.

"I'm not telling you that you can't see him anymore. I'm saying that your judgment right now is clouded. *Nobody's* perfect, Kay, and *that's* the point I'm trying to make here. Have you even talked to Dr. and Mrs. Denner yet about whatever it is that's bothering you? They *seriously* may not be aware of whatever's got you so angry. What if they've been lied to by Social Services *just* like you were?"

"Don't be stupid," she replied.

"You know what? I'm getting fed up with your attitude," Alex stated.

"You know, if you loved me, you'd be on my side about this!"

Alex couldn't believe Kaelyn played this card. It was a low blow, and it hurt his feelings.

"You need to leave," he said in a calm but stern tone. Kaelyn was about to say something, but Alex wouldn't have it. "*NOW!*"

Kaelyn jumped in surprise at Alex's scream. He was red around his eyes as tears now surfaced.

"Alex," Kaelyn whispered as she regretted her previous words.

"You *clearly* don't know me! I just poured my *whole heart* and my *whole soul* into you! I need you out of here *NOW*!"

"I should never have come here! This whole thing between us is just one big mistake!"

Kaelyn saw a couple of tears slip from Alex's hold, and tears now fell from her own eyes. They'd just broken each other's hearts, and neither couldn't say anything further. Alex just turned his back on her to avoid further eye contact, and Kaelyn stormed out. When Kaelyn got home, Vinessa, Timothy, and the parents had been laughing about something, but they all quickly grew concerned when they saw a very troubled Kaelyn walk into the house as she slammed the front door closed. Timothy was the first to stand up and approach her.

"What's wrong?"

Kaelyn knew there was no way Timothy knew the truth, so she didn't have a problem with him.

"I just want to be left alone," she whispered with tears before she darted up the stairs.

Timmy turned back to the others in curiosity.

"She was on a date with Alex," Vinessa stated. "Looks like they either had a major fight, or they broke up."

Kaelyn locked herself up in the Chiller, and everyone knew it too when they heard her slam the door shut.

"Why do I have a feeling the only person she'll talk to is Daniel?" Alice asked.

"Vin, you want to try to get him over here?" Michael asked.

"Sure, hold on," she said as she now pulled out her phone to text Daniel.

CHAPTER
THIRTY

After closing at his job, Daniel showed up at the house, though he went straight up to the Chiller and he lightly knocked on the door. Vinessa and Timothy were nearby, but Daniel paid no attention to them at the moment.

"Kay, it's me. What's going on?" he asked tenderly.

When he didn't hear any response, he then called her by his pet name for Kaelyn.

"Princess?"

"Not here!" was the only response he got from her.

Daniel, Timothy, and Vinessa quickly realized she wanted to go somewhere private with Daniel to talk about whatever was bothering her. Daniel then turned to Vinessa.

"Can you please get an outfit put together for her for tomorrow?"

Vinessa nodded and went to her room to do as Daniel had asked of her. Then he looked to Timothy.

"Can you please let Alice and Doc know that I'm taking Kay to my place for the night? I promise to take good care of her. She doesn't want to talk here."

Timothy nodded and went downstairs to do as Daniel requested.

"I'm going to take you to my place, princess, okay? We can talk freely there," he said towards the Chiller door. "Just you and me."

"Fine," was all he heard from her before she unlocked the door.

Vinessa quickly returned with a small duffle bag, and Daniel took it from her as he smiled briefly.

"Thanks."

"You're welcome," Vinessa replied as she now walked away and down the stairs.

At that moment, the Chiller door opened, and out walked a red-faced, teary-eyed Kaelyn with one of Matthew's hoodies on over her head. Daniel watched as she stormed down the hall, and he knew she was trying to keep herself together for the moment. He followed her for the time being without saying a word. When they got to the bottom of the stairs, though, Kaelyn was already out the door. Daniel turned to his parents first before leaving, though.

"I promise I'll be careful with her on my bike, okay? Had I known what was going to happen tonight, I would've borrowed Max's car."

"It's fine, Daniel," Alice said. "I know you care about her in the same way we do, so I know you'll be careful with her on your bike. You don't need to ask permission anymore to drive her around on it."

Daniel was quite shocked to hear this from Alice, but he was glad to know they trusted him with Kaelyn's life on his bike.

"Thanks," he spoke. "I'll get to the bottom of what's bothering her, and I'll report back—*if* it's not too private."

The group nodded in understanding, and then Daniel walked out the front door, and he gently closed it behind him. Daniel then saw that Kaelyn was already on his bike, with her helmet on, and he knew she wanted out of here as soon as possible. He then put on his own helmet when he got to her, and when he sat down after he secured her duffle bag, Kaelyn wrapped her arms around his waist and locked her hands in front of his abdomen. He was glad Vinessa had texted him because he knew Kaelyn needed him right now, and he was there for her. He started up his bike, and then they took off together.

When matthew heard from Timothy what happened while he was at work, he immediately went straight to Alex's before going home. When he saw Alex's mother's car in the driveway, he knew he would have to play nice until he got Alex alone. When he rang the doorbell, Mrs. Parker answered it, and she smiled.

"Well, hello there, Matt! Come on in! Alex is upstairs," she said.

"Thank you, Mrs. Parker," he replied when he stepped inside and headed upstairs.

Alex's bedroom door was closed, so Matthew knocked on it.

"Come in!"

When Matthew entered the room, he saw a look of surprise on Alex's face, and Alex said only one thing.

"Fuck."

Matthew knew Alex thought it was his mother at first and that he wasn't expecting anyone else. When Matthew closed the door behind him, he immediately approached Alex.

"Yeah, you're so fucked, but you're *so* lucky your Mom's home. What the *hell* did you do to my sister? I hand her to you on a silver platter and—"

Matthew paused when he realized how done up the room was for romance. He looked over at the bed, saw how messy the covers were, and he gave Alex the death glare. Matthew pounced on him, but Alex did his best to defend himself, though he was no match for Matthew. Matthew grabbed him by the collar, threw him onto the floor, and he balled his free hand into a fist.

"Give me *one good reason* why I shouldn't beat your ass after I gave her to you! I *trusted* you, Alex!"

"Hold on a damn minute, man! *She's* the one who broke up with me!" Alex exclaimed with tears in his eyes.

Matthew's fist froze in mid-air as he was surprised by this.

"Then why is *she* the one who's crying like someone just broke her heart?"

"If you get off me, I'll explain," Alex said calmly.

Matthew was silent for a moment before he threw Alex back onto his feet.

"You have *thirty* seconds to explain yourself, and this *better* be good," he warned with his arms now folded. "Go."

When Alex straightened his shirt out, he spoke up.

"We had a big fight about your family. She feels like her whole life's a lie, and she feels betrayed by your parents. I don't really know all the details because she said she made a promise to Denver."

Matthew remained silent as he took in Alex's explanation.

"I'm telling you, Matt, I've *never* seen her so angry before."

Matthew just sighed now.

"So Denver told her."

Alex was a bit confused.

"How'd you … ?"

Matthew knew what he was asking.

"I found out today when Denver visited me at the Zone. He didn't want to tell me, but I figured it out when I saw his family photo in his wallet. Kaelyn had her own copy, and I saw it the day I got her hired. Hers has 'Kota' written on the back in purple, and Denver's doesn't. She also looks like a carbon copy of their mother. Social Services lied to Kay about their parents' murder and told her that Denver died with them in a car accident. Since Vin is Denver's best friend, she'd seen that photo, so she recognized Kay at the group home from when we picked her out."

Alex was shocked when he heard Matthew's explanation.

"So, wait, your family *did* know?" Alex inquired.

"I didn't know until today, but Vin overheard our parents. They *did* know but kept us out of the loop because they signed some damn contract with Social Services." Matthew sighed for a moment before he spoke again. "I'm sorry she broke up with you, man. She's clearly not thinking straight."

"I'm not so sure about that," Alex spoke. "She said we were just one huge mistake, and that … after giving myself completely to her? I just … I love her, but I'm not sure she loves me. You don't say what she said when you love someone."

"I don't think she's thinking about love right now. As you said, she's hurt right now, and I don't blame her for feeling this way either."

Matthew looked over at Alex's bed now. He never realized how romantic Alex was. He made a note of the paper-made roses pinned to the translucent, net-like curtains of the bed, and he saw candles all over the place, only they were no longer lit. He then looked down at the trash can between the bedside table and the bed, and he saw a bag in it with tons of rose petals, which he knew were real. He knew Alex wasn't a "user" or a Casanova, but he couldn't help but be even a little jealous.

"I'm sorry you had to come up here and see this. I know this kind of thing bothers you when it comes to your sisters—"

"It's fine," Matthew interrupted quickly with a raised hand and a sigh. "I wouldn't want Kay with anyone else. As long as you're using protection, I'll forget I stepped into this."

Alex didn't know what to say.

"Yeah, well, that was a mistake. I shouldn't have given in to my emotions so easily."

Matthew knew that Alex was beating himself up over this whole mess.

"You're only human, and you didn't give in so easily. I know that you'd only give yourself up to someone you really love, or you'd wait until marriage. I respect that, Alex," Matthew spoke as he now walked towards the door. "Thank you for not making me punch you. That was the last thing I wanted to do to you."

Alex just nodded as Matthew now walked out and left Alex to his thoughts. When Matthew got home, he saw that the family was in the living room, just talking, until they saw him.

"I promised Denver I'd keep this a secret, but I can't because we need to talk to Kay together tomorrow. I already know you know, Vin, but Kay's angry with all of us," Matthew stated as he sat down with Vinessa, Timothy, and their parents. "Kay knows the truth about her parents. She knows they were murdered, and she knows her brother's still alive."

Alice and Michael now looked at each other.

"How did she find out?" Alice asked.

"And how did *you two* know?" Michael added in question as he looked back and forth between Vinessa and Matthew.

"Vinessa recognized Kay in the group from Denver's picture of their birth family," Matthew answered. "Kay is the spitting image of her mother. You could call her a carbon copy or a twin."

"It's true. They're identical," Vinessa added.

"Wait, Denver's the brother?" Alice inquired.

Now Vinessa and Matthew were confused.

"I thought you knew this?" Matthew asked.

"Uh, no, Social Services only told us her parents were murdered, and they said for protective and safety measures, they couldn't reveal who the brother was," Alice explained. "So, wait, Denver's really her biological brother?"

"Yes," Vinessa answered. "That's why I was so adamant about us fostering Kay. I couldn't let her slip through our fingers, not when Denver was out of town at the time and looking for her. She's better off with us than with another family, and we all know it. Wait, Matt, when did *you* find out about this?"

"Today at the Zone when Denver came in to see her. It wasn't his intention to tell me, but I connected the dots when he opened up his wallet to pay for his shakes. I saw his family photo. He didn't take me for a fool, so he came forward with the truth, though he wanted me to keep this from Mom and Dad here," Matthew explained calmly.

"Why?" Timmy asked in curiosity.

Matthew sighed as he leaned back into the armchair he sat down in.

"He knows about the contract, doesn't he?" Alice asked.

"Yes, he does," Matthew answered as he met Alice's gaze. "And Denver's not stupid. By the time he realized his search for his sister was over, he knew he couldn't rip her away from us. He *knows* she's safe with us and that she isn't going anywhere unless Social Services learns that Kay found out the truth. He said he didn't want to rip her away from this happiness that she has with us. Kaelyn wants to adopt the Denner name, and Denver wants this for her as well."

Alice and Michael exchanged looks as Matthew continued.

"He admitted he couldn't be a parent to her. He said he might wait until after we adopted her before he brought up the truth to her, but I guess he changed his mind and told her anyways."

"That explains why she was so anxious," Vinessa stated.

The room was silent for a few moments as no one knew what to say next until Matthew thought of his conversation with Alex.

"I spoke with Alex on my way home. Kay broke up with him, and he said she was *furious*. He said she knows we know the truth, and right now, she feels betrayed. Alex tried defending us, and that only made things worse. Now she feels like she doesn't know *who* she can trust," Matthew further explained, which caught everyone's attention.

Michael was none too pleased about this situation. Neither was Alice.

"She trusts Daniel," Alice answered. "He was the only one who could get her out of that room upstairs."

"I'm still not convinced that was a good idea," Michael spoke as he looked to his wife. "After all, Daniel hasn't trusted us since day one. He's going to side with her when it comes to knowing the truth and her right to it."

Vinessa knew she had to butt in and defend Daniel at this point.

"That's not entirely true," Vinessa replied as she met her father's gaze. "He's very thankful for you and Mom for taking him in and for claiming him as a son, and he'd, believe it or not, take a bullet for you. You raised him long enough to understand how you think and how you feel about everyone and everything. It's just that you don't know *him* well enough to understand who *he is* because he's got some strong beliefs and opinions that completely contradict what yours are, so to avoid fighting and conflict, he just guards himself."

Everyone was surprised at how Vinessa defended Daniel.

"You and Mom and Matt all think the same way, so he can't get close to you like he wants to without the fear of judgment and being disowned. When Kay isn't around, the way he acts with you isn't *at all* how Daniel acts with Kay when he's alone with her. Who he is with you and who he is with Kay are like two completely different people. I've seen this in action. They're very much like Denver and me. They're very open and honest with each other. They accept each other for who they are, and they'd probably go to the ends of the earth to protect each other, like Denver and I would, like Daniel and Max would, and like you and Mom would."

Alice, Michael, and Timothy were quiet as they took in Vinessa's words.

"I have to agree with Vin on this one. Daniel was right to take her out of here for the night. He understands she needs a little space from everyone, and I know he'll calm her down, at least enough to get her to talk to us," Matthew added. "It's true what Vin said about how they are with each other when they think they're alone or when they think they're not being watched. They challenge each other to do the right thing."

"We'll give her the night and until she returns tomorrow before we talk to her," Alice stated.

"Yeah, and somebody needs to get Denver over here," Michael added. "I don't care who does it, but *somebody* will do this."

"Since I broke Denver's promise, I'll tell him," Matthew said as he stood up and went into the kitchen with his cell phone.

"What are we going to do about this?" Alice inquired towards her husband. "If Social Services found out Kaelyn knows the truth, we could lose our license to foster."

"Wait, what?" Timothy asked.

Michael sighed as he closed his eyes for a few moments before he spoke up.

"We signed documents stating that if Kaelyn ever found out the truth about her past, Social Services would take her back, and we'd have to forfeit our right to foster permanently."

Timothy was stunned when he heard this.

"I *knew* it!" Vinessa exclaimed as she stood up from the couch. "*That's* why I didn't tell you guys I knew who Kay was!"

"*We* are going to do nothing," Michael stated as he now grabbed everyone's attention. "*We* are going to wait this out until *we* talk to Kaelyn and Denver … *tomorrow*. In the meantime, we'll tell *no one* what we all know. This means *no* Brienna, *no* Derek, *no* Alana, *no* Andy, *no one*."

Michael's tone meant business, and everyone knew it too.

"*Do I make myself clear?*" he asked.

Everyone remained quiet, though they nodded to show that they understood and acknowledged his request.

CHAPTER
THIRTY-ONE

When Denver's phone rang, he stirred in his sleep, but Amber was closer to it, so she answered the phone for him.

"Thank you for calling Denver's phone. This is Amber speaking. How can I help you?"

Matthew was a little confused by the voice on the other end of the phone because he hadn't met Amber yet, but he knew he'd dialed the correct phone number because she mentioned Denver's name.

"Uh, yes, Amber, my name's Matt, Matthew Denner. Is Denver available? It's urgent."

"I'm sorry, but Denver is currently unavailable. What message would you like me to leave for him? I'll be sure that he gets it when he wakes up."

"I'm sorry, but who are you?" Matthew asked.

"Oh, I'm Amber, his girlfriend, and you are?"

"Denver's best friend's brother," Matthew answered. "Are you *sure* you can't wake Denver up? This is about his birth sister, and it's very urgent."

When Amber realized this was about Denver's biological sister, she knew to wake him up.

"Hold on," she said as she turned to a sleeping Denver. "Baby?"

"Hm?" was Denver's mumbled response, though his eyes were still closed.

"You have an important phone call from Matt Denner. It's about Dakota."

"Put it on speaker," Denver requested.

Amber then put the phone on speaker.

"Okay, he said to put it on speaker, so he's awake and here. You can talk to him now," Amber stated.

"Denver? Denver, it's Matt."

"Yeah, what's up?" Denver asked as he became more coherent this time while his eyes opened.

"Kay's very upset, and I know I said that I wouldn't say anything to Mom and Dad, but I had to."

Denver was silent at first until he lifted his head off the pillow.

"Fuck, man, I told you not to do that!" Denver exclaimed with a sigh.

"You started it by telling Kay the truth. Look, this whole thing will get out of control if you don't come over. Kaelyn is upset with all of us, and we need to discuss it together so we're all on the same page. Dad is asking for you to come over tomorrow. Can you?"

Denver sighed as he now sat upright.

"I have a doctor's appointment tomorrow, dude," Denver replied. "And I kind of already have plans."

"It's okay, baby. Your sister's more important. We can change our plans up a bit. You can just call or text me when you're done with taking care of this situation," Amber replied.

Denver was a little surprised by how accomodating Amber was right now.

"Are you sure?" he asked.

"Absolutely!" Amber assured. "Dakota needs you."

"*You* are *so* amazing. You know that?"

Matthew felt awkward because Denver's phone was on speaker, which meant he heard their entire conversation with each other.

"I know," Amber answered with a big smile.

Matthew then heard Amber kissing Denver.

"I love you," Denver told her.

"Aw, I love you too, sweetie."

Once again, Matthew heard the couple smooch, but this time he felt he had to interrupt.

"I'm still here, you know?"

"I know," Denver acknowledged. "But you know what? I think I have to speak with your parents about Kay anyway because Dr. Hart wants to make an appointment with them and Kay. She suspects my CML's back since I had two nosebleeds back to back earlier today. I have an appointment with her tomorrow at noon to discuss all viable treatment options once she gets my test results back. I should be over at your place by two or three in the afternoon."

Matthew was surprised to hear the part of Denver's statement that talked about how Denver may no longer be in remission.

"Damn, man. I'll keep you in my prayers, buddy, but alright. I'll let Mom and Dad know you'll be here by three. I'll see you then."

"Later," was Denver's reply before Matthew then disconnected the call.

Matthew returned to the living room.

"Okay, so I've got good news and … maybe some bad news," he said. "The good news is, Denver said he'd be here by around three in the afternoon."

"And the bad news?" Alice inquired.

"He needs our prayers for his health." Then Matthew locked eyes with his father. "He's got an appointment with Dr. Hart tomorrow at noon to go over some test results, which is why he won't be over 'til around three. He also said Dr. Hart wants to speak with you guys and Kay."

Everyone saw the expression of dread now displayed across the patriarch's face. Vinessa had tears in her eyes, though.

"Oh, dear Lord," he spoke as he brought a hand to his face. "This is just *perfect*."

"Why would Denver's doctor want to speak with you guys about Kay?" Timothy asked with curiosity.

"Bone marrow, honey," Alice answered as she met his gaze.

Timothy was still confused by this, so Alice knew she needed to explain the situation further.

"It means that Denver's doctor suspects his Leukemia may have returned, and that's not good. They talked about bone marrow options the last time, just in case the alternative treatments failed. However, they weren't able to match him with anyone in the bone marrow donor registry. If Denver needs a bone marrow transplant this time around, then his best chance of recovery and remission would be through Kay because they're brother and sister."

Timothy nodded in understanding, though Dr. Denner spoke up again.

"Can somebody please text Daniel and tell him to bring Kaelyn back here by three tomorrow?"

"I will," Vinessa said as she pulled out her phone and did as her father asked.

MEANWHILE, AT MAX AND DANIEL'S HOUSE, MAX DID HIS BEST TO calm kaelyn down while daniel did his best to support her.

"I just … I just don't understand!"

Max confirmed that Alice and Michael knew the truth about her parents and that they had to sign papers to keep it from her.

"They had to sign papers, Kay," Max explained. "If they would have told you the truth, and if Social Services found out about it, they would've permanently taken away the foster license."

"I'm sorry, but I have to say, *that* is just some fucked up bullshit. Social Services is acting like she's in the witness protection program, but she's not," Daniel argued.

"You can't blame them for being protective, though, because her parents *were* murdered, and the killer *was* going after her and Denver. The perpetrator may be in prison, but when it comes to minors, there's no such thing as being *too* safe," Max further clarified.

"Yeah, well, my name was changed completely," Kaelyn replied.

"Yours was, but Denver's wasn't," Daniel added. "His last name changed because of the adoption with the Knights. You were still just a baby, so it was much easier to change your name completely."

Kaelyn couldn't help but sigh at this.

"They also must've known Denver was old enough to remember his sister, and they must've known he was going to look for her when he was older. I also think that's another reason they're being safe with you. I don't think they want you reunited with Denver because of the possible compromise in your safety," Max stated. "If it would've been up to Mom and Dad, without losing their foster license, they would've told you the truth. I *promise* you that, Kay."

Daniel wanted to respond to that, but by the red face Kaelyn still had, he decided to change the subject.

"You know what you need?" he asked as Kaelyn looked over at him. "You need to relax. I can bring out the grass if you want?"

"No, she doesn't need weed," Max answered before Kaelyn did. "She's a minor, and you don't want to get in trouble for giving any to her."

"Wow," Daniel replied as he scratched his right eyebrow. "You need to relax too. I'll be right back."

Before Max could say anything, Daniel took off out of sight.

"Please tell me you're not *really* going to smoke with him?" Max asked.

"Why not?" Kay said. "It's not like I haven't done it before."

Max sighed as he leaned back into the couch.

"Aw, Kay, no," he said softly.

"I'm not the only one. Matt and Vin did it a couple of times with us," Kaelyn added.

Max didn't say anything, not until Daniel came back.

"What's the matter with you? Are you looking for more trouble with the law because that's exactly what you're getting when you're leading to the delinquency of minors like our sisters and brother," he said.

"Relax, Max," Daniel replied. "It's not like I'm out in public and destroying property or something. Besides, I've been sitting on some of my stash for a while, and it's time to get rid of it."

Max sighed as he knew Daniel wouldn't listen to him anyway.

"Fine, but if either of you takes so much as *one* step, even a *toe*, outside this house, I'm telling Mom and Dad," Max warned. "God, I can't believe I'm allowing this."

"That's fine by me," Daniel said as he made a bowl up. "Are you joining?"

"Hell no!" Max exclaimed. "Did you forget that I'm a juvenile probation officer? Like regular law enforcement, I've got to get tested every month. Besides, I would rather not be wasted when I've got to supervise you two to make sure nothing gets out of hand."

"Well, you can relax here. I'm not smoking, and Kay's a couch potato when it comes to grass," Daniel assured.

"Yeah, seriously," Kay added. "Besides, he's right. I can't think about this betrayal anymore. I need to take a beat."

Max sighed as he now stood up on his feet.

"I need a beer," he said as he now headed into the kitchen.

"Bring out the shot glasses and the Southern Comfort!" Daniel called to him.

Max rolled his eyes but did as Daniel asked. After an hour and a half with two bowls smoked by Kaelyn, Kaelyn finally picked up the Southern Comfort and poured three shots.

"Let's play, 'Never Have I,'" she suggested.

"Oh, no," Max said quickly. "I'm *not* playing that."

"Yes, you are," Kaelyn said as she sat upright. "Never have I ever kissed anyone in this room."

Max threw a dirty look at Daniel in surprise.

"You *told* her? What the fuck, Danny!"

"It's 'no secrets barred' with Kay here," Daniel answered as he downed his shot with a smirk.

"Yeah, no one knows but me, I promise," Kay added.

"Oh, you're going *down*, sister," Max warned before he downed his shot as well. "Fine, I'm next."

"Shoot!" Daniel said as he poured himself another shot.

"Never have I ever had vaginal sex," Max stated.

Both Kaelyn and Daniel grinned at this, and they both took their shot. Then all three of them refilled their shot glasses. Daniel spoke up.

"Never have I ever had anal sex."

Now it was Max's turn to down his shot, and Kaelyn had also followed suit.

"Whoa, Kay, *really*?" Daniel asked, very surprised.

"A fact I wish I could forget," she replied as she filled her shot glass.

"Sorry," Daniel apologized.

"Don't be," she answered as Max refilled his shot glass. "Never have I ever masturbated in front of anybody."

The only person to drink to this was Max, which surprised Kay.

"Oh, okay. So, you like an audience, don't you?" she asked with a grin. "I'll be your audience. I dare you to kiss Daniel."

CHAPTER
THIRTY-TWO

The room turned quiet as Daniel and Max gazed into each other's eyes. Neither of them made any attempts to move towards one another.

"I think I'm done here," Max spoke as he made another shot and then quickly downed it as he stood up on his feet.

"Aw, c'mon, it's not that bad. Just one little kiss?" Kay asked.

"Back off!" Max fired back.

"Okay, I'm sorry for asking," Kay apologized.

At that moment, Daniel stood up, and he walked towards Max.

"No. Please, Danny, *no!*" Max pleaded before Daniel grabbed his face and kissed him with more passion than Kaelyn thought she'd see.

Kaelyn was surprised by this move. She honestly didn't think this would happen. She was even more stunned when Daniel pushed Max back onto the couch, and Daniel climbed on top of him. For a minute, Max was consumed by Daniel's impulsive move, and he couldn't help but wrap an arm around Daniel's waist while his free hand found itself on Daniel's face. After a few more moments, though, Max then finally pushed Daniel off him.

"We *cannot, absolutely cannot* do this!" he exclaimed as both of them now stood on their feet. "This is *wrooong!*"

"Maybe, but I know you have feelings for me—" Daniel began, though Max wouldn't let him finish.

"We are *brothers*, Daniel, and *nothing* more!" Max growled with rage as he now looked toward Kaelyn. "I trust you'll tell *no one* what you just witnessed!"

"See what?" Kaelyn replied as if she genuinely didn't know what he meant by his statement.

Max then gave Daniel another glare, but he said nothing further. Instead, he grabbed the half-empty bottle of Southern Comfort and took off to his room, drinking from it until he disappeared behind his bedroom door.

"That was very intense," Kaelyn noted.

"Think so? Try living with him," Daniel answered as he offered her another bowl, though Kaelyn gestured that she had enough, so he put everything back in his stash. "He's always brooding. By the way, I gave up ganja a little while ago, so the rest of this stash is yours, but I'm keeping it here. So, anytime you want to hit it, let me know, and I'll bring you back here for another sleepover. Once this stash is gone, though, that's it. I'm not buying or selling it anymore."

Kaelyn was surprised that Daniel gave up the weed, though he'd already lit a cigarette a few times tonight, and now he'd lit up another one. She didn't care one way or the other, though.

"Thanks. I should go apologize to him, though," Kaelyn said.

"Trust me when I say you don't want to, not until the morning, anyways. Once he goes off to be alone with a bottle of liquor in his hands, and you bother him, he gets nasty. I wouldn't want you to see that side of him. Granted, it's rare, but *never* disturb the beast within him," Daniel cautioned.

Kaelyn trusted Daniel about Max, so she decided to listen to him and leave Max alone.

"We can make him breakfast in the morning and apologize then," she suggested.

"Perfect," Daniel replied as he took a puff of his cigarette and relaxed back into the couch. "We'll butter up to him and make him his favorite, eggs benedict. He makes the funniest, most adorable, better-than-sex face when he takes that first bite every single time."

Kaelyn giggled when she heard that.

"That oughta be interesting to see," she commented with a smirk.

"Oh, it's the greatest," Daniel added. "I fucking love it."

Kaelyn smiled, and the two of them enjoyed a few more hours of each other's company until Daniel passed out face down on one of the couches. Kaelyn couldn't sleep because, now that she was alone in her thoughts, she couldn't stop thinking about the betrayal. She was then momentarily distracted as she heard Max's bedroom door open. She saw him walk out with the bottle of Southern Comfort, and she also noticed there was probably about a quarter left of it. She thought for sure that he'd have drunk the whole bottle. He'd gone to put the bottle back into the kitchen, but then he noticed that Kaelyn was still awake.

"Kay?"

"Yeah, I'm still awake, but Daniel's passed out cold."

"Yeah, he's a little bit of a heavy sleeper," Max replied as he set the bottle of alcohol on the kitchen counter and walked towards the thermostat to adjust it. "But what are you still doing up?"

"Can't shut my brain off," Kaelyn answered in a solemn tone.

"Still thinking about the news you learned today?" he asked.

"How can I not?" Kay replied with tears as she met his gaze.

Max took out a big, fuzzy blanket from the hall closet and came over to Kaelyn. She watched as he sat down next to her and unfolded the blanket.

"Are you cold?" he asked her. "I'm freezing."

When Kay nodded, Max wrapped the blanket around the both of them.

"Thanks," she said.

Max smiled as he now pulled his foster sister into his arms for a cuddle-fest.

"I was going to come after you earlier to apologize, but Daniel said you—"

"Turn into a beast?" Max finished for her with curiosity. "Yeah, that's true when I'm drunk. I try to make sure I don't drink too much, though."

"Gotcha," Kaelyn acknowledged. "I'm really sorry about what I said before."

Max paused for a moment as he studied Daniel, who was still out like a light on the adjacent sofa where his arm dangled over the edge.

"Don't worry about it," Max stated. "He's right. I am in love with him, but I could never act on those feelings for obvious reasons. That would just be wrong."

"I understand," Kay replied as she rested her head on her foster brother's shoulder. "You both fell in love with each other before the Denners found you two."

Max turned to look down at her with astonishment, and she knew it too, but she didn't move her head from his shoulder. Her eyes stayed focused on Daniel.

"He told me about what happened with that bully from the foster family you both had, how you protected him in every way you did so that he wouldn't know the kind of pain that your older foster brother gave you." Max had tears in his eyes when he heard this. "You don't have to talk about it, but he needed to when he told me. He cried like a baby, said he felt insanely guilty for not sticking up for you until it was too late. I suspected then that he was in love with you, though his kiss with you tonight confirmed it for me."

Max didn't know what to say to this.

"I promise I'm not judging your love for each other, Max, and I promise I'm a vault of secrets. I'll take all this with me to my grave."

Max still had no words, and his breath turned shaky on him. He felt Kaelyn's grip around him tighten, but he knew she was trying to provide comfort. He returned the gesture and rested his head on top of hers. Both of them continued to watch Daniel sleep.

"What are you thinking about?" Max asked, which indicated to Kaelyn that he wanted to change the subject.

"I'm … thinking about how I should feel about this whole mess back home. If we want to get technical about it, though, it's easy to say that Alice and Michael didn't tell me, so they *technically* didn't break the contract. But still, I don't intend on confronting my caseworker about Social Services and how they've kept me from the truth. I don't want them to know I know because I don't want them taking me away. I don't wish to see Alice and Michael lose their license to foster because I want them to take in Dylan."

The room was quiet for a minute before Max spoke up.

"So, Danny told you about his sister?"

"Matt kind of … confronted him about why he wasn't at Jacob's funeral and stuff, and Vinessa and I were there when he explained to Matt why he wasn't there. We all agreed that we'd help him find some way to rescue Dylan. I've decided that I'm going to ask Alice and Michael to meet her on my sixteenth birthday. I want them to speak with Daniel and Dylan's mom and convince her to let us take Dylan home with us."

It stunned Max to hear these words from Kaelyn.

"What about you? Don't you want to be adopted?"

"Yes, but I'm not ready for that yet. Besides, I want to see Dylan be adopted first. I *need* to see this through, for Daniel."

Max removed his head from hers and then looked down at her.

"Why?" he asked.

Kaelyn now looked up into Max's curious gaze.

"Because I love him. He's my best friend and the first person I'll call brother."

"What about Denver?"

"He's indeed my biological brother, but I'm upset with him too."

Max was surprised to hear this.

"I'm upset with him for keeping the truth from me when we first met. He had *every* opportunity to tell me since then, but what does he do? He tells me today, today of all days."

"What's so special about today?"

"Today marks the fifteenth anniversary of when our parents were murdered."

Tears formed in Max's eyes when he heard this answer.

"Why did he have to tell me on this particular day? I'll tell you why. Because he said that he didn't want to be alone with his thoughts, which consisted of the recurring nightmare of him seeing our parents being killed."

"No wonder you can't sleep," Max replied as he did his best to comfort her. "I'm so sorry, Kay."

"Ditto," she spoke as she now looked back to Daniel. "And now I might be losing him too. *Again.*"

Max wondered where this conversation was headed, though she continued.

"He had a nosebleed today when he was with me, and he texted me earlier to tell me he had another one at the doctor's office." She met Max's gaze again with tears in her own eyes as her breath turned shaky. "They're running some tests. He'll get the results tomorrow."

"You won't lose him," Max tried to assure her. "Just like Daniel here, Denver's quite a stubborn person. Denver's a warrior, Kay, and now that he knows he found you, he'll do whatever it takes to fight. He'll do it for you because you're his sister, and he loves you."

Kaelyn couldn't help but break down in tears at Max's statement. He knew she was overwhelmed with so many emotions. Max just kept a tight, comforting hold on her until they both gave in to sleep.

"YOU *PROMISED* ME, DANNY." KAELYN FELT GROGGY WHEN SHE woke up the next day, and though she quickly realized she was alone in the living room, she heard whispered arguing between Daniel and Max. "You *promised* me that you'd keep this between us."

"I know," Daniel replied in a tone with remorse. "I'm sorry, Max. I'm so, so sorry."

Kaelyn slowly sat upright as she figured they were in the hallway between the kitchen and their bedrooms.

"*Why* did you tell her? You *know* that she's a fifteen-year-old girl who has her own history of being abused. You could've triggered her into a panic attack or something by telling her what happened to me. Besides, it *wasn't* your story to tell!"

"Max, *please*—" Daniel started to beg with tears in his eyes as he grabbed Max's face.

"Get your damn hands off me!" Max warned in a low voice with clenched teeth as he swatted Daniel's hands away from his face.

Kaelyn had never seen Max this angry before. He was so furious with Daniel that he was red in the face with tears in his eyes.

"Max," Daniel called again as he tried to touch Max's chest now, but Max shoved him away with more aggression this time.

"Touch me again, Daniel, and I *swear to fucking God* I'll take you down. You *know* I'm a blackbelt. *Don't fuck with me.*"

Kaelyn watched as Daniel threw his hands up in the air in defeat before he ran them through his hair and turned his back to Max. It was easy for Kaelyn to understand that she caused this fight by telling Max the secret that Daniel revealed to her in confidence. She didn't know if she should intervene or not, and she felt guilty for causing this.

"Why in the hell, after eleven years, would you break our promise to keep this between us?" Max asked as he got in Daniel's face.

Daniel's head was down with his eyes closed as he pressed both of his hands against the wall for support. Kaelyn knew he was trying to keep it together without breaking down. He parted his lips to speak but closed them just as quickly as he shook his head.

"Tell me why, Daniel, before I walk out of here and decide that I never want to speak to you again!" Max threatened.

"Because I saw Jordy!" Daniel blurted out before the first of his sobs escaped. "Because you weren't the only one he touched."

Max was stunned when he heard this.

"I saw him a few weeks ago when I was working. Clara assigned him to one of my tables," Daniel further explained. "He didn't seem to recognize me, though he was on a date with another guy. He looked at his date … with that stupid fucking smug on his face, the same one he gave you … and *me*. I thought that I could handle it, so I took their drink orders, but when I got back to the kitchen, I panicked. I mean, I *really* flipped out, like I couldn't breathe. Big Jim took over for me and told me to go home for the day, so I did."

Max was still speechless, though the first of his tears fell. Daniel kept his eyes closed, and he fought like hell to keep his tears at bay, but he failed miserably at this.

"You were testifying in court, so I went home to speak with Dad. I nearly crashed my bike because my anxiety was through the fucking roof. I thought maybe Dad could help me because he knew our kind of pain, but he wasn't home. I tried calling him … but his phone was off, which meant he was in surgery. I couldn't wait for him to call me back, and I couldn't wait for him to get home, but Kay was there. She was the *only* one who was home at the time. *I swear to God*, Max, the walls felt like they were closing in on me, and *I couldn't breathe*! It felt like I was in the middle of having a fucking heart attack!"

Daniel couldn't hold himself together anymore. He'd collapsed in the hallway, though Max's reflexes were quick, and he went down with Daniel as he now held him in his arms. Kaelyn stood up from the couch, and she quickly fixed her hair. She headed toward the hallway but stopped for a moment as she saw how Max cradled Daniel in his arms for comfort.

"I didn't know," Max cried in a whisper as he kissed Daniel on the crown of his head. "I'm sorry, Danny."

Kaelyn got down on the floor with them and crossed her legs in the classic Indian style. Daniel had his face buried into his hands, but Max held his face to his chest. Kaelyn couldn't help but mirror their tears.

"I'm sorry if I caused this fight," she apologized as she touched Daniel on his arm nearest to her as she met Max's gaze. "I realize I should've clarified what I meant when I said 'too late.' He didn't tell you before what Jordy did to him because he said you'd worked *so hard* on trying to protect him back then. He didn't want you harboring the same guilt that he'd carried for not sticking up for you sooner by not reporting your former foster brother earlier."

Max leaned his head back against the wall for a moment but then leaned forward and lovingly rested his head on top of Daniel's as he wept. Now he realized what Kaelyn meant by 'too late.'

"Oh, Danny," he called in a tender voice as he sobbed along with his best friend. "I'm *so* sorry. *Please* forgive me. I didn't know. I'm so, so sorry."

CHAPTER
THIRTY-THREE

Denver was stunned beyond belief as he sat across from Dr. Hart in her private, upscale office. He thought he'd won the war that seemed destined to prevail against his health, but he quickly realized just how wrong he was, and tears formed in his eyes as he knew he'd now be thrust into yet another battle. A shaky breath that escaped his lips told Dr. Hart he was scared once more for his life.

"I'm so sorry, Denver, but there's a good chance you might have built up a resistance to the FC treatment, so it probably won't work for you this time around," Dr. Hart said with sympathy in her voice. She knew the young man needed to find comfort in her words, so she added, "At least not alone, which means there's some good news with a little hope for you. Newly conducted research shows that adding Rituximab to the FC combination, which is now commonly known as the R-FC treatment, would increase your chances of a full recovery by twenty-five percent. Of course, I have to warn you that you *will* have one or more side effects within the first two hours of taking Rituximab, and they consist of a fever that comes with chills, a headache, an itchy rash, or just plain feeling sick. We'd also have to keep you under our watch, just in case you have a reaction, so that we can get it under control as fast as possible."

Denver sighed as he figured out why she suggested so strongly that he go with the new R-FC treatment. He looked straight into her chestnut brown eyes and parted his lips.

"How far is it?"

Dr. Hart knew there was no beating around the bush with Denver, so she just told him like it was.

"Considering you have far fewer red blood cells than you should normally have, I'd say you're in stage three."

"Oh, my God," was Denver's only response as he brought his right hand up to cover his eyes.

"Denver, I know that we've discussed this the first time and that you would prefer not to go through with this, but radiation therapy might be a big help this time around."

When Denver's head immediately shot up, Dr. Hart knew what he thought, and she already knew what he'd say next, as they already had this conversation before he completed his last round of treatments that put him in remission.

"No," he said in a matter-of-fact tone. "I won't do it."

"Not even if it was a last resort?" Dr. Hart asked, slight hope rising in her voice as she met Denver's gaze.

"It's not my last resort," he answered in a quiet tone as he pressed his elbows on his knees and looked into his right palm, slightly tracing it with his left thumb. "Not technically, anyway. I imagine it's still possible for me to have a bone marrow transplant?"

Dr. Hart knew where Denver was headed with this conversation. They'd talked about bone marrow transplants in the past, and Dr. Hart even encouraged his adopted parents to help him look for his sister since he was fourteen years old, just in case the chemotherapy he went through didn't work.

"I took the liberty of checking the bone marrow registry before our appointment. I'm sorry to say that at this time, we still don't have any matches for you. The sooner I can see your sister and test her, the better off we are, even though she only has a fifty percent chance of being a match. Being that you both have the same mother and father, though, she's still your best chance compared to a random donor not related to you."

DENVER SIGHED IN NERVOUSNESS WHILE HE SAT IN HIS CAR ONE HOUR later and looked up at the Denner house. He'd been in that house millions of times, but right now, the place seemed huge to him. This was it. He *had* to talk to them about Dakota … Kaelyn … his sister. After he stepped out of his car and locked it, he walked up to the front door and knocked on it. When the door opened, Vinessa beamed a bright smile toward him, like absolutely nothing was wrong.

"Hey, Den!" she exclaimed with excitement as she stepped aside. "Come on in!"

Denver smiled as he entered the house, and when he did, he saw that Matthew and their parents were already at the dining room table. Everyone, except Michael, smiled at the moment.

"Hello, Denver, we're still waiting for Max and Daniel to return with Kaelyn, but please have a seat," Michael greeted with a brief smile and a gesture to suggest he sit down next to Alice on her left.

"Thanks," Denver replied as he took the seat next to Alice while Vinessa sat down next to him on his right.

"Before we get started, Vinessa and Matthew have told us about a picture of your biological family. May I see it?" Alice asked.

"Sure!" Denver said, now taking out his wallet and opening it up.

He figured she needed confirmation before they all got started, and he was okay with this, so he removed the picture from his wallet.

"Here you go," he said as he handed it to her.

"Thank you," Alice said as she took the photo from Denver and looked at it. "Oh, my!"

Michael leaned into his wife on her left to get a good look, and both of them were pretty surprised.

"You two weren't kidding," Alice said toward her kids before she looked to Denver. "Kay *really* does look like your mother."

"What'd I tell you; carbon copy, right?" Matthew asked.

"It's uncanny," Michael commented as he turned his attention to Denver now. "Do you know why your parents were murdered?"

"Yeah, the killer claims if he couldn't have my family, nobody could," Denver answered.

"If he ever got out of prison, he could probably look you up, and because Kay looks just like your mother, your safety *and* hers would *both* be compromised. Do you understand what I'm saying?" Michael inquired.

Denver knew Dr. Denner was acting like he was supposed to be. He was acting like a father and protector. Denver respected this about him.

"Yes, Dr. Denner. I understand completely. I recognize that this is why Social Services wanted to keep Kaelyn's real identity and past a secret," Denver stated.

"Then why on *earth* would you reveal the truth to Kaelyn, and in the process, make her feel like she can't trust anyone?"

"Okay, before we go any further, I just want to say that I *really* appreciate you looking out for her. I'm thankful to see that she has a real father now. When I first came over here yesterday to see her, it wasn't my intention of telling her the truth. I came over here because yesterday was the fifteenth anniversary of what happened to our mom and dad. I didn't want to be alone. I didn't realize until after I began talking with her that I needed her to know the truth. She *deserves* to know the truth."

Michael was about to say something, but Denver put a finger up.

"With all due respect, Dr. Denner. I just have one more piece of crucial information that you *need* to know. Social Services didn't tell the Knights this, so I'm almost positive they won't tell you two either. It doesn't matter *how hard* you would've tried to keep the truth from Kay because the truth will come to light in a few years anyway."

The last part of Denver's statement seemed to confuse everyone in the room.

"What do you mean?" Alice asked as she handed the photo back to Denver.

Denver took back the phone and put it back in his wallet. He spoke up as he put his wallet away.

"I don't know if the Knights ever told you, though I did tell them I wanted my finances kept a secret, but … when I turned eighteen, I inherited my parents' house along with eight million dollars. My dad came from money, and he was a world-renowned neurosurgeon. His attorney, who also handles the estate, somehow tracked me down. He'll do the same thing for Dakota when she turns eighteen, and when he does, she's going to find out that she's getting the other half of the deed to the house, and she'll also get her own eight million dollars," Denver explained. "If it were up to me, I would've sold that house as soon as it was put in my name, but I can't do anything with it because I'm not the sole owner, so I *have* to wait until Kaelyn turns eighteen."

Vinessa already knew this, as Denver told her this in confidence a long while ago, but she kept her mouth shut.

"Wait, did I hear you right? Kay will be inheriting eight million dollars?" Michael asked.

"Yes," Denver affirmed. "Once she turns eighteen, she'll get a million, and once she turns twenty-five, she'll get two million. Every five years after that, she'll get another million. She'll get the last two million when she's forty-five."

Everyone was surprised to hear this.

"He wanted to make sure you and Kaelyn were financially set for life," Alice replied. "You and Kaelyn will never have to worry about money, and Kay will have unlimited career choices to choose from. From the start, you could instantly pay for all for college expenses, build your own home, have a top-of-the-line, brand new car, and *still* have loads of money to play around with."

"I know. Whatever worries Kay may have about the future, those are over," Denver stated. "She has a family, *and* she has a future."

"We signed a contract with Social Services stating that for as long as Alice and I kept the truth of Kay's past a secret from her, we could continue to keep our foster license *and* care for her with the possibility of adoption," Michael explained. "*If* she wants to be adopted, that is."

Denver understood what Michael said.

"Then that means there's only one option here," Denver replied. "Don't tell Social Services, adopt her, and we can all continue on our merry way."

"But you've been looking for her for years, Denver. Don't you want her back?" Matthew inquired.

"Matt, you know as well as I do that I can't be a parent to Kay. I can only be a brother," Denver stated. "I want you guys to adopt her."

Michael was pleased to hear this.

"Okay, good, we agree on that," Michael added.

"Hold on, Mike," Alice interrupted as she raised her hand while she continued to look at Denver. "You want us to adopt her?"

"Yes, I do. You all know as well as I do that Kay needs parents, a real family. I love her, and I want what's best for her. I told Kaelyn yesterday that I wouldn't dream of taking you guys away from her. If she wants to know me as her blood, then I'll still be a brother, but I could never tear her away from the happiness she has with you. She deserves the opportunity to claim a big family like yours. Please don't take that away from her."

Everyone listened to Denver's words, but Alice was the first to speak up.

"It's up to Kay if she wants to be adopted, and if she does, then we'll adopt her."

At that moment, a car pulled up into the driveway, which meant that Max and Daniel had returned home with Kaelyn.

CHAPTER
THIRTY-FOUR

Max was the first to appear when the front door opened, and then Kaelyn and Daniel followed him. After Daniel shut the door behind him, all three of them approached the dining room table. Kaelyn then removed the hood of Matthew's hoody off her head, and everyone saw the anger on her face. She was pretty disappointed in everyone at the moment. Once Max sat down next to Vinessa on her left, Kaelyn then spoke up.

"How could you?" she asked towards Alice. "I trusted you to be completely honest with me. Coming into this family, I had absolutely nothing to hide, but you did."

"Kaelyn, it's more complicated than you realize," Alice started to say, but Kaelyn wouldn't let her finish.

"I know it's a complicated situation. I know it's about my safety. Still, though, you could have been *honest* with me!" Kay replied.

Everyone saw the tears in her eyes, except for Daniel, as he stood behind her. He didn't need to see her face, though, to understand that she was hurt.

"It would've hurt like it did yesterday when I found out, but I *can* handle the truth," she continued. "I'm almost sixteen, and in two years from now, I'll be an adult. I'm not some fragile little seven or eight-year-old child. I don't *need* protection from the *truth*."

Then she turned to Denver and gazed into his eyes.

"*You* should've told me that first day I met you."

Then she turned to Vinessa.

"*You* should've told me that you've known my brother after all these years. *You've* seen his copy of our family photo *so* many times throughout the years. *You* spotted me in my group home. So, on that first night when I arrived here, *you* should've told me."

Vinessa felt guilty over this, though Kaelyn's eyes had moved on to Matthew.

"Hey, don't look at me," he said as he threw his hands in the air. "Never before have I seen Denver's photograph of your family until he showed up at the Zone yesterday when he was looking for you."

Then Kaelyn met Dr. Denner's gaze.

"Would you please sit down? You too, Daniel."

"With all due respect, I'm not comfortable with sitting down at this table right now. I need my space," Kaelyn replied.

Michael then exchanged looks with Daniel.

"I'm sorry, Doc. I love you, but I'm on her side with this."

"Do you want to go back to that group home?" Michael asked as he looked into Kaelyn's eyes. "Because that's exactly what's going to happen if Social Services finds out that you know the truth."

"No, I don't want to go back to the group home, and while I may be mad at them for hiding the truth about my past for most of my life, I don't want them knowing that I know the truth. *We* have the upper hand for a change, so it's time to turn the tables."

Alice and Michael exchanged looks with one another in curiosity.

"I might be the only one who disagrees on this, but I believe what we really need to do is return Kay to Denver."

"No," Kaelyn replied in a firm tone which surprised everyone. "I want to be a Denner. I want to be adopted."

Matthew stood up from his spot at the table and kept his gaze on Kaelyn while resting his hands on the table.

"I can't accept that," Matthew started, though Alice scolded him.

"Matthew!"

Matthew wouldn't let her speak any further, though, and he kept his eyes on Kaelyn.

"Denver has invested *so* much of his time and energy and money into looking for you. While you'd grown up in the system, you had a brother out there who wanted nothing more than to have you in his life. While you grew up thinking no one loved you, he was loving you and missing you and thinking of you *every day*. You shouldn't be adopted. You should be in your brother's care."

It stunned everyone to hear this response from Matthew. He was the quiet one of the group, usually going with the flow, though now everyone realized how he truly felt about the situation.

"Are you saying you think I shouldn't be adopted, or you don't want me to be adopted?" Kaelyn further inquired as she kept her gaze on her foster brother.

"Both," Matthew replied as he now headed to the key rack on the wall by the front door.

"Matt," Denver called. "I appreciate your support, but—"

"With all due respect, Denver, there's nothing you or anyone can say or do that will get me to change my mind on this matter. I've said my piece. Now, if you'll excuse me, I'm late enough as it is, so I've got to get to work."

Before anyone else could say anything, Matthew had grabbed his keys and walked out the front door. Kaelyn could hardly believe how cold he sounded when he spoke about his feelings regarding her case. Daniel spoke up once the front door closed.

"Don't listen to him, Kay," he spoke in a calm tone. "We all love you, and we all want to adopt you whenever you're ready, of course. Matt will come around, so just ignore him."

"Yeah, he'll come around," Denver added as he pulled out a card from his wallet and handed it to Dr. Denner. "By the way, Dr. Angela Hart, my oncologist, wants to arrange a meeting with you and Kay."

Michael wondered when Denver would get around to this topic.

"I assume this is about seeing if Kay's a match for bone marrow donation?" he inquired.

"Yeah," Denver answered with a nod. "I don't expect you guys or Kay to do anything you don't want Kay to be a part of, but Dr. Hart at least wants to meet with you."

"Count me in," Kaelyn stated.

Kaelyn's response surprised everyone.

"Seriously?" Denver asked.

"Yes, seriously," Kaelyn answered as she folded her arms across her chest and locked eyes with Denver. "I may be upset with you for not telling me the truth about our past when we first met, but I won't leave you in the dark. There was this girl in my group home who had Leukemia. She had the same diagnosis, and she'd gotten to the point that she needed a bone marrow donor, but the doctors couldn't find any matches for her. You're my brother, Denver, and I'd do whatever it takes to see that you don't suffer the same fate that she did."

Michael cleared his throat, which caught everyone's attention.

"There's just one problem with that," he spoke. "Kaelyn, you're only fifteen years old."

"So? I'll be sixteen before long," Kaelyn replied.

"Donating bone marrow is a voluntary procedure. So, that means Alice and I can't sign consent forms for you. The legal age of consent for bone marrow donation here in the United States is eighteen. The *only* way you will be allowed to give consent as a minor at this point is through a court of law. What do you think that would mean for us?"

Everyone remained quiet for a moment as Michael's eyes locked with Kaelyn's.

"Social Services would find out that I know the truth," she replied with a small voice as tears now filled her eyes.

Denver saw the fear in her face. He stood up from his spot at the table, and he approached her. Then she locked eyes with him. He tried his best to keep a brave face on. Daniel knew he was scared, though, but he stayed quiet.

"Then we can hold off on that for now. I still have a few treatment options. They've come out with a couple of new therapies since I last went into remission. I can do this, Kota. I'll fight like hell for you. I'll take every avenue I can in this because I …" Kaelyn knew what he wanted to say, and she saw tears form in his eyes. "I can't lose you again."

Kaelyn didn't know how to react to Denver's statement. His face and his voice tried to express reassurance, but his eyes told her he was afraid. He was scared to lose her, and he was petrified to die. Tears filled her eyes, though instead of saying anything, she turned to the front door and walked out. Daniel followed her to see if she was okay.

"Kay, wait!" he called, though she was already on the lawn when she stopped and turned to look at him.

"Please don't follow me," she asked. He saw how she was red in the face as tears fully streamed down her cheeks. "I need my space."

He stood frozen in his spot on the edge of the porch as he watched her take off in the direction of the beach. He knew she needed time to process everything and have a good cry. He also knew she wanted to be alone to do that, so he left her be. He walked back inside and then shut the door behind him. Everyone waited in anticipation for him to say something.

"She asked for space, though she headed towards the beach," he explained.

No one seemed to know what to say at this point, except for the family's matriarch.

"I probably would've done the same thing," she said as everyone looked to her now. "She deserves a little breathing room, so we'll give her that, but I want someone to check on her later if she isn't home by dusk. There'll be a big party happening on the beach tonight, and you know how I feel about those."

"I'll check in with her," Daniel offered as he leaned against the front door and folded his arms across his chest. "I'm not working this evening, so I'll keep an eye on her and make sure she's safe. I've got to ask, though. Is she seriously in danger if Denver's in her life?"

Denver knew where this conversation was headed.

"Davis Anderson's in a maximum-security prison and serving a life sentence for killing our parents," he answered.

Daniel froze when he heard that name.

"Wait, are you talking about *the* Davis Anderson that's locked up in Hell's Island Penitentiary?" he inquired.

Everyone was surprised when he mentioned Hell's Island, though Denver was most shocked.

"Yeah," Denver affirmed. "How'd you know he's there?"

Everyone watched how the color drained from Daniel's face, and Max now approached him.

"What's wrong?" he asked.

"Boomer," Daniel answered.

The way Max suddenly realized who Davis Anderson was made Denver and Michael uncomfortable.

"Do you know him?" Denver inquired as he approached Daniel and Max.

Daniel kept quiet as he didn't know how to answer this question. Everyone else in the room was also curious to see what Daniel's reply would be, though Michael was the first to speak up.

"Please answer the question, Daniel," he asked. "I'd also like to know because I really don't like the way you spoke to Max just now."

Daniel met Dr. Denner's gaze before he met Max's. Max didn't say anything one way or the other, as he knew it was up to Daniel to say what he wanted about Boomer. Then Daniel met Denver's curious gaze again.

"Yeah, once upon a time," Daniel responded as he kept his arms folded across his chest. "But does that even really matter? I was only four years old. I barely knew him."

Denver stood in silence for a moment as he gazed into Daniel's eyes. He wondered how Daniel knew Davis, though Daniel would've been a little kid, one who could barely remember the man as he just said. Daniel's answer sounded to Denver like his contact with Davis was limited. So, he shook these thoughts out of his mind.

"No. No, I suppose not," Denver noted. "He's insane, though. He likes to think of himself as mine and Kay's father. So, he's *crazy*."

Daniel and Max both exchanged looks of surprise before Daniel responded to Denver.

"What if he's telling the truth?"

"Maybe *you're* the crazy one," Denver chortled.

"Never said I wasn't," was Daniel's answer.

"Alright, you two," Michael said as he stood up from his spot at the table. "Denver, I want to thank you for coming here and speaking with us about everything."

Everyone, including Denver, now turned to the patriarch.

"Alice and I'll make an appointment with Kay to talk with Dr. Hart, but I can't make any guarantees about anything else right now. We'll all be praying for you and for Dr. Hart to help you get back on the path to remission as soon as possible. Will you keep us apprised of your progress, though?"

"Sure thing, Dr. Denner," Denver replied as he now met his best friend's gaze. "I'll text you later."

"Love you!" she called.

"Love you too," he stated as he waved goodbye to everyone.

Daniel knew this was his cue to step away from the door. Denver then opened the door and walked out. Daniel couldn't help but follow him, though Max grabbed him by the arm for a moment, and he caught a glimpse of desperation in Daniel's eyes.

"I *need* to *talk* to him," Daniel whispered.

Max knew he couldn't deny him this. He released his grip around Daniel's arm and watched for a moment as Daniel ran up to Denver. Then Max closed the door and was left with Vinessa and their parents.

"Hey, Denver, wait up!" he called.

Denver turned around to face him as he approached.

"What do you want, Daniel? I'm not in the mood to deal with one of your mood swings."

"I honestly wasn't trying to give you an attitude in the house. I meant it when I said that I never said I wasn't crazy. Sometimes I can be the craziest person you'd ever want to meet." Denver couldn't help but roll his eyes at this. "You never answered my question. What if Davis is right?"

Denver was quiet when Daniel asked him this.

"What if you and Kay really *are* his biological kids? That would mean you two would have an older brother out there that neither you nor Kay has ever known to exist until now."

"Davis has a son?" Denver inquired. "How do you know this?"

"I know his son," Daniel answered. "If you really are biologically linked, he might be a possible bone marrow donor for you. I can reach out to him if you want."

Denver then stepped inside Daniel's personal space and brought his face mere inches from Daniel's.

"*Davis* isn't my father. If, for some crazy reason, I *do* share half his genes, I don't want *anything* to do with his son. I want *nothing* to do with Davis *or* his family. So, I'd suggest that you *don't* reach out to your pal because if I find out who he is, I'll fucking kill him with my bare hands. Davis killed my parents, so I'd return the favor with killing his son. I'd do it in a heartbeat."

Daniel could hardly believe the words that came out of Denver's mouth. He felt the passion in his voice, and he also saw the rage in his eyes. His words cut pretty deep, though.

"What if you fail to respond to all of your other treatment options, and the only viable option was a bone marrow donation? What if Kay wasn't a match?" Daniel inquired. "What if your only possible match was your long-lost brother?"

"I would rather die," was all Denver could say before he turned toward his car. "Perhaps then the recurring nightmare of constantly reliving the horror of watching my parents die would finally come to a fucking end."

Daniel stood in silence as he watched Denver take off in his car. Once Denver was out of sight, Daniel turned in the opposite direction and headed toward the beach. He wanted to be upset with Denver, but he knew it wasn't his place. He hadn't realized until now that Denver was witness to Boomer killing his parents. He couldn't blame him for not wanting anything to do with a half-brother he might have if Davis was his biological father.

CHAPTER
THIRTY-FIVE

Once Denver returned home from his afternoon out, he couldn't help but fall into a depressive mood. Amber was there, waiting for him anxiously, though she jumped on her feet from the sofa when he walked in.

"So?" she asked. "What did the doctor say? You're in the clear, right? The nosebleeds were just a freaky coincidence?"

Denver didn't say anything at first. He just closed the door behind him and locked it but kept his right hand on the door. Amber saw that he avoided eye contact on purpose, and he kept his eyes on the floor.

"Amber," he whispered as he then closed his eyes.

Amber hurried over to him as she then realized Denver leaned on the front door for support. She knew that he needed her, and when she approached him, he looked into her eyes with tears in his own. Amber knew then that the test results were *not* in his favor.

"How far?" she asked in a quiet tone as tears formed in her own eyes.

"Stage three," Denver answered in a whisper.

"Oh, my God."

She wrapped her arms around Denver and pulled him into a tight,

295

comforting hug. Denver responded by also wrapping his arms around Amber and burying his face into the crevice of her neck.

"Why me?" Amber heard him ask in a muffled voice.

She knew Denver was about to break if she didn't say anything positive.

"I don't know, baby, but we'll get through this. We're going to kick your Leukemia's ass straight back to Hell."

***

AFTER THE SUN HAD SET, KAELYN WENT BACK TO THE HOUSE, AND when she realized she was all alone, she was glad. She went up to her room and started to paint, but she then heard the front door open and close when she finished her painting an hour later. She heard laughter and conversation, which she knew came from Vinessa, Timothy, and their dad. Vinessa was the first to ascend the steps, and she froze in the doorway to their room. Kaelyn only turned her attention back on to her artwork, and Vinessa knew this meant Kaelyn still wanted to be left alone. After Kaelyn knew Vinessa headed for somewhere else in the house, Kaelyn sighed, and then she looked over at her bed.

"Kaelyn, may I come in?" Michael asked as he knocked on her bedroom door fifteen minutes later.

She didn't want to speak to him or anyone, but she couldn't deny him his request.

"You're going to come in anyway, so you might as well," Kaelyn said as she now sat on her bed but kept her eyes on her foster father.

"You underestimate me, dear. If you don't want me to come in, I won't," Michael answered as he stood in the doorway. "But I do want to talk to you if that's okay."

Kaelyn watched as her foster father refused to step foot inside the room.

"It's your house. You can come in the room if you please."

Michael sighed as he folded his arms across his chest, and he now leaned into the door frame on his right.

"Kaelyn," he called with a soft voice. "This is *your* room. It will *always* be your room unless you don't want to be with us anymore."

Kaelyn sighed as she looked down at her hands.

"You can come in," she permitted in a quiet tone.

"Thank you," Michael replied as he now stepped into the room.

When Michael sat down next to her, Kaelyn flinched and moved to the end of the bed. Michael instantly realized this was too much too fast.

"Kay, you don't have to be afraid of me," he said.

"I know," she spoke as she avoided eye contact. "It's just … I'm sorry, but every father I've ever had has …"

Michael knew Kaelyn had a history of being abused. He also just realized this was the first *real* alone time he actually had with her.

"I … am *so* sorry you were taken advantage of to the point where you don't trust me to be alone with you. It breaks my heart, Kay," he said as he met her gaze. "Though I understand why you're hesitant in letting me in so close. I have to say that, unfortunately, I also know how it feels to be in your position. The first half of my childhood was spent in an abusive home."

Kaelyn remembered Vinessa had told her about this on her first night here in this house when she gave her the grand tour of the place.

"Yeah, Vinessa told me this when I asked her why you and Alice didn't have more kids of your own."

"Vinessa and Matthew only know because they asked that very same question once," Michael answered. "Originally, I only meant to share this information with all the abused fosters Alice and I've taken in. I never wanted Matthew and Vinessa to know what happened to me or know how weak I once was, but it didn't seem to bother them one bit, and their opinion of me didn't change. I just want you to know that I'm here because I truly understand if you need to talk about it. The men who've abused you will face Judgment Day someday, and they'll have to answer for their sins. A little birdie told me you want to start calling me Dad, and that makes me feel like there's hope and that you want to start anew, which is progress."

Kaelyn looked up at her foster father with tears that formed in her eyes.

"I do," she answered. "And I do."

Michael knew she was coming around now, and he smiled toward her with warmth, but he stayed quiet as he knew she had something to say.

"All I've ever wanted were parents I felt safe with, parents to love me and accept me as I am. I know you're a good guy, a good father, and I want you to be mine. On my second night here, Daniel actually approached me about you. He said he knew I saw how you handled him the night before, and he wanted to make sure that his bad actions didn't reflect negatively on my view of you. He had nothing but good things to say about you, and coming from someone like him, that kind of meant a lot to me. I've been trying to get over my trust issues, and it helps when everyone you know speaks highly of you and Alice, and I'm always being told I couldn't have ended up with better parents."

Michael couldn't help but smile at her words.

"You're safe with us. I'd never let anything bad happen to you, and neither would any of your brothers, *including* Denver." Kaelyn now avoided eye contact, which told Michael she wasn't ready to discuss her biological brother. "You're accepted, and you're most *certainly* loved. We all love you, and we want to keep you. We want to adopt you."

Kaelyn now looked back up at Michael with joy in her eyes.

"Really? Wait, what about Matt?" she inquired.

Michael somehow knew she was going to bring Matthew up.

"Matthew was both right and wrong about what he said. He feels very strongly about family, so that's why he's on Denver's side about this whole complicated situation. Both Alice and I didn't want to give Timothy up, but Matthew reminded us that Tim's mother deserved a second chance because she'd gotten sober, she got a job and a decent place in a safe neighborhood. Matthew also understands that Denver deserves that very same chance. Matthew's heart is in the right place, but his head isn't. He doesn't understand how quickly this situation could turn dangerous. Of all the fosters we've taken in, you're the one who's in a unique position, one we've never encountered before."

Kaelyn listened carefully to his words. She kept eye contact with him as well.

"Your parents' murderer is a dangerous man. Your caseworker told Alice and me that he's also responsible for killing your mother's family by arson. Your mother almost died in a house fire with all her sisters and their parents, but he made sure she didn't by pretending to rescue her and take her to the hospital, where she then supposedly met your father. This criminal was obsessed with your mother. For as long as Denver carries his first name, his safety is compromised until the criminal is dead, but something tells me the man would rather come after you. After all, you're the spitting image of your mother."

Kaelyn was now scared. Her caseworker never told her *anything* like this. She knew Michael was brutally honest with her. She didn't know what to say, though. She just kept listening to his words.

"As you know, Denver's been *very* adamant about us adopting you. All he wants is to see you safe and happy. He's made his peace with this situation, I think, but I'm not sure it's in your best interest to volunteer for bone marrow donation."

"I really don't want to talk about that right now," Kaelyn replied as she avoided eye contact.

Michael saw the tears of disappointment in her eyes. He decided to respect her wish.

"Matthew, in time, will understand that adoption really is the best choice for you at this point. He still loves you just as much as we do. Just ignore his anger for now, and he'll come around."

Kaelyn understood and nodded.

"Let's do something, just you and me," Michael suggested as he now changed the subject and looked at her artwork. "I've got an idea!"

Kaelyn watched as he stood up and walked towards her easel and canvas pad.

"Do you mind if I draw on one of your blank pieces?" Michael asked Kaelyn.

"No, not at all!" Kaelyn said.

"Okay, great, because you're my subject!" Michael exclaimed as he turned the easel away from her, pulled up a chair, and turned to a blank page.

Kaelyn watched him for a good half hour though she couldn't see the artwork until he finished drawing.

"Okay, come take a look," Michael said.

Kaelyn got off the bed and moved towards the easel. She quickly realized Michael drew caricatures of her and him surfing on the waters and laughing.

"Wow, this is amazing!" she exclaimed as she was in awe of how real yet cartoonish it still looked. "I didn't know you could draw!"

"My two skills in art lie in architecture and caricatures," Michael admitted. "Hey, are you working tomorrow?"

"Actually, no, why?"

"Let's go surfing, just you and me. What do you say? Alice said you're one of her quickest learners yet."

"Well, I'm not that good yet," Kaelyn started to say, but Michael spoke up again.

"Ah, don't worry about it. You're fine! You've got all the basics down. Now you just need the practice. It's all about the fun, dear!"

Kaelyn smiled wide at this and nodded. They both knew this was what they needed to strengthen their bond as father and daughter.

"Okay, I'm down with that," she said.

"Alright, then set your alarm for daylight because we're going to catch the sunrise. This weekend is supposed to be a fantastic weekend for surfing!"

Kaelyn watched as Michael stood up and returned to the door.

"Wait!" she called, which caused him to turn around and face her. "Thank you for cheering me up … Dad."

Michael was delighted to hear this.

"That's what I'm here for, dear," he said. "I don't know if you ate anything on the beach, but we didn't have any set dinner plans, so be sure you get something to eat before you head to bed, alright?"

Kaelyn nodded in acknowledgment.

"Good night," he finished.

"Good night," she replied.

Michael smiled with warmth for a few moments before he then disappeared down the hall. Kaelyn was starting to feel good about this situation, especially when Michael told her they wanted to adopt her. After a good minute of silence, there was another knock on the door. Kaelyn looked up in response and saw her sister.

"Hey, Kay, is it too soon to ask you if you want to have a Girl's Night Out with me, and with a few of my friends, at a bonfire on the beach?" Vinessa asked.

"Actually, no, I'd love to go to the beach," Kaelyn replied.

Vinessa now beamed with joy.

"Yay, get dressed! I'll see you downstairs!"

"Okay," Kaelyn replied as Vinessa now closed the door to give Kaelyn a few moments of privacy.

Fifteen minutes later, the girls were on their walk to the beach.

"Hey, I just wanted to formally apologize to you for not telling you sooner about the truth of your past," Vinessa began to apologize, though Kaelyn interrupted.

"No worries. Dad gave me a little more information that's since made me realize it was better for Denver to tell me the truth. At least the family can claim plausible deniability, should you ever be called into court about it or something. I know you guys all meant well. I'm sorry if I blew things way out of proportion."

Vinessa beamed another one of her famous bright smiles, though she hugged her sister this time.

"I'm so glad we worked this out!" she exclaimed. "And you don't need to apologize for feeling the way you have the right to feel. I love you, Kay!"

Kaelyn felt a lot of sisterly love, and it was just what she needed right now.

"Aw, I love you too!" Kaelyn replied as she returned the hug and gave Vinessa an extra squeeze. "I'm *so* hungry. Do you think we can stop by Chey's Fries and Pups? I could *so* totally go for a hot dog with some loaded fries."

"Uhm, *yes*!" Vinessa replied with a giggle. "They close in a half-hour, though, so we betta gets to steppin'!"

"I'll race ya," Kaelyn challenged with a smirk. "Loser pays!"

"Oh, you're *so* on!" Vinessa replied as she now let go of her sister and ran off.

Kaelyn was quick to catch up to her in a sprint, though both girls giggled as they then ran neck and neck towards the boardwalk.

CHAPTER
THIRTY-SIX

Both girls called it a tie when they reached the line for Chey's Fries and Pups, so they decided to split the bill. Kaelyn paid for Vinessa's platter of mini corn dogs, while Vinessa paid for Kaelyn's loaded French fries oozing with delicious cheddar and white cheddar cheese sauce, sour cream and bacon, all topped with creamy cucumber ranch dressing. They agreed to share each other's dishes while they waited for Vinessa's friends at the bonfire. Fifteen minutes later, the other girls showed up, and Kaelyn and Vinessa shared their food with them as well. Hip-hop music was blasting, and beer was being passed around among the people. Kaelyn was down with the way things were going tonight. She was quick to grab a beer, and Vinessa smirked.

"I know how you feel, girl," she said as she also grabbed a beer.

"We've also got some grass," added Callie, another blonde friend of Vinessa's.

"That's perfect! That's a way to start my night," Kaelyn stated as she opened her beer and took her first sip from it.

"Girl, you know it!" Vinessa exclaimed.

All the girls enjoyed themselves for quite a while. Before they realized it, eleven o'clock rolled around, and Vinessa spoke up again.

"Alright, ladies, Mom said if she caught us here past eleven, we'd be in big trouble, so Callie, you still on for the sleepover?"

"Yes, but Sadie's driving us back. I'm too high," Callie answered with a giggle.

While Callie was eighteen, she still recognized that they had to be responsible for getting home safely. Sadie was a seventeen-year-old brunette, and she was the only one of the seven girls who stayed completely sober tonight.

"Then we better get out of here and leave now because you know I only have a junior license. I can't get caught driving past curfew," Sadie reminded before she turned to Kaelyn. "You comin' with us?"

"No, thanks. I'm just gonna finish my beer and head back to the house," Kaelyn replied as she turned to Vinessa. "Text me when you get to Callie's?"

"Yup," was Vinessa's response as she hugged her sister. "Have a good night, sis."

"You too."

Kaelyn watched as Vinessa and her friends took off, and then she looked around her to study her surroundings. She sensed the mood of the party changing, though dead straight ahead, she caught something she hadn't expected to see. Two model-like girls had Daniel pressed against a large boulder that started at the edge of the boardwalk. One of the girls, a redhead, was after his lips and his neck. The other girl, a brunette, was eager to unbuckle his belt as her lips were on his chest.

None of them had any drinks, though they undoubtedly enjoyed each other's presence. Daniel's head rested against the rocks, and his eyes remained closed as his hands were in the girls' hair, and he had a huge grin of pleasure plastered across his face. Kaelyn decided that before he'd open his eyes and catch her here on the beach, she'd turn around and walk away in the opposite direction. She walked along the edge of the water with her flip-flops in one hand while she carried her beer in the other.

She drowned out the hip-hop music playing in the background as she looked out upon the waters. She heard waves crashing against the rocks in the distance, and the water came in up to her ankles. A gust of wind picked up and whipped her hair around in her face. She smiled as the scent of the salty air brought upon her a sense of peace. After she took another sip of her beer, she realized she was walking around people who were either getting high, making out with their significant others or both. She just kept walking until she got to the cove, though. At that point, she heard a very familiar voice. It belonged to Jen.

"Oh, Matt!" moaned Jen in pleasure.

Kaelyn then walked around the boulders to find her foster brother making out with their co-worker. Matthew had Jen pushed against the rocks, and she had her legs wrapped around his waist. Kaelyn saw that Matthew buried his face in Jen's neck.

"Oh, Matt, you're so big!" Jen moaned again. "Oh!"

Neither of them knew Kaelyn was in their presence, though she wasn't visible either. She remained hidden behind the rocks. Kaelyn couldn't believe what she heard, though. She also couldn't believe she still had her eyes on the couple.

"Oh, yes, bite me!" Jen demanded.

Matthew growled into Jen's neck, and Jen moaned even more.

"Call me your dirty little whore!" Jen added.

Matthew got a little more aggressive as he also made sounds of pleasure.

"You dirty little whore!" he exclaimed. "Ugh, you feel so good!"

Kaelyn realized this wasn't a make-out session, after all. Jen and Matthew were having sex, and it was pretty passionate. She couldn't understand why Matthew kept going back to Jen if he hated her so much unless it was just about the sex. Kaelyn refused to watch any more of this because Matthew was her foster brother. So, she walked away and decided this was something to keep to herself. When she walked back to where she was, she ran into Alex, and he had a woman wrapped around his waist, and she was pining over him. Alex stopped in his tracks when he saw Kaelyn, and she did the same when she saw him.

"Really?" Kaelyn asked.

"What?" Alex said with an attitude. "You're the one who dumped me, and I've decided I'm not going to dwell on it."

Kaelyn couldn't believe this.

"You're better than this, Alex," she replied, which then received a sigh from him.

"Goodbye, Dakota," Alex said as he attempted to walk away, but Kaelyn stopped him in his tracks.

She pulled him by the collar of his shirt, and the woman wrapped around his arms defended him.

"Hey, watch it!" she replied in a whiny voice.

"Back off, *Barbie!*" Kaelyn warned through clenched teeth with fire in her eyes.

The blonde chick immediately stepped back, and Kaelyn now had a tighter grip on Alex.

"Don't *ever* call me that again," she warned.

"Or what?" Alex answered as he tried to free himself from her grip, but Kaelyn's grip was so tight her knuckles were white. "That is your name, *Dakota.*"

Kaelyn then poured her can of beer over Alex's head. Alex was shocked by this, and knowing that she caught him off guard, Kaelyn shoved Alex hard enough that he stumbled backward and landed on his ass and elbows. Alex was speechless by her strength.

"*David,*" was all Kaelyn said as she glared down into his eyes.

Alex realized he should never call Kaelyn by her birth name, and he sighed and spoke once he got back on his feet.

"Alright, alright! I'm sorry for calling you that," he apologized. "But did you have to soak me in alcohol?"

"Yes, because you're being an asshole. What's happening to you, Alex?"

"*You're* what's happening to me!" Alex fired back as he stepped towards her and was now mere inches from her face.

Kaelyn pulled her face back a few inches and slapped Alex on the cheek, which threw him off. Kaelyn couldn't help the tears in her eyes, though she made sure Alex didn't see them, as she turned her back to him and walked off in silence. Later on, she sat on the porch swing and then saw Matthew come home. He walked up the steps of the porch, and Kaelyn realized Matthew hadn't seen her there because he just walked right up to the front door and took out his keys. It was dark outside, though, and the outside garage light was off.

"I couldn't figure out why you continue to see Jen," she spoke, which caused Matthew to jump nearly out of his skin.

"*Jeee*sus!" he exclaimed as he placed a hand on his heart while he turned in the direction of the porch swing. "What the hell, Kay?"

Kaelyn just ignored his question as she continued talking.

"Then I realized … she's your dirty little whore, and the sex must be *really* good."

Her statement angered Matthew, and he walked towards her.

"Are you *spying* on me?" he questioned as he approached her.

"No, no, absolutely not!" Kaelyn replied with a relaxed giggle. "I just happened to come across you and Jen having—"

"First of all, you shouldn't have even been on the beach tonight. Tonight was an open party."

"Oh, don't I know that," Kaelyn replied with a huge grin. "But whatever, it was still entertaining. Wouldn't you agree?"

Matthew knew that Kaelyn was drunk and high, and he sighed.

"*Never* go to one of those parties again," he warned. "And *don't* ever watch me like you did tonight."

"Aw, why not?" Kaelyn asked with a pout. "Hot, passionate sex is such a big turn-on."

Matthew knew that she was teasing him and poking fun at him, and he was pretty annoyed with her. He stepped even closer to Kaelyn now. Then he placed his hands on the back of the swing on both sides of her head.

"*Promise* me, Kay," he commanded as his face was now inches from hers.

"Why *should* I?" Kaelyn replied. "If you can go to the beach, and Vinny can go, why can't I?"

"Wait, Vinessa was there?" Matthew inquired. "Is she still there? Why are you just telling me this now?"

"Would you relax? Damn!" Kaelyn replied. "She's at a sleepover at Callie's. Besides, she got permission from Mom for us to be on the beach until curfew. Then she left with her friends and headed to her sleepover."

Matthew sighed in frustration.

"Vinessa knows I don't allow her at those open parties without a chaperone. Even Daniel agrees about keeping all the Denner women from going to those kinds of parties without one of us because those parties are crowded with unsavory characters."

"Yeah, *maybe* … but you were too busy fucking your dirty little whore to notice either of us were there," Kaelyn replied.

"She might be a bitch, but you don't get to call her ... you know what? I'm not going to bother fighting with you on this. Just stay out of my life!"

Kaelyn couldn't believe he'd said that. His words cut deep.

"Well, *that's* going to be next to impossible because everyone's agreed on adoption."

Matthew couldn't believe the smile that remained on her face. He thought for sure the last part of his statement would have her in tears, but he guessed wrong. The smile on her face pissed him off even more. He racked his brain, trying to figure out how he could get rid of her, but then the idea suddenly hit him.

"Not anymore," he argued as he now kissed her on the lips with a lot of anger and passion.

Matthew took Kaelyn by surprise with this, and his lips on hers sobered her quite fast.

"What the hell?" she replied in shock as she pushed him away from her and stood up.

"Go ahead," Matthew dared with a massive grin now plastered to his face. "Tell Mom and Dad. Then I'll be rid of you *for good*."

He was pleased with the new reaction of tears in her eyes, but he was thrown off balance by what happened next. Kaelyn slapped him hard across the face, and the sheer force of her hand completely turned his head to the side. Stunned, Matthew stood frozen, and he was silent for a few moments before he slowly turned his face toward Kaelyn's again. When their eyes met again, sparks instantly flew between the pair, and now Kaelyn brought Matthew's face towards hers. Matthew knew she was pulling him in for a kiss, so he grabbed her by the waist and pressed her body against his. Neither of them couldn't help but moan into the kiss when their lips locked. It was fervent and wild with passion. Kaelyn pushed him towards the front door, and she opened it when she broke from Matthew's hold.

Matthew followed her inside, and he closed the door. When the coast was clear, Kaelyn led him to the Chiller room with a firm grasp on his shirt. When she closed the Chiller door, Matthew then pushed her against it and locked it as he brushed his lips with Kaelyn's. She immediately gasped in pleasure and grabbed Matthew by his hair. He couldn't help but unbutton her shorts, and then he pulled them off as he still held her against the door. Kaelyn quickly realized how hot and sexy Matthew was, for she'd never seen him in this light until now. Matthew grabbed her by the legs, and she jumped onto his hips while she wrapped her legs around him. He then carried her away from the door and towards the nearest sofa.

CHAPTER
THIRTY-SEVEN

A little while later, Kaelyn and Matthew found themselves on the floor, side by side and naked under the covers from the sofa. They were both out of breath, so they remained where they were until they returned to their normal steady breathing. It amazed Kaelyn to see how different Alex and Matthew were in the way they had sex. On the other hand, Matthew felt awkward, and he was speechless, for he didn't know what to say to her. After a few minutes of silence, she looked over at him, and he got up.

"Uhm," she began as he started getting dressed, but then she too realized she didn't know what to say.

Once he put on his khaki shorts, he looked down at her.

"What?" he asked with curiosity.

Kaelyn didn't like how cold he sounded. She sat up but kept her body covered with the blanket from the sofa.

"What's up with you?" she asked.

Matthew didn't know how to answer this question because it was a complicated one.

"Nothing," he replied, which he decided would be the simple way to answer this question. "Would you, uh, mind getting dressed? I can't talk to you like this."

Matthew turned his back to Kaelyn so that she could remove the blanket freely while getting dressed. He remained silent as he listened for the shuffling of her movements. After about a minute, she spoke up.

"You can turn around now."

Matthew looked over his shoulder, and when he confirmed she was fully dressed, sans her flip-flops, he then turned around to face her.

"Are you going to tell Mom and Dad about this?" Matthew asked as he folded his arms across his chest.

"Oh, that's a big, fat hell no!" she exclaimed in a whispered tone. "This gets out to *no one*!"

"Good," Matthew replied with a serious tone. "Because this can't happen again."

Kaelyn stood there all confused, and Matthew couldn't help but stare at her gorgeous body, so he cleared his throat.

"Wait a minute," Kaelyn began as she was perplexed. "Please tell me you didn't just use me?"

Matthew was stunned by her words, and her words cut deep. He scoffed as he avoided eye contact, though Kaelyn caught something in his eyes before he left her gaze.

"What do you want from me, Kaelyn?" he inquired as he met her eyes again. "Do you want me to be your brother or your lover?"

Kaelyn didn't know what to say to this.

"You don't know, do you?"

Kaelyn couldn't answer any of his questions, except the last one, where she shook her head in silence.

"Yeah, that's what I thought," he spoke with sarcasm, which she didn't like. "I suggest you figure it out before Mom and Dad start the adoption process."

Kaelyn watched as Matthew turned his back to her again, but she called out to him this time.

"Matt."

He then turned around again, this time with annoyance written on his face.

"*You* started this by provoking me," he stated as he approached her and kept his eyes locked with hers. "Look, don't get me wrong. This was … *amazing* … but I know you well enough to know that as soon as I walk out of here, you'll regret this whole thing. You've made it quite clear that you want to claim us as your family legally. So, why don't I just make it easy for you? I *don't* want to be your brother, but if that's what you really want, then your wish is my command."

Kaelyn was shocked by Matthew's words, and she watched as he walked away to grab his shirt.

"So, wait … you *honestly* don't want me to be your sister?" she questioned. "After all this time?"

Matthew sighed as he froze in his steps for a few moments before he spoke again.

"After what just happened, I could never see you like a sister, but if that's what you need, then fine. I'll treat you like a sister, but only on one condition. *Don't* shut Denver out. *You* may not need him, but *he* needs you." Kaelyn just stood there in silence, though Matthew knew that she wanted to say something. "What?"

Kaelyn just shook her head no while she looked away with a hand on her hip.

"I know you well enough to know you have something to say, so just say it," Matthew said as he went over to the door and picked his shirt up off the floor.

Kaelyn then looked back over at Matthew, and she sighed before she spoke up.

"You called me your sister on day one," she finally spoke. "You were *happy* about it. Something's changed with you, and I can't figure out what it is. You've been quite distant lately, too. What's going on?"

Matthew sighed as he found it hard to believe she still couldn't put two and two together. He realized he'd have no choice but do a show and tell. So, he dropped his shirt and turned toward her. Before Kaelyn realized it, he'd grabbed her face with sweet tenderness, and then he gave her a slow, passionate kiss. Kaelyn, completely thrown off by this, stumbled backward as he kissed her, but Matthew made sure she didn't lose her balance. When he finally pulled his lips from hers, his eyes were closed, and he pressed his forehead against hers.

"What's changed is who I want to be when I'm around you," he whispered as he still held her face in his hands. "All I want is to hold you, and kiss you, and make sweet love to you all night long. I want to be your lover, your protector, I want to be everything to you, but I *can't*. While we're living under the same roof as brother and sister, I can't do what I want and be what I want to be with you because it's wrong. If you went to go live with Denver, then everything would be fine. I know deep down, though, that you living with Denver isn't an option."

Kaelyn was at a total loss for words. She finally understood what his problem's been, though. He was in love with her.

"I'm in love with you, Kaelyn, and I'm not supposed to be, which is why I've been spending most of my time with Jen, and it's also why I'm going to ask her to move in with me in a place that she and I can call our own. As evidenced by what just happened, it's clear that I no longer have the strength to keep my hands off you. The longer you're here with us, and the more I get to know you, the harder it is that I'm falling for you. I'm afraid that if we continue to live together under the same roof, I'm going to make a mistake in front of the others, and we both know that can't happen."

Kaelyn couldn't help the tears that flowed down her cheeks.

"This stays here, with us, in this room, and it goes *nowhere* else," Matthew said as he let go of her face and pulled away from her.

Kaelyn watched as Matthew turned around for the final time and grabbed his shirt once more. Then, he walked out of the room without looking back, and he closed the door behind him. It was easy for her to see that Matthew tried like hell to fight his feelings for her. They both knew deep down, though, that what they did was so wrong. After fixing the room and taking a quick shower, she went back downstairs and then grabbed a throw blanket from the couch. She returned to the porch swing and swung on it while stargazing until she fell asleep.

A FEW HOURS HAD PASSED, AND MICHAEL WOKE UP KAELYN.

"Hey there, sleepyhead," he said. "What are you doing, sleeping out here?"

"Oh, I couldn't sleep last night, so I came out here to watch the stars, and … well, I guess I fell asleep."

"Well, I'm glad you got some shuteye. Are you still good to catch some waves at dawn?" Michael asked.

Kaelyn instantly perked up at this.

"Yes, that's just what I need to start my day!" she exclaimed as she jumped to her feet.

"Alright, well, let's get inside and change into our suits and grab our boards," Michael suggested. "Oh, and you might want to try going to the bathroom before we leave. The restrooms at the beach won't open until eight."

Kaelyn nodded, and they both headed back inside. Before they knew it, they were on the beach with their surfboards, and both were fresh and ready for the day. There were even a couple of other surfers on the beach, also prepared for the sunrise. Kaelyn and Michael stood there for a few moments, though, and admired the sun now peeking out from behind the eastern mountains.

"This is *so* beautiful!" Kaelyn said in awe.

"I know. This right here is one of my favorite spots because the sun is majestic here, both in its sunrise and sunset. It's magnificent, really," Michael added. "We'll wait 'til the sun hits the water, and then we'll go in."

Kaelyn giggled in excitement, and once the sun's rays reflected off the ocean, they both then ran off into the waters. That was how they spent their early morning. They spent a couple of hours bonding over their love of being on and in the water. Between Alice teaching her how to ride the waves with the surfboard and Michael showing his passion for surfing, Kaelyn quickly grew to love the sport as well. Before either of them knew it, the shops on the beach started opening up, and then the boardwalk came to life. At about nine o'clock, both Michael and Kaelyn were ready for some breakfast. After ordering omelets and blueberry crepes, Kaelyn spoke up.

"Can I ask you something?" she asked as her face turned serious.

"You can ask me anything, dear."

"What all do you know about Denver?"

Michael knew she was curious to learn more about her biological brother, and he knew it was only natural, so he was more than happy to answer any questions if he had the answers to them.

"Well, everything I know about him is through Vinessa and his adopted parents," he said. "Denver's a sweetheart, and you know this, but he has PTSD from witnessing your birth parents' murder and from being torn away from you when you were adopted out of the system. Even though he was only four at the time, he still remembers all of it as if it happened yesterday. He can recall every detail of both events, and if he forgets to take his medication, he'll suffer from nightmares and wake up in cold sweats in the middle of the night. I've seen it happen when he's slept over at our house."

Kaelyn was heartbroken to hear this.

"Alice and I go way back with his adopted parents, Mr. and Mrs. Knight. They've tried years and years of therapy and hypnotherapy to make him forget, but his soul is …"

Kaelyn watched as Michael froze in mid-sentence before he then resumed what he was saying.

"The Knights said Denver was mute when they first adopted him until he protected his adopted sister, Rori, from their babysitter on one awful day. Even then, he only talked to Rori and sometimes called her Dakota after waking from his nightmares. He refused to talk to anyone else until he met Vinny. He'd go to the ends of the earth to protect her and his adopted siblings, and I think it's because he *can*, whereas he couldn't protect you or your parents."

"What were you going to say about his soul?" Kaelyn asked.

"I was going to say damaged, but I think that might be too strong of a word," Michael answered.

"Maybe tormented might be a better word?" Kaelyn suggested. "Or perhaps scarred?"

"Either one works," Michael replied. "Why do you ask about him? Are you having second thoughts?"

"I don't know," Kaelyn replied. "Matthew said last night that just because I may not need Denver, it doesn't change the fact that Denver still needs me, and I think Matthew might be right about that."

Michael nodded in understanding.

"Do you think that would be wise?" he asked. "Getting involved with Denver, I mean?"

"I don't know," was Kaelyn's response. "I'm honestly thrilled to know he's alive and that he didn't die with our parents, but the whole 'murderer' part of the story scares me."

Michael watched as Kaelyn folded her arms across her chest as she leaned back into her chair.

"Truth be told, Kaelyn, I don't want you to be too worried about that," Michael said. "I'm sorry if we all made a big deal about your safety. Social Services has reassured Alice and me that *if* the criminal escapes from prison, the state will notify them *right away*, and Social Services is obligated to notify us. Several of your adopted siblings are on the police force, and one of them *is* the chief, so you're *well-*protected. You also have the rest of us Denners for protection detail as well. Besides, *that man* is locked up in one of the most secured prisons in the States. Only one man had ever escaped in its history, and that was well over a hundred years ago. Davis Anderson is locked up tight until his number is up."

Kaelyn was silent for a few moments as she didn't know what to say.

"I just want you to get that worry off your shoulders. Miss Wayne told us that you're *always* worried about the future, but I want you to focus on the present. Your future is safe from harm and secured from financial woes. You can choose any college, university, or Ivy League school of your choice without *ever* falling into debt. You'll be able to choose any profession of your choice. You'll even be able to purchase or build your own dream home, and you'll be able to buy yourself a brand new car and travel the world and go to places you dreamed of someday visiting."

Kaelyn continued to listen to Michael's words, and she smiled.

"So, tell me, Kay. If you had the option right now to go anywhere in the world, where would you want to travel first?" he asked.

Kaelyn mirrored her foster Dad's smile and spoke up.

"I'd first go to Peru and visit Machu Picchu, and then Brazil. I kind of would love to spend a year in Spain too. I also want to travel the world and all four oceans via cruise, and then I'd want to end the cruise with backpacking throughout Europe," she answered.

Michael knew this answer made her happy, as she now smiled from ear to ear, which was the biggest smile he'd seen on her in a while.

"There you go," he replied as he pulled her from her train of thoughts to focus on him. "It's time to stop worrying and start living."

Kaelyn's smile returned to a soft one, and now their food arrived.

"Would you be upset with me if I said I wanted both you *and* Denver in my life?" she asked as she picked up her fork but froze her hand when she kept her eyes on her foster father.

"Honestly, no, because I understand why. He's your biological brother, and you're naturally curious about your family. He's the only one who can answer questions about your parents that Social Services couldn't possibly answer, let alone anyone else. However, if you have him around, word that you two are reunited *cannot* get back to Social Services. Alice and I *don't* like going behind their backs like this, but we don't want to lose you either. If they find out you know the truth of your past—"

"They'll take me away from you, and I'd never get to see any of you again. As much as I'd love to call them out on their lies, I promise I won't let them know what I know."

Michael was glad to know they were on the same page.

"Okay, good," he replied.

Kaelyn watched as her foster father picked up his fork and knife, and she paid attention to the way he cut his omelet.

"I have a question for you," she stated as she took note of how he cut his omelet into small square pieces, though he looked up at her in response. "Would you take in anymore fosters after me?"

He sat back in his seat for a moment as he studied the hope in his foster daughter's face.

"Alice and I want to have a discussion with all of you about that. I guess now's a good time as any, but it stays between us for now until we can get the whole family together, okay?" Kaelyn nodded, but she didn't like the sound of where this conversation was headed. "After Alice and I signed that contract about keeping the truth from you, we had a long talk. To be honest with you, we were uncomfortable with keeping the truth from you. Alice and I don't like lies and secrets."

Kaelyn remained quiet, though she kept her gaze on Michael.

"We've decided you'll be the last foster we'll ever take in. Once we adopt you, we're not going to renew our foster license."

"Oh," was Kaelyn's shocked response as it grew silent between the two of them. "Okay."

Kaelyn now watched as her foster father looked down at his food with a smile. He then leaned in toward his plate and began eating.

CHAPTER
THIRTY-EIGHT

A month had passed before anyone saw Denver again, except for Amber. She spent so much time at his place that she had her own key and practically lived there. With the news of no longer being in remission, Denver had grown depressed. He quit both his jobs and refused to leave his apartment, even for doctor appointments. Amber tried everything to cheer him up, though she failed at every attempt. She got desperate enough that she finally reached out to Rori, whom she'd become close friends with since Denver introduced the two of them. When Rori came over, Amber felt like she had no choice but to reveal Denver's diagnosis, which Denver insisted on keeping from his family until he was ready to tell them. When Rori learned the dreadful news, she couldn't help but run to her big brother's room, and she saw him lying on his bed with his back to her.

"Denver!" she called as she approached him. "Denver, you need to get your ass out of bed right now, and you need to get on the phone with Dr. Hart's office. If I have to drag your lazy ass out of bed and take you to your appointments myself, I'll—"

"What's the point?" Denver inquired as he turned his back to her and now eyed the opposite wall.

Rori and Amber exchanged looks before they walked back into the hall together.

"We need Vinessa," Rori whispered. "She's his best friend, and she's great at pulling him out of this mood. Do you know where she lives?"

Amber nodded, though before she could get a word in, Denver spoke up.

"I can hear you," he stated in a monotone. "And nothing you do or say is gonna change my mind."

"Oh, yeah?" Rori replied as she turned in his direction with an arm on her hip now. However, Denver's back was still to her. "How 'bout we bring Kaelyn into the fold?"

Denver looked over his shoulder as he sat up for a moment.

"Leave her out of this, Rori. There's nothing she can do for me. She'd have to be eighteen years old to donate bone marrow, and that's a few years away. All it would do is raise a red flag to CPS, and they *will* remove her from Alice and Doc's care. She *deserves* a family, and I'm not ripping that away from her. So, leave her out of this, and just leave me alone."

Once Denver resumed his position with his back to both ladies, they exchanged looks again, though Amber had an idea.

"I'll go get them," she mouthed silently so that Denver wouldn't hear her.

Rori nodded in acknowledgment and walked back into Denver's room. Amber got her California driver's license now, and sometimes Denver let her drive. So, she took his car keys and left.

WHEN AMBER PULLED UP TO THE DENNER HOUSE AND PARKED THE car, she saw that Vinessa, Kaelyn, and some guy were all hanging out and laughing, until Vinessa's eyes fell on Denver's car. Vinessa didn't know the girl that came out of the car, though. Amber walked across the sidewalk and approached them as she took the steps to the porch.

"Vinessa?" she called as she met Vinessa's curious gaze.

Both of the ladies were sitting on the swing while Daniel sat on the porch banister with an arm relaxed around a support beam.

"Yes?" Vinessa replied as the smile left her face. "Who are you, and what are you doing with Denver's car?"

"I'm sorry that we haven't officially had the chance to meet yet, but I'm Amber."

"Ah, so *you're* the new girlfriend." Amber was at a loss for words when Vinessa spoke, though Vinessa continued. "You know, he never lets anyone drive his car. How'd you get him to give you the keys?"

The unusual harshness in Vinessa's tone told Daniel and Kaelyn that she was jealous of Amber. Kaelyn wanted to say something, but judging by the fact that Denver wasn't here, she sensed that something was wrong.

"Sometimes he lets me drive, but right now, he doesn't know I've left. I need your help."

Vinessa immediately stood up from the swing.

"He's depressed again, isn't he?"

When Amber nodded, this also prompted Kaelyn off the swing.

"What's going on?" Kaelyn asked with worry.

"Rori's at the apartment, trying everything she can to get him out of bed and go to his doctor. He stopped his treatments and he won't eat or drink anything anymore."

"Why didn't you tell me sooner?" Vinessa asked with an angry tone as tears filled her eyes.

Daniel jumped off the banister and stepped in front of his sisters. He sensed Vinessa was about to go into a hissy fit.

"Come on, 'Ness," he spoke as he stepped in front of her. "She's here, isn't she?"

Had it not been for the few birds chirping around in some nearby tree while a car made a windy noise as it passed by, the silence would have been deafening.

"Take me to him," Vinessa demanded as she kept her eyes locked with Amber's.

"I'm coming along," Kaelyn stated.

"I'll take you," Daniel said to both his sisters.

"I'm going with her," Vinessa said as she now took off towards the car.

Amber and Kaelyn were at a loss for words, though Daniel spoke up.

"I'll take Kay with me then, and we'll just follow you and 'Ness."

Amber nodded in acknowledgment and then turned back toward the car. Kaelyn followed Daniel to his car, and when they backed out of the driveway, they followed Amber and Vinessa.

Kaelyn couldn't help but stare over at Daniel. He felt her eyes on her too.

"What?"

"You're full of surprises," she commented, which only elicited a scoff from Daniel while he kept his eyes on the road. "You care about him."

"What makes you think that?"

"You could've let me ride with Amber and Vin, but you wanted to come along, which means you care about him."

Daniel became quiet for a time, though Kaelyn knew he was deep in thought. Before she knew it, she saw worry and fear flicker in his eyes.

"He's our brother," he muttered in a calm, quiet voice, though she still heard him. "We can't let him give up."

Kaelyn was amazed by Daniel's response, and when she saw the tears in his eyes, which he fiercely held onto, she knew Daniel loved Denver. She never knew Daniel to think of Denver as a brother, for she never saw the two hanging out. Neither did Daniel—until now.

WHEN THEY ALL ARRIVED AT DENVER'S PLACE, THEY ALL HEADED UP the stairs together and walked into the apartment. Vinessa was the first person to dart for her best friend's room, as she knew he'd be in bed. Kaelyn and Daniel followed, and Amber did the same after she'd shut the front door.

"Denver, I'm gonna kill you!" was the first thing that came from Vinessa's mouth as she stomped into his room.

Denver sighed deeply in frustration as Rori let Vinessa approach him. She was the last person he wanted to see right now because he knew she wouldn't give up on him until he was on his own two feet and back in the doctor's office. Before he knew it, she'd approached his bed and punched him in the arm as hard as she could.

"Ow!" he exclaimed in total shock. "What the hell was that for?"

Everyone saw her punch of fury too.

"*That's* for not telling me you've stopped your damn treatments!" Daniel wanted to step in and calm down Vinessa's aggression, but even he knew not to fuck with Vinessa right now. "I didn't go to every door of every house in our community, and I didn't start a few charity runs through my cheerleading squad at school, and I certainly didn't raise hundreds of thousands of dollars for your medical treatments just for you to throw it all the fuck away!"

Then she threw another punch in the same spot on his arm. This time he got out of bed and stood in front of her.

"And *that's* for keeping me out of the loop!"

It was a rare sight to see Vinessa red in the face, so red that tears even threatened to escape from her hold. Just as Denver was about to say something, she threw him another angry punch.

"And *that's* for breaking the friendship pact we made a long time ago when you promised you'd *never* give up without a fight!"

Everyone watched as Vinessa burst into tears, and even Denver couldn't help but mirror them. He pulled her into his arms and silently held her for a few moments before he spoke up again.

"I'm sorry," he apologized in a calm voice. "I didn't mean to hurt you or upset you. But … the Leukemia's just gonna keep coming back until we find a match in the bone marrow registry. Knowing my luck, not even that would probably save me, even if I hadn't stopped all my treatment. So, tell me, what's the point of fighting for just a little extra life that'll probably be spent in pain and misery? I'm dying, Vin, and it's time I accepted it."

"But I love you!" Vinessa protested with anguish as she clung to her best friend and wept in his arms. "And I'm sorry for hitting you."

"I love you too, Ba-Ba," he replied as he held her and leaned his temple against hers. "And I forgive you."

Everyone in the room had tears in their eyes, even Daniel, though he kept his at bay. When Denver finally pulled from the hug, he then sat back down on his bed.

"There's something I need you to understand."

"Don't even go there!" Rori exclaimed as she now stood next to Vinessa.

Kaelyn approached Vinessa's free side, and Amber sat down next to Denver.

"We're not giving up on you," Amber spoke in a tender, loving voice. "Don't give up on yourself."

"I'm sorry if I've hurt you in any way," Kaelyn added. "I hope I haven't made you feel like I don't want you in my life because I do. I never knew you were still alive until you told me the truth a few weeks back. I want very much to get to know you as my brother. Please don't give up now."

Denver just wanted to break down and cry at her words, though he remained calm instead.

"You guys don't know what it's like to have Leukemia. It's truly an exhausting disease. You don't know what it's like to feel so weak all the time with never-ending fevers and nosebleeds and pain in the joints. I could go on, but in short, I'm just … *tired*."

It was quiet in the room for a few moments until Daniel walked toward the group.

"Can I have the room?" he asked the ladies.

All of them nodded and left the guys alone. Kaelyn stole a glance over at Daniel in the hallway for a moment before she closed the door.

"You've got a lot of women who love you," he noted as he turned to Denver.

"Yeah, I know, and they're all so stubborn too," Denver stated.

"They'll do practically anything for the people they love," Daniel added. "And I will too."

Daniel debated on whether or not he should start the conversation about the elephant in the room or if he should wait.

"Yeah, they will," Denver replied, not thinking anything of the last part of Daniel's statement. "So, listen. I know you're here to talk me into accepting a bone marrow donation from your friend. I highly doubt he'd even be a match."

Daniel was a little confused by this news. He submitted his test a couple of weeks ago.

"When's the last time you talked to Dr. Hart?"

"I don't know, a few weeks ago," Denver answered. "Why?"

Daniel didn't say anything at first. He just took his phone out of his pocket, and Denver watched as he punched in some numbers.

"What are you doing?" he asked.

Before he knew it, Daniel turned the speakerphone on, and then someone on the other end picked up.

"Hart's Oncology and Associates, Michelle speaking, how may I help you?"

"Hey, Michelle. It's Daniel Denner. I've got Denver Knight here in the room with me."

When Denver realized what Daniel was up to, he tried in a hushed voice to tell him to hang up, but Daniel refused to.

"Oh, that's wonderful! We've been hoping someone would be in touch. I'll transfer you over to Dr. Hart's line. *Please* don't hang up. Just bear with me for one moment, okay?"

"Anything for you, darling," Daniel replied with a mischievous smirk as he knew this was torture for Denver.

Denver tried to take the phone away from him, but Daniel kept it away from him.

"Hang up the phone now, or I'm gonna beat your face in!" Denver threatened.

"Never in a million years!" was Daniel's reply as he continued to keep the phone out of Denver's reach.

Just then, a voice came on the line.

"Denver?" Denver froze in his steps when he heard Dr. Hart's voice while his eyes locked with Daniel's. "Denver, I know you're there. We've been trying to reach you. Listen, we have a bone marrow match for you. We need you to come in right away. Come in today. Anytime today. My door's always open for you. Please?"

Denver was shocked when he heard this. He couldn't believe he had a match, and it wasn't Kaelyn. Now Daniel handed his phone over to him.

"I'll call you back," was Denver's only answer before he ended the call and threw the phone on the bed.

Daniel went to take back his phone, though Denver grabbed him by the collar of his shirt and threw him against his armoire.

"Dude, what the hell?"

"What gives you the right to reach out to my doctor's office and try to interfere with my medical treatment? Huh?"

Daniel didn't know what to say when he saw daggers in Denver's eyes.

"Answer me!"

The bedroom door opened again when Denver's angry voice was

heard from the living room. Daniel knew by the corner of his eyes that it was Kaelyn.

"I'm fine," he said out loud to her. "Why don't you ladies go for a walk in the park?"

"Are you sure?" Kaelyn asked.

"Leave us," Denver warned as he now met her gaze.

Kaelyn didn't know what was going on, though she nodded in acknowledgment of Daniel and Denver's request. Neither of the guys said anything, and they seemed to be in mutual agreement of waiting until the ladies left the apartment. When they heard the door open and shut, Daniel spoke up again.

"What I'm about to tell you *must* stay between us. If this gets out to anyone, even Kay, and *especially* Social Services, I fear Kay will be taken from all of us."

"What does any of this have to do with you interfering with my medical treatments?"

"You and Kaelyn are important to me. Kay's helped me to see who I want to be as a person, and she's helped me come a long way. You did too after you said what you said last month. I can't lose either of you. You two are family an—"

"Cut the bullshit, Daniel!" Denver interrupted as he once more shoved Daniel into his armoire. "Kay might be your foster sister, and someday soon, she'll be your adopted sister, but that doesn't make us brothers!"

Denver's words cut straight through Daniel's heart in a way that he hadn't expected. For reasons unknown to Denver, he saw the tears flicker in Daniel's eyes. For a moment, Denver didn't know what to say, didn't know how to react to this surprising new side of Daniel.

"Take out the contents of my left front pocket." This confused Denver, though Daniel kept talking. "I'm serious, man. Do it."

So, Denver did as he asked and pulled out two coins and a mini worn-out wooden cross.

"Go ahead and take a good look at them."

Curiously, Denver did, and when he let go of Daniel to look at the coins, he realized upon closer inspection that they were sobriety chips. One was a tri-plated chip in a deep rich red with the number three, and the other was a silver and gold plated chip with the number one.

"The red one's from NA, and I got it because of Kay. The other one's from AA, and believe it or not, I just got it yesterday because of you."

Denver was stunned. He never knew Daniel to have possession of any sobriety chip. Daniel was one of the biggest partiers in town who was also an asshole that moonlighted as a hardcore drug dealer.

"I carry them in my pocket at all times, especially when I've got the cravings," Daniel continued as he now took them back but kept his eyes on them for a few moments before he put them back in his pockets. "You're the only one that knows, so please keep that between us."

Denver nodded as he gave Daniel his space and turned toward his bed to sit down on the edge.

"This may sound strange, but I need you to go into my phone and check my email."

Denver looked over at Daniel with a raised eyebrow.

"Why?" he inquired.

"Because I know for a fact that you're not Kay's only biological brother, and you need to see it for yourself." Denver didn't like where Daniel was headed with this conversation. "Go ahead and look in my email. Go back to the 12th, and you'll see what I'm talking about."

Reluctantly, Denver did as he was instructed and soon found an email with the subject line regarding DNA test results. He clicked on the email and soon realized it was a DNA test for Daniel and Kaelyn.

"A month ago, you said something to me that struck a chord. Then I couldn't get it out of my head, and I had to do my research." Denver listened to Daniel, though his eyes were on the cellphone screen as he scrolled down to the bottom, where it gave the conclusive results. "I read your parents' court case against Davis Anderson. I read all the available documents. He has a record of raping your mother three times, and of those times, you and Kay were both—"

Before Daniel realized it, Denver was back in his face with both his hands resuming their grip on his collar.

"Go ahead," Denver challenged in a low and threatening tone. "I *dare* you to finish that sentence."

"I'm sorry, Denver," Daniel apologized calmly, though tears threatened to break free. "I'm sorry Davis Anderson left my erratic hairbrained mother and me. If he hadn't left my mom and me for his disturbing obsession with your mom, your parents, they would both be alive."

Denver was at a loss for words, and his own tears developed now. Anger flooded his veins until it came to a boiling point once he fully realized that the son of the man who murdered his parents was here and standing before him. He couldn't help himself. He threw Daniel to the floor and punched him right in the kisser. Daniel was shocked by this, but before he had a chance to recoup, Denver threw another punch.

Denver was filled with a rage he couldn't control, and although Daniel could easily rip him off and fight back, he didn't want to beat up a cancer patient, not one that he suspected to be his biological brother. So, he just let Denver take his anger out on him. As he threw punch after punch, Denver couldn't control any of his other emotions too. He soon screamed with tears that ran down his face. After the 11th blow, Denver pulled back his fist and realized how badly he'd beaten Daniel's face in. He knew the girls would ream him out for it when they returned from their walk. Daniel didn't move for a good minute, though he moaned in pain. Daniel could only open one eye, and when he did, he only looked straight into Denver's eyes.

"I know you hate me," Daniel whispered. "And I know you'd like to kill me … but would you at least take my bone marrow first?"

It was at this moment that Denver realized Daniel was his match, the match Dr. Hart couldn't wait to discuss with him. He still hovered over Daniel, only now, he wept. He honestly didn't know what to do with all the information he'd just learned in the last five minutes.

"Go!" he spoke as he picked Daniel up off the floor and pushed him back onto his own feet. Then he snatched Daniel's phone from the bed and shoved it into his chest. "Just fucking go! Get out of here!"

Daniel felt woozy, but he knew he needed to get out of there, stat. He made his way toward the door and left as soon as he could. When Denver saw him leave, he slammed his bedroom door shut, and then he locked it. He wailed in defeat as he slid down the door. He felt so guilty for what he did to Daniel, yet he was so angry after learning Daniel was Dakota's biological half-brother while he was also the son of Davis Anderson, the man who murdered their parents.

"Why?" he howled between his never-ending sobs with his head pressed against the door. "Why!"

CHAPTER
THIRTY-NINE

Denver sat in his chair in Dr. Hart's office as his leg bounced up and down as he waited for her. Amber sat with him in the chair next to him and tried to hold his hand for comfort, though that didn't seem to calm down his nervousness. It would be a good ten minutes before Doctor Hart walked into the room and greeted them both with a warm smile.

"Hey, you two, how's everything going?"

"I'm okay," Denver replied.

"Are you sure? You've been ignoring a lot of the phone calls I've made. I was about to make a house call if I got voicemail again."

"I know, and I'm really sorry for that," Denver apologized. "It's been a rough month."

Doctor Hart nodded in acknowledgment before she turned to look at Amber.

"I know who the donor is," Denver stated, which surprised Dr. Hart.

"Really?" she asked. "He explicitly told me he wanted his bone marrow donation to be anonymous."

"Seriously?" Dr. Hart nodded to Denver's question. "He came to my apartment yesterday and told me."

Dr. Hart was silent for a few minutes as she thought on this. Then she spoke up.

"He's an interesting individual. He came to my office out of the blue one day, introduced himself as Dakota's foster brother, and said he got my card from you after you laid it on the dining room table for Dr. Denner to contact me with. He gave me a story that, quite frankly, chilled me to my bones. He's a few years older than you, and he's very healthy. He gave me a letter to give to you, and he hoped you'd accept his donation as anonymous."

Amber and Denver exchanged curious looks before Denver met Doctor Hart's gaze again.

"He told me that he believes you to be his long-lost biological brother. He says he only found out about you just a short time ago and says he understands that you don't want anything to do with him. He told me that he'd promised to respect your wishes."

Denver watched as Dr. Hart then took an envelope out from his file, and she proceeded to hand it to him. However, Denver shook his head in denial.

"I don't have a biological brother, and if I did, I wouldn't want his bone marrow. I *refuse* to accept a vile monster who *murdered* my parents and destroyed our lives!"

Amber sighed as Denver stood up from his chair.

"Denver," she called. "I highly doubt he's biologically related to you. It's just … this young man wasn't raised by his natural parents. He only has two biological sisters and didn't even get to grow up with either of them. He wishes he could know for sure if you two are related."

"With all due respect, I don't want anything to do with him," was Denver's answer as he finally spoke up.

Amber and Denver both watched as Dr. Hart reached out to him with an envelope in hand. Rather than taking it, he just looked at it in silence.

"I really think you need to read this. If this letter doesn't change your mind, then we'll just wait until we can find another match. I have to be honest with you, though. Something tells me that he's the match we need for you and that we won't find another one in the time that we have left. Dakota surely can't be a donor without approval from the court, and a case like that could be months. You need healthy bone marrow *now*."

"I can't," Denver said as tears surfaced as he paced back and forth between Dr. Hart and Amber. "He showed me the DNA test results for him and Dakota yesterday. They're half-siblings!" This stunned Dr. Hart, though Denver continued. "Do you know what this means? It means David Anderson raped my mother, and the bastard got her pregnant with Dakota! After I told him to leave my apartment, I had to see it for myself and look up the original court case records."

Denver then moved toward the desk and leaned on it as he then approached Dr. Hart.

"I can't do this. I don't want anything to do with Daniel. I don't think I can ever look at Dakota again without being reminded about these facts. It's like a never-ending nightmare that I can't wake from!"

Dr. Hart couldn't help but mirror the tears in Denver's eyes, and neither could Amber, though she stood up and lovingly placed one of her hands on his arm while the other one now rested on her growing belly.

"Baby?"

Denver turned in Amber's direction and met her gaze. Then he looked down as she gestured for him to do so.

"Oh, God," he said in a calm voice as he realized his words may have had an impact on Amber, as she was pregnant from a rape. "I'm so sorry."

"It's okay," she replied. "I promise you didn't offend me. I just wanted to remind you that a child conceived from rape is a blessing in disguise. I'm so sorry your mother went through the struggles that she did, but you need to know that half of your DNA that comes from the monster doesn't define who you are, and it doesn't define Daniel or Kay either. You have a love and respect for her, and she's your full sister. Does Daniel not deserve at least the same level of respect?"

Denver didn't know what to say to this. He just sat back down in his chair in silence. He knew Amber was right. Dr. Hart once more tried to hand him the letter, though this time, Amber took it from her, and she sat back down in the chair next to Denver. Then she gave it to him.

"After what you did to him yesterday, I think you owe it to him to read this letter."

Denver didn't say anything, but silently he had to agree. He took the letter from her, opened it, and read it:

July 19th, 2021

DEAR DENVER,

I USED TO THINK THAT I WAS THE ONLY SON OF THE CONVICTED criminal, Davis Anderson, until I recently found out that there was a possibility you could be my brother through him. I had always wanted a brother growing up, but I was horrified to learn through the court records on Davis Anderson that he'd raped your mother and killed your parents. I know I could never forgive a man who'd harm my family in any way, but then again, he was my family, biologically speaking anyway. He left my mother on my 4th birthday, and I never saw him again after that, nor did I ever want anything to do with him. I'm so sorry for what he did to your family.

I know my words could never be enough for you, but really, I am truly sorry for everything that transpired. When I learned about your Leukemia and the fact that you needed a bone marrow donor, I was drawn to the idea of being your donor if I could. I know you don't want anything to do with me, but that's fine. As much as I would've loved getting to know you and finding out if we really are brothers, I can totally respect the fact that you'd want nothing to do with me. I have a half-sister through him and a half-sister through my mother, and both of them are incredible, inspiring young women, and they're enough for me.

If you're reading this letter, then that means it's been confirmed that we're a match with our bone marrow. I wanted to write this letter to you because I wanted to communicate with you in a way in which you didn't feel a need to respond. You see, I haven't always been the best person to be around, but I wanted to do something meaningful for someone, and it's a humbling experience to learn that my bone marrow has value to someone who really needs it, someone like you. I know you don't want to know my identity, so I'm writing this letter to you anonymously, and my bone marrow donation is also going to be provided anonymously, should you choose to accept it. However, I do want to give you a little background information about who I am.

I'm twenty-three years old, though I'll be twenty-four in three weeks, as I was born on August 8th, 1998. You already know that Davis left my mother and me on my 4th birthday, but what you don't know is that four years later, I was taken away from my mother and put into a foster home, which was a total nightmare. I'd suffered a range of abuse from my foster parents and a terrible foster brother, though I'd also met my best friend in the same foster home too. We stayed by each other's side throughout our childhood, and he's still my most trusted confidant. Had I not met him so many years ago, I wouldn't be where I am today. I still see my mother occasionally, but when she's hospitalized for her mental disorder and suicide attempts, I look out for my little sister.

She's fifteen years old, and her name's Dylan. I love her more than my own life, and if it ever came down to it, I'd give my life for hers if it meant keeping her safe and out of harm's way. She doesn't know it, but I'm actually trying to get her out of my mother's care and into the care of the loving family who adopted me and took care of me. It's not easy, but my little sister is worth the effort, and I'd do anything for her. Dylan deserves to be happy, and she deserves to feel safe, and I'd do anything to make that happen.

It's my hope and prayer that you'll come to accept my anonymous donation. I understand that you want nothing to do with me, and that's fine. I might feel the same way if I was in your shoes, so I get it. Just know that I mean you and your loved ones no harm. I'm not my father, and in fact, I have an adopted father who's a hell of a man, and it's my hope that I can someday become half the man he is. Please accept my words from the bottom of my heart when I say that I only want you to live a good, long, healthy life. If doing so means giving you my bone marrow, then I'm ready whenever you are. If you need time to think about it, then that's perfectly okay too, but please know this—I'm here for you, no matter what.

Sincerely,
A.D.

"A.D.?" Denver spoke out loud in curiosity as his eyes were still glued to the letter.

"Anonymous Donor," Dr. Hart explained simply. "Though, not anymore, I guess, since he came forward."

Denver nodded in acknowledgment, though he closed his eyes at this point.

"God," he mumbled to himself. "I feel like such an asshole."

The room was silent until Amber grabbed Denver's hand. Then he looked at her with tears in his eyes.

"I fucked up," he added as he took his hand from Amber and hid his eyes behind it.

"Everyone makes mistakes," Dr. Hart stated, which made Denver look into her eyes.

"Not like me. I royally screwed up yesterday. I … punched his face in, multiple times." Now a look of horror displayed itself on Dr. Hart's face, and he knew what she thought. "I was such an asshole to him. I need to reach out and apologize."

"You better," Dr. Hart warned. "We need him."

Denver nodded as he stood up from his chair and wiped his tears.

"Will that be all for now, Doc?"

"Actually, there is one more thing," Dr. Hart answered as she moved to open a drawer of her desk.

Denver and Amber watched as she took out a huge lockbox. Then she stood up and handed it over to him. He was confused, but he took it.

"Give this back to Daniel. I told him I'd be doing the surgery pro bono, but he insisted on paying me cash for it."

"This is heavy," Denver noted. "How much cash are we talking?"

"His entire life's savings. There are over two hundred thousand dollars in there."

Denver and Amber both grew bug-eyed when they heard this.

"You mean to tell me he had over two hundred thousand dollars saved up, and he emptied his entire savings for me?"

"He called it an investment." Denver was blown away by this news. "He's invested in you."

CHAPTER
FORTY

Later that day, Denver decided to head over to Max and Daniel's place on his own and see if Daniel was available. He knocked on their door but heard loud music being played inside the place, so then he rang the doorbell, and that seemed to garner some attention. He patiently waited until someone answered the door. It was Max, and he didn't even have a shirt on. In fact, based on the fact that he saw countless beads of sweat roll down Max's face, neck, and body, it looked like he was working out.

"What the hell do *you* want?"

"Is Daniel here?"

"You stay the hell away from Daniel," Max warned, but then he saw Daniel's lockbox in Denver's hands. "And what the hell are you doing with his lockbox?"

"He gave it to Dr. Hart, but she told me she's doing my surgery pro bono."

"What surgery?"

Max's response threw Denver.

"The bone marrow surgery," Denver answered with confusion written on his face. "Didn't Daniel tell you that he's my match?"

"No, he didn't, but I'm not gonna let him do it."

"I deserve that," Denver replied in a quiet voice as he looked at the lockbox in his hands. "Though something tells me Daniel won't let you stop him from doing what he wants to do. The bone marrow donation surgery is over two hundred thousand dollars. He emptied all his life savings from his bank account, put it all in this box, and handed it to my doctor."

Max's eyebrows lifted in surprise when he heard this.

"Wait, did you say two hundred thousand?"

"Yeah. Is he here? I need to talk to him and apologize."

Max was silent for a few moments before he opened the door, which Denver took as an invitation. He stepped inside and watched as Max closed the door. He quickly noticed the furniture in the living room had all been moved towards the walls so that he had plenty of space to do his karate workout. Max closed the door and reached his hand out for the box.

"I'll take that," he said in his normal voice.

Denver handed him the lockbox and watched as Max shook his head while he put the lockbox on the dining room table.

"I can't believe he gave all his money to your doctor. He told me he was saving up for his sister's future."

"Dylan," Denver replied. "Yea, she must be something special if he had two hundred thousand saved up for her."

"I didn't even know he had that much saved up. He's good with money and investments, though. How do you know about Dylan?"

Max placed both hands on his hips as he kept a watchful eye on Denver.

"He told me in a letter, which my doctor handed over to me this morning. Actually, he told me quite a few things that really surprised me, things I never knew about him. He wrote it anonymously, though he changed his mind yesterday on keeping his bone marrow donation a secret."

"Oh, you mean when you bloodied up his face?" Max asked as he approached Denver with fury in his eyes. "You're damn near lucky I have morals about hitting someone who's already dying. Otherwise, you'd be leaving my house in a goddamn body bag for what you did to him, and I'd be going to hell with no regrets."

Denver didn't know what to say to this. Max's face was a mere few inches from his, and he knew Max meant business. After all, he was a blackbelt in karate, so he didn't doubt Max could kill him with his own bare hands.

"Did he tell you why I beat him?"

"No, but you better tell me why, or you're not seeing him," Max warned.

"I think if he wanted you to know, he'd have told you."

"Don't fuck with me, Denver. I'm not in the mood for games."

Denver sighed as he backed away from Max to put some distance between the two of them.

"He told me his father's Davis Anderson, the man who murdered mine and Kay's parents. I know you know who I'm talking about too. Last month, you two looked at each other at Alice and Mike's house when he called Davis 'Boomer'. So, before you say you don't know what I'm talking about, just know that I already know."

Now it was Max's turn to be lost for words. Denver slowly paced back and forth in front of him.

"He came after me that day, said he knew Davis Anderson's son, tried to tell me he'd talk to his buddy and see if he matches for a bone marrow donation. You know what I told him that day?" Max shook his head no. "I told him I'd kill his friend if I ever found out who he was. I wanted *nothing* to do with Davis or the idea that he may be my biological father through rape."

Tears instantly filled Max's eyes when he heard the last part of Denver's statement, though he remained quiet.

"Do you have any idea how traumatizing it is to a little four-year-old boy to see his parents brutally murdered?" Again, Max shook his head no as Denver pointed to his own head. "You have no idea how fucked up in the head I am from what I saw. It's all I see when I close my eyes. *Every* fucking night. It's so bad I've got to take medication for it."

It was silent in the room for another moment as Denver shook his head in disbelief while he brought his hand up to his face to wipe the tears from his eyes.

"When he approached me yesterday," he continued as he looked back at Max. "When he told me who Davis was to him … and showed me DNA test results which prove Kay's his half-sister … and told me that he read all the court records regarding Davis and my parents, and told me that he found out that Kay and I are actually products of rape, that Davis is really our biological father, after everything I've seen, after Kay and I have spent our childhoods apart … after all the night terrors I've had about Davis and my parents … can you blame me for flipping out the way I did?"

Denver sighed again as he now approached Max, though it was Max's turn to speak up.

"I'm sorry, *truly* sorry for what Davis did to your parents. They didn't deserve it, and you and Kay didn't deserve to be separated the way you were. Daniel isn't Davis, though."

"I know," Denver said with tears in his eyes again. "He's nothing like Davis."

Max brought a hand to Denver's shoulder. However, Denver was surprised by his gentle touch. He looked at the hand on his shoulder before his eyes locked with Max's, which also showed nothing but kindness now.

"Neither are you or Kay." Max saw his lips quiver. "I hope you'll believe me when I say I know it isn't easy learning the truth of how you came to exist in this world by rape. My mother abandoned me when I was only two days old. She couldn't stand to look at me after she realized I was only a reminder of what had happened to her. So, she dropped me off at a fire station and never looked back."

Max paused for a moment to keep his emotions together, though he too had tears in his eyes.

"My father isn't the man who raped her, and he isn't the man who was involved with the Mexican drug cartel. No, my father's the man who raised me, the man whose name I adopted, the man whose name is one that I'm incredibly proud and honored to bear. You got lucky with not one but two fathers—the one whose name you were born with and the one whose name you bear now. You might have Davis' genes, but he is *not* your father. *Never* entertain that idea. *Ever*."

Denver was at a loss for words, but he nodded.

"You've got a brother, though," Max added. "And a damn good one at that. He's a little crazy at times, but he's got his reasons. He's fiercely protective of the people he loves and cares about, and he'd do anything for them. He took the money he was saving for his sister's college education and her future, and he invested all of it into you and making sure you at least get a chance to live. What does that tell you about who you are to him?"

"I know," Denver acknowledged. "I don't deserve his kindness, but I do owe him a major apology."

Max nodded in agreement as he let go of Denver and gave him a little space.

"He's up at the cabin with Dylan," he spoke as he now placed his hands back on his hips. "Just a friendly warning, though; she's a little spitfire. You'll have to go through her to get to him, and I guarantee you she won't make it easy for you."

"Thanks," Denver replied as he moved toward the front door and opened it. Max followed him and then leaned against the door. "For everything."

Max had no other words, though he nodded as a response. Denver knew what it meant and that no other words needed to be spoken, so he just left.

It would be a couple hours before Denver would arrive at the Denner cabin up north. He fully expected to be met with Dylan at the front door, but no one answered the door. He looked inside all the windows on the porch and soon realized Daniel was curled up on one of the sofas. He checked to see if the front door was unlocked, and it was, so he opened the door. He looked around the cabin and couldn't find anyone else around. He wondered where Dylan was, though he headed over to the living room and moved his eyes onto Daniel, who was sound asleep and snug as a bug under a thin and brown microfiber blanket.

"Daniel?" he called in a soft voice.

Daniel didn't budge, but he didn't have to move and turn his head to see who the voice belonged to.

"How'd you find me?"

Denver knew he was awake but also knew Daniel wasn't about to move and look at him either. So, he sat down on the wooden coffee table in front of Daniel.

"Max." Daniel was silent, which indicated to Denver that he was not in a mood to talk. "We, uh, had a little chat."

"What do you want?"

"To apologize for the way I acted and reacted yesterday."

Daniel still didn't move, but his tone changed.

"I already forgave you yesterday, before I left."

Denver was blown away by Daniel's words. He couldn't help the tears that formed in his eyes.

"I didn't come here for your forgiveness. I don't deserve it."

"Well, you have it anyway."

"Why?"

It grew quiet in the room again until Daniel finally moved so he could look over at Denver.

"Because you're my brother and because you're dying."

Denver nearly broke down when he heard those words.

"I'm sorry, man. I'm so sorry for what I did to you yesterday."

"Honestly, it's all good," was Daniel's response.

"How can you say that?" Denver asked.

"Because I love you, and you're the very last person I ever want to fight with. I just want to be there for you in whatever way you need me, and if you need me to stay away, then—"

"I don't feel that way anymore," Denver interjected.

Now it was Daniel's turn to be surprised.

"I read your letter."

Daniel was quiet for a moment, though he positioned his body to relax on his back with his hands now on his stomach.

"And I stand by every word I said, no matter what."

"Except for the anonymity part," Denver added with a soft smile.

Daniel mirrored Denver's smile as best he could and nodded.

"I had every intention of staying in the shadows, but when I saw how depressed you were yesterday, I couldn't bear to keep it a secret from you anymore."

"I get it," Denver replied with a nod of understanding as he wiped the tears from his eyes. "I felt the same way when I told Kay who she really was to me."

It grew quiet between them again, though Denver couldn't stand the awkward silence.

"So, uh, where's this famous Dylan I keep hearing about?"

"In the woods hunting for frogs and rabbit for dinner. She's pretty good at it too. She'll be back soon."

"Gotcha. Listen, I'm sorry for the way I grossly misjudged you. You're not at all who I thought you were yesterday or before that."

Daniel remained quiet as he kept his eyes on Denver. He knew it was awkward for Denver to apologize, but he also knew Denver was serious about his words too.

"I'd completely understand if you're not up to this, but if you're willing, I'd like to start over with you and get to know you for real."

Denver watched as Daniel brought his hand out toward him, and then Daniel spoke.

"I'd be honored, but let's do it the right way and start it with you getting what you need."

"You'd still do that for me, even after what I put you through?"

Daniel moved his hand again and gestured for him to take it.

"I'm here for you, no matter what."

Daniel's final words moved Denver to tears. They smiled once more at each other. Denver accepted his brother's offer and finally took his hand.

To be continued …

Turn the page for a special sneak peek of the final
installment of Jenah Pierce's Finding Dakota series …

FINDING SANCTUARY

Coming soon in 2023!

1

Two weeks before surgery

A few days before Daniel had gone with the girls to see Denver, he'd made his way over to the Morning Star Ranch to see Alex when he was working. He wasn't at all surprised to find Alex tending to the horses, though he was surprised to discover how eerily similar the horse Alex was brushing looked like his own Ginger.

"Who's this majestic beauty?" Daniel inquired as he approached Alex and brought his palm onto Delilah's neck in one gentle move.

"Uh, since when do you like horses?" Alex spoke with a question of his own.

"Believe it or not, but before Max and I met the Denners, we were in a foster home together, and it was on a farm with horses."

Delilah nickered softly as Daniel gave her a gentle rub, and then he brought his free hand out as an offer to finish brushing her. Alex was suspicious at first. However, Delilah seemed pleased by Daniel's presence, and Alex saw no animosity in his eyes, only tenderness. He decided he'd keep a close eye on Daniel, though for now, he handed him the brush. He watched as he realized Daniel was showing him his soft side.

"The horses were beautiful," Daniel continued in a calm, steady voice. Delilah's ears twitched and moved in his direction as he spoke, almost as if she was listening to him. "Max and I … well, we bonded right away. Our foster brother, though … he hated our bond. Max and I would spend hours in the stables or out in the field with the horses.

We had this one horse, her name was Ginger, and she had a gorgeous reddish-brown coat. Black mane and tail, quite like this beauty right here. Man, did her coat have an incredible shine to it under the sun!"

Alex didn't know what to say to this. He remained quiet while he listened to the passion in Daniel's voice, though Daniel paused for a moment. Alex saw the smile on his face, which quickly disappeared in his pause.

"She was so sweet with us but so terrified of our foster brother." Alex didn't like where this conversation was headed. "Jordy abused her. He tortured her and the other horses and blamed it on me. I loved that horse, me and Max both. Jordy was a monster to us too, but I'll never forget the morning I woke up to a nasty beating by Mr. Jenkins. You see, Jordy had poisoned Ginger and the other horses in the stables because he hated them, and for reasons I won't go into at this time, he hated how Max and I spent so much time with them. So, he poisoned them and blamed their death on me."

Alex was mortified to hear what Jordy did, and he saw a sadness in Daniel's eyes which he had never seen before. He guessed Daniel's heart still grieved for the loss of the horses he loved.

"Max refused to have anything to do with horses after that, or any animal, and me? Well, Ginger was my favorite. She was the first horse I ever saw being born. I watched her grow into the beauty she became. I fed her, and I brushed her, and I cared for her. I miss playing chasing games with her in the field." Daniel turned quiet for a moment as he fought to keep the tears at bay. Then he spoke again. "I miss her."

Delilah nickered again, and this time she'd moved her muzzle towards Daniel. He brought a hand up her nose, and he gave her a soft rub.

"You want a sugar cube?"

Alex watched as Delilah's ears twitched again. He knew that she knew what Daniel meant. She nudged Daniel's body. Daniel chuckled as he took a small bag out from the back pocket of his black jeans.

"How'd you know to bring sugar cubes?" Alex asked. "Was the other horse the same way, Ginger?"

"Pretty much," Daniel answered in a quiet voice as he looked at Alex for a brief moment before returning his focus onto Delilah. "And Kay kind of told me all about this one. Delilah, right?"

"Yeah," Alex replied as he watched Daniel feed Delilah a few of the sugar cubes from his hand. "I'm surprised she likes you so much."

"That's because I'm nothing like Jordy," Daniel mumbled under his breath, though Alex caught what he said.

"I'm sorry for what happened to you and Max, along with Ginger and all the other horses," he apologized with sympathy.

Daniel then continued brushing Delilah.

"Thanks, but if you can, I'd prefer you kept that bit between us. If Max ever found out what I said—"

"Your secret's safe with me," Alex interjected. "Even from Kay, if you don't want me talking about it with her."

"She already knows," Daniel stated. "She knows pretty much all about mine and Max's past. She's my best friend, the one who doesn't judge me and lets me be myself."

Alex had no words, though he saw how Daniel's eyes developed tears. He could hardly believe Daniel was this kind to him.

"She doesn't know it, but she challenges me to be a better person. She makes me *want* to be a better person. None of us have known her for very long, but I've learned some new things, and I'm just—" Alex stayed quiet as he continued listening to Daniel, though Daniel met his eyes now. "She's my sister, Alex, and it's because of her that I'm trying to turn over a new leaf. All I wanna do is be the older protective, caring brother she didn't get to have while growing up. She deserves the best, and you want to know something else?"

"Hm?"

"You're the best man for her."

Alex was thoroughly surprised by this.

"Did you forget that she dumped me?"

"No, I didn't forget. I heard about what went down between you two and why. I know you tried to tell her that I was a drug addict and shit."

Alex didn't know what to say to this, and Daniel sensed it.

"Dude, relax. I'm not gonna bite your head off because … well, because you're right. I *am* a drug addict, though I'm in recovery now. I don't expect you to be my friend or anything, but I'm looking out for Kay. I mean it when I say you're the best man for her. I came here to talk to you about it because I think you need to see her and talk her into taking you back. She's going to need you in the coming months. You're going to be the only one she'll trust."

Alex was thrown off by the last part of Daniel's statement.

"What the hell are you talking about?" Alex inquired as he stood in front of Daniel now.

"Remember when I said a few moments ago that I learned about some new stuff recently?" Alex nodded his head in curiosity. "Well, trust me when I say some shit will hit the fans in the coming months, maybe even weeks. She'll need you."

"What do you know?"

"Enough to break her heart," Daniel whispered. Alex didn't know what to say to this. He caught a flicker of water in his eyes, though it disappeared just as quickly when Daniel sighed. "Do you love her?"

Alex threw him a look that Daniel understood.

"Then please … go talk to her. Besides," Daniel continued with his hands on top of Alex's shoulders. "She *wants* to talk to you. She just doesn't know how to. Just please keep this conversation between us. She'd be upset if she knew I was intervening on her behalf. This is just a talk between us, man-to-man."

It grew quiet between the guys again, though Alex focused solely on Daniel's eyes. He sensed Daniel was on the fence about something. Daniel removed his hands from Alex's shoulders, and he tried to focus on giving Delilah another sugar cube, but all his thoughts were on his long-lost brother and sister.

"You've got a look like you're worried about what's coming," he verbally observed.

"The less you know right now, the easier it will be for Kay to turn to you when she feels she can't trust even me. I've discovered a few secrets of hers and Denver's past that intertwines with mine. They're dark truths, and I haven't figured out how to tell her or *if* I should tell her. Those two have been through so much bullshit already. It's hard to keep my mouth shut because I'm a firm believer in honesty, but the things I've learned, they're too much … even for me."

Once Delilah took the sugar cube from Daniel's hand, he brought his hand up to the white diamond between her eyes.

"I can't stand keeping secrets. I hate it. At the same time, though, I don't want to devastate Kay any more than she already is. When she finds out what I know … and what I did to get the truth … and when she learns I didn't tell her my discoveries right away …"

Alex wasn't very fond of Daniel, but he knew Daniel was close to Kay. He knew the brotherly love was there. Then it suddenly hit him. It was brotherly love, real brotherly love.

"So, wait, when you say your past is intertwined with theirs—"

Daniel threw him a look that dared him to go ahead and finish his question. Alex wasn't dumb, though. He shut up while he took a step back from Daniel.

"Please don't ask me questions about that," Daniel asked calmly.

Alex realized why Daniel was acting this way. If he would come outright and tell him, then Alex would know the truth, and Alex knew he wouldn't be able to hide it from Kay.

"I get it. If I know the truth before she does, she won't trust me either."

"Will you pl—"

"I promise I'll go and see her. Truth be told, I'd already planned on seeing her soon anyway, though I can't promise you she'll take me back," Alex interjected. "I'll do what I can to be there for her. I'd do anything for her. I love her."

2

The night before surgery

Daniel stared hard at the tall bottle of Southern Comfort that was positioned at the center of the coffee table in front of him. In one hand, he had his one-month AA chip, which he twirled between his fingers, and in the other hand was a lit-up cigarette from which he smoked. He was alone in his living room, hoping that his heavy metal music of choice would drown out his thousand-mile-a-minute thought process. So many things were on his mind, and even though they were random, they all seemed to run together. He was used to the alcohol and the drugs drowning most of it out, but now that he was sober, he had a difficult time escaping from all his racing thoughts.

'Should I dump that bottle of SoCo or drink my money's worth? When should I tell Kay I'm her real brother, and should I do it alone or with Denver? Why the fuck does Jordy keep showing up all over town? And what the fuck do I do if he recognizes me? Should I come out to Mom and Dad? Will they still love me, or will they disown me? I'm probably fucked, either way, so is sobriety even worth it? Can a boulder please just fall out of the sky and kill me now?'

There was a knock at the front door that distracted him from his thoughts, a welcome reprieve. He took a puff of his cigarette as he put down his AA chip and stood up. Then he headed over to the door, and he opened it. He was surprised to find Denver standing there before him, though he opened it wider. Denver accepted this wordless invite and stepped inside the living room, though he was quick to notice the ongoing debate Daniel had on the coffee table.

"What's up?" Daniel asked as he closed the door and looked over at Denver while he turned the music off.

"I could ask you the same thing," Denver answered as he walked over to the coffee table. "I was going to say pre-surgery jitters, though it seems that's the least of our worries right now."

Daniel knew where Denver's thoughts were.

"Seal's not broken yet. I bought it a few days before I'd decided to try sobriety," Daniel replied as he took another puff of his cigarette while he moved back over to his spot on the sofa.

"Why do you say that in a way that feels as if you've already lost the strength to fight your urges?" Denver inquired as he sat down next to his brother and watched him focus on the Southern Comfort.

"I haven't yet, but to be honest with you, I'm not too far from the edge," Daniel confessed in a quiet voice as he took another puff of his cigarette.

Denver paid close attention to his brother's face. The swelling on Daniel's face had gone down, though the bruises remained. He sensed that something was wrong with his brother.

"Talk to me, Daniel. What's going on?"

"I miss Jacob," Daniel began. "There's too much noise, and I've no idea where to begin explaining every racing thought in my head. That SoCo used to take it all away. With Jacob, though, I didn't have to explain anything. He was already in my corner, and he knew when I felt like I was drowning. I don't know how he knew, but he did."

Daniel's eyes remained fixed on the bottle, though Denver also saw the tears forming in his brother's eyes. It was weird for Denver, calling Daniel his brother, though at the same time, the idea of having a biological brother was growing on him. Daniel took another puff of his cigarette before Denver cleared his throat.

"I'm sorry Jacob can't be here," he spoke in a soft voice. "I know I can't compare to him, but … I'm in your corner too."

Daniel's teary-eyed gaze now met his, and it was as if Daniel had a non-verbal reply for him that came straight from the soul. Denver wanted to read it as awe and relief, though he couldn't be too sure if that were the right way to describe it. He felt a sense of purpose-driven loss from Daniel, though.

"I mean it when I say I'm in your corner," Denver continued. "I can see you're struggling to stay afloat. Will you let me be a lifeline?"

At first, Daniel didn't have the words. He was desperate for help without a bias, though he also didn't want to talk to a stranger. Denver watched as Daniel threw him a subtle nod before he spoke up.

"I wouldn't know where to begin."

"Start with what pops in your head first," Denver suggested.

The room grew silent as Daniel took another puff of his cigarette while he focused on the bottle once more. He wondered if his brother would be an ally, though he had previously seen him at Club Ivy, one of the most popular gay clubs in the next town over.

"Can I ask you a question?" he asked.

"Anything."

"A few months ago, before you went out on your last trip looking for Kay, you were hanging out at Club Ivy, dancing with a guy."

"Yeah, I was there to show support to a good friend of mine that was coming out. What about it?"

"So, you're not … ?"

Denver knew where this conversation was headed, though he also knew that Daniel knew he had a girlfriend.

"No, I'm not bi or pans or anything of that sort, but I'm not hating on anyone whose sexuality isn't the same as mine either. Love is love. Whatever your sexuality is, it won't bother me. I'm cool with you not being straight. Seriously. I mean, hell, my best friend is bi."

"But your best friend is V—" Daniel began with confusion on his face, though he paused as he noticed how the smile on Denver's face spread softly. "Wow. How the hell did I miss that one?"

Daniel could hardly believe the news he'd just learned.

"As of this moment, we are the only two people in the world that know this," Denver added.

"I get it," Daniel replied. "I know nothing."

It was silent between the brothers as Denver nodded, though he was curious now.

"Am I the first person you're coming out to?"

"Max and Kay and Dylan already know I'm bi," Daniel answered as he put out the cigarette in the ashtray and left the butt there. "That's it, though."

"And I'm assuming the reason why you haven't told anyone else is the same reason Vin hasn't come out?"

"Pretty much," Daniel spoke. "We're not the only ones, though. I'm just tired of keeping it in, but I really don't want to lose Alice and Doc."

Denver saw the tears making their return to Daniel's eyes. It was easy to see that Daniel was petrified of losing Alice and Dr. Denner's love and support.

"My biological mother neglected me, and our biological father is a murdering, raping, revolting son of a bitch. My foster parents were controlling, narcissistic, abusive pieces of shit, along with their filthy perverted son. Alice and Doc have been the only two decent parents I ever had. I can't tell you how long I've wanted to call them Mom and Dad, but I'm afraid that if I do, they're going to reject me because of my bisexuality. I'm going crazy with keeping this part of me a secret anymore, but I can't handle them possibly turning me away or putting me down. I just can't."

Daniel's voice broke up on him toward the end of his statement. He brought his fingers up to the inner corners of his eyes and fought hard to keep the tears at bay. Denver knew he was about to cry, so he placed a hand on his back for comfort and support.

"Hey," he called softly. "If you need me to be there when you tell them, I will. I'll stand by you, and if they reject you, I promise I'll be by your side as you walk away from them. You'll always have Max and Kay and Dylan too. All of us, Daniel, we're *fiercely* protective of everyone we love and care about, and Vinessa would stand by you too."

Daniel sniffled while he returned his brother's gaze.

"You'd really do that for me?" Daniel asked.

"Of course, I would," Denver answered. "You're my brother."

"I thought you didn't want a brother?"

"That was before I found out that you'd emptied your life savings from a bank account to invest it all into my own life, even though your intention for your money was for Dylan's future. Dr. Hart refused it, so I hand-delivered it to Max that day I came to see you at the cabin. With everything you've done for me and how far you've been willing to go, I can't even express how much that means to me."

Daniel didn't know what to say to this. He was relieved to know that Denver was in his corner, though.

"You've opened up my eyes to who you really are," Denver said as he stood up and offered his hand to Daniel. "I'm genuinely proud and honored to call you my brother."

Daniel accepted Denver's 'bro code' handshake as he also stood up from his spot on the sofa. However, Denver took his free arm and pulled him into a hug.

"I love you, Dan."

These words took Daniel by complete surprise, and his tears had surfaced again, but he returned Denver's hug.

"I love you too."

After another moment or two, they each pulled from the hug, and Denver placed his hands on Daniel's shoulders while he met his gaze.

"Let's go celebrate you coming out."

Daniel scoffed before he spoke up.

"I didn't exactly leave the closet, not yet anyway."

"You came out to me, so that's something," Denver replied. "And it's okay to take baby steps with something like this. We should still celebrate, though. Let's hit up the Ivy. Besides, I think we could both use a night out to blow off some steam."

Daniel thought about this for a moment and realized he did need a guy's night out.

"Sounds good. Do you mind if I change first?"

"Go for it."

"Cool. I'll be back in a few."

Denver nodded as he sat down again, and Daniel went back to his room. While he heard the closing of Daniel's bedroom door, Denver's eyes focused on the AA chip before him. He picked it up, and his eyes remained fixed on it until Daniel reappeared a few minutes later.

"Here, put this on," Daniel stated as he threw him a leather jacket and fixed the collar to the sleek black blazer he now wore. "The jacket will make you look more badass."

Denver realized Daniel was trying to dress him up, but he didn't mind because he saw how Daniel's demeanor changed when they had decided to get out of the house and hang out. With the AA chip still in his hand, he stood up and put the leather jacket on. He noticed that even though Daniel changed out of his outfit, he still wore only black.

"I might be shooting myself in the foot here, but uhhhh … do you own any other colors besides black?" he inquired, which got a hearty chuckle out of Daniel.

"Black is my specialty," Daniel answered as he rolled both of the sleeves of his blazer up past his elbows. "It's all about how you wear it. Hey, do you still wear liner?"

"Sometimes," he said, but then he noticed Daniel already had his own eyeliner on, and he watched as Daniel took out a pencil from the front pocket of his blazer.

He also picked up on the fact that Daniel's facial bruises—from their fight—had magically disappeared, which Denver knew was due to the makeup Daniel now also wore. Daniel walked around the coffee table and approached Denver, and then he brought the eyeliner pencil up to his brother's eyes.

"May I?"

"That's a little weird … but sure," Denver answered while he still held the AA chip in his hand and played with it.

Daniel chuckled as he spoke while he pulled the cap off the pencil and drew around his brother's eyes.

"The idea is for us to be unfuckwithable. You've always been the cool, popular dude that everyone loves and supports, whether you're in or out of remission. Of course, you've also had some pretty psycho moments too. Me, though, I'm just the badass Denner that no one can stand 'cause I'm a total jackass. Under normal circumstances, you and I wouldn't be caught dead hanging out with one another. Imagine the surprise on everyone's face when they see us walking into a room side by side. Also, we're smokin' hot, but you've got a girlfriend, and I'm saving myself for someone special."

Denver was surprised to hear the last part of Daniel's statement.

"Ah … so no hookup for you tonight then?" Denver inquired with a curious gaze.

"Nah, the Shirley Temples and the music will be enough for me."

"Y'know, I used to think Luna's made the best Shirley Temples."

"Until you've had Ivy's, right?" Denver watched as Daniel now turned even more excited, though Denver nodded. "I could drink, like, six in an hour. Ivy's is the fucking best."

"Well, we can drink however much we want until midnight."

Daniel became silent as he pulled the pencil away from Denver's eyes, but he'd also noticed those pre-surgery jitters Denver mentioned earlier. He put the cap back on the pencil and placed it on the coffee table before he looked to his brother again.

"Nervous about tomorrow?" he asked as he played with Denver's hair.

"Yes," Denver answered, though he pulled his head away. "What are you doing?"

"Relax, bro. I'm just fixing your hair. Will you let me have a little fun with this?" Daniel replied in question as he remained focused on Denver's hair for another few seconds.

Denver said nothing, but then Daniel pulled his hand away from his head and gazed into his eyes.

"The surgery will work."

Denver was surprised by Daniel's steadfast belief in this.

"How can you be so sure?"

"I don't know. I just … believe."

"Faith it 'til you make it, am I right?" Daniel only nodded. "Yeah, I'm not a person of faith."

"I know," Daniel replied this time as he placed his hands back on Denver's shoulders. "That's why I've got enough for the both of us."

It grew quiet among the two again, though now it was Daniel who had nervousness written all over his face.

"What're you thinking?" Denver asked him with concern.

Daniel removed his hands from Denver's shoulders. However, he placed a hand over one of Denver's, the one that he knew had his coin.

"That I need liquid courage."

"For what?"

"Making a quick stop at Alice and Doc's."

"Tonight?" Denver asked. "Like, right now?"

Daniel had no words, but he nodded as his breath grew shaky. It was Denver who now had his hands on Daniel's shoulders after he'd allowed Daniel to take back his coin.

"You don't need liquid courage," he spoke in a calm voice. "You just need to take a deep breath. Whenever you're ready, I'm right here with you, okay?"

Daniel nodded as Denver brought his hands to his sides. Daniel then bent down to grab his lighter and pack of cigarettes. Denver paid attention to how Daniel seemed eager to light up, and he watched as Daniel pulled a cigarette out and brought it to his lips. Once it was lit,

Daniel closed his eyes and inhaled the first puff of his new cigarette, though he was careful not to blow it in his brother's face.

"My car or yours?" Denver asked as Daniel opened his eyes and gazed into Denver's.

"I've got the bike tonight," Daniel answered as he twirled his AA chip again. "But I'll leave it up to you."

"Yeah, no, I don't do motorcycles," Denver replied as he walked towards the front door. "We'll just take my car."

"Fine by me."

"You ready?"

"I'll never be ready," Daniel replied as he took a new puff of his cigarette and met up with Denver at the door. "I just want to get this over with."

Turn the page for a special preview of Jenah Pierce's
upcoming Christian Romance novel …

COLLIDE

*Coming soon in summer 2022 with a full digital
format that will be free to read for a limited time!*

1

Malena Rose Whitmore, a young and beautiful twenty-five-year-old African-American woman, was elated as she printed the final edit of her second Romance novel, *Dreams of Tomorrow*. She couldn't wait to run it by her publisher downtown. She came from money, though she spent all her time alone in the mountains because she had no family. Her mother passed away three years prior to a six-year war with brain cancer, and she was an only child with no cousins, aunts, or uncles. She knew almost nothing of her father except that he was a donor at the sperm bank her mother went to, though she suspected she inherited one of her favorite features from him – her gorgeous, distinctive slate grey eyes.

Her mother had once been married, but that marriage ended long before her mother decided to embrace her independence. When she felt ready, she reached out to a sperm bank and fertility specialist, and she raised her daughter all by herself. Malena's grandparents were long dead before she was born into this world, so Malena was all her mother had for many years. Malena was content with her life the way it was, though. She inherited her mother's independence and strong will, and her mother had taught her how to use both well, so she didn't mind being alone.

Malena hummed with enthusiasm while she clipped all the pages of her latest manuscript together, and then she put it all inside an envelope before she tied it shut. She left it on her desk for the time being, as she knew she wanted to freshen up. Then she went to the bathroom, checked herself out in the mirror, and soon put on a fresh coat of her favorite Sugar Baby red lipstick. She also checked to ensure her hair was alright. Her mother had always told her to take care of her hair and appreciate its natural beauty and color, so she took special care of it. She made a minor adjustment to her tight, lustrous ringlets before returning to her desk.

She was just starting her life, and she was settled into a spacious, warm, and cozy cabin high up in the gorgeous Blue Ridge Mountains of Braedon, North Carolina. After picking up the envelope with her manuscript, she looked out the window nearest her. When her cabin was built, she ensured one side was constructed with a weatherproof sliding glass wall system from ceiling to floor. Most of her writing was inspired by gazing out the windows at the mesmerizing bluish haze of the mountains. She looked out upon the beautiful city of Braedon below her, a city she loved so much during her travels with her mother that she moved here and knew she'd never regret claiming it as a place to call home.

***

TWENTY-FOUR-YEAR-OLD KINGSTON ALEXANDER BEAUMONT WAS THE son of Braedon's top domestic relations lawyer, and he despised his life. He felt like he was born into a pool of money because it surrounded him, and he felt like it was suffocating him. It had been one whole year since his fraternal twin sister passed away from Cystic Fibrosis, and his parents were in the process of getting divorced. He felt all alone in the world, and this feeling had petrified him more than the idea of death itself. To make matters worse, his parents had ignored him since his twin got sick and his now ex-fiancé had cheated on him with his two best friends. Thanks to her indiscretions, he had to be treated for Gonorrhea and Chlamydia. He suspected his ex-best friends weren't the only guys she cheated on him with. No matter, though, because he didn't care for her or them anymore.

Kingston was currently in an empty meadow on the outskirts of town, drinking away all of his problems with a bottle of Jack in the afternoon. He honestly didn't care if he drank himself to death at this point. After drinking nearly the whole bottle, he decided to drive his car off a cliff high up in the mountains. He figured it was best to end life on his terms because he didn't want to live anymore. So, he stood up with the nearly empty bottle of alcohol in his right hand, and he stumbled his way over to his car parked on the side of the road.

As he sat in the driver's seat of his metallic silver Mercedes-Benz convertible, he looked through the rearview mirror to see his dull grey eyes. He wondered if his parents would even miss him after his life ended. He hadn't showered in a few days, so his dark hair looked greasy, unkempt, and dirty. Did he care, though? No.

MALENA GOT IN HER CAR AND HEADED DOWN FOR TOWN AS SHE listened to some of her favorite contemporary worship music. About two minutes into her drive, her cell phone switched albums, though Malena wanted to replay the same album from the beginning, and she thought for sure she could drive one-handed while using her right hand to flip through the music app she had on her phone. She had done it countless times before, including looking away momentarily to see what musician or album became highlighted as she thumbed through the music. So, she did just that when she saw the road was clear and the next turn wasn't for a good minute, but while she looked down, a metallic silver Mercedes-Benz convertible had driven out of the curve ahead of Malena. She didn't even realize that she'd crossed into its lane, and the driver of the Mercedes, Kingston, hadn't seen Malena either.

KINGSTON'S MIND WAS TOO FOCUSED ON WONDERING IF HE SHOULD just swerve to the right, slam into the guard rail, and flip his car over the cliff, or if he should wait until he was higher up in the mountains. When he finally noticed the black Acura TSX steering into his lane, he knew in a heartbeat that killing himself was a bad idea right now because it just may involve killing someone else. He tried to turn into the opposing lane to avoid the oncoming car, though little did he know, the driver also saw him last second and tried hard to move back into her own lane. Malena had driven faster, so when she'd changed course out of fear as pure adrenaline kicked in, she quickly swerved back into her lane, and her Acura met the Mercedes-Benz sideways and flipped after it slammed hard into the left front side of the other car.

Before Kingston knew it, his car screeched to a full abrupt stop, and the front of his car was totaled. He hit his head against the steering wheel just a split second before the airbag went off, knocking him out for a few minutes. After he came to, he coughed and shoved his airbag aside. He was glad to know he wasn't dead yet until he realized what had happened. He looked in his rearview mirror to find the Acura in the middle of the road and upside down.

He turned around in shock as then he smelled something he hadn't before: smoke. So, he'd jumped out of his car as fast as possible and moved away from the vehicle. He couldn't tell if it was going to blow up, and he didn't know if the driver in the Acura was okay, so he ran from his car and towards the other driver. As soon as he reached the Acura, his car exploded, and pieces flew everywhere. Thankfully, nowhere near him or the Acura. He got down on his knees and looked inside the vehicle. The driver was a lone female, though she was covered in blood with apparent wounds on her face, and she was upside down, still strapped into her seatbelt. He couldn't believe how such a sight as this sobered him as fast as it did.

"Oh, my God," he thought aloud.

He then directed his words toward the woman.

"Miss!" he tried to call. "Hey, Miss, can you hear me?" He

couldn't tell if she was alive, dead, or simply unconscious. "Oh, God. *Please* tell me I didn't just kill a woman."

"Yes, I can hear you. Who are you, and why are you freaking out? I'm fine."

Malena stood behind Kingston, but she quickly realized the young man couldn't hear her.

"*Please* wake up, Miss!"

He saw her cell phone on the car's ceiling and saw that it looked intact, so he grabbed it. His cell phone was still in his car when it blew up, so he knew their best chance for help would be this cell phone. He saw the screen was active from playing music, so he knew that calling for help wouldn't be challenging. Malena watched as he dialed 911 on her cell phone while he stood up.

"911, what's your emergency?" responded a dispatcher on the other end.

"Help!" Kingston begged as he realized how smoke rose from the hood of her car now. "Please help us! My car just exploded, but the other car is upside down. We need an ambulance up here. The driver in the other car isn't responding, and she's got a little smoke coming out from under the hood."

"Okay, sir, what's your location?"

"We're in the mountains on High Point Road, cliffside."

There was a moment of silence before the dispatcher responded.

"I'm dispatching the police and an ambulance."

"Please hurry! She's all bloody and looks like she's hurt real bad." He was overwhelmed to tears by the situation he faced. "Oh, God, I didn't mean to hit her. Please don't let her die!"

THANK YOU

Thank you for purchasing this printed version of *Finding Dakota*. As a token of the author's appreciation, you're eligible to access the full eBook version of her upcoming Christian Romance novel *Collide*, which will be free until May 31, 2023.

To access the full free digital eBook of *Collide* when it's available, go to www.JenahPierce.com and click on the dedicated title page for *Collide* under the Romance sub-genre. Enter the following passcode below and enjoy your read:

Collide-05-31-2023

ABOUT THE AUTHOR

Jenah Pierce was raised in the Lehigh Valley of Pennsylvania, and she's spent most of her adult life there, except for two years in San Diego, California. She developed a passion for writing when she was fifteen, and she has a heart for raising awareness on anxiety, domestic abuse, rape, self-harm, and suicide. She is romantically linked with someone who has an aggressive mutation of Cystic Fibrosis, so she helps raise awareness of this disease. She also lost her baby brother, along with an early childhood friend, to Neuroblastoma, a cancer of the adrenal gland that mostly affects children, so she is an advocate for this disease and all other childhood cancers. To learn more about Jenah Pierce and discover her latest projects, please feel free to turn the page or check out her official website and social media handles below:

ALSO BY JENAH PIERCE

ROMANCE-SUSPENSE

Whitney's Reprisal (excerpt to the *Broken* series)

Broken (#1 of the *Broken* series)

Dawn of Darkness (#2 of the *Broken* series)

YOUNG ADULT FLASH FICTION (free)

Lovely Blue Eyes (Christian Romance)

YOUNG ADULT WORKS-IN-PROGRESS (free)

My World (Christian)

Raising the Crown (Romance)

IN ORDER OF WHAT'S COMING SOON

Collide (Christian Romance)

Kayleigh's Heart (Young Adult Romance)

Nightmare in the Mirror (#3 of the *Broken* series)

Finding Sanctuary (General Suspense)

Stronger (*Broken* series finale)

Rachael's Voice (Christian)